THE WILD OHIO

THE WILD OHIO

BART SPICER

CUTTING EDGE

ISBN-13: 978-1-952138-23-2

Published by
Cutting Edge Publishing
PO Box 8212
Calabasas, CA 91372
www.cuttingedgebooks.com

TO RAYMOND T. BOND
Partner in Crime

FOREWORD

On July 14, 1789, a Paris mob stormed the Bastille. Worried Frenchmen, who were largely dependent upon the Bourbon regime they detested, made immediate plans to emigrate. To them, revolution was quite as hateful as the Bourbons. Some had fought with LaFayette for American independence and held a romantic view of America, forgetting that there had ever been a revolution here, thinking only of the new nation that had been created through a war with England. To many Frenchmen, America seemed the obvious refuge and American land companies were quick to agree. Within six months, the Scioto Company alone sold more than 100,000 acres of Ohio wilderness land and hundreds of Parisians left Le Havre for the new world.

The founding of the town of Gallipolis—the City of the French—is the basis of this book. Historically, the facts are sound, but essentially, this is a work of fiction. Some of the characters will be recognizable but most are imaginary people caught in an upheaval of history, fighting as people will always fight to maintain their identities and to build lives of some meaning. While history can force people to react with violence and fear, it is those same people whose reactions, in a very real sense, make history.

CHAPTER ONE

Three trail-weary bay geldings stood patiently in the shadowed thicket, stamping occasionally to keep the sandflies away. Near them, beside the quiet Virginia stream, a tall man bent forward to squint into a polished square of steel, holding a heavy razor poised while his fingers searched for stubble he might have missed. His weathered face was ruddy and smooth-grained in the wavery mirror. He flicked the lather from his razor and snapped the blade shut. Six-and-a-half feet when he straightened, he was a bull-heavy man with tired eyes that were the cold lead-gray of bullets. He swept back his damp grizzled red hair and turned to face the stream.

"Mr. Blanchard!" he shouted.

A slim naked figure, white in the afternoon sunlight, rolled lazily in the water. A seal-brown head rose. "Don't shoot, Colonel," he called. "I'll get there."

Duncan Crosbie grunted. He couldn't make up his mind about Mr. Blanchard. Sometimes he thought he could detect a disturbing note in Blanchard's voice, something that was uncomfortably close to mockery. He knew he had no real complaint about the young man. His behavior during the past few weeks had shown that precise balance of obedience and cheerfulness suitable in a junior officer. All the same, Crosbie thought he would have preferred one of his dour Scots or even a Bible-quoting Yankee to Mr. Blanchard. It was probably just that he didn't understand the Tidewater Virginia gentry—or like them.

Crosbie lifted his best linen shirt and slid it over his head. He rammed the wide skirts into his tight doeskin breeches. Probably Mr. Blanchard would display something very elegant in the way of shirts, he thought sourly. Even military regulations permitted a degree of personal taste. Crosbie's plain linen shirt with its absence of lace or ruffles was a shade too simple for a ranking colonel. He looked down at his gleaming jack boots with no satisfaction. They would serve until he reached Alexandria but then he would be expected to appear in buckled low shoes. His shabby pair would contrast badly, he suspected.

The uniform had been a brilliant thought, he told himself. Strictly speaking, Crosbie should wear the clothes of a civilian, since he was no longer on the active Army roster. But latitude was permissible, and Crosbie's civilian wardrobe contained nothing suitable for Alexandria. Thank God that Blanchard had raised no objection. Though for all his airs, quite possibly that elegant young gentleman had no more money than Crosbie. Blanchard had been on General Putnam's staff and Crosbie knew that Old Put placed no trust in the frivolous gentry.

He threw his shaving gear into a flat saddlebag and stripped off the leather cover from his saddle. The seat should be clean enough, he thought. He rubbed the saddle briskly with the underside of the cover to remove any dirt. His white doeskin breeches would be black in no time if he rode a greasy saddle.

Crosbie flicked the cover lightly at his tigerskin saddlecloth and straightened slowly. His long cravat hung limply from a willow twig and he reached for it absently. His fingers had barely touched it when he froze. Behind him a saddle creaked and Crosbie turned tensely, slightly crouched.

"I didn't go to fright you, Colonel," a thick voice said.

Crosbie glanced up, not moving. From the edge of the grove a lone horseman watched him, idly flicking his reins against the withers of his ungainly horse. The rider's homespun breeches dangled loosely outside his bullhide boots and he wore a thick woolen coat cobbled together by a tailor with no knowledge of his trade. The horseman's right hand was out of sight, hidden by the full skirt of his coat. Crosbie noted the two worn cavalry holsters strapped to the saddle. He stepped back warily.

"I didn't hear you coming," he said coldly, speaking with a full, heavy voice, hoping it would carry to Blanchard, warn him in case a warning was necessary.

The stranger laughed quietly, baring long yellowed teeth. "I don't reckon you did." He lounged back easily in his saddle. "You're right late, Colonel. I been waitin' quite a spell."

Crosbie said nothing. He was not expected in this territory. He was sure of that. Only General Putnam knew his mission. Not even Mr. Blanchard knew why they were headed for Alexandria or why they had made such a hurried trip from the Ohio country. If Putnam kept the news from a favored aide, he was most unlikely to tell this seedy clodhopper.

The stranger flapped his reins at Crosbie. "You're too late, Colonel," he grinned. "The Frenchies ain't goin'. They done changed their minds."

Crosbie stiffened angrily. Then his mission *was* known, he thought. Tavern gossip, probably. He felt a sudden flush of resentment at General Putnam and at the smirking stranger who sat clumsily above, laughing at him. "Who are you?" he demanded.

"Why, I'm a friend, Colonel," the rider said, laughing outright. "I just come to tell you to go on back. Git home. There ain't nothing in Alex for you."

"I'll be the judge of that," Crosbie said tightly. Where in hell is Blanchard, he wondered. He took down his cravat and folded it in long precise layers, his fingers trembling slightly.

"Nope," the stranger said flatly, all humor gone now. "I'm the judge. And the jury. Git goin'." His right hand came up slowly, pointed a double-barreled horse pistol at Crosbie.

Crosbie wrapped his cravat snugly and knotted it, looking steadily up past the pistol to the horseman's face. He is very serious, Crosbie thought. And his finger is very tight against the triggers. Crosbie measured the distance between them. If the first barrel misfired...

"Don't try nothin', Colonel," the stranger said nervously. His mouth tightened into a hard line. "I'll shoot you, so help me, I'll..."

The rifle made a flat spiteful crack in the still air. The horseman stared incredulously at his right hand. His pistol was magically gone and his right thumb with it. He looked bewildered, not yet feeling the pain.

The rider's left saddle holster faced toward Crosbie and the Colonel leaped for it in a lithe pounce that seemed impossible in such a heavy man. He snatched the pistol and pulled back both hammers.

The stranger sat his horse numbly, holding his mutilated right hand up before his eyes. As Crosbie grabbed his second pistol, the rider came alert. He pounded his bootheels sharply into his horse's flanks, drumming frantically to stir the beast into motion. The horse almost reared, then lunged toward the road in a frightened scramble that sprayed pebbles behind him.

The close branches of the thicket rustled and then parted as Blanchard stepped gingerly into the clearing. He held a long rifle in both hands to keep the branches from snapping back against his naked body. Crosbie forced his face into stern lines, trying not to smile.

Blanchard stopped before Crosbie, placing his bare feet cautiously and then froze to attention with exaggerated stiffness. He brought the long rifle up to "Present" and grinned widely. "Lieutenant Blanchard reports to the Colonel as directed, sir." His soft drawling Southern voice made it "suh." The rifle barrel towered high above his head as a military musket would never do. There were respectable muscles along his tall frame, but beside Crosbie's bulk he seemed almost frail.

Crosbie felt a faint irritation. Blanchard's satisfaction with his perfect shot was very evident. But Crosbie would have welcomed an opportunity to question the strange horseman. There was no point in mentioning that now. He would need Blanchard's complete enthusiasm in the days ahead and a reprimand would serve no purpose.

"That was a fine shot, Mr. Blanchard," he said equably. "I envy you that rifle."

Blanchard's grin widened. He slapped the breech as he might pat a favorite dog. "Old Leman made this beauty for target shooting, Colonel," he said, obviously pleased. "It would be just as accurate at five hundred yards."

Crosbie managed a meager smile. He turned to get his coat. After a moment he said, "We've a distance to travel yet, Mr. Blanchard."

Blanchard nodded. He leaned his rifle carefully against a tree and reached swiftly for the gourd of soft soap on the ground. He smeared a handful over his scant beard and worked it in. He snapped open a walnut case of English razors, picking out one without looking. Crosbie glanced at the case with familiar envy. Those seven Sheffield blades were worth a month's pay at least.

Blanchard drew the razor down his chin in a long firm stroke. He twisted his mouth to one side and spoke in a distorted tone. "That bucko with the pistols seemed right determined we were going straight back to Marietta," he said, keeping his eyes firmly on the steel mirror. He ran the blade under his jaw lightly and flicked a glance at Crosbie, looking slyly to see if he could surprise a reaction from the Colonel.

Blanchard had served often with aloof and silent commanders and working without knowledge or understanding of his objective was no novelty to him. But this was obviously different. It would be no ordinary mission that could be accomplished by two men alone—and two such different men. It still irked Blanchard that he had not been permitted to bring along one man to take care of the niggling little chores during their trip from the Ohio. And Crosbie was a new experience for him. The

Colonel was a quiet and competent soldier, highly regarded by General Putnam, but he was an upcountry Highlander at heart and didn't trouble to conceal his deep distrust of the people from the Tidewater. You would think the war might have changed all that, but Crosbie apparently needed proof on a personal basis before he could accept a gentleman as an equal. Blanchard went on with his shaving. The Colonel's face told him nothing.

Crosbie pulled on his long white uniform waistcoat and then shoved his heavy arms into his uniform coat. He settled the thick golden epaulettes easily on his shoulders and hooked back the skirts of his coat as regulations required, displaying the vivid red lining that denoted the Artillery. He clipped his gilt small-sword to his belt. A light linen shroud protected his black cocked hat and the brilliant red plume that was coiled safely inside. He put them together carefully, pinning the plume with a black cockade, and then adjusted his hat on his head, settling it down into place and sweeping back his grizzled red hair that threatened to escape from the short twisted queue behind his neck.

Crosbie could sense Blanchard's sharp curiosity and he knew that inwardly the subaltern was impatient to hear of their mission. But never once had he actually asked, not since that moment in General Putnam's headquarters at Campus Martius, the log fort at Marietta, when he realized that Putnam wasn't going to tell him. Crosbie gave the young man high marks for his restraint; it was a quality he respected. Putnam had insisted upon speed and secrecy and Crosbie had accepted those conditions. But there seemed to be no reason for keeping Blanchard in the dark any longer. Not when even a stranger knew of their mission.

He watched glumly as Blanchard dressed himself. The young officer wriggled into his boots and hauled them up over his tight breeches. "Sure feel stiff after moccasins," he muttered. He eyed Crosbie's unfrilled shirt and searched quickly through his saddlebags. The shirt he brought out was just as simple, and to Crosbie's mind, no finer than his own.

Blanchard's uniform was brighter than Crosbie's because the subaltern was a light dragoon and the glistening white facings of his coat were much more noticeable. But when Blanchard turned, the difference in rank was emphasized. Crosbie's solid shoulders were weighted by his heavy pair of gold epaulettes that dropped a thick fringe down his sleeves. Blanchard's simple, left-shoulder epaulette was small competition. For no reason, Crosbie felt better, seeing that.

Crosbie lifted his saddle gear from the ground and draped it on the heaviest of the three tired bays. He checked the primer powder in both his saddle pistols and turned the setscrews tighter around their flints. The extra pistol he had snatched from the threatening stranger was tossed into his saddlebags. He dropped his deerskin saddle cover on a pile of buckskin clothes at Blanchard's feet.

"How long do you think we might be staying in Alex, Colonel?" Blanchard asked innocently. All the way from Marietta he had skillfully framed leading questions, trying with obvious guile to make Crosbie drop a hint of their assignment. And he had seen them all fail as the huge taciturn Colonel ignored or evaded the issue. This time he did no better.

Crosbie picked up his saddlebags. "No longer than we must, Mr. Blanchard," he said briefly. His deep serious tones held only faint traces of a Scottish burr, but however faint, they were traces he would never lose. "We'll not be long about our business." He tossed his saddlebags up behind the saddle and took out a light sinew thong which he tied around his waist, tucking it out of sight under his sword belt. He hung a thin scabbarded dirk on the thong. The scrolled and jeweled sheath was almost hidden under his belt and only the narrow curved hilt of chased silver and pale blue enamel was visible.

Blanchard grinned at the dainty deadly weapon which was never out of Crosbie's reach. He looked up blandly into the trees and muttered, "And how could you tell he was the Crosbie of Craigsmuir without the *skene-dhu?*" He squinted up at the bushy trees with enormous interest.

Crosbie nodded calmly. "It's a noble dirk," he admitted. Such frivolous comments were merely Mr. Blanchard's form of light humor, but they left Crosbie always wondering whether there might not be the thin edge of mockery underneath. Crosbie's heavy hand touched the dirk lightly with the easy assurance of long familiarity. The stag's head carved in the carnelian at the top was the Crosbie seal. Here in his hand was the Crosbie dirk and to the huge Scot it was his scepter, his sureness. The dirk had been the Crosbie dirk centuries before Germanic kings had come to rule England and claim the Highlands for their own.

Blanchard stooped, picked up the buckskin hunting shirts from the ground, straightened their sleeve and cape fringes and folded them. He wadded moccasins and hide breeches with them and rammed the lot into the withe carrier that rode lightly on the back of their pack horse. He pitched in the curry combs he had used earlier and cleared the site of its travel gear.

He waited for the Colonel to mount, standing close to his stirrup with his long rifle cradled carefully in one arm. The Colonel leaned both arms against his saddle and looked at him, clearing his throat roughly.

Blanchard was a stout, biddable boy, Crosbie thought suddenly. He stood his ground firmly and he had that hard level eye that Crosbie felt was a basic requirement. Maybe Blanchard could play the courtier, but Crosbie had to admit he hadn't tried it. Crosbie smiled briefly, a swift passing brightness that surprised Blanchard.

"That was a fine shot, Mr. Blanchard," he said abruptly. "I offered no proper thanks. You may well have saved my life."

Blanchard stared in amazement. This was the first human reaction he had seen in Crosbie. The Colonel had been a silent, almost glowering companion for weeks. Blanchard shuffled his feet in embarrassment and he felt his face redden. His easy grace deserted him.

Crosbie folded his thick arms across his saddle and watched Blanchard. The light flush had robbed the young man of the surface sophistication that would always irritate Crosbie.

"We've been a long road together, Mr. Blanchard," he said softly. "It may be far more difficult going back again." He smiled again. "You don't know what our mission is, do you, sir?"

Blanchard knew the question was rhetorical. He shook his head in silence.

Crosbie glanced up at the clear cloudless sky. His sandy eyebrows almost met in a shaggy line as he frowned thoughtfully. "How long will you remain in the Army, Mr. Blanchard?" he asked with seeming irrelevance.

"Why..." Blanchard hesitated, "only until we return to Campus Martius, sir." He tried to focus on the subject. "In fact, General Putnam has instructions to separate me at any time."

"Aye," Crosbie said glumly. He remembered the pleasant little ceremony his officers had arranged when he'd been mustered out. A warming tribute, though slightly drunken. It had been the beginning of a bleak and trying period of adjustment, a time of bad investments and ultimate bankruptcy. "And what do you plan to do when you're a civilian again, Mr. Blanchard?"

Blanchard grinned. "Hadn't quite decided, Colonel. I'd thought some of going down to New Orleans to join up with General Wilkinson. Easy pickings there, I hear."

Crosbie's frown grew deep and somber. General Wilkinson was a scoundrel and there was no argument about it. But that wasn't what Crosbie wanted to talk about. "I had it in mind," he said heavily, "that you might be staying with General Putnam to help him build the Ohio Company."

Blanchard shrugged agreeably. "I helped him some putting it together, Colonel, but I've little stomach for the life. Sight too much work in clearing virgin land," he said easily. "I think there should be more fun with Wilkinson. More money, too."

Crosbie's expression settled into its customary stern lines. He fixed his eyes on a twig above Blanchard's head, trying to show none of the disgust he felt. For a moment he thought of saying nothing more about the mission. Let the sleek young dandy stew in his curiosity a while longer. But the momentary irritation passed and he looked again at Blanchard.

"General Putnam has employed me," he said soberly, "to escort a group of settlers to the Ohio country."

Blanchard's chin dropped. "Settlers? But…but…" He snapped his mouth shut. A quick angry redness touched his face and large knots of muscle bulged along his jaw line but he remained silent.

Crosbie noted Blanchard's reaction and he smiled thinly. "A meager secret, you'll be thinking. And it may be so. The reasons for secrecy are General Putnam's and doubtless they have basis enough." Crosbie stroked his chin slowly.

"General Putnam said nothing more, sir?" Blanchard asked in a tone of pure amazement.

Crosbie delayed a moment before he answered. Blanchard had been Putnam's aide during the war and he had remained with Old Pete while the Ohio Company was being formed. Blanchard should know, far better than Crosbie, what Putnam had in mind.

"Mr. Blanchard," he said in a slow solemn tone, "please attend to me carefully. I have accepted the responsibility for bringing these people safely—and quickly—to the Ohio country. The Ohio Company agent in Alexandria will furnish whatever supplies and equipment they need. And," Crosbie paused momentarily to emphasize what he was going to say, "General Putnam has informed me that this matter is vital to him and his associates in the Ohio Company. No one is to know who sent us and particularly no one is to know exactly where we are bound."

Blanchard leaned an elbow against his saddle. He shook his head as though he were dazed. "I don't understand this, Colonel," he said. "I thought I was in General Putnam's confidence..." He hesitated and glanced quickly at Crosbie, almost flushing. "Not that my feelings are hurt, but..." He gestured vaguely. "Can you tell me anything more, sir?"

Crosbie stiffened irritably. This was what always came of explanations, he thought. He should have given Mr. Blanchard his orders and let it go at that. Now there would be discussions, possibly arguments if Blanchard were that foolish, and afterwards Blanchard would probably sulk for days, nursing his injured sensibilities. But Crosbie didn't attempt to evade the issue. He drew in a long deep breath and tried to speak in an easy tone.

"There's little more to know, Mr. Blanchard. A safe and speedy passage for these settlers. That's our job. The reasons needn't concern us."

Crosbie observed the Lieutenant's tight hard mouth, the hand clenched on the saddle seat. He raised his palm to forestall Blanchard's angry response.

"I shall expect your complete support, Mr. Blanchard," he said quietly. "And I know too much of your professional ability to have any doubts on that score."

The complimentary manner, as well as the words, relaxed Blanchard. Crosbie felt a brief twinge of guilt but he refused to be disturbed about the minor hypocrisy; surely Old Pete insisted upon a high degree of ability in his staff officers.

"In strictest confidence, Mr. Blanchard," Crosbie said solemnly, "General Putnam added one thing more. I can hold you to respect that confidence?"

Blanchard nodded stiffly.

"Good," the Colonel said. "In some fashion, these settlers are a serious embarrassment to General Putnam. They must arrive in Ohio quickly and without undue attention from the public. It is, so General Putnam said, a matter involving his personal honor."

Blanchard's gaze widened slowly. 'Little more to know,' indeed. But what about the mounted stranger who's been prepared to shoot if Crosbie went on to Alexandria? Obviously that man had knowledge of their mission, more knowledge than Blanchard had, possibly even more than Colonel Crosbie had, but the vital fact was that he knew anything at all when General Putnam had insisted upon secrecy. After a long thoughtful moment, Blanchard whistled softly to himself and smiled nervously at Crosbie. "How many settlers do we herd along, Colonel?"

Crosbie's answering smile was wide and genuine. "Couple of hundred, I imagine," he said. "Women and children and all their baggage. It'll be difficult, Mr. Blanchard."

"It will that, sir," Blanchard said soberly. He and Crosbie had spent more than two weeks making the trip from Marietta. Two weeks through hazardous country. How much longer would it take to nurse a migration, complete with children, back along that route? "Where do we take them? Marietta?"

Crosbie reached for his stirrup leather, twisted it and brought his left toe up to the iron. "Not sure," he grunted. "Somewhere down the river, I think. We'll pick up a guide at Marietta."

Blanchard secured the lead-rope for the pack horse and then mounted, holding back to let Crosbie lead the way from the grove to the dirt wagon road. Wide soft meadows bordered the road, and far back, clear of the dust, lay low white houses surrounded by thin stands of shade trees.

"Mighty pretty country," Blanchard said lightly. "I was born and raised not far from here. Down in Albemarle County."

Crosbie muttered something. He was not pleased to be reminded of Blanchard's Tidewater origins. He knew the lieutenant was gentry-born. He was willing to overlook it if he could.

"Reckon these settlers brought any nice young girls with them, Colonel?" Blanchard asked.

"They're Frenchmen," Crosbie said briefly.

"My, my," Blanchard breathed happily. "Might just take one of them out to the Jockey Club some fine afternoon. That's a wonderful place for ..."

"Mr. Blanchard!" Crosbie snapped. "There'll be little enough time for the work we have to do. I'd be making no plans for racing if I were you."

"Sorry, Colonel," Blanchard said softly.

Crosbie settled back heavily in his saddle, wondering what made him lash out at Blanchard like that. He turned to face him. "I'm counting on you to find the wagons we need," he said more amiably. "And the supplies. We'll prepare the list when we find out what the settlers can furnish for themselves. En route, you will command the advance party and the scouts. And you will probably have to train them yourself before we leave Alexandria."

"Yes, sir," Blanchard said.

Crosbie reined in to let Blanchard come abreast. "We've little time, Mr. Blanchard," he said. "It's June now and the summer seems long, but we'll be hard put to it to get these people settled before the first snow."

"It's little enough time," Blanchard said with understanding. "I know the trouble of moving troops, sir. I imagine this will be even slower." He grinned widely at the Colonel. "I'll not add to your burdens, sir."

The note of mockery was not far beneath Blanchard's tone, Crosbie suspected. But there was nothing he could take exception to in the words themselves. He nodded soberly and let his heavy gelding move ahead of Blanchard's horse.

As the wagon road approached a turn it dipped down into a long shallow valley. From that point the road ran straight for Alexandria and they could see the town far below, spreading along the riverbank. A long-legged black horse left a pale ribbon of dust as it held to a fast rocking trot up the easy slope toward them. Crosbie glanced back at Blanchard, signaling him to stay back where he was. Blanchard sucked in a deep breath and held it a moment. What now? Was the Colonel expecting trouble from every traveler they met? Crosbie lifted the flap of one saddle holster and cocked the pistol. He left the pistol in his holster with the flap hanging open. Behind him he heard Blanchard bring the hammer of his long rifle slowly back to full cock.

The three bay horses maintained their long swift walk and the distance between them and the black horse diminished quickly. The rider—a stranger—reined in abruptly, halting a few yards ahead of Crosbie. He touched his ornate laced hat with a grimy forefinger.

"Warm day, gentlemen," he said. His thin dark face smiled but his cautious eyes studied their uniforms closely. "You've come for the Frenchies, eh?" he asked with a suspicious inflection.

Crosbie's bushy eyebrows pulled down sternly. "It's a warm day, sir," he said curtly. He walked his bay level with the black, holding it at the edge of the road. Then he motioned for Blanchard to pass.

"My apologies for being so rude, Colonel," the rider said. He crowded his mount closer to Crosbie, trying to make him swing out again to block the road. "All Alexandria has heard you were coming, sir." He smiled again, clearing his throat with a pompous sound. "My name is Budd, sir. Oliver Budd. A name not unknown in these parts. If I could be of assistance in any way..."

"Thank you, Mr. Budd," Crosbie said flatly. "We've no need of assistance at the moment."

"You may think differently soon, Colonel."

Crosbie stared at him bleakly. "Possibly, sir," he said, holding his voice to a mild, indifferent tone. His eyes moved over the rider, observing his soiled blue riding coat, his unpolished boots, his shaggy unkempt horse. "I doubt it."

Budd flushed quickly. "You'll change your tune, Colonel," he said nastily. "Officers ain't the lordly ones. Not now. You'll find that uniform does you no good with the people here." His harsh thin voice cracked angrily and his dark poorly shaven face was tense.

"We'll proceed, Mr. Blanchard," Crosbie said quietly, watching the rider.

"Now, just a minute," Budd said hastily. "I have something to…"

Blanchard flipped his right hand, heaving the lead-rope and dropped the end across Budd's lap. It touched one hand and Budd looked down at it, not moving. Blanchard smiled at him. "We'll be going along, Mister. Just move back." His soft voice was smooth, almost purring.

Budd turned his head to Crosbie, then looked back at Blanchard as he felt the lead-rope scrape across his hand.

"Back, Mister," Blanchard repeated softly.

Budd stared sullenly. He contracted his reins, forced his horse to the edge of the road. Crosbie let his gelding walk forward. Blanchard waited a moment, then spurred his mount and hauled at the lead-rope. He smiled pleasantly at Budd as he passed. "Another time, Mister," he said lightly.

CHAPTER TWO

Alexandria in 1790 was already a city of brick, an enduring city of grace and traditional solidity. Colonel Crosbie and Lieutenant Blanchard rode slowly through the outskirts without halting, turned at Royal Street and walked their weary horses toward the City Tavern.

"You'll have the housekeeping assignment, Mr. Blanchard," Crosbie said as they drew near. "Get us two rooms if you can and for God's sake, find someone to wash our dirty clothes before we founder."

Blanchard nodded. He shouted at a tanned barefoot boy, threw him the lead-rope of the pack horse and swung down to the brick sidewalk.

"Plenty of oats and not too much water," he said to the boy. "And get your back into it when you rub them down. The pack goes up to my room." He turned to Crosbie. "Will you want to go up now, sir?"

Crosbie considered a moment. He leaned down toward the stable boy. "Sonny, do you know where the head man of the Frenchmen is staying?" A wide copper coin appeared magically in his thick fingers and the boy beamed.

"Shorely do, seh," he grinned. "He's down to Doctor Gaines's house." He pointed a freckled finger down the street. "Jest go down two streets thataway, then a couple toward the river. You cain't miss it. Three stories high with gre't big ole belly winders."

Crosbie smiled. He dropped the penny into the waiting palm and dismounted. "Take my horse, too, sonny."

He stretched heartily and settled his sword belt around his waist. "I'll just go along now, Mr. Blanchard, and see what our problem looks like. I'll be back for supper, most likely. Be sure we get something decent."

Blanchard nodded casually as Crosbie turned away, but his gaze was curious as it followed the Colonel's tall figure out of sight. A strange man, the Crosbie of Craigsmuir, and one who attracted even stranger happenings. Crosbie passed the tavern entrance, heading toward the Potomac, and walked in stiff jarring strides, his spurs rattling gently and his heavy boots making the loosely set bricks wobble uncertainly in the sidewalk.

Colonel Crosbie paid little attention to the city as he worked his way toward the river embankment. Royal Street ended abruptly at the high berm above the water and he turned right automatically, his mind occupied with the practical details of his mission. The greatest problem, he felt, would lie in the number of people he would have to take by wagon to Pittsburgh or Redstone Old Fort and down the Ohio from there. If the Frenchmen were no more than a handful, Crosbie would have anticipated no trouble. But hundreds were a different matter. A broad-wheeled Pennsylvania wagon would carry four tons of freight. Food they could buy en route, provided they took…

Crosbie went by the low green orchards along the embankment, the pleasant brick and clapboard houses with their tiny lawns facing the river where small boats plied busily and fought for the available docking space—Chesapeake fishermen, Baltimore sloops, square-rigged stumpy British ships, light shallops and pinks, cutters and longboats. As he walked briskly along the shore, Crosbie heard a thin cat-like squeal near him, unconsciously noting it without focusing his mind on the noise. It came again, higher and sharper this time, knifing into his brain like a sudden scream for help. Crosbie stopped short.

He listened, leaning forward slightly in concentration. The sound was muted and strangled when he heard it again. It seemed to come from the peach orchard beside him, from a point just above the water. Crosbie moved closer, edging toward the trees, drawn by the whistling screech.

Leaning with evident contentment against a stunted peach tree, a small dark-haired boy grunted with effort, his face contorted and strained. The wild skirling sound blasted again through the orchard, a full true tone with a complete purity that could only have come through accident. The small boy eased his clenched fingers, raised his head and smiled ecstatically at the sky. Crosbie's somber tired face broke into the same wide grin. He stepped around the low tree.

"A pibroch," he muttered softly, almost to himself. "Surely it is a pibroch."

The boy held both short arms tightly around a distended silken bag, his right elbow tied tightly with a roman-striped silken ribbon to a flat ornamented bellows. The boy's chubby fingertips wouldn't spread quite far enough to reach all the holes of the chanter pipe and he had partially blocked the bottom two with stumpy twigs. While Crosbie watched, the boy's elbow pumped swiftly to inflate the bag. Then he squeezed, shooting the air through the drones and chanter pipes with an uneven pressure. Crosbie scowled heavily at the resultant screech.

"A *musette*," he said scornfully. "A spindly Frenchified *musette*."

The boy glanced up, wide-eyed, suddenly alarmed. He scrambled to his feet awkwardly, holding the *musette* half hidden behind the tree. Crosbie relaxed his dour scowl and almost smiled.

"Now don't skitter off, boy," he growled pleasantly. "It's not a pibroch you've got but it's the same family." He eyed the frail instrument under the boy's arm. "A lady's *musette*, I'd say."

The boy's solemn dark eyes lost their panicked tension and were now only bewildered. He bobbed his wildly tousled head in a clumsy bow.

"C'est un cornemuse, monsieur," he said in a boy's nervous treble. *"La musette..."*

Crosbie's faint smile became a quick darting grin. The few words of Parisian French sounded suddenly warming and familiar to him, as though he had walked through a hidden doorway into a familiar world again. French and Gaelic had been his boyhood tongues and his fluent English was an acquired language that would always be harsh and unpleasant to his ear.

"You'll be one of the Frenchmen, then," Crosbie said amiably, dropping into French with a feeling of relief that surprised even him. "What's your name, boy?"

The boy offered a tentative smile. "I am Jacques Carel," he said. He stared at Crosbie's gaudy dress uniform, at the gilt epaulettes and sword hilt, at the brave plume. "But you, *monsieur le général,* you are not..."

"I am no general," Crosbie said heavily. "I am a Scot." That would explain almost anything to a normal French boy. Scots could be—and were—men of all ranks and attainments in France, buffoons or generals, traveling mountebanks or dukes of the realm. But no matter how honored, how apparently stable, they were always suspected of erratic impulsiveness.

"L'Ecossaise." Jacques nodded wisely. That was enough for him to know. A man in a glittering unknown uniform who spoke a Parigot with the ease of a Paris gamin—that was puzzling. But a Scot! Indeed yes, why not? One realized that Scots were always puzzling. It did no good to worry about such things.

Crosbie's curiosity about the boy's instrument was still keen; at least it made the same sort of sound as a pibroch, even if it was a silly toy. The *cornemuse* was a frilly version of the *musette,* a bagpipe that operated with a bellows to pump the bag rather than a stout pair of lungs. But the principle was the same in either case. As a young officer in the French army, Crosbie had often seen the stalwart Auvergne pipers on parade when the French troops assembled, but he'd never been curious enough to investigate their pipes. This delicate affair that Jacques carried under his arm was probably one of the ridiculous toys the Queen and her ladies played with at *Le Petit Trianon*. Not that Crosbie moved in such circles, but one heard reports. He knelt slowly, moving cautiously so as to minimize the strain on his tight doeskin breeches.

Jacques pumped the bag tight again and tried another note as the Colonel watched. Crosbie waved him to silence and had him pump again. This time Crosbie fingered the stops of the chanter pipe.

"Pump harder, boy," he smiled. "Eh, Jacques, is it? Well, pump harder and keep the pressure even and I'll play ye a tune to dance to."

Jacques flailed his right elbow, bringing the silken bag to dangerous tension maintaining it while Crosbie's solid fingers stumbled slowly up and down the chanter, finding the notes. Not the full nine-note range of pibroch, but fair enough. Crosbie took a deep happy breath, moved closer to the boy. His fingers, almost without effort, found the positions.

"Charley Is My Darlin'" is a children's tune, a light and gay ballad. But it is also a lament for the Stuart cause. And even a hardened Scottish soldier of fifty, tough and solid with his years, may sometimes feel a dampness under the eyelids and a vague dark sorrow. Crosbie cleared his throat roughly and made his fingertips dance over the chanter, and Jacques laughed for happiness.

Crosbie rose stiffly, stretching the kinks out of his back. He nodded to the laughing boy. "Aye, Jacques," he said, "it's the pipes for a lively tune." He pulled at his tight waistcoat to erase the wrinkles and ruffled the boy's hair with one big hand. "When we get to Marietta," he said, suddenly recalling his mission, "then I'll show you a set of pipes fit for ..."

A thin crackling sound behind them took the boy's rapt attention from Crosbie. Jacques stiffened briefly, stared wildly about, poised for flight. Then he stopped and dug one foot at the turf in obvious embarrassment. Crosbie pivoted quickly on his heel.

The woman was still young, not much past thirty, Crosbie thought. She was rosy and plump in a tightly laced bodice that emphasized a firm and full bosom that needed little emphasis. Normally her round face would be smiling and the fine lines at the corners of her eyes would come from laughter and not the worried tension that marked them now. She snatched swiftly at the hesitant boy, holding him with a firm grip while she stripped the gay elbow ribbon from his arm and captured the frail *cornemuse*.

"Jacques," she almost wailed, "*la cornemuse de la bonne maman! Vous êtes...*"

Crosbie interrupted with his gruffly fluent French, anxious only to delay the scene until he could make his escape. Obviously the boy had taken a treasured instrument, one forbidden to him without adult supervision. And Crosbie's playing had led Jacques's mother straight to him. In a way then, it was Crosbie's fault, too.

"And I've appointed Jacques piper to our expedition," Crosbie went on, desperately trying to distract the woman. "He's even got the name for it, hasn't he? Jock. A fine name for a piper. We'll have Jock skirling for us each evening. That is, after a few days' practice..."

Crosbie's voice dwindled away as he became more aware of the woman's quiet twinkling regard. To see him she had to tilt her head far back and thick soft plaits of hair fell smoothly down her back, reminding Crosbie... of what? Something about a dark-haired girl with unruly hair. Something about a quiet almost solemn expression that was but a flimsy mask for gaiety. It was France, surely. Or was it Spain, that girl in Burgos ? But the words died in his throat as he looked into her eyes.

"I am grateful, *monsieur*," she said demurely, still keeping her tight clutch on the boy's arm. "My son misses the proper instruction of his poor dead father…" The tips of two teeth barely showed on her lower lip and she let her eyes drop wistfully, lamenting her widowed estate, but being sure that the Colonel understood her availability.

Crosbie flushed slightly, but he pulled himself sternly erect, bowed stiffly. "Colonel Duncan Crosbie, ma'am, at your service."

The answering curtsey was deep and smooth but somehow incorrect. It showed instruction and control but little practice. "Madame Carmelite Carel," she said softly. Her hand forced her small son into a clumsy bow. "And my son, Jacques…"

"Jock and I are already old friends," Crosbie said firmly. He felt foolish, damned foolish, but then every man has felt foolish in just that way and for just that reason. The wench was giggling at him, he felt sure of that. Under the demurely lowered eyelids would be a wide and wicked grin, hidden by the inclination of her head. He could see only the shadow of her expression. But there would be time. Time enough for anything on the road to the Ohio and by God, Duncan Crosbie was just the man to…

"Possibly, ma'am, you could tell me how to reach Doctor Gaines's house?" he suggested slyly. He could pretend a complete ignorance and then she might come with him.

The response was more than Crosbie hoped for. The lowered gaze came up again, sparkling as he'd suspected, the lips parted and firmly round, an expression of intense excitement.

"You have come to meet the Marquis?" she asked swiftly in that fast crisp tongue of the Parisienne. "Then we are finally to start? Finally to leave…"

"I know of no Marquis, ma'am," the Colonel said stiffly, still determined to maintain the discretion he had pledged to General Putnam. "But if he is the leader of the French *émigrés*…"

"Yes, yes," she broke in excitedly. "In a sense, he is the leader, the man of experience and position. But are we to go, *mon colonel?* Are we finally to leave this ... this ..."

Her clutching hand had released Jacques and fastened avidly on Crosbie's arm. It made a small patch of warmth that he found oddly distracting. He smiled down at the vivacious face and touched her hand with one huge fingertip in an awkwardly gallant gesture.

"It is a matter for discretion, ma'am," he said in a half whisper. "But you and young Jock might begin to pack, if you were of the mind." He nearly winked at the small rosy woman. "It might not be a waste of time, though I promise nothing, you understand."

"Ah, such evasions," she protested archly. She waved the dainty *cornemuse* in a mock threat. But the warm hand on Crosbie's arm patted lightly at the uniformed sleeve. "Shall I then send Jacques with you to lead you to the Marquis? Or should I ..."

"If your duties permit, ma'am," Crosbie growled, "I should be honored by your company."

"But it is I who would be honored, *mon colonel,*" she said, her eyes dancing with amusement at the stiff and determined soldier. "To guide to the Marquis the bearer of news for which we have waited and hoped."

"I am known as Duncan to my friends, ma'am," Crosbie said, plodding forward with a sure, though rusty approach. By God, it had been more than a year since he'd tossed his bonnet at a girl. And the easy way of it might have escaped him, but the goal was there, clear and sharp. It remained only to move forward firmly.

The light warm hand smoothed at the fine cloth of his best uniform.

"Duncan," she said softly and to Crosbie's ear it was "Dooncahn," the long rolling vowels of French that were so much the same as Gaelic, and to Crosbie, just as welcome.

He moved forward erectly, proud and gay with the sprightly woman worn like a favor on his sleeve, letting her lead him gently by the arm. The little boy pranced along beside them dividing his attention between the forbidden *cornemuse* his mother still retained and the glittering full dress uniform of the huge Scottish Colonel. The dour fixed lines around Crosbie's thin mouth gradually smoothed away as they walked through the warm afternoon shadows.

CHAPTER THREE

Lieutenant Blanchard drew a long relieved breath as he watched Crosbie's jarring strides carry him quickly down Royal Street. After some two weeks of constant association, he was glad to be free of Crosbie for a time. Not that he disliked the Colonel, he told himself. As a matter of fact, Blanchard decided he liked him better than most. He liked the slow deliberation with which Crosbie approached a problem, and the clear potentiality of speed and sureness that lay under the Colonel's dour and diffident attitude. Crosbie was a fine soldier, no mistake about that, but he was getting a little long in the tooth now. He probably couldn't remember back to the days when he'd worn only the left-shoulder epaulette of a lieutenant. Meaning no disrespect to that good gentleman, Blanchard grinned to himself, but Crosbie just wasn't the company for a young subaltern. Not during the first few hours in a wild sweet town like Alexandria.

Blanchard stood in the warm sun, batting his eyes lazily, looking up at the front of the tavern while he waited for the stable boy to get the pack and saddlebags. The City Tavern didn't look as monstrous big as it had when Blanchard's father had brought him here years ago, but it was a good sturdy size and shape, two stories of brick with carved doors and trim around the windows. It was still the best tavern in town, unless maybe the Bunch of Grapes had improved lately. When the stable boy staggered around the corner, all that Blanchard could see was the bulging withe carrier and the two sets of saddlebags that rode precariously beside it. But the boy was willing; he reached a hand for

Blanchard's rifle, obviously intending to add it to his burden. But no hand but Blanchard's ever touched his precious Leman. He swung it around out of reach and then took a step forward to relieve the boy of some of the load. But a rotund bald-headed man in a long wrinkled white apron scuttled out of the entrance and reached the boy first.

"I'll take care of it, Lieutenant," the man said in a hoarse amiable shout. "Just you leave it to me." The man shoved the stumbling boy ahead of him, helping him on his way with a kick, and all the while smiling widely at Blanchard and bobbing his polished head to usher him inside.

"A nice sunny room, now, Lieutenant?" he asked coaxingly in that barely audible shout. "A comfortable and clean..."

"Two rooms," Blanchard said crisply, watching the boy force the withe carrier up the narrow staircase.

"Oh," the man hesitated. "Well, now I just haven't got... for a fact now, Lieutenant. There's only one empty room up there. 'Course we got some space in the loft but I wouldn't think you'd want anything like that. Will there be two of you, did you say?"

Blanchard halted with one foot on the lower tread. The bald-headed man kept bobbing his shiny pate in a distracting rhythm.

"Nice big bed up there, Lieutenant," he shouted. "Plenty room enough for two, if, eh..." the innkeeper permitted himself a discreet snigger. "That is, if it ain't, uh... so to speak..."

"It ain't," Blanchard said sourly. "I'll share with Colonel Crosbie." He waved the man on. "Well, let's get up, man. I want something to wash the dust out of my throat."

The entrance hall was narrow and Blanchard stepped back to let the aproned innkeeper precede him. Through the wide double doors to his right he had a clear view of the spacious high-ceilinged taproom, and there was just a faint whiff of rum and cinnamon, of beer and brandy all fused together in a wonderful aroma. Blanchard turned away with regret. Just a few more minutes and he'd be back downstairs to investigate the pleasures of the company. There was a pleasant bustle in the taproom and the low relaxed tones of men talking about things of no importance while they held glasses and mugs full of negus or punch or whatever it was, drinking a little now and again and murmuring amiably when someone said something, but not really thinking of anything except going home for dinner pretty soon, but not so soon as to make it necessary to hurry with this drink.

Blanchard passed the doorway slowly, then stopped and went back. That soiled bright-blue coat, wasn't that familiar? And those grimy sleeve bands that slender hands were elegantly rolling back along the coat cuff, where had he seen them before. He almost stepped inside, but he stopped when he remembered. Of course, that was Mr. Oliver Budd, the greasy unshaven horseman on the big black hunter. The man who knew more about their mission than Blanchard did. And didn't like what he knew. Well, he would keep for a while.

Blanchard went up the narrow dark stairway with long steps, hitting every other tread. The bald-headed innkeeper stood in an open doorway, waiting for him, wiping his perspiring fat hands on his unclean apron and bobbing inanely. Blanchard felt like kicking him. He fumbled in his pockets, found a coin and flipped it to him. The man caught it with a surprisingly agile movement.

"We have a new shipment of fine French claret, Lieutenant," the man offered hopefully. "Just in yesterday. Only one dollar a bottle and the very best ..."

"Rotgut," Blanchard muttered sourly. "What rum have you got?"

"Barbados, Lieutenant. The real Barbados. And a little Medford. But I can sell the Barbados for a dollar a gallon as a special price to you, sir."

"There's nothing special about the price," Blanchard said flatly. "But bring up a gallon. Now what about supper?"

The man wiped the back of his hand across his mouth. "Well, sir, we've only a joint of beef ready. I'm afraid we don't have a steady demand for much better. But I could find you some fowl if you could wait a bit. A nice turkey now. Or some ..."

Blanchard shuddered involuntarily. Turkey, good God! He and Crosbie had been living on little else. But a thick cut of beef now ...

"The beef will do," he said with an attempt at casualness. "A couple of chickens, and a dozen soft-shelled crabs. What about oysters? Do you have ice?"

"Well, yes, we've got ice, Lieutenant. But you don't want oysters right now. They won't be worth eating until Autumn."

"Yes," Blanchard said. "I'd forgotten. Well, just the things I mentioned then. You'll have time enough. I'll wait for the Colonel."

Blanchard tossed his cocked hat carelessly on the bed, balanced his prized Leman near the wide window and picked up the bulging withe carrier. He opened the fastenings and upended it onto the bed, letting the rumpled mass of clothes and travel gear fall onto the counterpane. The Colonel's linen hunting shirt seemed the biggest item, Blanchard thought. He tied both arms of the shirt up tightly around the neck and used the body of the shirt as a receptacle for the soiled laundry. The grimy buckskin he pitched into a corner. You couldn't do much with buckskins. If they got too gamy for your taste, you bought a new set. If not, you kept them until they wore out or got too stiff from constant wetting, or too greasy. But hardly anyone ever tried to wash them.

Blanchard had his fat bundle trussed up when the bald-headed innkeeper edged through the open door with a gallon jug of rum and two thick ill-made glasses in his hands. The jug had already been unstoppered and the cork rode lightly in one of the glasses. Blanchard dropped his bundle and accepted the jug happily. He took the first sip back-country style, finger through the handle and resting the belly of the jug on his elbow and raising it slowly while he held his mouth ready. The rum was a warm spreading knot in his stomach, a fine rosy feeling after weeks without a drop. He beamed at the bald-headed man, took one of the glasses and poured out a brimming measure.

Blanchard sat on the edge of the featherbed and balanced his cocked hat rakishly above one eyebrow. "Excellent rum," he said pleasantly, "but the price is no bargain."

The innkeeper spread his soft red hands helplessly. "These days, sir, what with …"

"Never mind," Blanchard broke in. "If you've got any money these days, you're a scoundrel. Only scoundrels have any money." He closed one eye and looked at the bobbing bald head over the rim of the glass. He drank a large gulp of rum and said, "And I'll wager you've got a lot of money."

The innkeeper's appalled expression delighted Blanchard. Damned strong rum, he thought. I'll have to go easy on that. He drank down the rest of the glassful and settled his hat squarely. "Well, my fat wealthy landlord, I'll be in your tap-room if I'm wanted." He toed the bundle of dirty clothes. "Have your washerwoman get these things ready by tomorrow. No delay."

The fat innkeeper shook his head sadly. "She's run off," he said glumly. "Only yesterday. I swear I don't know what's come over people these days, not wanting to do a fair day's work for their wages any more. Shiftless and …"

Blanchard booted the bundle out the door.

"Lieutenant, there's these no-good Frenchies that do washing," the landlord said eagerly "Hardly any of them got any money. They take in washing, do cooking and …" he tried to nudge Blanchard with a pudgy elbow … "some say they got other tricks, too."

Blanchard looked away from the smirking man. Every time he looked at that face, he wanted to cuff it away. One more look and he would.

"Whereabouts are these washing Frenchies?" he asked coldly.

"Just up the street, Lieutenant," the landlord said quickly. "I sent that shiftless boy out to get your chickens, but just the minute he gets back, I'll send him ..."

Blanchard muttered, "Never mind." He went out into the hallway, kicked the bundle again, sending it rolling soundlessly down the stairs.

He clumped noisily down after the bundle, an irritated frown cut deeply between his eyes. Hell, his feelings weren't injured; he'd done his own washing many's the time during the war, but this was different. A man didn't want to be bothered with picayune details like laundry when his mouth was all fixed for those aromatic drinks down in the taproom. He kicked the fat bundle again, pretending it was his portly, shouting landlord and immediately felt better. He picked up the bulging hunting shirt and walked out the door to the sidewalk.

Alexandria seemed clean and exciting after the open country and Blanchard went down Royal Street with an easy stride, holding the bundle wide to keep it away from his curved dragoon's saber. The half-pint of rum he'd had in the tavern was beginning to have its effect and this piddling chore had ceased to be an annoyance. Blanchard whistled softly between his teeth and looked sharply at the houses on both sides of the street as he passed.

The landlord was right. From the first corner beyond the City Tavern, Blanchard could see a small sign in a window across the street. In fairly large letters, printed by an unsure hand, it said, "Washing and Mending." And under it in small letters, "Blanchisseuse." That would be French, he figured, but it probably didn't refer to the "other tricks" the smirking landlord had mentioned. No use hoping, he told himself. They wouldn't come right out with it. Not on a main street that way.

The door was flush with the brick sidewalk and Blanchard noticed it was standing partially open. He shoved the fat bundle against the door and followed it into the dim room.

An attempt had been made to give something of a commercial air to the room, two spindly kitchen tables having been pushed together end-to-end, making a counter just inside the door. A pair of chairs stood behind the counter and on the seat of one was a small wad of sewing with a needle jabbed into the mass and a fine ivory thimble riding the needle. The rest of the room was too dim for Blanchard to see anything at first, but his eyes gradually became adjusted to the light and then he saw something move in the adjoining room. He dropped his bundle on the makeshift counter and crossed to the inner door, his spurred boots making almost no sound on the carpeted floor.

What he could see was delightful. He edged nearer, being purposefully careful now to move quietly. The girl was bending over a low shelf that held neat stacks of laundered garments. Each stack appeared to have an identifying tag or label, but the girl was having trouble finding the one she wanted because the room was so shadowy. She turned a little. The light wasn't strong enough but Blanchard could make out the tumbled mass of wild dark hair, the thin simple gown that clung lovingly to smooth round curves, and in that posture, the low-cut bodice that was no concealment at all. The angle was wrong, though, and Blanchard saw only the soft upper slopes of her small breasts. Something glittered on one hand as she moved.

Afterward, Blanchard always blamed the ruin whenever he remembered the next few minutes. And it was a memory that came in a flush of wild embarrassment. He stepped lithely forward, brought his right hand into position and laid his warm suddenly trembling palm on the tightest part of the gown. Laid it on softly and patted. Just once. There was no time for more.

The girl straightened and whirled toward him. First amazement—that was brief—then glowing rage colored her face. Blanchard saw then that the simple gown was not so simple. Or rather, the simplicity of the draping silk was cunning artifice.

And the tangled lustrous hair was a carefully designed coiffure. The glitter on her hand was a cluster of emeralds. But the wilder glitter was her flashing eyes. Blanchard saw little more before the bejeweled hand slapped across his face with a sting like a whip. The fatuous, rum-hopeful grin was wiped away. His paunty cocked hat spun unnoticed to the floor and Blanchard took one involuntary step backward.

He heard an infuriated spate of words that held no meaning for him. There was a brief—and blistering—pause. Then the girl raised her voice and called, "Lucie!"

A young woman appeared in the doorway and murmured something in a softly questioning tone. Blanchard could not see her very clearly but she seemed to be simply dressed in gray and wore no jewels to glitter in the dim light. Her pale blonde hair was plain and uncurled. The dark beauty spat more furious words. Then the elegantly simple gown whirled across the room, followed by the blonde young woman named Lucie. A door slammed explosively and Blanchard stood foolishly alone, his mouth gaping.

Only vaguely he realized a brisk voice was speaking to him. That must have been minutes later but he was still half dazed. His hat seemed to float in midair just under his eyes. He took it automatically and settled it on his head.

"The bundle outside is yours, young man?"

Blanchard blinked his eyes and turned. The waspish voice came from a slight, grey-haired woman who stood primly with folded hands, her small mouth tucked in pursily.

"Uh…yes, ma'am," Blanchard stammered. He backed toward the outer door, almost catching his spur in the carpeting. "No starch, except in the ruffles, if you please, ma'am," he mumbled.

He didn't wait for her answer. The open doorway was a brilliantly lighted refuge and he backed awkwardly through it, bowing stiffly to the prim old lady.

Once in the open again, Blanchard pulled in a deep breath, held it and then let it whistle out while he shook his head slowly. A fine looking girl like that and he had to go and ruin everything. His toes curled in his boots at the thought. And that rapid spatter of words, that was French wasn't it ? So she'd be along with the rest of the Frenchies. All the way to the Ohio country. Blanchard pounded angrily along toward the tavern. Most probably the prettiest girl of the lot and what good that do him? What chance would he have now?

Blanchard's natural good humor had almost returned by the time he reached the tavern. He went straight into the taproom this time and eased himself into a polished armchair at an empty table.

Well, so he'd insulted her. That was bad. But maybe it wasn't too bad. From what he'd heard during the war, maybe it wasn't such a bad start after all. Real gay types, these French girls, he'd been told. Just maybe...

"Something with ice in it," he told the waiting boy. "And bring me a pipeful of tobacco."

He leaned back in the chair and stretched both legs far out. The tavern was doing a fair business. A quiet knot of respectable looking townsmen sat at the table just inside the door, and a rowdier collection of young blades had their heads together over the board beside them. They looked like they were cooking up some devilment, Blanchard thought. For a moment he considered joining them. But Colonel Crosbie would be along soon. It wouldn't be worth the trouble of moving. Those other men at the table next to the scullery door were a scurvy lot for a good taproom. Most innkeepers wouldn't let such a pack inside his door. One of them had a sailor's stocking cap crammed over matted hair and maybe that explained matters. A sailor could do a useful favor for a landlord, provided both of them were willing to risk the penalty for smuggling. That new shipment of French claret now, or maybe the Barbados rum, were both of them properly taxed, or had the fat shouting landlord rushed them into his cellar during the dark of the night? Blanchard yawned heavily, reached for the frosted mug the boy had placed on his table. He sniffed happily at the pungent mint odor. What did he care about the rascally landlord anyway? Or the smuggling sailor?

Blanchard grinned into his drink, sniffed again at the mixture of brandy and rum and mint all chilled beautifully by the chunk of ice floating in the mug. He sipped slowly, letting the icy drink roll over his tongue. He settled even lower in his chair until he was barely supported on the seat. And just as he shifted comfortably, a heavy shoe cracked against his booted ankle.

It was a wide-toed, rough leather shoe buckled with tarnished brass, and it had not struck Blanchard accidentally. He lifted his gaze slowly, observing the twisted yarn stockings, the stained canvas pantaloons with filthy spots where tarred fingers had slovenly wiped. A wide leather belt with another stained brass buckle, a greasy shirt that might once have been white and above it all, a red-eyed leering face with straggly hair over each ear and a red knitted cap pulled down tightly. Small bloodshot eyes were set deep in the mottled flesh; the bulbous pocked nose looked like a radish that has been nibbled and then discarded. The heavy-set sailor grinned wolfishly with a slack, tobacco-stained mouth, displaying broken yellow teeth. He leaned forward, blowing his stinking breath into Blanchard's face.

"Not enough room for you, Bucko?" the sailor snarled. He glanced down at his shoe beside Blanchard's boots, drew it back and kicked again.

But this time Blanchard's foot was out of reach, lifted in a sudden reflex. The sailor's heavy shoe thudded against the puncheon floor, skidded under Blanchard's boot and was momentarily pinned there by his spurred heel.

Blanchard's hand gripped the heavy pewter mug with a convulsive fury but he forced a thin cold smile. The sailor staggered off-balance, then righted himself again with an ungainly lurch.

He steadied himself with a hand on the table, his face only inches away from Blanchard's.

The shapeless snaggle-toothed mouth poured out a flow of snarling obscenity, words that hardly seemed justified in Blanchard's view. The sailor's huge scarred fist tightened on the table but he delayed his attack stupidly while he worked himself into a blind red rage. And that was a mistake.

The unexpected intensity of the sailor's rasping screeching curses had startled Blanchard and he wasted a moment searching for a reason behind the attack. But the senseless lashing obscenity, the obviously manufactured affront, turned his mind another way. In a dark unthinking part of his mind, Blanchard remembered the man in the soiled blue riding coat. Mr. Oliver Budd. Mr. Budd had been in the tavern when Blanchard arrived. Blanchard had seen him, and to be visible from the doorway, Mr. Budd must have been sitting at the table near the scullery door—the sailor's table. Then the reason was clear to Blanchard. He didn't know what was behind it, but Mr. Budd was the connection. Blanchard's hand twitched, almost reflexively, jerking in a flat low curve controlled carefully.

The icy minted drink splashed on the sailor's forehead, soaking his tangled hair, blinding him for the brief moment it took Blanchard to get to his feet. He shoved hard at his table, skidding the heavy oak forward against the sailor's legs. And that was luck for Blanchard.

He came erect in time to see the sedate city men scatter from their table and edge toward the door. He stood alone watching the heavy swearing sailor fighting his way around the table. But the sailor wasn't alone any longer. Two dirty bullnecked men were on either side, flanking Blanchard neatly. He saw a flash of steel blade in a hand and he swept his arm wide, driving the solid armchair across the room where it would impede the knifeman. Then he snatched for his sword hilt, dragging the heavy curved blade out of the scabbard.

The low-set man on his blind side ran at him, ominously silent like a mute trained to kill on signal, head pulled between his lumpy shoulders, both arms wide and curved to grab. His tarred hands closed on Blanchard's sword arm, dragging him almost to the floor. He held on desperately, head snuggled against Blanchard, waiting for the others to get Blanchard while it was safe.

A driving knee freed Blanchard briefly. The sailor snatched a wooden piggin of small beer from a table and swung it hard against Blanchard s head just as the Lieutenant was whirling away from the other. The hollow piggin rang loudly in the room, a clear sharp tone like a billiard stick meeting a ball. And Blanchard crumpled slowly. His eyes were still open, his hand was clenched tightly around his sword hilt, and he saw the burly sailor holding the cracked piggin and waiting for him to fall. For a moment, Blanchard had the weird illusion that he too was standing apart, watching a tall dragoon officer as he crumpled slowly to the floor.

He was unconscious when he reached the floor and later he remembered the low roaring growl only because he had thought it was a foghorn like the conches blown along the Chesapeake during the winter months. It had the same mournful, outraged tone and it built in volume the same way, rising to a peak of pure distilled fury. Blanchard remembered nothing more.

But the heavy shoe of the sailor never reached his head. It was pulled back ready to strike but it hesitated when the growling bellow sounded. The sailor looked up, startled, stared unbelievingly at Crosbie's huge frame filling the doorway. He tried then to kick Blanchard, bringing his foot forward swiftly, but Crosbie was on him with a cat-like pounce that shook his steady leg.

The sailor didn't get a second chance. Crosbie's big fist slammed him away, sent him reeling down the room toward the scullery door. One of his squat assistants jumped for the Colonel, holding his knife low between thumb and forefinger, aiming for the stomach. Crosbie turned his hip quickly, let the blade pass and clamped hard fingers on the wrist. He held the low-set man like that for a moment, then spun quickly, hauling him off his feet and whirling him through the air. The spinning feet smacked sickeningly against the third man, catching him solidly above the ear. Then Crosbie let the knifeman go, sliding him into a tangled knot with the other man.

Crosbie's infuriated roaring growl sounded constantly, but now it carried an aggrieved tone, the note of a reasonable man who finds himself required by circumstances to do things he really doesn't approve.

The sailor pushed away from the scullery door, dug a short tarred knife from his pocket and advanced toward Crosbie. His two assistants at the far end of the room climbed to their feet, one helping the other and both crept quietly toward the front window, obviously retiring from a fight that was becoming too serious for them. The sailor eyed them, saw them slip through the windows. He took another look at the towering Colonel, at the bulging power under the wide glittering epaulettes and watched grimly as Crosbie flicked the dainty murderous dirk from his sword belt. The sailor spun quickly on one foot, diving toward the scullery door, moving with the ungainly motion and incredible speed of a land crab.

Crosbie roared deep in his throat. The sailor was too far away to reach and he was damned if he'd run after him. He took two long steps and then halted. As the sailor reached the door, bent low to turn toward the back entrance, Crosbie lunged suddenly forward, hurling the dirk in a straight line. The sailor screamed once, a high contraction of fear in his throat. The dirk sliced above his head, pinning the knitted cap to the wall, hitting the timber with a thud. The enameled hilt glistened against the drab wall, the cap dangling gayly from the point as a few scattered snips of greasy hair sifted lightly to the floor.

The only sound was the sailor's heavy footsteps as they pounded swiftly across the scullery floor and out into the yard.

Crosbie stood quietly, breathing with heavy labored motions of his chest. He walked stolidly across the room, pulled his *skenedhu* from the wall, needing almost his full power to get it free. The taproom customers watched him cautiously as he returned to Blanchard's inert body.

Crosbie put away the dirk and a long soft sigh murmured in the silent room. But no one spoke as the Colonel bent to lift Blanchard. He raised the young man, let him fall forward across his shoulder and stood again, being careful to retrieve Blanchard's cocked hat as he rose.

The customers remained silent with a silence that had something of the air of the habitual about it, a watchful silence that stored up every minute detail for the recounting that would begin the moment Crosbie left the taproom. At the door, Crosbie paused, half turned and raised his hat to them briefly. Then he went out, carrying Blanchard lightly across his shoulder.

CHAPTER FOUR

Blanchard strode stiffly, silently, along the quiet street beside Colonel Crosbie. The Lieutenant's hat was thrust well back on his head to keep the hard band from chafing the tender lump above his ear. Neither martial nor neat but it did save Blanchard from sharp twinges of pain. The dull throbbing ache behind his eyes would remain for another day or two.

He had explained nothing to Crosbie, not even his conviction that Mr. Oliver Budd had spurred on the sailor and his filthy friends. Crosbie had carried him to their room, revived him with a careless dash of water and then merely ordered him to set his clothes to rights. The dour Colonel had snorted when he observed the gallon jug of rum beside the bed, and his attitude of grim, disapproving silence had clearly indicated that he believed Blanchard had become involved in a drunken tap-room brawl. And Crosbie let it be understood that he would have seen Blanchard properly disciplined if he had still been a Colonel on the active list.

Somehow, Blanchard couldn't help feeling the reaction of an unjustly accused boy who determines to say nothing to excuse himself in the face of adult misunderstanding and cruelty. He knew he was being silly but knowing helped not at all; he said nothing and he drank rather more with dinner than he had wanted, just to demonstrate to the Colonel that he decided such matters for himself.

Crosbie had to force himself to speak to Blanchard afterward and his words were coldly formal. Crosbie had that afternoon called upon the leader of the French *émigrés,* a Marquis d'Aucourt, at Doctor Gaines's house. The Marquis was then leaving to dine with friends, and he had agreed to invite his colleagues to meet with the Colonel later that evening.

Those were the facts and Blanchard knew nothing more. Crosbie had not mentioned the half-hour the dandified Marquis had made him wait before deigning to receive him, nor had he referred to that nobleman's initial unwillingness to disturb his friends for an evening conference on such short notice. Crosbie considered that he had controlled his temper admirably. He had urged the Marquis, that was true, but only in quite respectful terms. And he promised himself to remain respectful as long as he could. But he was conscious of a black sourness of depression in his mind about the future.

The tall slim Lieutenant turned to the Colonel abruptly, as though he meant to speak. He lifted his hand and let it fall again, a gesture of invitation that seemed to fail before it had well begun. Crosbie glared at him silently and Blanchard shrugged.

He matched his strides to Crosbie's but save for that he tried to ignore the Colonel. He gazed around Alexandria as though he were seeing it for the first time. In fact, he had almost forgotten what he knew of the city. As a boy he had attended the races here with his father before the war. Then Mr. Washington had been Steward of the Jockey Club, but that had been long ago when the President was merely another Potomac planter, more distinguished than most, perhaps, as a Colonel of militia, but hardly the man one would have expected to command the first army of the new republic, or to become President. In those days Alexandria had appeared much larger to Blanchard and the short distance between Hunting Creek and the Potomac had seemed miles wide and crammed with houses cheek by jowl. Now the distances were shrunken and most of the houses were depressing little brick boxes.

Crosbie made a smart turn at Duke Street and Blanchard had to stretch to keep pace with him. Crosbie pointed silently toward a large house down the street and stepped off the brick paving to cross over. The house was built of mellowed red brick, larger than most of its neighbors, with three stories and brick string-courses. Two huge round-arched dormer windows commanded the street. Crosbie led the way to the door, lifted the brass knocker and let it fall.

Blanchard followed the Colonel inside, waited as an elderly Negro disposed of their hats and ushered them down the hallway to a wide carved door that was set ingeniously into rollers and slid back at a touch.

Blanchard could see nothing of the room beyond as Crosbie halted in the doorway to make his bow, and a very elaborate and complicated bow it was, too. Crosbie's sudden graceful movements were a constant source of surprise to Blanchard. By rights the man should have been as clumsy as an ox but here he was, making a bow that was going to make Blanchard's seem stiff and ridiculous by comparison. Then Crosbie moved inside and it was Blanchard's turn.

The room was dazzling with the light from two chandeliers, and Blanchard returned the bow of a wiry gentleman in magenta satin. He felt the bow come off as awkwardly as he had feared and the resultant confusion made Blanchard suddenly aware that his uniform was drab and travel-worn when compared with the satin coat and breeches, the silk clocked hose and the high-heeled pumps of his host. When he came erect again, Blanchard's face was impassive, held in a frozen mold, but his ears were flaming red and he scarcely heard the murmurs as he and Crosbie were jointly presented to the gathering of some twenty men, most of them as richly attired as his periwigged welcomer.

Only a few names stayed in his mind. The Marquis was the elderly dandy in magenta satin and gold lace. There were two

Counts, one young and smiling, the other middle-aged with the raddled face of an aging *roué,* both wearing the preposterously dressed court wigs that always made Blanchard itch to throw a rock. The younger even had a tiny heart-shaped patch at the corner of his shapely mouth. Settlers, Blanchard thought suddenly. Settlers, my God! Settlers bound for the wild Ohio! With wigs and satins and patches and probably a wagonload of fine wines that must not be jostled!

A young and solemn priest in somber black broke the gaudy pattern, but Blanchard was even more surprised to see him. Not that he had any particular religious opinions, but priests of the Roman Church were not held in favor west of the mountains. That was a reaction to the French and Spanish attempts to seize the western country; but whatever it was, the feeling was deep and the French would have been well advised to establish themselves before bringing their priests to them.

The introductions proceeded in a hazy blur, and only when he was presented to Doctor Gaines did Blanchard realize the language used was entirely French. Gaines was a round ruddy man with the nose of a tosspot. Exploded veins made thin purple hen tracks across his cheeks as well, but his hand was firm and steady as he gripped Blanchard's.

"No French, eh, Lieutenant?" he charged amiably. "No more have I. The Father," he thumbed toward the young priest, "he translates for me."

Blanchard nodded glumly. A fine conference he was about to join. He wouldn't understand a word.

"Just you stay close to me," the doctor muttered. "We'll follow the meaning when Father La Font tells us." He pulled Blanchard down to the chair beside him as the gathering settled around a wide dining table. He leaned across to whisper hoarsely in Blanchard's ear. "Been wondering what these people were going to do. Glad to have their company, but they're a damned queer kind of settler, if you ask me."

Blanchard agreed heartily. But he noticed that Colonel Crosbie seemed adjusted to them. He'd responded to each introduction with some useful phrase or other, and now he took his position at the head of the table, right next to the Marquis, as though he meant to see to it that the conference proceeded on intelligent lines. Blanchard was just as happy to leave it to the Colonel.

"The Marquis is all right," Doctor Gaines whispered. "Laddi-dah enough to choke you but a right good man. Soldier who knows the business. Keeps his people behaving themselves. Most of the time, anyway. Can't say much for the Counts, but I don't see much of them."

Not all the men were so elegantly attired as the Marquis. Some actually seemed as out of place as Blanchard felt. There were a lot of red-heeled pumps, some even with paste gems mounted in the buckles and heels; but Blanchard noticed several pairs of slippers no more ornate than his own and down at the other end of the room, a neatly dressed group of men, all fairly plump and soft of jowl, who wore the simple leather shoes of townsmen. It was a motley mixture but possibly it was reasonable. Blanchard didn't feel capable of judging. He turned with Doctor Gaines to look at Crosbie as the Colonel rose beside the Marquis to address the meeting.

Crosbie's frame of mind was similar to Blanchard's. He understood the language well enough but he could hardly credit what he heard. Even Blanchard could tell that this was a strange group and a puzzling one, but to Crosbie it held implications of disaster. Here were gathered the chosen leaders of a people who planned to establish a settlement in the wild Ohio wilderness. Nearly three hundred of them in Alexandria already and more to follow from France. Possibly five or six hundred all told. In a way it was no wonder that General Putnam wanted them in Ohio. That many people settled in one new town would be a powerful inducement to others who were thinking of moving to the Ohio country. But these were clearly the wrong people. Their numbers might be impressive, but that was the only impressive item.

A wilderness settlement needs workmen, farmers mostly, a few hunters who know the woods, and all of them trained to provide their own protection against marauding Indians. These genteel townsfolk led by their dainty nobles were a grim joke. They would not survive the first winter.

But Crosbie tried to reassure himself; the working folk among the French would probably not have been invited to mingle with their social betters, not even to plan the last step of their long journey. No, the farmers, the men of real usefulness, would all be waiting elsewhere this evening until the Marquis decided what they were to do.

Crosbie's address was brief and almost curt. He identified himself, mentioned his service in the French Army and explained his present position as their guide and protector. He referred to the hazards of their coming journey and asked for their complete support. He then suggested that the meeting be devoted to an informal discussion of their preparations for traveling, of what equipment they had on hand and what was lacking.

Crosbie had seated himself before the Marquis realized that he had finished. This was the traditional moment for a few stirring observations upon the courage and resourcefulness of the French settlers, and *Monsieur le Marquis* had settled himself into his comfortable chair prepared to endure a tiresome speech. He rose quickly, made a few graceful and meaningless comments flattering to Crosbie while he collected his thoughts.

Blanchard understood nothing that was said and he leaned slightly toward Doctor Gaines, hoping the young priest behind them might offer a translation. He noticed that the Marquis spoke in a low deep tone that was much like Crosbie's voice. And there were other similarities, too, now that he looked for them. The posture of both was that trained military erectness that isn't quite stiff but never comes naturally. And the Mar-Monsieur de Flaville were so thoughtless of their comfort as to move the wagon away, leaving them exposed to the pitiless glare of the hot sun. Such a moment was not the most propitious for asking the Marquis's assistance, but Crosbie was beyond diplomacy.

"We must leave within the hour, sir," he said in a hard clear tone. "Will you call your people together now and tell them?" Crosbie pulled his lips back in a tight grimace that might have been meant as a smile and added, "Please," in a tone that made it a command.

The Marquis choked on a mouthful of food and Crosbie seized the opportunity to remind him that it was to him, the Marquis d'Aucourt, that the Frenchmen looked for example, not to Crosbie.

The reminder was sufficient and the Marquis's training in the tactful acceptance of unwelcome orders stood him in good stead. He put down his half empty plate with an air of long-suffering that further annoyed Crosbie. He waited until the Marquis brought out a slim silver whistle and blew to attract attention. Then he turned his horse and walked him back to his position on the knob of high ground.

The big horse threaded his route warily through the throng, kneed lightly against the town's artisans in their yellow buckskin breeches, checked shirts and skimpy flannel jackets, past the lunching gentry who had dressed themselves for the journey in cocked hats heavy with lace, bright-colored long coats with lace at wrist and throat, striped silk stockings and buckled pumps. And the ladies had been no wiser, Crosbie noticed, in their brocades and taffetas with high hats and feathers. In deference to the demands of the trip, the courtly folk were wearing only small shapely wigs that hugged the head rather than the towering monstrosities of urban routine. One, Crosbie observed, had even adopted a plain brown wig. But thank God not all the Frenchmen were that stupid. All of Mr. Blanchard's young men, for example, were dressed simply. Monsieur de Flaville had even acquired a buckskin hunting shirt somewhere, probably from Blanchard, and the others wore sturdy corded fabric and leather.

The single hour he had allowed the Marquis stretched to two, but eventually Blanchard had all the wagons in place against the far wall stared at him with worried frowns. Beside Crosbie, the older Count was openly yawning, patting his gaping mouth with an embroidered scrap of lace. Another elderly gentleman seemed to be sound asleep. Crosbie noted that Blanchard was watching the Marquis as if he understood and approved of every fatuous word, betraying his total lack of understanding only by a sort of glassy look in his eyes. It would do the young brawler good to sit there for a time, but Crosbie made a note to find someone qualified to serve as interpreter for Blanchard, otherwise his subaltern would be of no use to him in herding the French *émigrés*.

An abrupt silence marked the conclusion of the Marquis's speech and it caught Crosbie napping, with no sure idea of what his host had been saying. A thin old man with a delicate lined face began to rise from his chair with one hand lifted for attention, his mouth half open. There was no time for more formal speeches. Crosbie spoke brusquely, an impatient edge to his voice.

"Winter is our problem, gentlemen," he said roughly, not looking at the old man who stood hesitantly with his fingers trembling against his open mouth. "All of you—particularly the women and children—must be under your roofs before October. That doesn't leave time enough for..."

"But, Colonel," the Marquis protested, "it is but June now. Surely the entire summer is sufficient."

Crosbie thought for a moment he detected a flicker of amusement, possibly even contempt in the Marquis's eyes, and a sudden flare of anger gripped him. Then, scrutinizing the Marquis's face, he wasn't sure. That bland weathered face was so unmoving, so judiciously unruffled.

"No, sir," Crosbie said flatly. "It will not be sufficient." His wide hard hands gripped together on the table and over his large knuckles the red freckled skin slowly whitened. "This is a question of judgment," he went on deliberately, "and I must insist that you accept my judgment without challenge."

Even Blanchard understood the quality of the silence that followed. A few gentlemen straightened themselves haughtily and some of the townsmen drew in sibilant breaths, but all of them waited for the Marquis to reply.

Crosbie eyed him grimly, not relaxing his heavy frown, even when the Marquis smiled at him pleasantly.

"I too have been a soldier, *mon colonel*," the Marquis said equably, "and I know the value and purpose of discipline. My associates are agreed that we must sacrifice ourselves to the common good and I speak for them in assuring you of our willing compliance with your guidance."

Crosbie nodded curtly to his wordy host. He turned slowly and surveyed the colorful gathering, pausing a brief moment to look at the face of each man.

My God, Blanchard thought suddenly, the Colonel's bullying the lot of them. Whatever the trouble is, he's going to beat them down. Just look at those red faces, will you. But Crosbie is going to get his own way with this.

Crosbie sat heavily with a laborious intentness on his face and when he spoke, it was with an abstracted and deliberate air, as though he attempted to define the philosophic concept of Plato to a group of unlettered idiots and had no real hope of success.

"There must be no misunderstanding about this," he said slowly. "The Marquis has mentioned the discipline of the military and properly so. We need not be quite that formal, but my commands must not be questioned."

Red anger flared in the eyes of the nobles at the table. Voices spoke sharply, rising high, objecting to Crosbie's assumption of power. The spate of noise reached a peak and Crosbie raised one huge hand from the table, held it flat above the board and brought it down sharply with a crashing explosion that effectively silenced them. Blanchard chewed desperately at his inner cheek, fighting to maintain a straight face when he wanted to grin in delight.

Crosbie shifted irritably in his chair. "Your safety, gentleman," he growled. "Your safety and the safety of your families. That is my only concern. Three hundred people can move with comparative safety to Ohio provided they all act in accordance with a central authority. I have been employed to bring you safely to the Ohio country and I plan to do just that. You may not approve of me as a commander. You may possibly have other objections about your expedition." Crosbie paused long enough to let the few angry men murmur and nod. Then he added, "But you will accept my orders if you want to reach Ohio."

Blanchard greatly enjoyed the ensuing hubbub. He could see that the Colonel had thrown some sort of challenge and he watched the grim Scot sitting stolidly, unmoving at the table while the Frenchmen yapped around him. Finally the Marquis's gold lace and magenta satin rose again and he soothed his friends with a long and eloquent speech that was entirely lost on Blanchard. Whatever he said, it comported with Crosbie's intent, Blanchard guessed. The Colonel nodded several times in answer to questions, spoke once briefly and then when the Marquis was finished, the assembled Frenchmen seemed to regard Colonel Crosbie in a far more respectful light.

Doctor Gaines leaned to whisper in Blanchard's ear. "Knocked 'em down, wiped the floor with 'em and now they all love him. He's a real catamount, your Colonel."

Blanchard winked in answer. He tried to figure where the discussion was leading now, but the angry heat was gone and what talking was done seemed to be quiet and perfunctory.

"Wagons," Doctor Gaines told him. "Your Colonel's trying to find out how much gear they brought with them. And how many of them are women and children who won't be able to walk the whole distance." Gaines chuckled roupily. "Just wait till they find out the Colonel doesn't plan for them all to ride in style. Bet there won't be a dozen here who've walked a mile in the last ten years."

Whenever the objection to the necessary walking came, Blanchard missed its significance. By then Colonel Crosbie had established his control and the demurrances were few and short. Even the most beribboned of the nobles and the fattest of the townsmen were beginning to regard their overland journey as high adventure. The discomforts referred to weren't yet real enough to bring much reaction from them.

The young thin-faced priest behind Doctor Gaines slid his chair forward and whispered in a heavily accented voice that Blanchard could barely understand. "This is most strange to me, *monsieur le docteur.* The Colonel Crosbie is unpleased to hear when the Marquis tells him we have brought flowers. The tulip bulbs from Delft which I myself obtained at tremendous cost, the cuttings of roses from *Le Petit Trianon,* given by our gracious Queen, the true hyacinths of Artois. But this beauty is nothing to the Colonel Crosbie. He speaks angrily of the seeds of grain, and of young poultry and brood stock."

The doctor smiled thinly at Blanchard and shrugged, an easy Gallic shrug that indicated the Frenchmen had baffled him often before and from them he had taken the one gesture that best expressed his lack of comprehension.

"The Frenchies have a paper, a kind of prospectus..." the doctor began. Then his fingers tapped at Blanchard's sleeve. "There it is. Old fellow reading it is the Chevalier de Valcoulon. Wait till you hear this..."

The young priest sat back momentarily, not bothering to translate again a document which the good Doctor Gaines had heard many times before.

"Don't remember it all," Gaines confessed. "This part now is where he's telling about the 'cotton in great profusion' and then a little further on, 'sugar equal in flavor and whiteness to the finest Muscovado' and something about 'tobacco superior to that of

Virginia' and a lot more about how good the grapes are for making wine. Then there's something about how healthy it is to live in those swampy forests and how easy it is to drift down the river to New Orleans whenever you have a mind to take a little holiday."

Blanchard stared at him with no belief. Then he shook his head. "This is nothing to joke about, doctor," he said stiffly. "These people are bound for the Ohio country not..."

"I'm not joking," the doctor said sharply, hardly bothering to whisper. "They got that thing in Paris. They believe every lying word of it and they believe it's talking about Ohio. And that's what it says, too. None of them figure they'll have to turn a hand to make a living. Not a one of them."

Colonel Crosbie listened with the same bewilderment, hardly knowing where to begin his reply. The pleasant elderly Chevalier reading the prospectus lingered over the phrases, tasting them happily again, and the company nodded complete approval. When the reading was over, Crosbie silently held out his hand for the paper.

The title was, *Prospectus pour l'establissement sur les rivières d'Ohio et de Scioto en Amérique.* It had been issued by the *Compagnie du Scioto* which obviously referred to the Scioto Company of Associates that had undertaken to sell an immense tract of land just west of the Ohio Company's property. Crosbie knew nothing about the Scioto Company and he had no curiosity about it.

"Your land is a wilderness, gentlemen," he said, softly, tossing the prospectus on the table. "It is covered with trees crowded so tightly together that the sun can't get through to the ground. You'll see the truth when you arrive. The problem now is to make sure that you do arrive. And safely."

Several of the gentlemen at the table were about to speak but each decided not to chance the uncertain temper of the Colonel. There would be ample time later to get a full explanation. Crosbie took advantage of the momentary lull to set the departure date for a week hence and he added his urgent recommendation that all unnecessary baggage be discarded before then.

The priest whispered hissingly in Blanchard's ear and he followed the solemn consideration of the baggage problem, with lengthy discussions about clothing, wigs, musical instruments and furniture that left Blanchard as bored as the Colonel. Both of them fidgeted, Blanchard wishing the priest would not bother to be so helpful, Crosbie being unwilling to interrupt with what was essentially a matter of his own preference. After all, the vital points had been raised and he could now endure a few more hours of dull debate if by so doing he could display his willingness to work in harmony with the French.

The elderly Chevalier broke in on the endless chatter with a soft smile for Crosbie and the gently offered announcement that he had compiled a list of talents available to the new settlement.

"Truly a concentration of proven abilities such as few great cities are able to muster," the Chevalier said in his high singing voice. "Permit me, sir, to read."

Gaines banged a warning elbow in Blanchard's ribs. The doctor's searing brandy breath was just beyond Blanchard's nose. "Listen to this," he said in a voice of unholy glee. "Father La Font ..." Gaines pulled the priest forward where Blanchard could hear.

"First, *Monsieur le Marquis* François d'Aucourt, premier scholar of the Military School of Paris, a soldier of high repute," the priest intoned. "Next, *Monsieur l'Abbé Boisnautier,* canon the Church of St. Denis in Paris, whom His Holiness has appointed to become Bishop of our new settlement when suitable quarters are prepared for him."

Gaines winked at Blanchard and shook his head.

The list included doctors, lawyers, teachers and scholars of all degrees, gardeners, coach makers, hair dressers, wig makers, goldsmiths, stone cutters, watchmakers, sculptors, glass blowers, architects, makers of precision instruments such as barometers and compasses.

The Chevalier beamed rosily at Crosbie, obviously expecting a statement of congratulation. And the Marquis rose from his chair, went around the table to assist the old gentleman into his seat again, patting his shoulder.

"An inspiring collection, is it not, *mon colonel?*" the Marquis demanded. "A city in miniature with limitless possibilities."

"Very true," Crosbie muttered through lips that had grown stiff and cold as he listened to the names and occupations of the people he was leading into a wilderness. "Inspiring indeed. Have you ... I mean to say ... well, what of the workmen? The farmers and stockmen, the laborers?"

The Marquis waved an expansive hand as he took his seat again. "Five or six, of course," he said. "You understand that it would not do to exclude all of them. And one rascal of a stowaway boy, too. So we have at least six. But no more."

Crosbie nodded, his eyes fixed on the tabletop. Six workingmen out of three hundred. And how many of the women would be able to card and spin their own flax and wool, to butcher their meat, develop their own kitchen gardens? How many would live through the first winter to see another spring? Five. Good merciful God! Five men! And a stowaway boy!

Blanchard glanced at his Colonel, saw the shocked tension and understood clearly where the trouble lay. This would be hard on Crosbie, he knew. The Colonel was the worrying sort. Well, it wouldn't solve anything to sit here brooding. Blanchard drew a deep breath and cleared his throat.

"Colonel Crosbie, sir," he said in his soft Southern voice. "If I might ..."

Crosbie lifted his head slowly, looked at him. "Of course, Mr. Blanchard," he said heavily. "What is it?"

"You made some mention of forming a detail of scouts, sir. I thought you might want to ask some of these gentlemen here and maybe find me one who could speak a little English ..."

Crosbie nodded slowly. He forced himself to consider the matter of an advance party, mounted pickets, the number necessary to protect his wagon train. The answers came automatically even to his stunned mind and he made the announcement. The clamorous response was deafening. Every gentleman under fifty was on his feet demanding the right to speak.

The Marquis was compelled to rap the table sharply before he could regain control.

"All my bloodthirsty young men wish to join with Lieutenant Blanchard," he laughed. "I shall appoint my son, *le Comte* de la Foure, to consult with you, sir." He bowed to Blanchard and with a graceful gesture indicated the younger of the two Counts, a slim figure in white silk. "And also," said the Marquis, eyeing Blanchard with a sharp glance, "Monsieur de Flaville. Since they are inseparable, you may as well begin with both, eh?"

De Flaville rose eagerly. He stood a few inches taller than the Marquis's son, though he was even thinner, but with a surprising breadth of shoulder. "Monsieur de Flaville," said the Marquis, "and my son were until recently cadets of the *Garde du Corps* and both have some facility with the English tongue. Though rather less than they have with the blades, *c'est vrai,* Charles?" he said gayly, almost nudging de Flaville.

Blanchard came to his feet slowly and bowed to the two young men across the table. He liked the looks of de Flaville, he thought. Good length of muscle on him and a sort of merry face that didn't seem to be afraid of laughing now and then. The French cadet's mouth was long, thin and mobile, curved in a line that could become a smile at the least provocation. Blanchard also approved of his clothes, for while most of the gentry here were as gaudy as Spanish parrots, de Flaville wore a simple brown velvet coat with a tidy spill of silver lace. He also wore his own hair, thick and long, that curled in a lion-blonde mane on his neck. In the faint light Blanchard could not be sure whether the light shadow on his upper lip was a blonde mustache or merely an illusion.

But the Marquis's son was a completely different sort of man and Blanchard instinctively disliked him on sight. Facially, he resembled his father closely, but the cheeks that were hard and weathered in the father were soft, plump and powdered in the son. The preposterous clothes were very probably routine to a man of the Count's position, but nothing could make Blanchard admire lace and ribbons and embroidery on a man. But there was a hard sharp glint in de la Foure's glance that persuaded Blanchard to hold his decision in abeyance. Coldly, he watched the two young Frenchmen resume their seats.

The broad carved door rolled quietly back into the wall. Through the opening came two Negro footmen bearing silver trays loaded with glasses and a third behind them with an immense steaming bowl that smelled wonderfully of rum and honey. The assembled gentlemen came hurriedly to their feet and Crosbie rose with them when he saw the short brisk woman standing just inside the door.

"Ah, my dear," Doctor Gaines snorted, "Happy inspiration, indeed. We'll all be grateful for a drop of something cheerful."

The prim little lady offered a chilly smile. "I'll trust you to see it is merely a drop, Doctor Gaines," she said waspishly. She swept low in a deep curtsey and the gentlemen bowed. "The ladies grow mortally impatient. I trust your business is nearly concluded?"

"Shortly, my dear. Shortly," the doctor growled. "Permit me to present Colonel Duncan Crosbie who has come to take these good people to the Ohio country. And his aide, Lieutenant Nicholas Blanchard."

Blanchard bowed again, feeling his face redden brilliantly. The slight gray-haired woman had seen him before—at the laundry where he'd told her something about starch in his shirts. His face had been red then, too. But surely a woman who lived in a house like this would not be reduced to operating a laundry? Everything seemed completely muddled. They weren't only strange, these Frenchies, but they and everything concerned with them were completely incomprehensible.

"Colonel," the lady murmured, inclining her head toward Crosbie. She observed Blanchard's flushed face with a tight smile. "Lieutenant Blanchard and I have met before. But then he was in too much of a rush to bow."

"Humble apologies, ma'am," Blanchard mumbled in deep embarrassment.

"He had just been engaged in conversation with your niece, Mademoiselle Adrienne," she observed to the Marquis in a clear piercing tone that made Blanchard shrink. "So I suppose we must forgive his ... distraction."

"Most grateful, ma'am," Blanchard said deep in his throat. I wish the Colonel and the Marquis would quit staring at me like that, he thought. He clasped his sweating hands tightly behind his back. And only then did the prim lady's words register in his mind. The Marquis's niece! The dark-haired girl who had slapped him ! And her name was Adrienne.

Crosbie rescued his lieutenant with a comment to the lady, addressing her as Mrs. Gaines, which cleared up another mystery for Blanchard. Crosbie promised he would not detain the gentlemen much longer and ultimately Mrs. Gaines withdrew, taking her cold, appraising gray stare from Blanchard as she curtseyed again in the doorway. She turned spryly and left the room, but not before her eyelid flickered at Blanchard. The young lieutenant was even more appalled than before. Had she winked? Or was she ...

None of the gentleman sat again. The footmen handed around aromatic glasses of hot punch and most of the Frenchmen tried to corner Colonel Crosbie, deluging him with questions about the new country across the mountains. Blanchard drained a glass quickly, took another in company with Doctor Gaines.

"Met my wife before, eh?" the doctor muttered. "Old rip. Walk carefully, young man. My wife's a managing woman. Likes nothing better than arranging people's lives for them. She's adopted a dozen or more of these French families, put them to work doing laundry and cooking and gardening and such when their money ran out. She even started classes in English for the children." There was prideful approval in Doctor Gaines's manner, despite the complaining attitude about his wife's managing. "But at heart she's a matchmaker," the doctor went on. "You have to keep alert all the time or she'll marry you off to someone sure as ... as ... well, she'll do it certain if you don't take heed."

"Thank you, sir," Blanchard said. Then maybe it had been a wink Mrs. Gaines had passed him. Maybe she understood about his mistaking her for a washerwoman. And maybe she could repair a little of the damage he'd done by ... by ... well, patting the Marquis's niece like that.

"You don't look as if that worried you much," the doctor growled savagely.

Blanchard noticed that the Marquis's son and Monsieur de Flaville were working through the crowd toward him. It was time he had a talk with the young men who were to form his scout detail.

He looked down at the scowling doctor, thinking of the grim future the man saw for him in his wife's matchmaking habits. "No, suh," he breathed softly, "I don't reckon it does worry me much."

The doctor regarded him with thoughtful scorn. "It should," he said. "It certainly should. That girl's a hellion if ever I've met one, Marquis's niece or no ..." he paused briefly. "She'll give you trouble on the trip, I fear. Mademoiselle Adrienne is a spoilt minx and totally out of sympathy with the notion of leaving Paris to go pioneering in a wilderness." Doctor Gaines shook his head. "If you've got to make up to one of these French girls, son, you'd be better off with that sweet little blonde one, Lucie. One who calls herself Mademoiselle Adrienne's maid…"

But Blanchard wasn't really listening any longer. There had been a second girl, he remembered vaguely. But she had been no more than a pale shadow beside the vividness of Mademoiselle Adrienne.

CHAPTER FIVE

Colonel Crosbie stood wearily beside his big bay gelding, leaning both elbows on the saddle, watching the bustle around him with eyes that were red-rimmed and gritty with sleeplessness. The dull insistent ache of fatigue would stiffen his muscles soon, but it was good to stand still for a moment and try to forget the strain and anxiety of the past week.

The wide bare field in front of him was a noisy confused mass of mingled wagons, horses and milling, shouting people. Probably most of the idle population of Alexandria had turned out to see the Frenchmen off. And they would have good reason to be pleased at their departure, Crosbie thought, for he had recently learned that many of the *émigrés* were completely without funds and only the generosity of the Marquis and the citizens of Alexandria had stood between them and dire need.

From his vantage point on the slight knob beside the road, Crosbie could appraise the state of preparedness of the wagon train without running his horse to death. He had set sunrise as the moment of departure but he was ready to accept what he could get. He had already prodded the Frenchmen to the point of open rebellion. Now, Crosbie was wise enough to station himself in plain view, but keeping clear of the confusion and letting the leaders of the French take command if they could. Crosbie tightened his grip on his saddle grimly. It was now two full hours past daylight and the mob below showed no signs of organization. Crosbie tried to warn himself against the tension of the irritability he was beginning to feel. If the wagon train cleared

Alexandria today, if the last wagon, the last straggling child with his led goose actually got out of the city, then it would be a good day. Nothing more could be expected.

But Crosbie had to struggle against a conviction of hopelessness. It was almost one-hundred-and-fifty road miles to Winchester Old Town on the Potomac. That stretch would be the easiest and the safest. After that, Fort Cumberland and the narrow wagon road through the Narrows of Wills Creek that General Braddock had chopped to the Youghiogheny where he had crossed to his defeat. Long before Crosbie's wagon train reached Fort Cumberland, he would have to be sure that his people were trained to withstand the dangers of the wilderness. And he could make none of the Frenchmen understand his deep concern.

A clattering swirl of motion caught his eye and he turned toward the road. And the tight grim mouth relaxed, almost smiled. At least he need not be too much concerned for the safety of his wagon train as long as Mr. Blanchard continued to do his job so well. The eight well-mounted young men behind him made a gay sight as they cantered up. The Comte de la Foure rode a shiny black racer that was far and away the best horse of the troop, though Blanchard's agile gelding would be more useful in broken country and de Flaville's stocky sorrel had a depth of chest like his master's, bespeaking endless stamina. All were dusty and travel-stained, for they had spent the past three days out with Blanchard, discovering for themselves the problems of scouting operations in heavy forest. Crosbie wasn't sure where Blanchard had taken them and he didn't want to inquire. He had a deep suspicion that his lieutenant had combined sport with business and made a breakneck visit to his home in Albemarle County. Probably good training, too, Crosbie was ready to admit to himself, but it would never do for him to condone such frivolous conduct on a military exercise.

Blanchard turned in his saddle, shouted back at his detachment, then faced forward again. He swept his heavy dragoon saber up to the salute as his troop passed Crosbie, held it until the Colonel raised one hand in response. Blanchard returned his saber to the scabbard, yelled, *"Allons-y"* in an atrocious accent that brought a full grin to Crosbie's mouth. In seven days Mr. Blanchard had acquired a large and magnificently faulty French vocabulary and one that interspersed the ribaldries of his young scouts with stately phrases he had picked up from the Marquis. But Blanchard's eager attitude toward mastering the language overcame all objections, and his frequent errors were accepted as light-heartedly as they were made. In fact, Blanchard's popularity among the French had been of great use to Crosbie. Almost from the first, Crosbie had felt compelled to adopt an aloof demeanor, a dour, biting delivery as he gave his orders. But Blanchard tempered the sharpness and he kept Crosbie well advised of the prevailing sentiments of the Frenchmen. Of the men among them at least. Crosbie had a far better guide to the feelings of the women in Madame Carmelite Carel.

Young Jock had become a fair hand at the *cornemuse* now and Crosbie was constantly grateful for having the boy's lessons as an excuse to visit his mother. Carmelite was ... well ... sweet. Restful in the way one's family should be but seldom ever is. Cammie understood him well, too well in fact. But she was good for him, took some of the grinding weight off his mind, made him laugh as he hadn't laughed since he was a boy. She had spirit, too, and more than her share of courage. It was no usual thing for a young widow to embark upon an undertaking like this, to transplant herself and her child to a new world, a wilderness world.

"It seemed right for Jacques," she had explained, eyes searching Crosbie's face, their gaiety subdued for the moment into earnestness. "I wanted for him a better life, a better chance than he would ever have at home. There was just enough money to pay for our passage and to purchase our land ..." she paused, then questioned, "I was right, was I not, Dooncahn?"

And what could he say but, "Yes, Cammie, you were right." What else was there to say under the circumstances? She needed to believe in what she was doing. Who was he to take that belief away from her? Too, her advice about these peculiar Frenchmen had been enormously helpful to him.

Blanchard's mounted detachment dispersed as it neared the wagons. The young riders tied their mounts and swaggered among the crowded gathering, seeking their friends and families. It was a lively, noisy scene and just looking at it increased Crosbie's annoyance. Another delay. But was it? There at the rim of the mob was Blanchard, laughing with a cluster of heavy-set men in simple workingmen's clothes. That, too, was a lively and noisy scene, but underneath the gaiety was the sure hand of organization. After a few minutes a blue-bottomed wagon rolled out from the field, led by the Marquis's son, trundled slowly across the rough ground and stopped when it was some fifty yards down the road from Crosbie. The Colonel's tension eased slightly. Blanchard was shouting, joking happily in that egregious accent with his garbled phrases that set the Frenchmen howling in laughter, but he had the people with him for that moment. And Blanchard was taking advantage of his moment to get the wagon train lined up.

That first wagon was a reassuring sight to Crosbie. It was one of the Pennsylvania wagons designed by the wainwrights of Conestoga for difficult terrain. They were odd to look at, almost repulsive with high ends like an unseaworthy boat, with the stretched canvas tops that resembled nothing so much as an unmade bed. But those high wide-treaded wheels could find traction in any footing, those pot-bellied underbodies, invariably painted blue by the Dutchmen who made them, were easily capable of carrying four full tons with no danger of shifting on bad country and the wagon could make fifteen miles a day over a good road. They had cost the Ohio Company agent nearly eighty dollars each, which was an ungodly price for a wagon, but they were worth every cent. Crosbie had been able to get only six of them and he had spotted them in the line of march among the weaker wagons he had found available in Alexandria. The lead wagon had four heavy horses straining at the traces and a light boy on the off-wheeler to drive. It was loaded to the tight canvas with French possessions but more important in Crosbie's estimation was the supply of picks and shovels, ropes and axes, riding in the wheel-box, tools which the Frenchmen would learn to use if they were ever to reach the Ohio.

Blanchard himself led the rearguard wagon up to the road, halting it at the edge of the field where it could roll into place when all the other wagons had finally begun to move. Blanchard stopped on his return, reined in beside the Colonel and doffed his hat.

"Slow work, I'm afraid, sir," he said, speaking softly with a sympathetic note as he observed the strained lines of Crosbie's face. "They're all skylarking around. Be most of the day getting them started."

Crosbie nodded. "Keep them at it, Mr. Blanchard," he said, trying to keep the bitterness out of his voice. "We can't push them any more right now. Just do the best you can."

Blanchard wiped his arm across his forehead and put on his cocked hat. He tried to think of something pleasant he could say to the Colonel without seeming over-presumptuous.

"Picked out a right pretty campsite for tonight, sir," he said diffidently. "Little brook comes into the river just there. About nine miles out. Didn't figure we could get any farther than that today." Blanchard rubbed his chin thoughtfully. "Figured maybe you might like to ride out and have a look at it?"

Crosbie glanced up sharply, hearing the softness of Blanchard's voice and suspecting the sympathetic concern that underlay it. "Do you know your job, Mr. Blanchard?" he snapped.

Blanchard straightened in surprise. "Yes, sir."

"Then you've picked a suitable place," Crosbie said in a voice that sounded unnecessarily stern, even to him. "Surely I don't have to follow you around, too?"

"No, sir," Blanchard responded angrily. He bowed stiffly from the saddle and spurred his leggy gelding forward.

Crosbie banged his tight fist at the saddle seat, not feeling the impact. This has gone far enough, he told himself furiously. Blanchard is doing his level best. He couldn't keep chivvying him this way, trying to take things out on him. It wouldn't do.

But the dark taste of failure stayed in his mouth. Only a miracle could bring this wagon train in to Pittsburgh with no losses. There was no end to the danger ahead, the countless streams to be forded, the trees that would fall to block the road, the wild animals that would travel in packs almost beside the wagons, eager to snatch a goose or a chicken, or even a small child if one was offered. Not to mention the Indians.

Crosbie knew the shadowy fears in his mind came largely from his deep tiredness, a weariness that reached to the bone and undermined his confidence. He addressed himself firmly, trying to quiet his misgivings, but none of his sober logic banished the cold premonition of failure that bedeviled him.

His payment was to be five hundred acres in the Ohio Company tract, selected by himself. And a cow, a few fowl. Five hundred acres of untouched wilderness that any wise soldier familiar with the smooth tailored farmlands of Europe would scorn on sight. Yet to Crosbie, those five hundred acres meant the beginning of a new life, one last chance to find for himself the essential meaning of his fifty exile's years.

If he failed there would be no five hundred acres, there would be nothing, no other opportunity that he could anticipate. He was a soldier by training, by conviction, almost by birth. He belonged in the Army, but there was no place in the permanent Army establishment for a ranking Colonel of Artillery, not in an Army that totalled one understrength regiment of Infantry and one lone battalion of Artillery plus some worthless militia units in which the rank went only to politicians. Crosbie's future would be decided by the success of his present mission and considering the sort of people he had to protect, he dreaded the outcome.

Crosbie eyed an approaching wagon sourly. The two horses pulling it were too light for draft work and that was not his fault, but the Marquis's. D'Aucourt had purchased his own stock and his choice was dictated by some romantic preference that yielded no ground to the dictates of common sense. Those horses would have to pull a plow later on, but they were almost delicate and nervous enough for racing. The wagon also was frail in comparison with the lumbering Conestogas but it should do well enough. Beside the wagon, the Marquis rode elegantly on a deep-chested black, a half-brother to the magnificent mount he had purchased for his son, a dainty high-stepper that looked wonderful on firm footing and would probably break an ankle on the first exposed root it could find. On the far side of the wagon Blanchard walked along, leading his horse. The lieutenant was looking up with a wide silly grin on his face, trying to make conversation with the slender dark-haired girl who sat on the wagon seat, ignoring him completely, almost burying her pert little nose in a book. She was the Marquis's niece, Crosbie remembered. Something in the wind there. Have to keep Blanchard away from her if possible. Trouble enough without that.

The Marquis's plumed hat swept low in an extravagant salute as he pulled up beside Crosbie.

"My niece, Mademoiselle Adrienne, is feeling rather bored, *mon colonel*," he said softly. "Mr. Blanchard has told us of the pleasant spot he has selected for our bivouac tonight. I thought we might go ahead and prepare..."

"No." Crosbie spoke without heat, in a toneless voice. "The wagons stay together. From now on." He replaced his hat carefully and looked squarely at d'Aucourt. "I regret, sir," he said as pleasantly as he could manage.

The Marquis shrugged as though he were slightly amused, letting his lip curl in an expression that he knew would annoy Crosbie. "As you wish, sir."

Crosbie's glare was dark and baleful. He made no further effort to be pleasant. He looked away from the Marquis, turned toward Blanchard and shouted,

"Mr. Blanchard!"

"Sir." Blanchard glanced up, startled.

"Get the rest of those wagons rolling, mister. This one is second behind the lead wagon. Put it there."

Blanchard nodded briskly and swung up into his saddle. He had noticed the Marquis's supercilious mouth, realized the Frenchman must have done something to infuriate Crosbie. He leaned down to seize the headstall of the off-wheeler and then he walked the wagon forward into place behind the lead Conestoga, paused only to raise his hat before cantering back to the milling crowd in the field.

The long grinding day continued as it had begun. The frolicking mob in the field paid little attention as Blanchard or another of his detachment led the wagons into place one at a time. The moment a wagon reached the road, the driver deserted and dashed back to rejoin the party.

Only the Marquis's young dark-haired niece remained with her wagon, seated stiffly on the padded seat, holding both hands cupped tightly together around her book, a faint frown between her full dark eyebrows and a dreamy withdrawn expression on her face that made Crosbie suspect she wasn't concentrating on her pages. Far from being helpful, her presence at the wagon was an added nuisance, for Mr. Blanchard found innumerable petty errands that took him to the lead Conestoga, past the quiet seated girl who gave no indication of seeing him. Only once was she distracted from her book. A blonde girl in a modest gray dress approached the wagon carrying a large portmanteau. It must have been heavy for she carried it with an obvious effort; once she appeared to stagger under its weight. The sun was blazing hot and she did not even wear a hat on her smooth pale hair to shelter her from the blinding mid-morning rays. Again cursing the childlike stupidities of these people, Crosbie was about to dispatch one of his men to help her when Mademoiselle Adrienne glanced up from her book and saw the girl. In an abrupt whirl of billowing skirts, she slid down from the high wagon seat. Crosbie could hear a scolding note in her voice as she snatched away the heavy portmanteau and remonstrated with the girl who had been carrying it.

"... when you've been ill, too!" Bits of the conversation drifted to Crosbie's ears. "Lucie, your wits have deserted you."

The fair haired girl surrendered the portmanteau unwillingly.

"It was forgotten, Mademoiselle Adrienne," she protested. "At the house of Doctor Gaines. Madame Gaines said ..."

What Madame Gaines said was lost to Mademoiselle Adrienne. The blonde girl swayed suddenly, put out one hand and clutched at a wheel of the wagon for support.

Adrienne caught her by the other arm, helped her into the wagon and rummaged out a bottle of wine from a hamper behind the seat. She found a cup, filled it and held it while the other girl drank. She went right on scolding, though Crosbie could no longer hear her words.

He thought sourly that all he needed now was sickness among his charges to make the whole business more impossible than it already was.

An hour before noon the French folk in the field assembled around small flaring fires to prepare a meal, like children at a picnic, like the offensively naïve gentry who played at the rustic life with Marie Antoinette at *Le Petit Trianon*. Small boys and girls dashed to the wagons to riffle through them for food and cooking utensils. Crosbie stayed where he was, refusing every invitation sent him, even Cammie's. He forced a bleak smile for Jock, patted him lightly on his head and sent him back to his mother with strict instructions to practice the *cornemuse* for an hour after luncheon. But Crosbie ate nothing and neither did Blanchard nor any of the scouting detachment who by this time had begun to assume something of the harried intensity of their commander.

Crosbie hoped that in the somnolent atmosphere following the midday meal he might be able to start the wagons rolling without too much distraction from the French. To collect the *émigrés,* inform them of the need for action and to get their support, he would need the Marquis. Crosbie choked back his resentment and swung stiffly up into his saddle. His epaulette-laden dress uniform had been carefully packed away and only the plumed hat remained to designate his rank. The hat he wore as a signal, much as he would have preferred a coonskin cap. The Frenchmen had been enchanted that morning when Colonel Crosbie gave them their first glimpse of a frontiersman's field gear. Even modest ladies crowded close to finger the long fringed buckskin leggings and exclaim at the extravagant dimensions of the enormous hunting shirt that had room enough for three men Crosbie's size. His moccasins were decorated with a smattering of beadwork on the toe, quite sedate as such decoration went, but he was offered dozens of profitable trades in footgear for them.

Crosbie rode slowly through the milling crowd, halting his heavy gelding often to keep from ramming some roistering celebrant. No one was drunk that he could see and that was a good sign. True, there were bottles of wine in evidence, but wine was as common as water to the Frenchmen and had been from birth, for only fools will dare to drink the poisonous water of France. All of them looked sober enough, Crosbie thought. The elation was brought on by the prospects of a journey to their "estates" along the Ohio, not by an excess of ardent spirits.

The Marquis was taking his luncheon with friends, eating from a porcelain plate, using a delicate silver fork as daintily as though he were picnicking at home. Hovering close to the gentlemen stood the short stocky boy, François Valodin, the stowaway who had clearly attached himself to the Marquis and his son, doing the rough work for them, always eager and smiling and always watchful, keeping his flat brown eyes fixed upon the Marquis, anticipating his needs and somehow, Crosbie suspected, measuring himself against d'Aucourt as if by his constant observation he could find a way to compete with the other Frenchmen. A strange boy, but no stranger than any of the rest, Crosbie thought sourly.

The small group stood in a patch of shade thrown by one of Crosbie's Conestogas, chatting with animation as if at a party. The conversation stopped short when Blanchard and young Monsieur de Flaville were so thoughtless of their comfort as to move the wagon away, leaving them exposed to the pitiless glare of the hot sun. Such a moment was not the most propitious for asking the Marquis's assistance, but Crosbie was beyond diplomacy.

"We must leave within the hour, sir," he said in a hard clear tone. "Will you call your people together now and tell them?" Crosbie pulled his lips back in a tight grimace that might have been meant as a smile and added, "Please," in a tone that made it a command.

The Marquis choked on a mouthful of food and Crosbie seized the opportunity to remind him that it was to him, the Marquis d'Aucourt, that the Frenchmen looked for example, not to Crosbie.

The reminder was sufficient and the Marquis's training in the tactful acceptance of unwelcome orders stood him in good stead. He put down his half empty plate with an air of long-suffering that further annoyed Crosbie. He waited until the Marquis brought out a slim silver whistle and blew to attract attention. Then he turned his horse and walked him back to his position on the knob of high ground.

The big horse threaded his route warily through the throng, kneed lightly against the town's artisans in their yellow buckskin breeches, checked shirts and skimpy flannel jackets, past the lunching gentry who had dressed themselves for the journey in cocked hats heavy with lace, bright-colored long coats with lace at wrist and throat, striped silk stockings and buckled pumps. And the ladies had been no wiser, Crosbie noticed, in their brocades and taffetas with high hats and feathers. In deference to the demands of the trip, the courtly folk were wearing only small shapely wigs that hugged the head rather than the towering monstrosities of urban routine. One, Crosbie observed, had even adopted a plain brown wig. But thank God not all the Frenchmen were that stupid. All of Mr. Blanchard's young men, for example, were dressed simply. Monsieur de Flaville had even acquired a buckskin hunting shirt somewhere, probably from Blanchard, and the others wore sturdy corded fabric and leather.

The single hour he had allowed the Marquis stretched to two, but eventually Blanchard had all the wagons in place strung along the road in a long line at the edge of the field and the Marquis had pushed his people out to the road.

Crosbie signaled for Blanchard and his detachment, ordered them to make sure that every wagon had at least one driver and then gave the command to start.

Blanchard relayed the order, rearing his horse high and shouting, *"Allons-y,"* in an accent that brought bellows of laughter from the French.

Crosbie waited where he was until the last wagon had rolled onto the road and then followed slowly, paying no attention to the solid wall of dust that hugged the road. Nine long miles to the first encampment. In that stretch how many of the gay people walking along beside the wagons would attempt to climb up for a ride? And how successful would he be in stopping them? Suddenly Crosbie decided not to try. Not today. The French would have to learn a great many disciplines of the trail, but some of the teaching could wait. Crosbie touched spurs to the flanks of his gelding and trotted him up along the train of wagons, keeping well downwind so as not to increase the volume of dust that had already begun to coat the walkers.

The road was lined solidly with townspeople out to wish the Frenchmen a pleasant journey. All of them recognized Crosbie and some shouted pleasantries as the dour Colonel trotted past. He waved stiffly in reply, cursing them silently for delaying his departure and hoping fervently that none of them would decide to visit the Frenchmen at the camp site and further impede them.

Blanchard's detachment rode beside the wagon train, each placed where he could be most helpful in event of minor difficulty. There would be no need for scouts fanned out ahead until they were past Fort Cumberland. For the first stage of the journey they would be more use if they were kept close at hand. Crosbie made a mental note to say something to Blanchard about his fine work.

Then he forgot his good intentions as soon as he saw Blanchard. The tall Southerner was riding slowly beside the Marquis's wagon again, leaning far out of his saddle to talk to someone out of Crosbie's line of vision. But he didn't have to see. That girl again. He couldn't have her reducing his only dependable aide to a stuttering, ten-thumbed boy like this.

"Mr. Blanchard!" he bellowed.

Blanchard straightened with a guilty start, touched his hat to the wagon and cantered, red-faced, toward Crosbie.

"I'll *go* ahead to inspect the campsite," Crosbie said crisply. "Take station at the rear and keep the wagons closed up."

"Yes, sir," Blanchard said. "We make two turns before we reach it, sir. I've placed Monsieur Bonvouloir and Monsieur de Clugny at the crossings and Monsieur Prenet is at the site ready to guide the wagons into position. Ground's a little marshy in spots. We'll have to site the wagons carefully."

"Good," Crosbie nodded. Blanchard's matter-of-fact report did much to ease his tension and for a brief moment he was on the verge of apologizing for his evil temper. But he restrained himself, said merely, "Good work, Mister." He returned Blanchard's salute and then put his gelding into an easy canter along the road.

The first turning of the road was not the sort that should have confused anyone, being merely the junction of a path with the main road, but Blanchard had been wise to put a man there, as a precaution. With these erratic Frenchmen it would always be best to assume they would fall willingly—probably gaily—into any error that presented itself.

The route to the campsite was clear and simple. Young Monsieur Prenet was busily occupied as Crosbie approached. In the scout's hands were long branches torn from the hemlocks that bordered the open space and he was pacing off the firm ground, mounting a branch for a marker at each place a wagon would halt. In the center of the site was a low flat area and if it was not too damp, that would do for tethering the horses and oxen. Blanchard had chosen well, Crosbie conceded. He did not disturb Monsieur Prenet at his work, but walked his gelding up on a hillock that commanded the campsite and dismounted there.

He was in perfect position to watch the wagons roll from the road into the camping ground and he decided to wait there for the first few wagons to appear.

The afternoon sun struck him squarely between the shoulders and Crosbie stretched with a long weary yawn that surprised him. He was even more tired than he'd thought and he would have to make sure he got an adequate amount of sleep tonight no matter what else happened. He bent to rub at a chafed spot on the side of one knee where his stiff buckskins had rubbed the skin. In a few more days the hide clothes would be soft and easy as his skin but just now they were dry, stiff from neglect. Crosbie found the butt-end of a treasured segar he had stuffed in his shirt that morning and he fingered it lightly, sniffing at the aroma, wondering if he wanted to smoke badly enough to bother getting out his tinderbox. Ultimately he decided not to bother and he tucked it away again carefully. He leaned both his elbows on his saddle in that habitual resting posture of the mounted soldier and half dozed until the first lumbering Conestoga wagon left the road with a noisy rumble and approached the campsite.

Crosbie came alert with a start, noticed approvingly that Mr. Blanchard had collected his scouting detachment beside the lead wagon so that he could easily regulate traffic and still be able to send a man with each wagon to lead it to its proper space. A shouting mob of young children ran about underfoot, but Blanchard's control of the situation was evident to Crosbie.

Apparently some Alexandria folk with nothing better to do had followed the wagon train. Four men on poorly tended livery nags turned off the road with the lead wagon. They seemed to agree that Crosbie's vantage point was the place to watch from and they turned their mounts toward him, kicking them heavily to force the clumsy beasts to climb the steep grade. Crosbie eyed them distastefully and then looked away. He couldn't very well order them to leave, much as he wanted to.

The Marquis's light wagon reached the turnoff next and from what Crosbie could see, only the girl was driving. The fair-haired girl in the gray dress rode beside her. She seemed to have recovered from her illness of the morning. Crosbie felt a fleeting sense of comfort in that. Sickness in the wagon train could slow them down beyond the limits of safety.

Crosbie mounted quickly, intending to ride down to the wagon, not liking the prospect of a young and inexperienced girl being left to manage a wagon over rough ground. But Mr. Blanchard had anticipated that, too. A slim rider in a buckskin jacket came up beside the wagon, leaped to the seat and took the lines from the girl. That would be Monsieur de Flaville, Crosbie thought. He relaxed then and sat his horse quietly, fully prepared to find that Blanchard could direct the wagon train without his help. He suppressed firmly the small twinge of annoyance at the thought.

The four townsmen had reached the summit of Crosbie's hillock and came toward him slowly, almost cautiously as though they could feel the Colonel's disapproval. Crosbie turned away, pointedly ignoring them.

Down below him, the Marquis's wagon was led to its bivouac. Before young de Flaville could fix the brake, the Marquis's niece had slipped from the seat onto his horse. Mademoiselle Adrienne was clearly an adept horsewoman, Crosbie noted, for she hooked her knee around the pommel of the saddle tightly and kicked the horse into a gallop, riding away from the wagon with a wild flurry of skirts that rippled like a battle flag. Something in the spontaneous gaiety of the maneuver caught Crosbie's sense of humor. He almost laughed aloud at de Flaville as the young soldier, awkward in his spurred boots, ran after the laughing girl who had stolen his horse. But the laughter died quickly in Crosbie's throat at a gesture from one of the strange men beside him.

The four were fanned out wide with one rider slightly in the lead. He wore a large cocked hat with a greasy tricolored cockade above one eyebrow. His thin sallow face was wrinkled in a wide smile and he raised his hand as though he were an old friend sure of his welcome. The man's salute caused Crosbie's gelding to move nervously to one side. Crosbie tried to remember who the man was. Probably someone he had met casually in town since nothing about him seemed familiar. Crosbie half raised his hand when one of the men twitched suddenly in his saddle.

Crosbie's normal alertness was dulled by his deep weariness. He stared with slow comprehension at the rider who had abruptly brought a battered musket into line, centered on Crosbie's chest. And he continued to stare helplessly as the bulky flint hammer slammed down on the frizzen. The priming powder flashed in the pan and something scalding ripped along Crosbie's right arm.

Crosbie's excited horse swung around quickly, making the Colonel grab for the pommel to keep seated. He heard only dimly as another musket was fired at him. When he regained a lost stirrup, he let his reins drop and fumbled at the tong ties of his left-hand saddle holster. Sweat was running into his eyes, blurring his vision as he kneed his gelding in a wide circle.

He snapped an unaimed shot at the cockaded hat, knowing he had no hope of hitting the man, meaning only to distract him from a sure aim. A third musket flared and banged as he pulled his trigger and the heavy musket ball ripped along the bulging muscles of the Colonel's chest, tearing into the wounded right arm. Crosbie fired the second barrel of his pistol, then threw it desperately at the cockaded hat.

The swirling movement of the horses, all frenzied by the firing, carried Crosbie away from his attackers briefly and he could see two men with muskets reloading in frantic haste while the leader, the only one armed with pistols, again aimed slowly and carefully. Crosbie heard only the drumming clatter of horses' hoofs as he leaned far forward to make the smallest possible target.

A great wave of pain and nausea darkened his view of the hilltop. Another shot banged with deadly meaning, but he felt nothing. Crosbie spurred his heavy gelding savagely, not caring where he was taken so long as the horse moved. His left hand groped clumsily for his *skene-dhu;* the jeweled dirk was his best weapon now.

He felt the impact of a collision as his gelding crashed head-on into a lighter horse. Crosbie whipped wildly with his blade at the vague figure that was all he could discern. A hoarse frightened scream stabbed in his ears as the horses recoiled.

Crosbie shook his head, looked up with normal vision briefly, seeing clearly for the split second it took to recognize the gigantic shape beside him, a mounted man standing tall in his stirrups to swing full-armed with a clubbed musket. Crosbie tried to raise his wounded right arm, ducked and whirled his horse, knowing as he did so that he was moving too slowly. But he felt nothing when the musket struck him. He heard a sharp rattle of shots, two or three at most, but the crack of the clubbed musket on his head drove him unconscious from his saddle.

CHAPTER SIX

Duncan Crosbie lay stiffly quiet listening to the monotonous rumble of horses' hoofs, the high-pitched squeal of ungreased axles. Above him was the soft flapping of cloth in a light breeze and Crosbie maintained his rigid immobility, knowing without knowing how he knew, that movement would bring a welling surge of pain. He could not remember back to a time when he had not been lying stiffly on his back, holding his body tense and still and his eyes tightly shut. The dim quiet space smelled of sweet grass smoke, of pine needles and axle grease and, very faintly, of a lady's boudoir.

He could hear his own breath rasping through his throat. He moistened his lips, running his tongue along a mouth that was papery and fever-hot. He could hazily recall being lifted some time long ago and being carried to the accompaniment of soft curses across uneven ground. And he began to remember the pain, the knifing red waves that swept across his nerves and brought, ultimately, a blessed unconsciousness.

He was lying on a feather mattress that rocked in a gentle swaying motion that could only have come from a moving wagon. Crosbie opened his eyes warily, ready to retreat again to an assumed blindness if the pain returned. But the only unpleasantness was his inability to focus in the light. He kept his eyes parted a careful distance waiting patiently as only a sick man can wait.

The taut canvas was merely a few inches above his face; his feather bed had sensibly been placed on top of the load, leaving him a barely adequate space. Forward, the canvas top must have been rolled back for he could occasionally smell a trace of warm pine-scented air that seemed as invigorating as rum punch. Crosbie took a deep expansive breath, forgetful of the pain. The quick throbbing stab in his chest warned him to be more careful, but the depth of pain was nothing he could not endure. The blinding, drowning quality of fiery agony that he could remember seemed to be gone now and the constant ache was only rarely acute.

Crosbie's last clear memory was the hilltop with its confused pattern of whirling horses and murderous shots aimed at him by men he had never seen before. With a conscious effort of mind he realized that he had been seriously wounded without knowing any reason for the attack. But that problem could not be explored now; he was far too weak to consider anything. His pain-dulled mind drifted hazily. Crosbie let his eyes close slowly and he dropped into sleep again.

Later he woke to the soft murmur of voices, the cool freshness of a hand on his forehead. His eyes opened upon darkness that was frightening for a moment before he realized he had slept through the afternoon and it was now evening. The interminable screeching, jangling, thudding rhythm of the wagon train had ceased now, and he could hear the faraway sounds of preparation for dinner, high irritated women's voices calling for errant children, the thin clanking of pots and dishes and the easy relaxed tones of men who have done their work for the day and felt they had earned a peaceful moment. Close by Crosbie's ear a jug gurgled deliciously. He licked his feverish lips and a low voice laughed indulgently.

"Only the least touch, *mon lieutenant,* the greedy man would have it all, but *le rhum* is not for invalids."

That was Cammie, Crosbie thought vaguely. She was talking to Blanchard, most likely. Crosbie was pleased with the logical way his mind was working, but his acute thirst was not at all pleasant. His right arm wouldn't budge when he tried to move it. The elbow and forearm were bound solidly to his chest with a long tight wrapping. And though he could make his left hand move slightly, he could not reach far.

A delightfully cool arm cradled his feverish head close to the swelling softness of a woman's breast. That was Cammie, all right, Crosbie told himself. His hot mouth pursed in anticipation and the thin rim of a metal cup touched his lips at just the right angle. Cammie shifted it in perfect rhythm so that he could drink as quickly as he liked without waiting and without slopping. The Colonel had it in mind to say something appreciative, but he forgot in the brief space of time it took to regain his pillow.

The warm sting of weak rum-and-water stimulated him and in a short moment he was listening with full understanding to Blanchard's voice, speaking its atrocious French with complete mastery of the words, but none of grammar or accent.

"... broken now. If the wounds might not infect, he should be healed," Blanchard said firmly. He leaned forward and the monstrous shadow of his shoulders blackened Crosbie's bed. "Should he not?" he insisted, prodding Cammie to answer.

"Of course" she said softly in a tone that was gentle reassurance. "He is mending rapidly. The Colonel is ..."

"Wide awake," Crosbie said in a hoarse croak. "Your French is improving, Mr. Blanchard."

"*C'est à rire!*" Blanchard laughed. "But I'm getting right handy with the swear words, Colonel." He reached forward, touching Crosbie's left hand with one finger, hesitantly. "How do you feel, sir?" he asked softly.

Crosbie ignored the question. "How long ..." He had to swallow tightly to speak further. "How long have I ..."

"Twelve days, sir," Blanchard said. "For a while there you looked right bad but Madame Carel pulled you through. You should have seen her getting that slug out of your shoulder. One of the doctors wanted to bleed you but she wouldn't even let him get his foot in the wagon. She cut out a musket ball the size of Jock's fist that was snuggled right up against your rib." Blanchard shuddered and Crosbie saw his shadow jitter on the canvas. "I don't think I could have done it as well and I know I wouldn't trust either one of those fancy French doctors, not if it was me."

"Twelve days!" The exclamation burst from Crosbie's mouth after a thoughtful moment. With a dreamlike sense of unreality he remembered his own worry—it seemed a long time ago now— because a fair-headed girl had come close to fainting with the heat and might be ill. Illness could cost his wagon train precious time, time that could not be made up. And now he himself had been twelve days an invalid. "Where are we now?" he demanded, almost fearing the answer.

"Well…" Blanchard hesitated.

A cool soft hand stroked across Crosbie's forehead. "We have proceeded, Dooncahn," Cammie said gently. Despite the wish of the Marquis and others to return to Alexandria and wait until you were well again. The gallant lieutenant demanded we progress and take care of you in the wagon."

Crosbie clenched his teeth and a flickering spasm of pain caught at his chest. "Quite right, Mr. Blanchard," he said. "Absolutely right. Why did they want to go back?"

"Just worried about you, sir, is the way I figured it. Didn't have much faith in me, I reckon."

"Where are we now?"

"We're doing fairly well, Colonel. We'll make Halfaday Creek tomorrow. That's not fast, but I thought I'd better take it slow and let the folks get used to traveling."

"Good," Crosbie said as forcefully as he could. He thought Blanchard was being strangely reticent about something but he couldn't quite focus his mind on it. Probably just a normal diffidence about his first command. "Who's staying with the wagons now?"

"Well," Blanchard fumbled. "I asked the Marquis to take your place. He sort of liked the idea, but I've been sticking pretty close, too. Charlie de Flaville takes the advance party out when I'm not around. He's getting a real feel for the country. He'd make a good dragoon. And," he added with scrupulous justice, "the Count makes a useful man, too."

Crosbie didn't pursue the subject further. Appointing the Marquis wagon boss was a clever stroke of policy and Blanchard had obviously considered his problem carefully. Blanchard could rejoin his detachment tomorrow or the next day anyway, now that he was conscious again.

"What ... happened back there?" he asked weakly, his mind suddenly filled with the clear memory of the wild fight on the hilltop outside Alexandria.

"You got rescued," Blanchard grinned. "Mamselle Adrienne did it. All by herself. She swiped Charlie's horse and she was just galloping around, cutting the fool, when those buckoes jumped you. She had a little pearl-handled lady's pistol, about the size of a baby carrot, but it had two barrels and she charged those muskets like she was Light Horse Harry Lee himself. Right up to them, holding her fire till she was a couple feet away. Scared me, I can tell you. I couldn't get a shot in at all for a while. Well, she cut loose and winged one of them. I found a hat a while later that had a bullet hole a fly could hardly squeeze through, but it was right spang in the center of the cockade. Three of them got away, though."

Crosbie felt a hot fury at remembering the scene and a lively gratitude at Adrienne's rescue. He swallowed painfully and said in a thin voice he didn't recognize, "You'll express my thanks, Mr. Blanchard. I'll repeat them later." He closed his eyes wearily. Then he recalled what Blanchard had said. "Three of them got away. What about the other? Did Mademoiselle Adrienne get him?"

"I reckon I nailed him, sir," Blanchard muttered. "Had to wait so long for a clear target that I only got in the one shot..."

"I'm grateful, Mr. Blanchard," Crosbie said, trying to keep his voice level, to choke back the surge of emotion. "This is the second occasion I've had to..."

Blanchard glanced sharply at Cammie who was sitting back now, looking forward toward the wagon seat. He bent to Crosbie's ear, keeping his voice down to a hissing whisper that was barely audible to Crosbie. "And the same man both times, sir."

"What!"

Cammie glanced around when Crosbie bellowed. Her soft white hand went automatically to the Colonel's forehead and she smiled the faint distracted smile of a mother with a worrisome small boy who takes his first illness with bad grace.

Crosbie noted Blanchard's tense face, his glance that flicked toward Cammie and then toward the rear of the wagon.

"Cammie, me dear," he said hoarsely, "please be good enough to ask the Marquis to come in if he has nothing more important to do."

Crosbie watched Blanchard tightly as Cammie stooped to touch her warm lips to his unshaven cheek. The boy's face is gaunt, he thought suddenly. The lines are getting deeper around his mouth and his eyes look like chips of gun flint. It's been a strain for him, but he's holding up well enough. Cammie clambered slowly out of the wagon, waved and then disappeared in the growing darkness.

"Well, sir?" Crosbie said crisply.

"Thank you, Colonel," Blanchard said swiftly. "I didn't want anybody here to know. I was afraid they might insist on going back to Alex if I told them. So I just kept it to myself and made them go on."

"Very good, Mr. Blanchard," Crosbie nodded. "But how do you..."

"The man I shot was wearing a bandage where his right thumb used to be," Blanchard said in a half whisper. "That's why I was sure. I shot that thumb off back by the river the day we came into Alex. Remember?"

Crosbie nodded again, very slowly. The slight motion of his head tired him excessively. He could hear Blanchard's voice whispering beside his ear, a tight sibilant tone saying things he wanted to hear, but Crosbie's mind refused to concentrate, no matter how vital Blanchard's information might be. His fever was almost gone now but its aftermath left him weaker than he realized. Against his will, his eyes closed and he fell abruptly into a deep dreamless restful sleep.

In the coolness of morning he wakened, hearing a robin chirping, thinking for a moment that he had been roused by the bird, but changing his mind when Cammie slipped her strong warm arm tenderly under his head and held a steaming cup to his mouth. He gulped greedily, trying to restrain his suddenly ravenous appetite and failing completely. Cammie chuckled softly and Crosbie felt his head move pleasantly as her breasts shifted under his weight.

"There is more, Dooncahn," she crooned in a gently maternal voice that somehow reconciled Crosbie to his helpless state. He waited avidly for the refilled cup and this time he drank more slowly, savoring the aromatic broth, feeling stronger and more restored with every sip.

Outside a bullwhip snapped sharply in the stillness and a shrill voice shouted far in the distance. The noises of the stirring camp reminded Crosbie of his situation. He gulped the last of his broth and raised his head.

"Blanchard," he said thickly. "Where is Blanchard?"

"He will come," Cammie soothed. "Now is the time of departure and he is most occupied, but he will come. It is almost as though I have a grown son to help me, the way he has taken on himself the responsibility for this wagon." She eased Crosbie's head back to his pillow and let her fingers trace along the point of his heavy jaw. "We must now ask Monsieur Grennelle to bring his implements for shaving. You have the face of a great red bear."

"Yes," said Crosbie, not listening. "Please tell Mr. Blanchard to come at once."

Cammie slid down to the wagon bed and stooped to pass through the circular opening in the canvas. "He will come, Dooncahn."

But the coolness of the summer morning vanished under the hot sun as Crosbie endured the dainty twittering Monsieur Grennelle who stroked his razor across the grizzled red stubble with delicate precision, all the while keeping up a constant flow of anecdotes designed to establish Monsieur Grennelle's eminent position in the world of barbers, leeches and *friseurs*. Even lesser court officials had been graciously appreciative of his flawless technique with razor and curling iron. Crosbie felt a faint revulsion at the man's flabby white hands but he endured the caressing touch until he was shaven. Then he swore mightily at Grennelle to make him leave without dusting him with scented powder.

Crosbie's ill temper increased rapidly as he lay silent and alone under the warm canvas, hearing the bustle outside but feeling strangely remote and detached from the activity. When the Marquis d'Aucourt poked his snuff-brown traveling wig in through the rear port, Crosbie almost snarled at him.

"We are all enormously gratified, *mon colonel,* to hear of your rapid recovery," the Marquis said with obvious sincerity. "I confess I was so distressed about your grievous wounds that I thought it best to turn back until you were well again, but I see now…"

"Ridiculous," Crosbie snapped. "We have no time for such foolishness, sir. I've tried to impress that on you."

"And succeeded, too," the Marquis smiled, "with the able and forceful assistance of Mr. Blanchard."

The Marquis's equable temperament and his unfailing courtesy merely added to Crosbie's irritation. No one would give him a legitimate excuse for flying into a rage and the considerate behavior of the Marquis made Crosbie unpleasantly aware of his bad manners.

Crosbie recalled himself to sanity and made a few comments of reasonable graciousness. He suddenly remembered something he should have thought of much earlier.

"I have heard from Mr. Blanchard, sir, of the part your niece played in my rescue." Crosbie brought a thin smile to his dry cracked lips. "Please convey my deepest gratitude and respects."

The Marquis waved an expansive palm. "She will be enchanted, Colonel. But she too is aware of how much we owe to your tireless efforts." The Marquis drew a quick orator's breath and the compliments continued to shower on Crosbie's weary head. "One might almost say she was merely acting in her own interest, for surely we could ill-afford to lose ..."

D'Aucourt's endless encomiums were cut off abruptly by the screeching drone of a bagpipe. A sure hand rippled easily through "Charley Is My Darlin' " and a wide grin, mostly of relief, broke across Crosbie's face.

"Jock, me sonsie jinker," he bellowed. "Bring your toy in to me." To the Marquis, he said, "I'm making a piper of the lad. He has a poor instrument, but some small talent, I think."

The Marquis politely murmured something about the pleasure a Scottish exile might be expected to find in hearing the pipes again. The Marquis made it clear that his tastes were slightly less catholic. He bowed again and took himself off to carry Crosbie's message to his niece.

Jock slid into the wagon from the front seat and climbed to the feather mattress, bracing a leg against the side slatting. He bowed solemnly to Crosbie, pumped mightily and fingered the chanter pipe, producing a halting, squealing version of "The Campbells Are Coming." Crosbie winced inwardly but he managed to compliment the boy on his meager improvement since his last lesson.

The small boy squirmed around on Crosbie's bed so the Colonel could reach the chanter with his left hand and after a few false starts, Crosbie corrected Jock's errors. Shortly, the Campbells were called to action in a fashion even they could approve.

"That's a braw tune," Crosbie said, suddenly tired by the effort of sitting up. "And you play it passing well, but you'll never do it justice on a fluttery toy like that. Wait till you hear it on a real pibroch." Crosbie eased himself flat on his pillow and sighed. "I'll show you a proper set of pipes when we reach Marietta."

"Marietta," Jock echoed. "That is to be our new home?"

"*Pas du tout,*" Crosbie murmured. "Marietta is but the headquarters for the Northwest Territory. It is there that the log fort of Campus Martius commands the river and keeps the Indians quiet. But our destination is farther down the river. A place to be called Fair Haven, I believe." A place that should be built by now, Crosbie thought, with cabins and some sort of stockade for defense. But no point in worrying about that. His job ended when the *émigrés* arrived. How they were to be housed was General Putnam's problem.

"This place we go to," Jock asked excitedly, "it is in the real wilderness?"

Crosbie nodded wearily. A depth of wilderness that no child bred in a European city could possibly imagine. Where trees lifted to hundreds of feet and blotted the sun so that all of living was a shadowed, almost frightening affair. But wilderness or no, it was a land treasured by the Indians and they would fight to keep it.

"And will there be the noble savages, too, as *Père* la Font has said?"

"Aye," Crosbie said through clenched teeth. "Noble," indeed. The frivolous foolishness of the Frenchmen was deeply rooted in the idiot's prating of the philosopher Rousseau, and they took their opinions, even their phrases, from him. None could understand that Rousseau was a European with no knowledge of the Ohio country. The noble savages he wrote about, those simple and generous folk who would live in idyllic content and peace if they were treated decently, these were concepts that testified to Monsieur Rousseau's sense of human values, but they would get his countrymen killed unless they learned better very soon.

Jock twiddled with the *cornemuse*, pumping it aimlessly, "Will they not be charmed to hear me play the *cornemuse?*" he laughed. "I shall learn a savage dance for them."

"They have heard the pipes before," Crosbie smiled. "But they were not charmed."

Jock's sobering face urged Crosbie to explain.

"The pipes are frightening to them now, me boy. They heard them skirl when the Highlanders broke the back of Pontiac's uprising, at Bushy Run where Bouquet brought the Highlanders against them to avenge Braddock's defeat. Bouquet was a crazy little Swiss, no bigger than a muskrat, but he served the Sassenach king as well as any could, and so did his Highland troops. Aye, the noble savages have their stories about the pipes now. They'll not hear them again without remembering and being afraid." Crosbie grimaced at the canvas, his face strained and bitter. "It was another eighteen years before the Sassenachs permitted the wearing of the tartan again in Scotland, but I've always had it in my mind that even an Englishman had to honor Bushy Run."

After a long silent moment, Crosbie stirred on the soft bed. He smiled at the boy and shoved him gently down, sending him to practice in the last wagon where he could disturb no one, sending away also the eager admiring gaze, the utter trust which stood clear in the boy's eyes and which would always embarrass Crosbie. To the Frenchmen, he might seem wonderful, but in his own estimation, Crosbie was almost a fraud. He was sure that a thousand men of the frontier were as well equipped as he to bring the wagon train safely to Pittsburgh. His special qualification was his knowledge of the language and that was a minute advantage; even Mr. Blanchard had already picked up enough to do his job—and probably enough more to make himself pleasant to Mademoiselle Adrienne as well.

Crosbie closed his eyes and tried to doze. The constant fretfulness he felt was due to his wounds and the irksome necessity for lying still. In time of physical weakness one is easily discouraged and every obstacle seems larger than it actually is. Crosbie understood that well, but the shadow of failure was dark and cold in his mind.

The strident noise of departure was impossible to ignore and Colonel Crosbie was brought out of his dreamy haze by hoarse shouting, the loud snapping of whips and the high shrill yelps of the children. He felt a sudden lurch that shifted his feather bed and then his wagon rolled slowly forward. From the sounds, Crosbie knew that all the other wagons were also rolling simultaneously; obviously Mr. Blanchard had sited them so cleverly that the usual delays had been eliminated.

Further, Mr. Blanchard had wisely ignored Crosbie's order to report immediately, for in the flurry of inevitable minor crises attendant upon departure, Blanchard's presence and active assistance would be urgently needed in the bivouac area. Blanchard had delayed and properly so. Now if the young subaltern had the additional wisdom to make no reference to his delay, then Crosbie would be willing to give him a high score in the difficult art of military tact.

Crosbie's wagon lurched over broken ground, steadied on a rutted road and the customary jangling thudding rhythm sounded along the wagon train in a soothing hum. Only when all the wagons had reached the road did Blanchard appear, riding up in a swirl of dust. He tied his leggy gelding to the rear of Crosbie's wagon and climbed in stiffly through the port. He carried his long rifle carefully, its breech mechanism protected from dampness by a fringed and beaded leather case. He rested it against Crosbie's mattress.

"Morning, sir," he said, coughing to clear the dust from his throat. He took off his cocked hat to wipe his streaming forehead.

"Did we make a good departure, Mr. Blanchard?"

"Middling, sir. A youngster got himself lost for a while. Most of the cows are holding their milk and the hens won't lay. Women have a hard time getting breakfast, but everybody's learning." Blanchard drew a deep breath and smiled a lean tired smile. "But that's not what I wanted to talk about, Colonel. One moment, sir."

Blanchard slipped through the loaded wagon, poked his head out of the front port. He returned a moment later and sat with his head close to Crosbie's.

"I sent the driver away and tied the reins. The wagon wheels will follow the ruts all right and I don't want to have anyone close enough to hear us."

Colonel Crosbie glanced sidewise under the knotted slant of his eyebrows. Blanchard's posture was tense and the lines of strain around his mouth were deeply cut. Crosbie watched as he thrust a hand inside his leather hunting shirt and brought out a folded parchment sheet.

"I told you the man I shot was the same bully-boy I winged earlier," Blanchard said soberly, unfolding the heavy sheet. "I found this in his pocket."

Crosbie took the sheet, held it up against the canvas top to look at it. A crude map, done with quick sure lines of fine ink on expensive parchment.

"That shows the road we're taking, Colonel," Blanchard said tightly. "The map has three crosses on it. Different places. It's hard to figure just what the places are because there aren't any place names on the map, except for Fort Cumberland and Pittsburgh. But one of the crosses could be our first campsite, the spot where those four men jumped you."

Crosbie nodded. He folded the map again and returned it to Blanchard. He turned to look at Blanchard's sober, steady eyes. "You're positive it was the same man, Mr. Blanchard?" he asked harshly.

"Positive," Blanchard said flatly. "There's something else, too. Maybe I should have mentioned it before." Blanchard's gaze dropped in momentary embarrassment. "Well, I was a mite riled, I reckon and I never did say anything about it."

"About what?" Crosbie growled.

"That afternoon at the City Tavern when I got in that fight," Blanchard said. "There were three sailors sitting at a table. Well, maybe an hour before that I saw Mr. Oliver Budd sitting at that table. He was with some men. I'd like to say they were the same men, but I'm just not sure. I did recognize Budd, though."

Crosbie frowned in puzzlement. He shifted cautiously on the bed so he could more easily see Blanchard. "I don't..." he began.

"Maybe I'm wrong, Colonel," Blanchard broke in quickly, "but we met Mr. Budd about the same time we met that other man. Maybe he was heading out to meet him. And that fight in the tavern was none of my doing. And then the map."

"What do you make of it, sir?" Crosbie demanded, a cold chill touching him briefly along the spine.

"I think someone means to prevent us from reaching Pittsburgh safely, Colonel," Blanchard said, almost defiantly. "Maybe it sounds funny, but..."

"I'm not laughing, Mr. Blanchard," Crosbie said coldly. "Where is the next spot marked on the map?"

"It's hard to tell, sir. Some place this side of Fort Cumberland, I'd say." Blanchard looked at Crosbie and his face was suddenly less tense, as though he had managed to transfer his worries to Crosbie.

Crosbie's lips barely moved as he spoke. "A plot against us seems illogical...pointless. But for the time being we'll have to assume your judgment is correct, Mr. Blanchard. We don't dare assume anything else." He rolled back in his bed until he was facing up at the flapping canvas top, feeling a tight fury, a deep distaste and revulsion at Blanchard's news. "What steps have you taken?" he asked hoarsely.

"I've ordered all the firearms loaded and I've organized a sort of Infantry platoon from the able-bodied men. The Marquis is the boss of that. And I'm keeping the scouts busy. I got the Marquis to tell our people to stay close to the wagons, no hunting or wandering about."

Neither Crosbie nor Blanchard was conscious of the partisan decision implied in referring to the French *émigrés* as "our" people.

Blanchard gestured angrily with the parchment map. "I didn't show this to the Marquis. I've tried to tell him we have to watch out for Indians but he only curls his lip, and that son of his laughs and..."

"Very good, Mr. Blanchard," Crosbie said. He, too, knew and resented the Marquis's manner at times, but just now it would have to be ignored, as would the manners and habits of the Marquis's son. "I have had it in mind for some time to commend your energy and forethought, Mr. Blanchard," he said formally. "I cannot speak of them too highly."

Blanchard flushed brilliantly. Praise from Crosbie was praise hard-won...

"Very... ah... gratifying, sir," he fumbled.

"You'll say nothing of this to anyone," Crosbie added crisply. "Keep your advance party out well forward and maintain a connecting file at all times. Form a wagon barricade at every stop and post a double guard. That's all we can do."

"Very good, sir," Blanchard said, stooping to retrieve his rifle. "I'll get forward with the scouts, sir."

Crosbie heard Blanchard back out of the wagon through the rear port. "Not a word, Mr. Blanchard," he said warningly.

"Not one, sir." Blanchard dropped to the ground, untied his horse and pulled himself up into the saddle. He trotted toward the head of the wagon train.

Crosbie lay silent and gloomy after Blanchard left. The long day passed slowly and he was compelled to respond pleasantly to the constant sympathetic inquiries about his health. Normally he might have given vent to the raging anger inside him, but today he could not see or hear any of his French party without a deep feeling of pity and concern that erased his irritation and most of his fury. They were now "our" people and even more so to him than to Blanchard, for Crosbie bitterly understood the meaning of exile.

If the French émigrés reached their lands without serious trouble, if all went well, Crosbie would probably part from them with no regrets. Though now that he thought of it, that wasn't too likely. Not in the case of Cammie and Jock at any rate. He had drifted into intimacy with Cammie during the long busy confusion of preparing for their journey. Separating now would be difficult at best. But he would have to reach a firm understanding with her. In his fifty years Crosbie had never felt the need or desire for marriage and he wasn't sure that he did now. But young Jock needed a father and after all, Cammie was a widow; someone had to look out for her. And she was Cammie, soft, sweet, doubly endearing to Crosbie in the way she could make him live again his young gay days in France before the Army had done its sour work on him.

His thoughts of Cammie, of Jock, of possible happiness far ahead, were childish evasions, Crosbie realized. He didn't want to think of a possible conspiracy against the French settlers. No sane man would have any real grievance against these gay, useless people. The facts, as Blanchard outlined them, were ominous enough. The mere hint of coming attack made stringent preparations necessary. But while the thinking part of his mind accepted the danger, another portion, the hopeful self-occupied portion, rejected the possibility of a plot against the Frenchmen.

The wagon train lurched through marshy fields of fever-few daisies, rolled in and out of three muddy little streams, rumbled across gravel beds, and through it all Crosbie lay stiffly quiet, not seeing, not hearing, his big hands clenched tightly on his chest. A deathly paleness came to his face as he grew aware that he was ruined completely if a successful attack were to be launched against his wagon train. If it should be successful he could never claim his five hundred acres from General Putnam.

As the wagon jolted beneath him, Crosbie's mind was busy with plans. Blanchard had done his job well, very well indeed. But he needed help. Crosbie would get up as soon as the wagons halted for the night at Halfaday Creek. Possibly he wouldn't be able to do much at first, but he would most certainly not lie abed when possible danger threatened his people.

Crosbie shifted his left hand slightly, barely touching his wounded shoulder and a low savage moan escaped from his clenched teeth at the sharp stab of pain. He lay quiet then, swearing monotonously, meaninglessly, at himself.

CHAPTER SEVEN

Lieutenant Nicholas Blanchard rode his tall bay slowly into the clearing along Halfaday Creek, sitting half turned to keep a balancing hand on the doe carcass slung behind his saddle. It had been a lucky shot that brought down the deer at three hundred yards. The wagon train needed meat constantly but Blanchard had issued strict orders against hunting expeditions. The safety of the *émigrés* was far more important than a full belly. The small doe would give the Frenchmen something to flavor their soup tonight. And Colonel Crosbie would probably relish some of the liver now that he was beginning to take an interest in things again.

The camping site was high ground, overlooking the junction of Halfaday Creek and the Potomac. Carrying water up that steep slope would be a trial but it was the slope that most pleased Blanchard. Two sides of his camp would be protected by the bank and he could form a sturdy barricade of wagons on the other sides.

It was rich land along the river, bottom land that would return a crop worth having if a man cleared away the trees. The meadow grass was high and green and from a distance It looked fine, but Blanchard knew it was fouled with acrid dog fennel. For one day, it wouldn't hurt the stock but any longer and they'd refuse to eat. Blanchard was prepared to hear complaints about the rank and bitter milk the cows would give tomorrow. But the animals would be safe here and that was the first consideration.

Blanchard pushed the doe carcass backward, letting it drop to the ground just above the flowing creek. There it could be butchered tidily without offending any of the squeamish French.

Four wagons had already been sited by Charlie de Flaville, and Count de la Foure had the others closed up tightly along the rutted road, moving at a slow crawl, waiting to be guided into their places. In less than two weeks the discipline of the wagon train had become almost a matter of instinct. Not that everyone pulled his own weight, but the ones who worked brought such zeal and energy to their tasks that Blanchard now was free to supervise.

In the center of the sun-dappled clearing, the Marquis, tall and wiry in a crisp white linen shirt, was mustering his platoon of guards. Seven gentlemen, one nobleman and three workmen formed an uneasy rank, grounding their muskets, fowling pieces and rifles gingerly and listening with frowning intentness as the Marquis spoke to them. Blanchard grinned widely at the sight. He'd have to make sure Charlie and a couple of the other scouts stayed alert tonight. The detail the Marquis had assembled wasn't exactly anything he wanted to trust his neck to, though they'd probably shape up well enough in time. Blanchard was developing a conviction of optimism about his Frenchmen.

Blanchard dismounted slowly and drew a picket string from his saddlebags. He pegged the string in the ground, tied it around the gelding's neck and then stripped off his gear. He used a fat fistful of grass to wipe the gelding's back and legs. After an hour or two he could have some water but right now the leggy bay was too hot and tired. Blanchard walked back to the doe carcass, took out his heavy knife and in three practiced motions, had the steaming liver in his hands. He gathered up his sweated saddle and bridle, laughed at his gelding who was pretending alarm at the scent of blood, and walked stiffly across the meadow to Cammie's wagon.

Far down the slope of the riverbank he could see Cammie and Jock with a long giggling line of women and children struggling with water pails. The low sun was still bright and warm, a faint breeze from the river was cooling the bivouac and all the settlers were lighthearted after the grinding monotony of another day's march. A pleasant scene, Blanchard thought, but his soldier's instinct nagged at him, an oddly persistent apprehension based upon nothing tangible. He pitched his saddle gear under Cammie's wagon, put the doe's liver on the wagon seat where the dogs couldn't reach it and pulled out his long rifle from the wagon. He turned then, heading for the rim of high ground that bordered the campsite.

The lead Conestoga with its supply of vital tools was placed almost in the center of the bivouac, but all the others were strung out in a loose defensive ring along the high ground. As he crossed the clearing, Blanchard noticed a couple of his scouts hauling at Cammie's wagon, backing it a few feet until its rear port almost hung out over the river bank. Make it nice and cool for the Colonel tonight, Blanchard thought, but he better not try to climb out unless he wants to swim back.

At one point the ring of wagons touched the solid mass of timber that surrounded the clearing. That would be a danger point, Blanchard noted. Have to post two pickets there and maybe another one farther out. If I wanted to jump the wagon train, right there is where I'd hit and I'd have a good chance of snatching a couple of scalps before anyone saw me.

He grinned at de Flaville when the blonde young Frenchman took the Marquis's arm, turned him and gesticulated forcefully toward the line of trees. A formal military education should have taught them where to place pickets even if it couldn't teach them about the skulking kind of warfare the Indians fought. Blanchard waved and went on, reminding himself to make sure that the timbered point was well patrolled tonight.

He walked slowly toward Halfaday Creek, taking long strides to stretch his stiffened muscles, feeling the low afternoon sun warm against his back, strangely pleased at being by himself for the first time that day. In the clearing children were screaming and galloping like young colts in the high grass, trailing across the meadow in long tireless chases that led from the high ground to the steep river bank and back again, but never straying beyond the line of wagons. Some of the men were carrying stones and mud to shape together for fireplaces and others were lazily chopping wood, somehow making a game of it and stopping often to make a telling point in those endless political discussions the French seemed to love so much and which Blanchard could never understand. The stowaway boy, François Valodin, gathered flat stones to form a low table which would serve for the *poque* players that night. The regular card games was religiously attended by the Marquis's son who seemed to lose every hand as far as Blanchard could determine. François acted as steward to the gamblers but occasionally he sat in the game himself and when he did, he invariably won.

The stock was fed and staked out to graze for the night. The Marquis had assigned his guards and then released them for dinner. Charlie and the scouts would wait in position until they were relieved. Blanchard watched the Marquis stalk briskly across the clearing, his laced shirt flapping in the breeze. As he watched he saw Adrienne slip away from the wagon, ease herself cautiously down the bank and disappear. The pale face of her maid, Lucie, was framed in the back opening of the wagon and her soft voice called, "Mademoiselle Adrienne!" in frightened, urgent tones. Adrienne either did not hear or did not wish to hear. Blanchard moved quickly through the tall grass to the bank of Halfaday, just in time to see her pass below him, her yellow dress a bright banner against the dense green foliage, the pale gravel and the hard-running, steel-shining water of the creek.

Blanchard stood there silently, leaning his chin on the muzzle of his rifle, not moving as Adrienne picked a slow stumbling path up along the creek. For a long moment he thought of nothing but the easy grace of her slim body as she climbed fallen tree trunks, skipped nimbly across marshy spots and ultimately passed from sight around a sharp bend. In two weeks, he thought angrily, two long grinding weeks, he hadn't said more than a polite good-morning to Adrienne. Not that he hadn't tried. But somehow she always managed to have someone with her whenever Blanchard found her and she was always so deep in a confoundedly intimate conversation that he hadn't the courage to break in. She'd be talking with de Flaville, most likely about France. That light-hearted ... and obviously light-minded ... Paris Doctor Gaines had warned him she was so reluctant to exchange for a new home in an uncharted and certainly uncivilized wilderness. Or she'd be laughing merrily with the Count de la Foure whenever Blanchard came around, laughing at something witty de la Foure had just bent to whisper in her ear. Or laughing at himself, Blanchard suspected with an anger that surprised him. For the first time he thought bitterly that if the war had not come just when it did he, too, would know Paris and that gay, elegant life Adrienne was a part of. All three of his older brothers had spent their year abroad, as befitted the sons of a Tidewater landowner. But the war had come, and ... well, he shrugged, he hadn't regretted it then. It was a fool's trick to regret it now.

He looked back at the clearing behind him, finding pleasure in the orderly, protected camp. And then he gripped his rifle, leaped down the bank, reaching the water in a sliding, scrambling plunge that nearly threw him into the stream. All these precautions to protect the wagon train and that fool ... that girl, goes wandering off, walking straight into whatever danger lay outside the protected circle of guards and wagons. Blanchard ran up the creek bed, staying just inside the stream where the gravel bed gave him an even footing. And he ran as though the devil chased him, watching carefully along both banks with eyes that were greatly sharpened by his long weary days of caution and fear.

A driving anger seized Blanchard as he sprinted up the stream, a fury that flared his nostrils as wide as a charging stallion's. But with a buried part of his mind he sensed it was an anger rising from fear for Adrienne, far more than any resentment at her idiotic behavior. But the anger within him focused more and more on Adrienne as he ran, as the blood pounded in his temples and his legs, wearied by sixteen hours in the saddle, almost wobbled under him.

He rounded the bend, running hard, his moccasined feet spraying water knee-high, his eyes seeing through a red haze of blind rage. He braked himself abruptly against a huge rounded boulder, leaped across the stream to grab Adrienne's arm, touched her lightly and then recoiled, suddenly seeing what he should have seen when he came past the bend, what he should have guessed before he even started.

Adrienne crossed her arms across her breasts when Blanchard released her. She didn't scream. She didn't say a word, though her mouth opened silently. Afterwards Blanchard remembered her silence with gratitude, always. He could see the billowing yellow dress draped across a leaning tree on the creek bank, together with a mass of foaming whiteness that seemed to be entirely ruffles. And Adrienne. Adrienne standing mute, frozen, wearing only a frilly something that Blanchard couldn't identify, a something of nearly transparent linen and lace that started somewhere around her waist and ended above her knees. He could see, too, that one of her hands was clutching the tiny pistol with which she'd gone to rescue Colonel Crosbie, back at the first campsite. The girl wasn't quite the helpless idiot he had thought her. She'd come armed, at any rate. Toy-sized though it was, the little pistol could inflict a nasty wound. Adrienne was a good shot, he knew that. She could have shot him, now, he realized with a shock.

It was a wonder she hadn't, hearing him come splashing up the creek like that, having him grab her ...

Blanchard stepped back hurriedly, going into the swift water to his knees, his face a fiery red with embarrassment and forgotten anger. His mouth worked silently as he searched his mind for a way to apologize in French. Every word he had learned slipped from his memory.

"*Mamselle*," he said quickly, stepping back still another pace to show his good intentions, "*vous êtes en* danger ..." Blanchard took a deep breath. "I mean it isn't safe ..."

Adrienne nodded silently and put the small gun down at the edge of the creek. She turned quickly to the tree, flipped the foamy whiteness into the air and wriggled under it, but not before Blanchard had a dazzling view of her smooth creamy back and just a suspicion of a rounded, jutting breast. Adrienne held her pale yellow dress up in front of her and nodded again to Blanchard.

Her eyebrows, full and dark like ... like wings, Blanchard thought, came together in a frown as she concentrated. "Is ... is there ... dangers from *les sauvages*, Mister Blanchard?"

Blanchard grinned hugely because she had spoken in his language, not her own. "You speak a mighty fine English, Miss Adrienne. Better than I can do with French ..."

Adrienne blushed quickly, a redness that had not come when Blanchard grabbed her, but painted her face and throat brilliantly now. "I ... I have been studying," she said. A little note of anger crept in, as though she did not like being forced to confess her activity. And to confess it in the hesitant words of an unfamiliar language seemed to increase her anger. "We are to be of a new country, Mister Blanchard," she said sharply. "It is but proper that I learn the language of it." Her tone forbade that he should find any personal implication in her new accomplishment.

Blanchard ignored the sharpness.

"You're doing right well, too," he said amiably, remembering the book she'd kept her nose buried in so often, remembering his own wonder at what she found so interesting about it. Then his face sobered abruptly. "But you're right, Miss Adrienne, there is danger. From now on. You'll have to stay with the wagon train. All the time."

"But I wanted to wash myself!" she said irritably, as if possible danger counted for little in the face of her desire for cleanliness. "All over. It has been so many days now that ..."

"Yes, well ..." Blanchard said unhappily. "I'm afraid we can't ..." He swallowed heavily and shifted in the swift water. "We'll arrange something, but not ..."

Adrienne pouted, Blanchard thought, but God didn't she look pretty, though! He cleared his throat roughly. After his error in Alexandria, he'd been trying to put his best foot forward and just look where his foot was now. Twice he'd been alone with Adrienne and twice ... well, he was done, that was a sure bet. But, was he? Wasn't she smiling? At least the visible signs of anger had disappeared from her face.

After a moment she said softly, "You might at least find my slippers, Mr. Blanchard." A little quirk teased one corner of her red mouth into the undeniable beginning of a smile.

Blanchard leaped out of the stream as if he'd been touched with a bull whip. He came to the bank a few feet from Adrienne and rested his rifle against the leaning tree, searching the ground anxiously for her shoes. Yellow, they were, like the dress, and satin, soft and fragile and completely useless. Blanchard stooped for them, touching them with fingers that were cold and stiff. He could feel a hard pounding pulse beating in his throat and a sudden trembling that made it impossible to pick up the slippers. He waited a moment for control.

Adrienne had her dress on when he straightened. Nothing much to it, Blanchard noticed. A couple of buttons, a sort of sash, and that was all there was. She was fully dressed now, smiling at him with no trace of disapproval that he could see, but Blanchard felt more awkward than ever, conscious of the change in her attitude but not understanding it at all.

"*Merci*, Mr. Blanchard," she said, lifting her bare foot from the ground, obviously expecting him to put on her slipper.

The fragile yellow satin nearly crumpled in Blanchard's convulsive grasp. "My friends call me Nick," he said in a voice that sounded strangled. He ducked to put on her shoes.

Adrienne said nothing and Blanchard could feel his ears growing hotter and redder under her scrutiny as he knelt at her feet. He felt she was enjoying the sight. He held the slippers clumsily while Adrienne slipped her feet into them. There was nothing to fasten or button and Blanchard was grateful for that. His fingers could never have managed.

Adrienne's hand touched his shoulder lightly as he rose. "Thank you," she said softly, "Nick."

She was in his arms then, a swift unthinking motion that made Blanchard exultant, for the motion was Adrienne's as much as his. He felt the melting softness of her warm mouth. His hands gripped her avidly and he kissed her fiercely with an aching, demanding tenderness that brought a low soft moan from Adrienne. Her breath quickened sharply with a tone that was almost pain as she gripped him intensely, gasping with sudden pleasure as his groping fingers touched her breast.

Then she pushed away abruptly, staring up at him with her head well back, her long black hair tumbled and wild under his fingers. Her gaze was both startled and unsure, as if what had happened was no part of her planning. Blanchard had never seen her unsure before. Eagerly he pulled her close again, but this time there was no soft yielding. Adrienne stiffened, she raised one hand with a cat-like swiftness and he felt the sudden sting of long sharp fingernails across his cheek. Then she twitched out of his arms.

"It is … as you have said … dangerous here," she said harshly. "Too dangerous, I think."

Blanchard forced a smile and took a hesitant step toward her. And then she was gone, running along the creek bed with a swift agility that startled Blanchard. Before his stunned mind could understand, she was out of sight around the bend, running back toward the campsite.

Blanchard remained unmoving, struck with a strange lassitude, a dream-like state he had no experience of before. He could still feel the softness and the warmth of Adrienne in his arms. It was going to take him a long time to understand that girl. First, she'd let him kiss her like that...had even seemed eager to be kissed. And then she'd changed her mind and scratched his face like an angry, ruffled cat. Maybe she'd just been teasing him. But when, he wondered? When she kissed him, or when she scratched his face?

Slowly, automatically, he bent for his rifle, found Adrienne's little gun on the bank where she'd dropped it. He picked that up, too. Then he walked blindly along the bank, somehow not stumbling, but giving no thought to his route. Though he walked without haste, he was breathing heavily, almost panting. He saw Lucie coming to meet Adrienne. Lucie's pale face wore a look of real fear as she moved timidly along the creek bank, searching. But she had not been too frightened to come after her rash young mistress, and she greeted her with almost frantic relief. Blanchard was glad to see that somebody else was trying to look after Adrienne, too.

He stopped at the overhanging bluff, trying to throw off his bewilderment before he climbed back up to the campsite.

CHAPTER EIGHT

Blanchard came fully awake suddenly, like a cat, his ears pricking up to listen, his sleep-heavy eyes strained to focus in the darkness. Above him was Cammie's wagon and the slow, even rumble of Colonel Crosbie snoring on his feather Blanchard rolled softly onto his side, staring out from under the wagon toward the thin ominous black line of thick timber that ringed the campsite and stretched a long solid finger of trees toward the line of wagons. Nothing. Nothing moved. Blanchard sighed heavily and rolled back in his blankets. From the corner of his eye he could barely discern the gray mound of the central fire which still had a faint cherry glow deep in its ashes. Within the border of wagons only the grazing stock moved, slowly, sedately.

Blanchard's eyes were gritty from sleeplessness. Foolishly he had permitted de Flaville to persuade him to play *poque* with the Marquis's son and the other scouts. It was a new game for Blanchard and it still made no sense to him. The boy, François, used a 20-card deck when he dealt and the winning hands appeared to be determined on a strange and erratic basis. Once Blanchard had been sure of winning when he held three high cards, but the Count had shown a hand full of *Piques* and won, despite his low cards. And tonight, as was customary. Count Edmond de la Foure had contributed heavily and the young sturdy boy François Valodin and de Flaville had shared a tidy sum. The stowaway boy would have all the Frenchmen's money by the time they reached Pittsburgh if he kept winning at that rate. But he'd get no more of Blanchard's. Once was enough.

Poque was obviously a foolish game and it would never gain any popularity, Blanchard was sure. He rolled over to loosen his blanket.

Beside him was a weird spindly shape he couldn't identify for a moment. But when his eyes grew accustomed to the night, he could make out the form of the Colonel's chair, a clever contrivance of heavy green wood and buckskin strips which Charlie de Flaville and a couple of the scouts had made so that Crosbie could half recline comfortably beside the fire and become a part of the wagon train again, giving a sense of sureness and security to the French. Though he and the Colonel had mentioned their fears to no one, somehow their serious misgivings were communicated to the *émigrés* by a mysterious sensitivity and by now there could be no man of the group who remained unaware of Crosbie's apprehensions. Even Blanchard was impressed when the Colonel insisted that he check the picket line every two hours during the night. Blanchard yawned and stretched widely, delaying the moment when he would have to roll out of his blankets and pull on his clammy moccasins again.

As he climbed out from under the wagon, Blanchard wondered vaguely why he bothered to follow the Colonel's instructions. He had made his rounds twice now, finding the guards alert and moderately cheerful, as guards always were early at night. But it was hardly sensible to lose sleep over them, Blanchard thought. Any new john knew that Indians always attacked at dawn. To them, a man killed at night was doomed to Hell, but the moment the sun peeked up, he was assured a position on the Indian Valhalla if he should be killed, always provided, of course, that he didn't lose his scalp. Valhalla had no room for hairless warriors. Blanchard grinned sourly at the thought and he brushed back his long tangled brown hair with impatient fingers.

The ground was black and gloomy but where the steep bank broke down to the river, a silvery mist was forming, a cold dankness that made Blanchard shiver. He wiggled his bare toes distastefully into his moccasins, picked up his rifle, powder horn and bullet pouch out of his blankets and came erect, miserably conscious of an ache in his back that must have come from a stone under his bed. He scraped his tongue back over his teeth and spat lustily, trying to get rid of the vile taste in his mouth.

Then a fluffy white dog whined in a high complaining tone and Blanchard was wide awake, poised lightly on the balls of his feet, waiting. Another dog and a third muttered and then one of them far on the other side of the campsite growled deep in this throat. Blanchard pulled back the hammer of his rifle to full cock, took up the slack of the trigger and waited again. A dog is a bothersome animal most of the time, but he can't endure the smell of rancid bear grease and that's what Indians use to keep from getting cut to ribbons by brambles and thorns when they travel fast through thick undergrowth. A dog was worth all the trouble he caused just because he couldn't abide the acrid stink of Indians. But Blanchard held his fire. No point in arousing the camp for a false alarm. But a lighter yapping picked up on the outer perimeter and died away abruptly as if it had been choked off. Then Blanchard squeezed his trigger. His rifle flared in the pan, then blasted a sharp spiteful sound. Blanchard cursed himself for not having made sure of his priming; his rifle had almost mis-fired. Without moving a step, he reloaded automatically, bellowing a loud, incoherent warning to the sleeping French.

High alarmed shouts came back from the pickets and Blanchard cursed more heavily then; the fools should know better then to call out like that. Their positions were known now to any enemy outside the circle of wagons.

The piercing gobbling shrieks that followed had a frightening intensity. A high wavering ululating scream seemed to jab through Blanchard's skull.

"Mr. Blanchard!"

That was the Colonel's voice, but Blanchard had too much to do right now. "Minute, sir," he shouted over his shoulder.

Count de la Foure was at the fire before Blanchard reached it, looking almost ludicrous in a frilled nightshirt that flapped about his heels. But he had his rifle and gear. Sometimes the Marquis's son was surprising. A woman Blanchard didn't recognize had laid strips of bark on the fire and by its meager light was spreading out mounds of bullets, fresh-run that afternoon, on a blanket. Edmond de la Foure had one of the scouts filling extra powder horns from the kegs in the wagon. Blanchard caught a glimpse of Lucie near Adrienne's wagon. Lucie was fully dressed in her voluminous gray gown. He wondered briefly how she had managed to dress so quickly. But there were too many other things to think about. Already the terrified screams of women and children were beginning to drown out everything else, but Blanchard listened for the steadiness of firing from the picket line. They hadn't been surprised, then, for he could discern at least six rifles firing outside the line of wagons. He grabbed de Flaville's arm, aiming him toward the timber that reached almost to the wagons. De Flaville was fully dressed and wide-awake by that time.

"They'll be in there," Blanchard shouted. "Take the scouts and lay for them." He held Charlie's arm and shook him hard to make him concentrate on what he said. "Don't go in the timber. Understand? Wait for them to come."

"*Bien,*" de Flaville grinned. "*Une grande bataille, non?*"

"*Grande,* enough," Blanchard muttered as he ran back to Crosbie's wagon. Crosbie was roaring like a wounded bull and Blanchard's tension relaxed at the sound. The old man really wants to get in the fight, he thought.

Crosbie's wagon was backed to the steep bank and Blanchard almost slipped down when he ran behind to climb inside. He hauled himself in with an undignified scramble that annoyed him excessively.

"Small raiding party, I reckon, Colonel," he said angrily. "They didn't get through the pickets and we're set for them now." Blanchard paused to catch his breath.

"*Les sauvages, mon lieutenant?*" The high excited voice was young Jack's, but Blanchard couldn't see him in the dark wagon bed.

"Aye," Crosbie said sharply. "All around us, Mr. Blanchard?" he asked mildly in a voice that contrasted sharply with his previous bellowing.

"No, sir," Blanchard said flatly. "We've got the creek and the river on two sides. I figure I'll take a detail and come on them from behind if they stand long enough."

"No rush about that, Mister," Crosbie said equably. "Any casualties yet?"

Blanchard ground his teeth, making hard muscles budge along his jaw. Every senior officer who ever lived always wants to prove how calm and brave he is in time of danger. Right now Blanchard wanted action, not serenity.

"Don't know, sir. I haven't ..."

"Can't be many," Crosbie said, almost placidly. "I hear mostly muskets out there. Can't hit anything with those old smoothbores even in daylight."

He sounds happy, Blanchard thought in amazement. Just because he can pick out muskets by the sound.

"We aren't much better off, Colonel," he snapped, raising his voice to carry over the din. "Only the guards and my scouts have rifles. The rest are mostly fowling pieces and pistols. I wish we had some of those muskets." This is mad, Blanchard told himself. I'm arguing about rifles when men are getting shot out there.

A sharply pointed silhouette poked through the back port and Cammie screamed, a tight hysterical note that made Blanchard dive quickly for his rifle.

"A thousand pardons, Colonel," a voice said almost inaudibly.

"The Marquis," Blanchard muttered. The pointed head was his nightcap, most likely. A very martial figure.

"I am leading a charge, *mon colonel*," the Marquis announced almost gaily. "I will ..."

"Damn your eyes," Crosbie roared. "Damn your insolent teeth, sir. You'll do nothing of the sort." He lurched upright, his eyes glittering in the faint light.

"I have some experience ..." the Marquis said in a voice as polite as the one he would have used in a drawing room.

"Damn your experience, sir," Crosbie broke in coldly— "Mr. Blanchard! You will shoot any man who disobeys an order from me. Is that clear?"

"Yes, sir," Blanchard growled.

"Now then, sir, please come inside the wagon. I want to listen for a moment." Crosbie laid down slowly and was silent.

About two minutes, Blanchard told himself. I'll give him that long. Charlie and the boys won't be in any trouble that soon. But any longer and I take command, Colonel or no Colonel. He said nothing as the Marquis grunted his way into the wagon, dragging a double-barreled fowling piece with him, a weapon that shone with silver filigree.

The gibbering screeching outside made a fearful racket. Blanchard suspected that most of the shooting was aimless and even dangerous for a shooter reveals his position when he fires, but he damned seldom hits anything at night. The firing dwindled and grew sporadic but the screaming was constant, as much from the frightened people of the wagon train as from outside.

Blanchard thought suddenly of the Indians he had fought, the half-naked bodies smeared with splotches of vivid color and the stripes of black that were a warrior's preparation for death, the mouths wide and distorted with the terrifying screams that were an essential part of the Indians' arsenal, the archaic arrows that were somehow more frightening than a civilized bullet could ever be. And the scalping. That was the last murderous indignity that made Indian fighting a matter of passion more than determination. And to fight them he had a pack of Parisians, professional men and artisans, courtiers and men of fashion. Only a few had any knowledge of warfare and all those few understood was the rigid sedate pattern that had no meaning here. And even they were not held in check because the Colonel wanted to listen. Blanchard gripped the stock of his rifle tightly, bearing down hard and keeping his mouth shut with a major effort of will.

It was Jock who broke the silence, seizing the opportunity to speak. "We will again make the savages run, Dooncahn?" his shrill voice demanded.

Crosbie eyed him with sober thoughtfulness, then chuckled suddenly. "We will," he laughed. He clutched Blanchard's arm, pulled him down beside him and whispered hoarsely, quickly, and when he had finished, he put his head back on the pillow and bellowed a stentorian laughter that nearly rocked the wagon. The Marquis seemed to shrink back, Blanchard! noted as he climbed out of the wagon to collect his scouts.

Within three minutes Blanchard slid softly down the steep river bank, followed by six of his scouts and young Jock, who clung tightly to Blanchard's hand. They moved with deliber- ate caution along Halfaday Creek, keeping just inside the water, walking in cadence so the sound of their movement was masked by the noise of the hard-running stream. They turned the bend carefully and Blanchard looked the other way as they worked slowly past the leaning tree where Adrienne had hung her clothes. Down in the deep gully of the streambed, the world was totally dark save for the glitter of tumbling water and the occasional ghostly glow of dead white bark on the overhanging trees.

Blanchard led his detail with the wariness of a timber wolf, feeling his route slowly, ever fearful of ambush, watching for an easy path back up to the high ground. Most of the ravines leading into the stream were choked with brush and Blanchard passed them by, choosing finally a slippery clay slide that a family of otters had once polished. By digging their toes in sharply he and his men climbed silently up to the forest.

Blanchard dared go no farther. None of his men could walk noiselessly in the forest even in daylight. At night they would be heard before they took three strides. He pulled young Jock around in front of him, backed him against an enormous oak and pushed him gently against the bole as a signal to stay where he was. Then he tapped the stock of his rifle twice in the prearranged signal to his men. Without waiting, he slipped into the woods, trying to get as far from the stream as he could before...

The shrieking skirl blotted out the gibbering shrieks. It struck with shocking impact and even Blanchard, prepared as he was, faltered in his stride when Jock blared on his *cornemuse*. Five high startling, keening notes. Then silence.

Blanchard drew a deep breath, steadying himself squarely.

"As skirmishers!" he bellowed, putting all his volume into the command. "Fix bayonets!"

And Jock picked up the sharp frightful tones of "The Campbells Are Coming," pumping smoothly and developing a solid wall of skirling sound behind Blanchard.

"Forward!" he roared, and even Colonel Crosbie could have done no better. Blanchard fired into the darkness ahead, as did the six scouts behind him, a meager volley, but effective enough with the wild demanding bagpipes to back it up.

The tense yipping shrieks of the attackers had been drowned by the first notes of the pipes. Afterwards they dwindled into a wailing sound that carried an undertone of surprise and fear.

The attack was over. As abruptly as it had begun, the firing slackened and then stopped. From the campsite came an exultant cheering.

Crosbie rolled up on his elbow, grinning wolfishly through the darkness at the Marquis. "They think it's a relief column," he chuckled. "I'll bet my breeches they all think the Highlanders are just outside the bivouac." He almost choked on his thick laughter. Cammie stroked his forehead distractedly. "And so do the Indians!" Crosbie bellowed.

"Ah, yes," the Marquis said politely. "*A ruse de guerre,* then, is it? Splendid, sir. Truly splendid. That … that appalling sound is made by little Jacques …"

"Aye," Crosbie said heavily, all laughter suddenly gone. "I must have been daft to send that boy out there to …"

The abrupt end of the noise made Crosbie aware of the volume of his voice. In quick embarrassment his voice died away and he reached to touch Cammie's hand. "I forget he is but a lad," he said with a quick surge of guilt. "He seems …"

Cammie's hands touched his lips, cutting off his words. Cool restful hands patted him gently and Crosbie relaxed enough to grin again at the thought of the bagpipes.

Within the circle of wagons, the campfires were quickly built up to brilliance and Blanchard came in with his small detachment, moving into the light only when he was sure he had been recognized. And even then he waited for de Flaville to come to him. For a moment he thought of raking them all over the coals for relaxing their guard now that the attack had been lifted. But he contented himself by posting guards again far beyond the ring of fires and then he carried Jock on his shoulder back to the wagon, not trying to make the boy stop playing his incessant battle-cry.

"Successful, Mr. Blanchard?" Crosbie asked quietly.

"Completely, sir," Blanchard said. He put his rifle down, balancing it cautiously, taking more time than the operation required, just to have something to do. He hadn't thought much of the Colonel's notion, that was a fact. But it wouldn't do to say so now. Blanchard had figured that taking the Indians by surprise from the rear would turn the trick; he'd placed no faith in that damned bagpipe at all.

"What casualties, Mister?"

"Charlie's going to find out," Blanchard said, his voice strained, his legs suddenly weary and trembling. He leaned against the side of the wagon.

"I couldn't find a scalp, Dooncahn," Jock said, jumping with excitement. "But I brought you a fine Indian bonnet."

"A fine souvenir, me lad," Crosbie said without thinking. "You'd best ..."

"Let me see it, Jock," Blanchard said quickly. He reached a searching hand across Crosbie's chest toward the boy, feeling a coldness move along his spine.

"It is for Dooncahn," Jock insisted, shrilly determined.

"Have a look, sir," Blanchard murmured in Crosbie's ear. "I'll be back in a minute." He leaped lightly from the wagon, all weariness forgotten now, and went to find de Flaville.

Crosbie took the bonnet from Jock with no interest other than a mild curiosity at Blanchard's attitude. But the same iciness touched at him when he fingers closed around the bonnet that Jack had brought him. It was a knitted woolen cap with a worn silken tassel. A fancy sailor's cap. The sort of thing the French *couriers de bois* out of Quebec sometimes wore in the woods. No Indian ever wore such a cap, except for fun, and certainly no self-respecting Indian would wear such a thing into battle. Crosbie returned the bonnet absently, saying nothing for a moment until he was sure his voice would betray none of the agitation he felt.

"A bonnie souvenir," he said amiably. "You treasure it, my lad. And to go with it, I'm presenting you with your piper's warrant in the morning. No soldier ever earned one more surely than you have this night." He patted Cammie's hand, drew her down and whispered, "The boy's a pack of nerves right now. Take him out and see if you can get him to drink some warm milk."

He suffered through Jock's vociferous objections to leaving, agreed they would discuss the entire campaign in the morning, ultimately had to plead a sudden weakness to make him leave. Luckily the Marquis chose to take it seriously and he, too, left with Jock and Cammie, leaving Crosbie alone in the dark wagon, staring out blindly at the black, ominous sky, waiting impatiently for Blanchard, trying not to think of the bonnet and what it might mean.

"What was it, sir?" Blanchard asked softly.

Crosbie started. He hadn't heard Blanchard as he came through the rear port.

"The bonnet?" Crosbie growled. "French, I guess. Probably a Huron could get it in Quebec."

"Yes, sir," Blanchard said with no emphasis. He clattered something in his hand. "These make just as much sense. The same kind of sense."

"What ..."

"We've got five men shot, none serious. The Indians lost one man. Charlie just found him. He was a Huron."

"Well?" Crosbie growled challengingly.

"Wearing Miami moccasins," Blanchard said. "Had a Shawnee tomahawk in his belt."

"Nothing from the Wyandots?" Crosbie asked sourly.

"No, sir," Blanchard said, "but I found three Cherokee fire arrows that never did get lighted. And I'm glad we didn't wait until they were lighted."

Crosbie ignored the implied rebuke. The facts were meaningless; they added up to nothing definite, but all the same ...

"French, Huron, Shawnee, Cherokee," Crosbie said in a thoughtful voice. "What do you make of that, Mr. Blanchard?"

Blanchard chewed at his lip. "Indians don't fight at night, Colonel, you know that. Not the ones who still worship the old gods. They can't get to heaven if they die at night. But the renegades don't care about that. They learned just enough Christianity to give them a free hand."

"Which means what?" Crosbie asked gloomily.

Blanchard shook his head. "Nothing by itself, sir," he admitted softly, "but I found a bare spot out there where three horses had run across a muddy stretch."

Crosbie nodded without speaking. Indians hardly ever brought horses into battle; they were too rare for such a risk. An Indian might ride close to a fight, but he would always send his precious horses to the rear before he attacked. Horses indicated white men, as did the presence of renegade Indians. Crosbie glared tightly at Blanchard.

"And I'm put in mind of something else, Colonel," Blanchard almost whispered.

"Yes," Crosbie growled. "That map."

"That map," Blanchard echoed. "One of the crosses marked on it could have been Halfaday Creek. It all makes me mighty uncomfortable, Colonel."

The two soldiers were silent in the darkness of the wagon, Crosbie's heavy breathing the only sound. Both knew that the wild country was constantly endangered by roaming wolf packs of renegade Indians, men of no account who were the dregs of the disciplined tribes, ready, even eager, to attack any vulnerable target. But Crosbie's wagon train was not vulnerable in that sense and the wolf packs never struck when there was much danger of resistance. But even more important, and this fact hung in the air like a poisonous vapor, the marauding renegades never came east of Fort Cumberland. Their wagon train had been attacked not from any casual hope of loot, but as part of a plan that was designed to stop the Frenchmen before they reached their lands in the Ohio country.

Neither Blanchard nor Crosbie felt it necessary to put any of it into words. They sat together and they sat silently until Cammie came to rouse them with steaming cups of coffee.

Only then did Blanchard let himself think of Adrienne again. He walked past her wagon on the way back to his own bed. She was safe enough, of course. He could hear her voice, and the answering murmur of Lucie's. He could feel again the wild excitement of holding her warm, yielding body in his arms. The stinging slash of her sharp fingernails still burned across his cheek. He remembered Doctor Gaines saying, back in Alexandria, "Spoilt minx. She'll give you trouble on the trip, I fear ..." Well, so she was, only maybe it wasn't exactly the sort of trouble the little doctor had envisioned.

CHAPTER NINE

As long dull weeks of slow cautious progress brought his wagon train closer to Pittsburgh, Colonel Duncan Crosbie could see unmistakable signs of strain and tension on his people. All were thinner and the fashionable pallor of their faces had tanned slowly. Now only the Marquis and a few of the ladies were dressed in a manner they considered fitting to their station. The others, seeing the effect of briars and vines, of constant wettings and inadequate launderings, had put away their finery for the duller but more practical homespuns of the country. At Fort Cumberland, while Crosbie was busy nursing his wagons across the ford at Wills Creek, many of the Frenchmen had gone ahead to the sutler's, eager to replace their flimsy satins and silks with leather and linen. Some, particularly among Blanchard's crew, seemed to compete in outward savagery with long shaggy hair, untrimmed beards and buckskins torn, grease-spattered and smoked to the color of an old hide.

Some of the horses—particularly the light, handsome animals chosen by the Marquis—were beginning to look gaunt and worn. That meant more walking for members of the Marquis's party, particularly the ladies, who had no saddle horses. It was rough country for ladies, and neither Adrienne nor her maid had proper heavy shoes. Somehow, Blanchard had contrived to find moccasins for them and that helped.

The three days the wagon train had rested at Fort Cumberland had been the last peaceful time for Crosbie. Ahead of them lay the Braddock Road, still called by the people at Fort Cumberland,

Nemocolin's road after the drunken Indian who had led Colonel
Cresap over the road long before Braddock. But it was the British
General who had altered the course to pass through the Narrows
of Wills Creek so that his wagons could avoid the worst of the
mountainous country. Crosbie grimaced when he said it, but he
gave Braddock credit whenever it was impossible to avoid a direct
reference. Beyond Wills Creek lay disputed ground and nothing
the Frenchmen had yet seen could compare with it.

When the ache in his chest built into a painful throb, Crosbie
reined in his heavy bay and dismounted cautiously, moving
slightly to stand in the shade of an enormous walnut tree, waiting for the wagons to come abreast. Three or four hours in the
saddle was all he could easily endure but he had put his time to
good account. Ahead and on both sides, young Mr. Blanchard
rode with his advance party, now well trained and cautious,
though still inclined to a dashing foolhardy approach to an
unknown danger. Between them Blanchard and Crosbie were
hard put to control them. Along the narrow rutted road the wagons rumbled, two abreast now, since that halved the length of the
train and doubled the protection Crosbie could give them on the
move. Crosbie still woke up at night, sitting tense and stiff with
the aftermath of nightmare in which he saw his long drawn-out
wagon train attacked without warning, attacked piecemeal and
hacked to bits. By doubling his wagons, Crosbie had doubled the
possibility of accidents to wagons and stock, but now every pair
of wagons had at least two armed men beside the road, as well as
Blanchard's men on each flank. Crosbie could do no more.

Behind him the wagons approached, seeming to Crosbie a
solid mass resembling a company drawn up for parade, with the
double line of wagons, women and children and the led animals
walking between them and the men close on either side, carrying
rifles, muskets, fowling pieces or pistols at the ready.

Crosbie reined in behind the second wagon and stiffly dismounted. The stowaway boy, François, ran quickly to him, took

his horse and tied it to the wagon. Crosbie grunted his thanks. That wise-eyed eager boy was never far from the Marquis's wagon. He seemed to know that his best chance of survival among the French was to be useful to the most influential man and his family. When he wasn't catering to the Count's evening gambling sessions, he was running errands for Mademoiselle Adrienne or working industriously over the Marquis's muddy riding boots. Crosbie swung up to the wagon box and sat heavily, feeling a slow throbbing ache in his shoulder, a sour sickness in his stomach. From the far side of the wagon, Adrienne smiled brightly up at him as she walked along, swinging a long slender ash stick that Crosbie had seen Blanchard carving some nights earlier.

Mademoiselle Adrienne seemed actually to thrive on wilderness travel. True, her blue gown did not follow the rounded curves of her figure quite as closely as it originally had, but the slight loss of weight had fined down the planes of her face, making it appear less the face of the pretty pampered child and more the face of a woman whose changing world was unfolding some surprising and sometimes frightening things. The sun had gilded her skin to the warm tone of a ripe peach. Mademoiselle Adrienne had a startling beauty and no one was more aware of that than Mademoiselle Adrienne, Crosbie thought sourly.

"How ... how do you feel, Colonel?" Adrienne asked in a halting English that carried still the inflection of her native French. She smiled at the big glowering man and flourished her polished stick. "It is a day of grandeur, is it not?"

"Aye," Crosbie growled. It irked him exceedingly to be riding when even the children walked. He settled sideways on the seat, easing the impact of jolts from his wounded side. As he turned he saw that he was not the only rider after all. In the back of the wagon, Mademoiselle Adrienne's maid lay on a sort of couch made of piled mattresses and quilts. She caught his glance and flushed. Probably remembering the often-repeated order about sparing the horses for their necessary task of getting the wagons to the Ohio country.

"You are ill?" Crosbie inquired gruffly. He had not intended to be that sharp.

The flush deepened on the girl's pale face. Swiftly she rose and without a word moved toward the back opening, sweeping aside the canvas curtain that kept the dust out.

It was Adrienne who replied to Crosbie's question.

"Not ill, Colonel. Lucie is resting. She was very tired. *I* insisted." Her voice was light but she emphasized the "I" as if she thought it quite sufficient reason for countermanding Crosbie's orders.

The blonde girl ducked under the canvas curtain and dropped to the ground from the slowly moving wagon.

"Stay where you are, Lucie," Adrienne called with a hint of anger in her voice. But the blonde girl came around the wagon and fell into step with her mistress, murmuring something Crosbie could not hear. Adrienne's protests subsided.

The girl did look ill, Crosbie thought. He felt a small touch of chagrin at his rudeness. He didn't enjoy ordering discomforts for the women. They should be sensible enough to understand that the orders he gave were designed for their ultimate safety.

"We will come to the bivouac soon, Colonel?" Adrienne was smiling again, ignoring the Colonel's vile temper, his deep frown.

Crosbie flicked a glance at the sky. It was late, he thought, later than Blanchard usually waited to camp. "A short distance now," he said gloomily, not looking at Adrienne. The saucy baggage had completely bemused his subaltern and Crosbie knew of three young Frenchmen who couldn't stay away from her. But she still sparkled her bold eyes and made her smile shimmer for Crosbie. Ah, well, he thought, flirting with every available man was probably little enough compensation for the loss of the gay Paris society she had left behind her.

As they maneuvered around a turn in the road, Crosbie could see Blanchard up ahead, sitting lightly on his leggy gelding, man and horse both harder and thinner than when they left Alexandria. Heavy lines were etched in Blanchard's face as he held his horse in the road, looking up toward a small clearing where two of his men were busy laying out the campsite. Crosbie immediately felt relieved upon seeing Blanchard. The young lieutenant's frivolous manner had sobered immensely in the past few weeks and Crosbie had come to depend heavily on him.

Blanchard walked his bay slowly toward Crosbie, lifting his dusty cocked hat gracefully to Adrienne.

Adrienne smiled her smile for him, too. She must be as tired as the others, Crosbie thought. The dust of the road had stained her silk gown and dimmed the luster of her black hair. But that smile was tireless and bright as a banner. Beside her, Lucie looked like a ghost in her shapeless grey dress. There was something wrong with that girl, certainly; her small face was almost translucent in its pallor. An odd sort of maid for the Marquis's niece to choose, he thought. And for such a journey. He heard Lucie murmur a greeting to Blanchard. She smiled up at him, then thrust forward one small foot shod in its newly acquired moccasin.

"I have not thanked you, Monsieur Blanchard," she said gratefully. "It is so much easier now to walk..."

Blanchard grinned and said it was nothing at all, he was glad that she was able to walk with greater comfort... and all the time his eyes were following Mademoiselle Adrienne, her untiring grace and her vivid, taunting beauty.

Crosbie turned aside to look at the campsite, thinking a little sourly that for all her appreciation of the new shoes, Mademoiselle Lucie was doing little enough walking in them. He did not see the girl sway suddenly, the pale face going paler still, put out one hand in a groping, helpless gesture and crumple to the ground at Adrienne's feet. But he turned in time to see Blanchard leap from the saddle, to hear Adrienne gasp "Lucie!" in startled, anxious tones. Then she was kneeling beside the girl, helping Blanchard to lift her. And from her nearby wagon, Cammie came hurrying across the trampled grass of the campsite, concern written plainly on her round, rosy face.

Blanchard carried the girl to the rear of the wagon and lifted her in to her couch of mattresses. There, Cammie and Adrienne took charge and Blanchard came around to where Crosbie still sat on the high front seat. He shrugged at the questioning look on the Colonel's face.

"I don't know, sir," he said softly. "Guess maybe the girl is sick." He hesitated, then added, "Hope it isn't the fever. I heard of a few cases back in Alexandria before we left..." He stopped at the thunderous look of rage that came in Crosbie's face. "Perhaps you could ask Cammie later," he suggested tactfully. "She seems to know a lot about such things."

Crosbie only grunted. But it was a good suggestion. He would ask Cammie later.

He got back to the more important business of the campsite.

"There's water enough, sir," Blanchard said in a flat tone, "but I don't like the way we're hemmed in here."

Crosbie nodded and slid across the wagon seat. "I'll look," he said quietly, assuming command as he saw Blanchard's confusion.

The clearing was small for their wagons. The cut-back timber had been burned off some years earlier and fields had been planted. It was rich valley land and someone had seen a vision of peaceful farming. The cabin had been built with a high-pitched roof to ward off the driving rains and snow that would come from the mountains through the gap in the hills. The meadow was small and the fields were full of stumps, and weeds and seedling timber were beginning to reclaim the land. A small farm, but a good one, Crosbie thought. Why had the owner left? His cabin was still standing, roofless now, but not worthless, and there had been a crop of corn to be harvested, but it was gone to tassel and was useless now. Why had he left? Indians, possibly, because the war had made this area unsafe. Or maybe just because the road was bringing in too many new faces for his taste. At any rate the cabin was deserted, the fields abandoned. Rings of blackened ash dotted the land where travelers had built their campfires for the night.

"Double guard again tonight, Mr. Blanchard," Crosbie said crisply. "Post them in the timber. It will do then."

Blanchard drew in a deep relieved breath and let it out slowly, almost sighing. "Yes, sir," he said dully.

"But not you," Crosbie snapped. He prodded Blanchard's chest with a stiff forefinger. "I'll patrol the positions. I want you to sleep. All night. I have a difficult job for you tomorrow."

Blanchard dropped his head and rotated it slowly, working out an aching stiffness from his neck muscles. "What sort of job?" he asked in a voice that was slow and listless.

"In the morning," Crosbie said bluntly. "Let's move the wagons into place and settle down." He turned back toward the road without waiting for Blanchard.

The wagon train bedded down slowly, but with the ease of long practice as the wagons were sited, wheels locked, stock unharnessed and fed, fires built and water drawn for the one big meal of the day. The wagons were lighter now and most of their grain and meal were gone. Only the horses and oxen actually pulling wagons were given an allotment of grain, the rest had to make do with grass alone and all were showing the effects of the journey. None of the cows had given milk for a month, the chickens looked more like scrawny corbies to Crosbie's jaundiced eye and the pigs were as lean and bad tempered as the dogs. Only the children thrived, Crosbie thought suddenly, as he saw Jock racing toward the shallow stream beside the abandoned cabin. The children were fat and healthy and so were some of the younger men. But this life was hard on the women and the older men. The long days of walking or riding, the short hours of rest which were never sufficient, and most of all, the constant tension of the new and frightening country had created its peculiar reaction. Most of the older ones would have turned back, Crosbie suspected, if they had anything to go back to. Crosbie muttered a quiet prayer that they would find in the wild Ohio country some reward for their efforts.

Crosbie straddled his thick legs wide and stood in the meadow until all his wagons had taken their positions around him. He was pleased at the despatch with which the Frenchmen made their bivouac. Even city folk could be trained, he thought.

Young Jock had gathered the children and armed them with long whippy branches torn from the trees bordering the stream. With disciplined precision, they deployed around the campsite, slashing lustily at the ground, beating carefully at the under-brush, the high grass. Any rattlesnakes or copperheads hiding within the bivouac would slither away from the swishing noise, either escaping into the forest or being killed by one of the men who would come racing at the first alarm from the children. Young Jock supervised his crew with shrill cries and wild signals with his leafy branch. Crosbie watched him carefully.

"You are pensive tonight, *mon colonel?*"

Crosbie whirled to glare up at the Marquis sitting high above him on his fine black horse. Weeks of travel lay lightly on the Marquis's slim shoulders. He alone of the Frenchmen wore his customary clothes now, a simple *cord-du-roi* suit with soft glove-leather riding boots and a plumed hat. His shirt was a cascade of thin lace ruffles and lace cuffs protruded elegantly over his light gloves. Just looking at him made Crosbie feel unwashed.

"A pleasant place, sir," he said easily, swinging a silver-handled riding whip against his long boots. "A peasant's hut, I imagine?"

Crosbie looked around at the cabin in momentary bewil-derment. "A peasant..." he hesitated. Then he smiled a wolfish smile. "A yeoman, sir," he said stiffly, using the only term the Frenchman would comprehend. "A free man who owned his land and followed no man but the man he chose."

"Ah?" the Marquis breathed. "But of course. A new land and new manners. It is very fitting." He touched his horse with a silver spur and trotted toward his wagon, lifting his whip in salute as he passed Crosbie.

With the coming of darkness, Crosbie made the first of his inspections of the guards. They were no longer as dependable as they had been at first. The novelty was gone now and fatigue was a constant enemy. But it was too early for any of them to be asleep. Crosbie walked wearily back to Cammie's wagon, the heels of his moccasins smacking solidly against the ground as he strode along, too tired to try to walk easily.

The campfires were beginning to die out now, except for the large one in the center where the guards stayed when they were off duty, and where six were gathered now, fumbling at a greasy *poque* deck while François hovered solicitously, waiting for someone to send him running for wine or more money. Crosbie walked through the lighted area, his immense frame grotesque in silhouette.

"Colonel Crosbie! Colonel!"

That was Blanchard's voice, but where was he?

"Over here, sir. On the road!"

Crosbie turned, waving his heavy arm to signify his willingness. But Blanchard didn't wait for him. He came running swiftly up the slight slope from the road. Behind him Crosbie could dimly see the misty whiteness of a woman's skirt against the dark sky. Adrienne again ...

"I told you to get some sleep, Mr. Blanchard ..." he began angrily.

"In a minute, sir," Blanchard broke in. "There's a wagon coming down the road. At least it makes that kind of noise."

"Take a detail," Crosbie snapped. "Mounted."

"I sent Charlie to get the horses," Blanchard said quickly.

As he spoke four horses moved across the lighted edge of the campsite coming toward them.

"Bring the wagon to me, Mr. Blanchard," Crosbie called out as Blanchard swung into his saddle.

Blanchard saluted absently.

"It is not something…dangerous, Colonel Crosbie?" Adrienne asked softly from the darkness.

Crosbie could barely discern the outline of her white dress. The minx had changed clothes tonight; something none of the women bothered about these days. Crosbie was about to snap at her when he thought suddenly that she might really be concerned for Blanchard's safety. He thought it unlikely, but if that was the case…

"It was nothing serious, Mademoiselle Adrienne," he said as gently as he could manage. "Otherwise they would not approach noisily." Crosbie spoke in French, hoping to reassure the girl.

"Of course," she breathed in evident relief. "That is so obvious."

"But it might be best if you returned to the fire," Crosbie said bluntly. He thumbed back the lock of his rifle and rested it in the crook of his arm easily.

Adrienne stayed silently beside him, not moving or speaking. Crosbie moved a few steps so that she was shielded from the road.

Blanchard's voice shouted once from far away, then for some minutes there was no sound. Crosbie fingered his rifle, touched his belt to make sure his long murderous dirk was close to his hand.

A horse trotted slowly down the rutted road and stopped below Crosbie.

"Colonel? Just travelers. One wagon with two men."

"Travelers?" Crosbie's tone was incredulous. "At this time of night?"

"Said they were pushing hard to get here," Blanchard said in a judicious voice, presenting the facts without opinion. "It is the only good place to camp for about five miles."

The wagon rumbled up the road, escorted by three of Blanchard's scouts. It halted when Crosbie shouted.

"Who are you?" Crosbie demanded.

"Name's Carver," a thin reedy voice said. "Me 'n my brother. Headin' fer Pittsburgh."

"Why do you travel at night?"

"Don't reckon it's none o' yer business, Mister," the high voice said sharply. "We know the road. Wanted to bed down here."

Crosbie was silent, thoughtful. It was unlikely that danger could come to his wagon train from two men who openly announced their arrival. But he was in no mood to take chances.

"We'd admire to join up with you folks," the voice said. "Me 'n Ben ain't much fer ..."

"No," Crosbie said brusquely. "You can stay here for the night but you don't join my train."

"It's a free road ..." the voice blustered thinly. "I reckon ..."

"Mr. Blanchard!" Crosbie roared.

"Yes, sir," Blanchard said softly.

"Park this wagon by the side of the road. Unhitch the horses and tether them near my wagon." Crosbie ignored low mutters from the strange wagon. "Then search the wagon. Take every weapon away from these men until morning. Is that clear?"

"Clear, sir," Blanchard said. "What about it, Mr. Carver? You want to argue?" Blanchard's voice was lively now, almost gay with the prospect of action.

Whatever was said was inaudible to Crosbie. He turned back to the wagon train, taking Adrienne by the arm and pulling her along.

"Now that you understand English. Miss Adrienne, this is no place for you. Not with what those men will be saying."

"But is it then safe for ..."

"Everything's all right," Crosbie said tiredly. "You just go along to bed now. I want Mr. Blanchard to get some sleep."

After a silent moment, Adrienne giggled delightedly and Crosbie realized what he had said. "Good night," he growled. He stumbled across a recumbent body and fumbled his way to his bed in Cammie's wagon.

He uncocked his rifle carefully and propped it against the bed, took off his hat and moccasins and stretched out full length on the mattress, sighing deeply with relief.

He would sleep for two hours, he told himself, then he would get up and check the guards again. But first he'd have to wait for Blanchard to report. And sleep seemed to pull at his eyelids, drag at his mind until he was bathed in warm drowsiness that gradually swept over him, drowning him ...

"Colonel," Blanchard whispered. "Awake, Colonel?"

Crosbie awoke with a start, feeling guiltily angry. "Of course I'm awake," he growled. "What is it?"

"Got our visitors bedded down," Blanchard said softly. "They had two rifles, two shotguns and eight pistols. Quite a load, I thought, but they say it's normal for two men travelling alone. Claim they're going to trail along with us tomorrow."

"They won't," Crosbie grunted. "Very good, Mr. Blanchard. Get to bed."

"Yes, sir," Blanchard said. "Good night, sir."

"Good night," Crosbie muttered. He rolled over in the softness of his bed, staring out across the campsite toward the strange wagon. No matter what their intentions, the brothers Carver couldn't interfere with his people now. And in the morning, he'd make sure they weren't close enough to do harm.

Cammie's soft voice spoke to him out of the darkness.

"You are concerned, Dooncahn? There is difficulty for us?"

His own voice sounded heavy and troubled as he answered.

"Nothing, Cammie," he said. After all, there was no need to worry her with his vague doubts and fears. No answer Cammie could give to all the questions raised by this long and perplexing day could solve them for him. But then, slowly, something stirred in his mind. Something almost forgotten in the press of later happenings. That girl ... Mademoiselle Adrienne's maid.

"Cammie ..." he fumbled for a way to phrase his question. If the girl should have the fever, that dreaded summer ailment which killed its victim as often as it spared, he had no wish to frighten her. "Cammie, that girl, Lucie ..."

"Yes, Dooncahn?"

"She's ... she is ill, isn't she? That business of fainting this afternoon. And I saw her do the same thing once before, back in Alexandria. What is wrong with her, Cammie?"

There was a moment of silence, a definite feeling of hesitation. Crosbie waited. To his amazement he thought there was a note of amusement in Cammie's voice when at last she answered.

"She is not ill, Dooncahn," she said. "Not really. You need have no concern. There is nothing wrong with Lucie that time will not cure. She is no danger to your wagon train."

He could make no sense of that, beyond, of course, his usual startlement at Cammie's immediate understanding of his motives. He told her so. He heard a soft breath of a sigh out of the darkness.

"I have been sworn to secrecy, Dooncahn," Cammie said. "By Lucie and by Mademoiselle Adrienne. They do not wish you or the Marquis to know. They fear you will send Lucie back to Alexandria. She has nothing there, you see. No money, no family, no one to turn to for help excepting possibly the good Madame Gaines. And she wishes, too, to be with the man she loves ..."

"Cammie!" He wanted to shout his protest, but Jock was there, close to him, and sleeping soundly. "Cammie, you are not making sense. Why should they fear we would send the girl back to Alexandria if she is not ill? And even if she were ill it would be impossible. I could not spare an escort for her. Cammie ..." he managed again to control the incipient roar. "Answer me! A simple answer and one I can understand."

"Of course, Dooncahn," Cammie soothed. There was that odd suppressed amusement again. "It is really *very* simple. Lucie is pregnant. She will have her child in four months. And by that time we will all be safe in our new homes, and Lucie will be married, and ..."

Crosbie could feel his face begin to burn in the dark as Cammie went on murmuring assurances, but he did not know whether it burned in rage or in embarrassment. Pregnant! He should have guessed, of course. All that fainting, the queer apprehensive way she looked at him when he found her riding in the wagon when she should have been walking with the others ... He should have guessed they were trying to hide something, she and that minx Adrienne.

And Cammie had said "... she wishes to be with the man she loves." That brought up another question. What man was it? One who travelled with them? One she expected to rejoin somewhere in the Ohio country later? The last seemed unlikely enough, God knows. Why had the man not married Lucie in Alexandria if he meant to marry her at all? Why not marry her now, for that matter, if he was a member of the wagon train? There was a perfectly proper priest ... But those questions Cammie would not answer. If, indeed, she knew the answers.

"I cannot tell you, Dooncahn," she said firmly. "Those are matters between Lucie and the man himself. It is not for me to interfere, and, I think ..." it was gently said but quite firm ... "not for you."

He accepted the rebuke. Perhaps he even deserved it. Nevertheless, he would find out about the matter. No doubt there had been gossip, there always was about such a thing. No doubt Blanchard had heard ...

Crosbie cursed silently. He did not like it. Whoever the man was he could hardly be a man of honor. The girl was no tart, that was clearly to be seen. She had the quiet gentle manner of a lady. Not the lady-of-fashion's arrogance that marked Mademoiselle

Adrienne, true, but still an unmistakable air of gentility. He realized now that it was that gentility which had made him think Lucie an odd choice for a lady's maid. She had nothing of the servant about her, for all her attempts at self-effacement. What sort of game were they playing, Lucie and Mademoiselle Adrienne? And how could they hope to conceal what could not be concealed much longer in any event?

Crosbie turned over too hastily, winced as his injured shoulder reminded him forcibly of its presence. Nothing could be done tonight at any rate. Tomorrow... well, tomorrow he would see. He was relieved that the girl did not have the deadly summer fever, with its attendant danger to other members of his wagon train, but still he didn't like this sort of thing among his charges, either. It was hard enough getting them safely through a wilderness without complicating factors like illegitimate pregnancies. A man who was responsible for such a thing would be a man you could not trust in other matters. He did not want with the wagon train men you could not trust.

He composed himself for sleep, listening to the deep regular breathing of Cammie and Jock, the faint stirrings around the campfire, the quiet movement of the night wind in the high trees. There was a long aching interval as Crosbie lay still. One by one the tensions of pain and fatigue eased away and he slept.

CHAPTER TEN

Lieutenant Blanchard prowled cautiously through the dense timber, stepping with exaggerated care and holding his long rifle at the ready. Ahead somewhere was a picket who had already spent nearly four hours in fearful watching. With the coming of the first greyness of dawn, the picket would be a doubly dangerous man. The first sound, even though it came from his rear, would be enough to drive him to an abrupt, thoughtless reaction. Blanchard, having in the past few weeks been shot at twice by his own pickets, moved like a timid panther as he patrolled the campsite.

When he had crossed the meadow to seek out the first guard, Blanchard had been pleasantly aware of the approaching daylight. His moccasins and leggings had been dripping with dew and his lungs full of sharply cold air. But here in the forest, night remained a tangible darkness. Even at noon, only a vestige of sunlight would penetrate the interlaced leaves and branches to reach the ground. A rustling to one side stopped Blanchard. He brought his cocked rifle up warily, waiting.

A sudden screech froze him in his tracks and before he could move, a thin wicked point thrust into his back. Blanchard stiffened. His legs tensed as he poised to leap.

"A noisy woodsman is a dead woodsman," a laughing voice said behind him. "Do I quote you correctly, Mr. Blanchard?"

Blanchard didn't move. He looked up toward the treetops as though something there fascinated him.

"If you could say that about Frenchmen," he said sourly, "there wouldn't be a one alive today."

The knife point moved away and Blanchard turned slowly.

"Charlie, you're a double-damned fool. Who told you to go on guard tonight?"

De Flaville shrugged. He stroked his pale blonde mustache in a habitual gesture. "Poor Grennelle," he grinned, "he was so sleepy, I found. And expiring for love of Rosa, the large maid of Madame de Ravalle. I was able to relieve him of one anxiety, but the other …" De Flaville shrugged again and laughed.

Blanchard uncocked his rifle and let it ease down until the butt touched the ground. He looked without expression at de Flaville's rakish, slanted grin, looked with no amusement.

"I don't look for a friend to put a knife in my back, Charlie, even for fun." There was no inflection to his voice and the flat cold tone was hard and demanding.

"A joke, is it not?" de Flaville said lightly, still grinning, though the grin was now beginning to feel tight and useless, even to him.

"No joke to me," Blanchard insisted.

De Flaville shrugged again and forced his grin wider. "Then I apologize to my commander, *monsieur*," he said amiably. "I became overwhelmed with my growing craftiness in the woods."

Blanchard nodded abruptly. "Maybe I'm tired," he said heavily. "Forget it. In about an hour, round up the guards and bring them in."

De Flaville saluted elegantly with his long hunter's knife, a gesture that Blanchard thought lacked much in tact.

He pivoted on his heel and walked quickly back toward the campsite, trying without success to choke back his rising anger. De Flaville had been about the most promising of the scouts and here he was playing a fool trick that no man of sense would consider funny. Even the Marquis's son would have known better. Blanchard paused at the central campfire, pitched on a handful of dry bark and shoved two heavy logs on top of the bed of coals. He bent to fan them with his breath and in his anger, he blew too heavily. A massive billow of ashes recoiled into his face, sending him into a mad paroxysm of coughing. Then he leaned back with clenched fists and cursed his present assignment, Crosbie, the fatuous Frenchmen as he had cursed them a dozen times before. He heard his ridiculous heated words and laughed at himself, laughed softly and humorlessly, but he laughed. Then he stood erect, kicked the fire again gently and went across the bivouac toward Crosbie's wagon.

Blanchard reached high through the rear port and poked his rifle at Crosbie's mattress, prodding it twice. Then he waited.

The old man always went through the same routine when he woke up, Blanchard thought, grinning to himself. The heavy regular breathing stopped abruptly, then was picked up again, stealthily, as if the sleeper had merely turned over or moved in his sleep. But the Colonel was wide awake, Blanchard knew, awake and fighting to bring his mind into function. And he was listening as keenly as any hungry Shawnee.

"Blanchard, sir," he said softly. "Coming on for dawn."

Crosbie cleared his throat and shifted on his bed. Blanchard waited patiently. The Colonel never appeared until he was fully dressed and ready for any eventuality.

Crosbie pulled on his stiff cold moccasins and slid out through the rear port. He raked his fingers through his tousled hair and settled his cocked hat with a solemn air of authority before he turned to Blanchard.

"Who checked the guards last night, Mr. Blanchard?" he asked gruffly.

"I did, sir. Took it on myself. I thought you looked awful tired last night, Colonel."

Crosbie ignored the sympathetic tone in Blanchard's voice. His bushy eyebrows drew low in a stern frown. "An order, Mr. Blanchard, is given to be obeyed..." Abruptly his voice dwindled and Crosbie cleared his throat roughly. "Well, in any event...ah, thank you, Mr. Blanchard," he said irritably. "But never again." He cast a keen glance around the campsite, inspecting it quickly. "What of the night?"

"Nothing unusual, sir," Blanchard said easily. "Count's game went on most of the night. I think maybe we better break that up before somebody loses too much and starts a fight." Blanchard stared across the bivouac, his young face heavy with fatigue. "Sometimes I think these people don't realize what danger they're in."

"They realize," Crosbie said firmly, "but they don't let it bother them. They know they couldn't do much to change anything and in any event, they're a great people for ignoring unpleasantness longer than you or I could." Crosbie rubbed a hard hand across his stubbled chin. "Any trouble from our visitors?"

"Stayed in their blankets all night, sir," Blanchard answered. "And the guards were awake. Most of the night anyway," he added with a faint smile.

"And you, sir," Crosbie glared. "Have you had any sleep?"

"Some, Colonel. Enough, I reckon."

"Today, de Flaville will take over your duties as leader of the advance party. You will remain behind with our visitors until after midday…"

"But, Colonel, I…"

"Until midday," Crosbie repeated stubbornly. "At which time you will take their spare wheel and one of the wheels from their wagon and carry them with you at least four miles. Our visitors can carry them back and that will put them a day behind us. I'll drop off their weapons along the way. Warn them that if we see them again, they'll not have their wheels returned again."

Blanchard laughed at the thought. But the laughter faded quickly.

"They'll have their weapons, Colonel," he warned.

"They've seen how we guard ourselves, Mr. Blanchard," Crosbie said. "If they had mischief in mind, they'll not try it now."

Blanchard removed his hat and ruffled up his hair where the band had matted it. "Colonel, do you think they ..."

"I don't speculate about them," Crosbie said, touching Blanchard's shoulder lightly. "I merely remove the possibility of danger. Now get your breakfast and sleep until the wagons move out. When you catch up with me, I'll tell you the next step."

"More, sir?"

"Aye," Crosbie said, moving toward the fire. "And still more after that." But he would not take up the matter of the girl, Lucie, now. That could wait. "Get to sleep, Mr. Blanchard," he said gently.

Blanchard walked toward his blanket spread beneath the lead wagon. He settled stiffly on the coarse wool, took off his hat so he could use it as a pillow. His rifle remained from long habit in the crook of his left arm and his right hand checked the location of his knife before he let himself relax. It was impossible to sleep, he knew, now that the *émigrés* were beginning to stir and the smell of breakfast cooking would bring him quickly out of any sleep, no matter how deep. Blanchard stretched languorously, coughed heavily to get rid of the metallic flavor of sleeplessness. He shifted his hip in a restless motion and then he was asleep soundly.

The Marquis brought two steaming cups of coffee from the campfire and walked toward Crosbie. As always, the Colonel felt an awareness of his own untidiness when he saw the Marquis. The Frenchman wore a simple brown suit and his snuff colored wig but his linen was dazzling in the sunlight. With no real interest, Crosbie wondered how he managed to get his laundry done when he was on the move. Probably didn't, he thought suddenly. A man like the Marquis would have a trunkful of clean shirts. He took the cup from d'Aucourt's hand and forced a smile of thanks.

"A most pleasant morning, sir," the Marquis murmured. He sipped delicately at his thick metal cup and sighed heavily, looking at the solid fringe of trees that ringed the campsite. "On such a morning," he said to the silent Colonel, "I once breakfasted *al fresco* with Madame de Flahaut in the *Bois*. A delightful creature," he said with another reminiscent sigh. "I regret to say that I was never able to repeat the occasion. Your minister, Mr. Gouverneur Morris, was a most persuasive man. It was he who breakfasted *al fresco* thereafter and I had my solitary meal."

Crosbie grinned wholeheartedly. The Marquis was a great one for the pleasant memory and if his life had been as active as Crosbie suspected, the Marquis had a barrel of fine memories.

"A tragic affair, sir," he agreed.

"Of no moment," the Marquis shrugged. "It was not a clear victory for Mr. Morris. The eloquent Bishop, Talleyrand, was an ardent competitor. I never felt that Mr. Morris long enjoyed the fruits which he won from me. Madame de Flahaut was rather a changeable lady."

Crosbie laughed outright at the Marquis's expression of mock regret. "It says much for your philosophic acceptance, sir, that you should come to America after our minister so grossly deceived you."

"I forgave him," the Marquis laughed. "And America was the one refuge of meaning to us after the Bastille fell." He stared off toward the trees and his voice was a low, soft sound, as if he thought aloud.

"When one is out of favor at court, life can be trying," he said haltingly. "And estates will not forever bear the burden of expenses at Versailles. I once thought it best for my son to grow up with the men who would in some sense control his future, but that was an error. Such men no longer control any future, even their own. Edmond was not enthusiastic about leaving France at first. It was his friend, young de Flaville, who saw clearly both the need to leave and the possibilities of a future in a new world. It was he who made Edmond see too, finally..."

Privately, Crosbie had grave doubts of the visionary powers of the Marquis's light-minded son.

"An intelligent and ambitious young man, de Flaville," he said politely. That much he could say with agreeable conviction.

The Marquis nodded. "A young man of courage, also," he said soberly. "Courage enough to attempt a new life and a new career after the fortunes of his family met with recent... and complete... disaster in France..." he paused thoughtfully, then shrugged his rueful acceptance of misfortune and change. "I had hoped," he said, "that Adrienne, my niece, and Charles..." he broke off again, as if suddenly aware that he had strayed far from the subject of discussion.

"The world is coming to an end for France," he resumed softly. "An era is dying and one must either remain loyal to the horror of the Bourbons or find a place among the rabble who will rise against them. I could find it in my conscience to do neither."

Crosbie nodded solemnly. "A difficult choice," he said, feeling a twinge of sympathy for the Marquis. "Did most of your people here find the problem equally difficult?"

The Marquis shrugged. "Pioneers are made up of a variety of types. Among us as among every pioneer group. Many share my views and find hope in the new idea which made this country free. But some bought their land with money that should properly have gone to their creditors. They hope to recoup in a new world. Many are people of decency, small tradesmen and craftsmen who were largely dependent upon court favor for their existence. The Revolution which is coming would have ruined them. To them, America is a land of hope also. We are a large group of people, *mon colonel*, and among us you will find a wide variety of talents, of backgrounds and of morals. It could not be otherwise, could it?"

Crosbie's shrug matched the Marquis's, but the Colonel did not share the Frenchman's indifference. The wide variety of people made his job immensely difficult. It was not a matter for casual dismissal.

"You will excuse me, sir," he said gruffly. "I have much to attend to."

"Certainly," the Marquis bowed. When Crosbie had taken his first step, d'Aucourt caught his arm lightly. "My son, Edmond," he said quickly, "do you find him useful?"

Crosbie stopped. The Marquis's face had lost some of its habitual composure and sureness. For the moment, he was a father and he wanted reassurance. Edmond de la Foure was a gambling, foppish idiot in Crosbie's view, but Mr. Blanchard found him useful. That should be enough for the Marquis. "Very useful," Crosbie said sharply.

The Marquis nodded, his eyes fixed on the gleaming tips of his boots. He bowed again and strode away toward the circle of people around the campfire.

It was not the bustle of the morning routine nor the smell of breakfast that awakened Blanchard, not even the growing warmth and light of the sun that hit him squarely in the eyes. A soft cool hand stroked once down his cheek and Blanchard started, fully awake at the first touch.

"Your ogreish Colonel insists you must now awaken," Adrienne said lightly. "I managed to put aside your breakfast."

Blanchard mumbled something incoherent. He cleared his throat, licked his dry lips and tried to make his eyes focus intelligently on Adrienne's face. He could see nothing but her wide flounced blue dress that seemed to surround him like an implausible cloud and above it her elfin, pointed mocking face. And if he could not see beyond the billowing dress, neither could anyone see him from the campsite. He lunged upward and forward swiftly, almost desperately and his mouth touched Adrienne's in a light darting kiss. He felt her lips move under his and then retreat.

"I shall now tell the fierce Colonel that his lieutenant is now alert and ready for duty," she said softly, moving farther back from Blanchard. "Your breakfast, *mon cher lieutenant*."

Blanchard lurched forward too slowly. Suddenly Adrienne was demurely seated some feet away from him with her massive skirt swirled around her, and now Blanchard was in full sight of the whole camp.

"Does the gallant lieutenant lack courage?" Adrienne whispered with sparkling eyes.

She was teasing him again, he thought. He grinned, refusing to rise to the bait. "He lacks food," he said, reaching for the metal plate that lay beside him.

He ate quickly, voraciously, wolfing down the stewed deer meat and journey cake, purposely devoting himself to his food and covertly watching Adrienne as he scooped up his food with his horn spoon. He finished the last of his stew, licked his spoon tidily and tucked it inside his shirt. His cup of coffee was cold and it wasn't coffee either; it had been a barley-and-coffee mixture some weeks ago but now it was parched corn with the merest flavor of coffee. Blanchard gulped it quickly and put the cup on his plate.

He slid his hand along the ground toward Adrienne's knee. "And now, about that matter of courage, Mademoiselle," he said with a spurious leer. "You were saying..."

Adrienne leaped up with a muffled shriek and just then Crosbie's heavy voice broke into Blanchard's consciousness.

"We move in five minutes, Mr. Blanchard," he roared. "Are you ready?"

Blanchard grinned ruefully at Adrienne, scooped up his hat and blanket and stood erect. "Ready now, sir," he called.

While he had slept, the stock had been harnessed, the Frenchmen fed and the campsite swept clean of gear. Even the scouts were gone, Blanchard noted, for only his horse remained in the plot of meadow where seven had been tethered last night. Blanchard tossed his blanket inside the lead wagon and went to get his horse. Crosbie walked his heavy gelding toward him.

"The weapons I'll leave wrapped in a canvas five miles along the road, Mr. Blanchard," he said. "You'll have no trouble with the brothers Carver, I'm thinking, but if you do, tell them they won't get their weapons back unless they follow orders. Understand?"

"Yes, sir."

Crosbie leaned down so he could speak softly. "When you leave, Mr. Blanchard, come quickly."

Blanchard's eyes widened. So far as he knew, there was nothing of immediate concern or danger. He nodded slowly. Crosbie trotted his bay forward, held up his immense arm and signaled the wagons forward.

Blanchard strolled toward the strange wagon, stopping ten yards away on a small rise of ground. He sat then, holding his rifle across his knee negligently.

The Carver brothers drove a wagon that was warped by hot sun and gaping at the joints. The once blue paint had weathered away and the bare wood had bleached a bone-white. Their horses were a small, mismatched pair with prominent ribs, shod only on the rear feet. A cheap rig, but one that would carry them to Pittsburgh if they were careful.

Behind Blanchard the wagons of the French *émigrés* moved out in orderly procession. Within twenty minutes, the last heavy Conestoga had lumbered down onto the road. Then the dark shaggy man standing beside the horses rugged at the head-stalls. Blanchard lifted his rifle, cocked it deliberately. He said nothing.

Out of the torn canvas port at the front of the wagon, another shaggy head, this one with an equally shaggy beard, poked out and muttered something Blanchard couldn't hear. The driver looked around apprehensively, saw Blanchard and released the headstalls as though they were molten metal.

"Now looka here, you," he blustered. He looked toward his bearded brother for assistance. The beard withdrew into the wagon.

"Come outside," Blanchard said gently. He counted five slowly to himself, then raised his rifle slowly, drawing a careful bead on the near horse.

"Fer Gawd's sake, Ben, get outta thet wagon. This here fellow is plumb crazy. He'll shoot the horses. Git down outa there, I tell yuh."

"He's right, Ben," Blanchard said. His trigger finger contracted slightly until he saw the bearded brother slide out through the forward port and scramble to the ground, keeping carefully on the far side of the wagon with his brother.

"Now unhitch the horses and tether them," Blanchard ordered.

The brothers muttered. They spoke of the rights of the road, of the overthrow of King George and all other tyrants, they spoke of the brotherhood of man. But they unhitched and they tethered their horses. And then they sat, at Blanchard's command, under the shade of their wagon while Blanchard stayed on his hill, his cocked rifle across his knees, his back to the rising warming sun.

The morning passed slowly for Blanchard, too slowly for safety, because the hot sun put him briefly to sleep a dozen times. But each short doze ended before he had relaxed his vigilance sufficiently to make it safe for the Carvers to charge him. As the sun rose nearly overhead, Blanchard rose and walked quickly around the wagon, keeping himself awake by movement. There was no spare wheel, he noted absently and then he wondered why he cared about their wheels. Memory came to him slowly. Then he ordered the shaggy brothers on their feet and set them to propping a rear axle and removing a wheel.

"I ain't gunna do it," the beardless brother said stubbornly. "I'm a free man and there ain't no son of a..."

"Suit yourself, brother," Blanchard shrugged. "You get the wheel and your weapons back. If you want to keep the wheel, you don't get your weapons." He turned his back on them, went slowly toward his picketed horse, delaying as long as he could without appearing to wait for their decision.

"What you-all aimin' to do, then?" the bearded brother asked fearfully.

Blanchard swung up into his saddle and turned his bay to face them. "I'll take the wheel and leave it about five miles down the road. You'll find your weapons with the wheel. That's provided I get the wheel. If I don't, you won't find any weapons waiting for you."

"Man alive, we couldn't make it without a couple rifles. You know that."

"Certainly," Blanchard said agreeably. "So take off the wheel."

The brothers moved grudgingly toward a rear wheel. One glared up with the last dying fragment of resistance. "How do we know you-all gunna leave us the wheel?"

Blanchard shrugged. He touched his heel to the bay's flank and trotted him forward toward the road.

"Wait! Heay now, wait!" The brothers wrenched the wide rickety wheel from the axle and rolled it down to Blanchard. After he had sent them back to their disabled wagon, Blanchard got down, shouldered the heavy oaken wheel and climbed back on his horse.

"Don't start off for a while," he shouted. "I might get nervous." He moved his gelding slowly along the road, following the fresh ruts the wagon train had left.

A brilliant solution, the Colonel's, he thought bitterly. I'll break my back with this wheel. And if I run into any kind of trouble, I'll spend an hour getting this wheel off my neck so I can shoot. Crosbie's a smart man sometimes, but he wasn't thinking much this morning.

Blanchard balanced the wheel carefully and put his gelding to an easy canter, eager to get rid of his ungainly load as soon as he could. His gelding snorted with pleasure and arched his neck happily. It had been nearly a month since Blanchard had let him run.

The Carver brothers weapons were lying right in the center of the road under a scrap of mildewed canvas. Blanchard slowed and as he passed the canvas mound, he pitched the wheel to the roadbed. Then he let his leggy bay resume the canter. He rose lightly in the stirrups, feeling the wind flap his long hair behind him as the gelding settled into his rocking pace.

Colonel Crosbie was riding tail guard on the wagon train, half obscured by the streamers of dust rising from the churning wheels. Blanchard pulled in his eager horse and slowed to match the Colonel's stride.

"All secure, sir," he grinned. "Our visitors won't be coming back."

Crosbie grunted sourly. He wiped his dusty face with a handkerchief that showed signs of hard usage.

"Do you know where we are, Mr. Blanchard?" he snapped.

"Why... why, I guess not, sir, not within twenty miles, anyway."

Crosbie waved, an annoyed gesture that silenced Blanchard. "We'll cross the Youghiogheny tomorrow at Stewart's Crossing."

Blanchard whistled. "Pittsburgh in less than a week, then."

"Aye," Crosbie glowered. "Pittsburgh in less than a week. With three hundred Frenchmen in wagons. General Putnam is to furnish boats of some kind for the remainder of the journey. I want them ready the moment we arrive. That's your assignment. You go ahead, see the Ohio Company agent and make sure they're ready for us."

"Yes, sir," Blanchard said soberly.

"I'll cross Turtle Creek and wait in Braddock's Field until you return, Mr. Blanchard. I don't want these people loose in Pittsburgh if I can help it. That's a wild place for strangers. I want to come straight in through the town to the landing, load onto boats and get away, all the same day. Understand?"

"I understand what you want, Colonel," Blanchard said slowly. "But I sure don't know whether it can be done. Three hundred people, all this stock, and the ..."

"You do it, Mr. Blanchard," Crosbie snapped. "Meet me at Braddock's field in about a week, five days would be better."

"Very good, sir," Blanchard said absently.

"Get to Pittsburgh as soon as you can. I've had your gear packed and some food put up for you. The pack is in the lead wagon. Pick it up as you go by. Good luck, sir."

Blanchard nodded, his mind busy with plans. It would be possible to give the Colonel what he wanted, but only barely possible. What if the boats weren't ready, what if...

"And Mr. Blanchard..." Crosbie waited for the lieutenant to look at him.

"Sir?"

"You had your breakfast, Mr. Blanchard, so you won't need to dally at the wagon train. Make your best time."

Blanchard reddened slowly, saw the Colonel grinning wickedly at him. He kicked his gelding into a trot and rode quickly down the long double line of wagons.

CHAPTER ELEVEN

Colonel Duncan Crosbie checked his heavy gelding above Turtle Creek gorge and sat there stolidly, staring down at the brown, tumbling water. Here General Braddock had crossed to his disastrous defeat at the hands of united Indian nations and their French leaders. The survivors of that fiasco had remembered well their difficulty in crossing Turtle Creek. Even General Washington had once mentioned to Crosbie the sign that had later been placed at the ford: "Turtle Crick—Meen Crossin."

Young de Flaville had sounded the creek along the length of the ford in hopes of finding a more shallow depth, but ten inches of rolling water was the least they would encounter. Crosbie rubbed his chin thoughtfully and studied the ground below him. If he doubled the teams so that every wagon had at least four horses pulling, then he would double his chances of crossing safely. He could use some of the heavier men to pull back on ropes so that the wagons could approach the steep descent to the creek very slowly. And on the other side, still more men to help with the desperate struggle to regain the level land. He could do nothing more, so far as he could anticipate, but somehow his plans seemed inadequate in his mind. Crosbie rubbed his wounded shoulder gently and the dull pain distracted him briefly. The reputation of Turtle Creek was ominous at best. A splendid force of armed men had here lost much of their equipment and only hours later had lost their war. There was nothing reassuring in that for Crosbie and even the hot welcome sun on his back could not relax him.

Below him de Flaville scrambled swiftly up the bank, pulling himself toward Crosbie by minute toeholds and his agile use of roots and bushes that protruded from the slippery clay.

"The road is clear, Colonel," he panted, "but most difficult, I should say."

Crosbie nodded at the young Frenchman. "Aye," he said heavily. "But we've no alternative, sir." He looked down at de Flaville and smiled thinly. The scout had spent nearly an hour splashing about in the swift water of Turtle Creek and he had slid down and struggled up the bank several times. But he stood ready to investigate again, and cheerfully, if Crosbie were still curious. As Crosbie remembered telling the Marquis, de Flaville was a hard-working and ambitious boy. Whatever regrets he might have over losing both family and fortune in France were strictly private regrets. Perhaps he, of all the *émigrés,* had the hard core of determination and the fatalistic acceptance of reality necessary to make a success of carving a future out of a wilderness ... Crosbie put idle speculation out of his mind. He turned to look at the waiting wagons lined up along the bank behind him.

He saw the Marquis and his son cantering up toward him and he turned quickly back to de Flaville.

"Take your young men across and form a picket line on the forward slope below the military crest. Understand?"

De Flaville wiped the streaming sweat from his face and nodded hesitantly. "But, Colonel, are we not close to Pittsburgh?"

"Aye," Crosbie grunted. "We're close, sir, but we are not there yet. Collect your men and move along."

De Flaville saluted casually, waved at Edmond de la Foure as he approached and ran with long quick strides down toward the wagon train to collect his men.

De la Foure doffed his plumed hat in a gallant sweep as he halted beside Crosbie.

"I am told, Colonel, that Pittsburgh is no great distance from here." The statement was accompanied by an urbane smile but something in de la Foure's tone put Crosbie on his guard. Too many frivolous requests had been prefaced by just such a bland comment of obvious fact.

"True enough, sir," Crosbie said agreeably. "Now, if you'll excuse me, I ..."

"A moment, sir," the Count said quickly before Crosbie could pivot his horse. "We have been a long time without certain small comforts and my father and I thought of riding ahead into Pittsburgh in order to purchase ..."

"No." Crosbie's voice was flat and hard. "No one leaves the wagon train. It isn't safe."

Edmond de la Foure replaced his hat deliberately. His eyes came up and met Crosbie's frankly and for the first time the blank stylized courtier's face became a real face, demanding recognition. His voice was remote and tightly controlled. "We have been pleased to place ourselves at your command, Colonel, largely because you understood best how to counter the dangers of our journey. But I see no reason to permit your arrogant interference with our personal lives. Therefore, I should warn you that ..."

Crosbie made a quick irritated gesture with one hand. He knew it was hopeless to discuss his well-based fears with a man who had no personal experience with wilderness warfare and lacked imagination powerful enough to visualize the danger to a divided force. He forced himself to speak without heat and he tried not to scowl at the elegant Count.

"You were once a cadet, sir," he said patiently. "Let me ask you this then: Would you choose to attack a force that had just left a place of protection or one that was arriving at such a place after a long tiring journey?"

De la Foure flushed angrily at the barely concealed contempt in Crosbie's voice. "The latter, certainly," he said curtly. "Does your hypothetical question mean that you anticipate still another attack upon our people?"

"I don't know," Crosbie growled. He leaned forward until his face was close to de la Foure's. "But do you want to be absent from this wagon train in the event of attack, *monsieur?*"

Crosbie's voice was mild, almost pleasant, but the Count felt the sting of his meaning. Thin lumps of hard muscle jutted along his jawline and he glared tightly at Crosbie. Without a word, he reined his horse around and trotted him back toward the wagon train.

Duncan Crosbie drew a long careful breath and sat his horse stolidly, allowing de la Foure time to return to his father and advise him of the change in plans. The young Frenchman had impressed him for the first time and Crosbie was aware that de la Foure was something more than the useless gambler he had thought him to be. Crosbie pushed his cocked hat back off his forehead and drew his leather sleeve across his streaming face. Long weeks of strong sun had baked his face to a fiery brick-red that showed deep successive layers of skin where the outer layers had flaked away. He would never grow smoothly, darkly brown as Mr. Blanchard had done, but rather would peel and blister continuously as his pale freckled skin was tortured by the late summer sun.

De Flaville and five young men trailed their long rifles behind them as they ran up the slope from the wagons and headed for the ford. Crosbie walked his tired gelding slowly forward, signaling for the first wagon to move out. Ahead walked the group of two dozen men who would attach their ropes and assist the double team when the wagon was ready to ascend the far slope. Behind were another dozen to tail onto ropes from the rear axle and retard the too-sudden descent of the wagon into the gorge. A small, wizened man, an experienced coachman, sat hunched high and monkey-like on the wagon box, holding the lines firmly, one foot hard against the brake handle. Crosbie could think of no more precautions, but a failure of an axle or a wheel, a momentary fright on the part of the city-bred driver, a sudden lurch of tire on stone under the swift water, any one of a thousand unforeseeable possibilities and a valuable wagon-load would be lost beyond retrieving.

Only a handful of responsible men stayed back with the other wagons. Women, children and most of the men gathered along the sloping route of the wagon rumbling toward the gorge, surging forward for a clear view of the deeply cut ravine, shouting gaily at the guards now passing out of sight over the far hill, sounding very much to Crosbie's ear like a school on holiday, paying no heed to the obvious difficulty of the ford. Their attitude might have been construed as a compliment to Crosbie, a proof of their great faith in his ability to take them safely through anything, but Crosbie's sour depression permitted no such construction.

The lead wagon lurched over the edge of the gorge and began its downward passage. Crosbie wheeled his gelding and walked him to the lip of the gorge to watch.

The men tailing onto the drag ropes were hauling back too hard, so much so that the wagon was skidding with braked wheels. Crosbie tried to shout to them, but the joyous din around him drowned his voice. Luckily the driver saw the danger and eased off the brake, letting the weighted wagon straighten itself out just as the fore wheels touched the water. The driver shouting wildly, waved for the men behind to cast off, lashed his horses vigorously and galloped them into the stream, creaking, bouncing, splashing in a high boiling froth of foam as they clattered across the creek. Before all forward way had been lost, the two dozen men waiting on the far side had their drag ropes looped around the front axle and were leaning against the wagon's weight, heaving erratically, slipping and sliding up the rocky clay slope, but taking enough of the load to permit the double team to haul the wagon slowly up the bank. Two of the men wisely followed along behind with thick logs, ready to throw them under the rear wheels if the wagon was unable to reach the top.

Crosbie cursed savagely to himself. He dismounted, tied his horse and stamped heavily along the rim of the gorge to the second wagon, determined to accompany each wagon so that he could signal for the men to cast off the drag ropes at the right moment. Another error like the last could be disastrous.

A rousing cheer told Crosbie the first wagon had safely cleared the gorge. Already many of the Frenchmen were wading through the hard running water to wait for their wagons on the far side. Crosbie ignored them; he could depend on de Flaville to keep them safely within his picket line.

Crosbie knelt to inspect the knots that secured the drag lines to the second wagon. This was the Marquis's and it had none of the sturdy timbers of the lead Conestoga. It was a soundly built farm wagon, nothing at all fancy, but it simply hadn't been constructed for wilderness travel. The underpinning showed no signs of wear that Crosbie could detect, no sprung joints, no dried, splintered wood, no wobbly bolts. Crosbie straightened with a grunt and stopped again to mop his streaming face.

"A fearfully hot day, is it not?" Adrienne said happily.

Crosbie glanced up, surprised to hear her voice at his ear.

The girl lay stretched within the wagon, only the top of her burnished hair and one sparkling eye were visible to Crosbie.

He fanned his red face with his hat as he glared at the girl. A proper minx and one who badly needed a good clout on the ear.

"But the day is not so vile as your temper today, is it, my dear Colonel?"

And the dark brooding spell that had hung over Crosbie suddenly lifted. He managed to keep his stern face set stiffly in its hard lines but within himself he grinned widely. He'd been a bear with a sore tail and no doubt of it. And that was quite enough of it, too; an irritable commander can do more to ruin a unit than any other single element. Crosbie placed his hat carefully on his breast, moved his feet skillfully into position and made a flourishing bow.

"After which cogent observation, my lady," he said in his most elegant French, "will you be good enough to alight while your carriage is transported? I note Mademoiselle Lucie has already done so; I saw her among the ladies watching from the rim of the ravine." He thought there was a brief flicker of alarm, perhaps even a sort of guilt in the bright gaze Adrienne turned on him at mention of Lucie's name. As if she were wondering just how much he knew about Lucie and the secret the two girls were plotting to hide. But it was only a brief wonder and Adrienne did not speak. "My arm, my lady," Crosbie finished.

Adrienne sat up and shook her head firmly. "I shall drive. I do not trust Jean." She leaned out the rear port and whispered lightly in Crosbie's ear, "My best ball gowns ride in the large portemanteau. I must see to their safety."

"True enough, my lady," Crosbie said heavily, determined to maintain his newly found equanimity. "Ball gowns must be protected at all costs. But Mr. Blanchard, Monsieur de Flaville, Count de la Foure and the Marquis ... not to mention half a dozen other gallants ... would never forgive me if I failed to protect you as carefully."

Adrienne colored briefly. She swept back her dark hair with an abrupt, peremptory gesture. "I shall drive," she insisted.

"It should be an exhilarating drive, my dear," Edmond de le Foure's voice spoke behind Crosbie. "I envy you the experience."

Crosbie stiffened angrily. He placed his hat on his head, squaring its brim with his heavy eyebrows. He made no answer to the young Count who stood watching him with a level gaze, ready for anything. Crosbie bowed curtly to Adrienne and walked forward around the light wagon where three shouting, sweating men were fighting a second restive team into place. Crosbie waited grimly, careful not to display his impatience or anger to the men. But his face was fiery and his hard gray eyes were chips of flint. His thin, almost lipless mouth was a firm tight line above his heavy jaw.

A small hand wormed its way into his clenched fist and Crosbie pivoted angrily. When he recognized Jock, he forced a meager smile and touched the boy's tangled hair with a gentle hand.

"Shall I play for you now, Dooncahn?" Jock asked in his high treble. "Something gay for the marching horses?"

"A noble thought, Jocko," Crosbie growled. He cleared his voice and patted the boy again, a genuine warmth in his smile now. "Take station where I've tethered my horse and pipe us a merry skirl when the wagon leads off, eh?"

Jock's eyes glistened at the unexpected permission. Usually Crosbie forbade the pipes when tricky work was to be done, for the savage skirl smothered all but the loudest commands. Today, however, with the French in holiday spirits, Crosbie would have to lead by visual signals anyway. Jock might as well have his share of the sport.

Crosbie's eyes were warm as he watched Jock race up the slope toward Cammie's room where he kept his precious *cornemuse*. A few more days now, Crosbie thought, and I'll get my luggage at Marietta. Then we'll see what the boy does with a proper pibroch.

Adrienne snapped her short driving whip unexpectedly and the double team lurched in the traces. Crosbie leaped quickly, hauled back the brake and stopped the wagon before it had gone two feet.

"I'll give the signal, mademoiselle," he snapped. With a hoarse bellow, he called the men around him, warned them of the need for a coordinated effort, arranged a signal for casting off the drag rope, another for taking up the forward ropes, still another as Adrienne's cue to whip up the horses in order to take immediate advantage of the slight momentum she would have when the wagon met the swift water. From the impish glint in her eye, Crosbie suspected Adrienne had her own ideas about his signals, but she would have no chance to put them into effect.

He waved his arm once and the drag ropes were lifted, drawn taut. Crosbie reached up to the wagon brake, shoved it clear and as the wheels began slowly to move, he jumped up to the box beside Adrienne.

"I'll handle the brake," he said curtly. "Keep the horses at a slow easy walk until you reach the stream. When I let off the brake, give them a hard cut with the whip. Understand?"

Adrienne glanced at him from the corner of her eye. She nodded once as she flipped the lines lightly. A small private smile picked up the corners of her mouth.

The wagon swung high before it dipped with a sickening lurch over the steep bank into the gorge. Crosbie leaned hard on the brake and looked back at the straining, cursing men on the ropes. With the wheels barely turning and a steady restraint from the ropes, the wagon was safe, he thought.

The far slope of the gorge seemed to be a sheer impassable cliff of slippery clay. Waiting below in the water were two dozen men spaced along their ropes, ready to hook on when the wagon was about to cross the tumbling water. The creek was narrow as Crosbie saw it, but sharp jagged rocks protruded along its bank and water spumed around them like a storm at sea. A beautiful, treacherous sight, Crosbie thought.

His wagon began that slow dangerous skid as soon as the locked wheels touched the clay. Crosbie eased the brake slowly and the wagon straightened itself quickly. But the strain on the men at the drag ropes was greatly increased now. Crosbie half rose to estimate the remaining distance to the bottom. Another thirty yards at least. Not too much unless the men on the ropes should stumble or ...

The wagon bounced high over a buried tree root. The wheel rode up over the root, crashed through the rotten fiber and cramped them back momentarily. The wagon tongue swung out quickly, hitting the near horse with a solid thump. The unexpected twisting of the tongue nearly wrenched the coupling pin in two at the king bolt. Crosbie dove across the wagon box and snatched the lines from Adrienne's hands.

"Whip them up!" he thundered. "Whip them!"

Adrienne rose with an excited scream, a thin delighted shriek that sounded high and constantly above the sharp snapping of her driving whip. She stood in the box, holding with one hand on the canvas top, her wild hair blowing like a tattered banner, yelling and cracking her whip. Crosbie kicked off the brake quickly, slapped the lines hard and shouted at the horses.

The cramped wheel skidded along the clay, scraping up a huge mound that threatened to trap the wagon. But the men at the drag ropes had cast off and the terrified horses pulled desperately in their sudden fear. The wagon wheel straightened out, swerved around the mound and then there was nothing to impede their progress, nothing except the boiling water waiting for them in the gorge below.

"Jump!" Crosbie roared. His vast arm nudged Adrienne toward the side of the wagon. "Jump now!"

Adrienne shrieked something inaudible, shook her head fiercely as she grinned exultantly at Crosbie. Then she leaped forward and swung her whip again and again above the excited horses.

There was no point in trying to set the brake again, even if the runaway horses could be slowed. Their only chance was to enter the water squarely and drive straight across, keeping up enough speed to counteract the force of the water. Not a good chance, Crosbie thought grimly.

He eyed the boiling water carefully and gently urged his double team a few inches to the right where a comparatively flat stretch of water lay below. His cocked hat whipped from his head with the speed of their descent and Crosbie suddenly felt sure and confident as the breeze struck his steaming face. He flicked a glance at Adrienne and smiled quickly when she cracked the whip again. A bothersome wench at best, but there was nothing puny about her spirit.

The lead team clattered into the rocky raging gorge and keening high above the screaming voices from both banks, Crosbie heard Jock's *cornemuse* blaring out a lively march tune that made his spirits soar.

The second team followed and then the front wheels, angled only slightly upstream as they entered the water. The stream bed flattened suddenly and the frail springs in the front of the wagon compressed, folded in on themselves and snapped like rifle shots. The rear wheels struck solidly, the rear springs cracked as the wagon skidded and lurched across. The front team was digging frantically into the abrupt rise across the creek, screaming in high frightened sounds that rose above the bagpipes.

Then a rear wheel buckled. The axle splintered. The wagon lurched heavily to the right, throwing Adrienne on top of Crosbie. He caught her easily as he braced himself on the box. And she let him support her as she leaned her weight into her whip, flicking it nastily about the ears of the lead team. The horses scrambled, sending muddy water spraying high over Adrienne and Crosbie. The damaged wagon slithered and scraped through the water.

"Once more," Crosbie bellowed. "One more crack."

Adrienne swung the whip again, laying the lash expertly between the ears of the off leader. And that was enough.

The frantic horses dragged the wagon up clear of the water and their driving hoofs heaved great gobbets of clay back over the box. But then the forward motion stopped. The horses dug for traction, slipped and lost ground, tried again and again until daring spirits among the waiting men leaped for their bits, calmed them slowly and then unharnessed them from the frayed and battered traces.

Crosbie wrapped the lines automatically around the brake handle, though no one would ever again drive the Marquis's wagon. He swung to the ground heavily, sinking in the mud nearly to his knees. Then he turned, holding his arms for Adrienne.

"My compliments, mademoiselle," he said sincerely. "A splendid effort."

Adrienne loosed her tight grip of the canvas top, moved one hesitant step toward Crosbie, smiling mistily at him. "My gowns, *mon colonel*," she murmured in a voice that was suddenly thick and indistinct. She wavered slightly, tried to catch herself against the canvas, then crumpled in a low swooping line that ended in Crosbie's waiting arms.

The Colonel walked up the far slope, carrying the girl carefully, ignoring the Marquis and all the cheering gesticulating Frenchmen around him. The savage exultancy of the bagpipes kept step with him up the ravine. Once he slowed to readjust his burden but he never considered letting one of the younger men take her.

His strength was beginning to desert him, he knew, but he could manage to reach the top of the gorge and then he could stop. The sudden excitement and effort had come too soon after his serious wound. His weariness had nothing to do with age at all, he assured himself. Merely the natural reaction after being shot, nothing more. He had never been in better condition. In the prime of life, to put it bluntly.

He glanced down at the glowing face, the wind-tangled hair of the girl he carried. A skinny little thing by the look of her, but a buxom armful for all that. Crosbie felt the swelling curve of her breast against his hand. Just might decide to give Blanchard a run for his money, he thought suddenly.

He knelt slowly at the rim of the gorge and put the girl down gently on the grass. After a long thoughtful moment while he struggled for breath, he stared closely at her. From far down the gorge he heard Lucie's voice calling for her mistress. He shouted an answer and saw the girl start toward them, walking swiftly. Crosbie turned away. There was work to be done; the wagon to be hauled up and repaired; the other wagons to be brought across. But he stopped briefly to look back before he let himself down the slope again.

CHAPTER TWELVE

Nicholas Blanchard stirred restlessly in the soft bed, rolling over to escape the brilliant sunlight that shone straight into his eyes. A slow solid pulse pounded in his head in a sickening rhythm and Blanchard tried to remain asleep. Long strands of hair drifted across his nose, making him sneeze into the sweat-drenched pillow. Slowly he opened one red-rimmed eye, feeling a sharp lancing pain from the strong light.

He was naked in the wide feather bed. Across the room, leaning against the rough wooden wall stood his precious Leman rifle and beside it were his powder horn and bullet pouch. Probably his clothes were somewhere out of sight but just then Blanchard had no interest in looking.

Blanchard grinned to himself, wincing as pain shot through his head. A rousing carouse it had been and no mistake about it, a fine drunken night full of singing and laughter and ending, as somehow such nights did, in a blood-tingling brawl with a pair of dock-wallopers. A proper soldierly affair all told, run quite according to regulations and now the required, regimental nausea as a souvenir of a perfect evening. But the fine edge was missing as Blanchard remembered the details. Getting too old for such business, he told himself.

It was all Benny Upjohn's fault, Blanchard recollected. Benny was a civilian now, a respectable citizen of Pittsburgh, well set up with a fine wife, a part interest in a boatyard and a steady income as agent for the Ohio Company of Associates. But long before he had been Captain Upjohn, dragoon troop commander with whom Blanchard had served for nearly three years. So it had been a reunion and Benny had been even drunker than Blanchard, if that was possible.

Blanchard rolled toward the edge of the bed, reached cautiously for the floor with one foot and then lurched upright, carefully keeping his eyes closed until he was erect. Between the windows with their diamond-shaped panes of scraped horn was a washstand with a chipped pitcher and he stumbled toward it. The pitcher held almost a gallon; half Blanchard drank in long thirsty gulps and the rest he poured over his head. He stood in the hard sunlight, rubbing his head with a rough towel, breathing deeply, trying to convince himself that he was now ready for a normal day.

By evening he would be at Braddock's Field to meet Crosbie and the wagon train. Until then he would take his ease and try to regain some of his vitality.

He sat heavily on the window sill and bent to pick up his rumpled buckskin from the floor. One moccasin was hung on the lock of his rifle and the other dangled from a beam far overhead. He must have done a very active job of undressing. Blanchard laced the thrums of his shirt, yawning widely.

In a way it had been a stroke of luck to find Benny Upjohn handling the Pittsburgh agency for General Putnam. Benny knew Crosbie, if only by reputation, and he had been full of sympathetic understanding for Blanchard and what was even more important, Benny saw the need for strict sure discipline in moving the Frenchmen to their boats. Benny had the boats ready and they were fine broad-horned bateaux, decked and roofed against the weather, fitted with heavy ringbolts and slings for carrying the livestock, and each was manned by an experienced boatman. When the Ohio Company set out to do a job, it left nothing dangling. Crosbie could bring his people in to Benny's boatyard which was half a mile from Pittsburgh, unload the wagons and get them on board without any possible confusion. Shouldn't take more than a day, two at the most, Blanchard figured.

He pulled on one moccasin, picked up his rifle and poked the other from the rafters, sending a whale-oil lamp swinging perilously with a careless touch. This was a better tavern than he'd thought—no stinking tallow lamps here. He couldn't see his cocked hat anywhere, but it just might be downstairs in the tavern. Blanchard balanced his rifle against the wall again and padded softly across the floor to the door.

Downstairs Blanchard paused at the open doorway. Overhead the painted tavern sign carried a clumsy portrait of an Indian girl wearing a fanciful headdress of feathers. A thick swarm of flies rose from the dusty street, swarming angrily through the heavy August heat. Blanchard turned toward the taproom and looked inside, leaning one hand against the low beams that supported the ceiling.

"Well, come on in, cock," a light voice shouted. "Don't just stand there like a dying duck."

Blanchard could see nothing inside the dim taproom. The smells of spilled liquor almost gagged him but he stepped inside, moving toward Benny Upjohn's voice, blinking his eyes to make them focus.

"Severely wounded, Mr. Blanchard?"

Blanchard's groping hand found the back of a chair. He turned it around and dropped into it gratefully. "Mortal, sir," he growled.

Benny Upjohn's laugh was a pleasant thing most of the time, but at the moment, Blanchard found it odious. When his former Captain bellowed for service, Blanchard felt the pounding ache start again behind his eyes.

"Softly, sir, for God's sake," he groaned.

"Softly, sir, for Nick's sake," Upjohn chuckled. "Meg, bring a rum flip and a thick cut of something sustaining for my poor feeble friend," he called to the barmaid. "And another rum flip for me while you're about it."

A soft warm hand that smelled of harsh lye soap touched Blanchard's cheek gently, moving along his stubbled cheek with a faint rasping sound.

"Your friend wasn't so feeble last night," Meg said in a thick voice. "Right active, I'd say."

Blanchard stared up at her blankly. A round faced blowsy girl with her wide mouth touched up with some French paint, stringy hair the color of apple cider, no longer young enough for the best taverns, heavy through the buttocks, immense in her breasts. She leaned forward to make her bodice spill outward and she smiled encouragingly at Blanchard, her tongue touching the corner of her full mouth in a knowing way. Blanchard restrained an involuntary shudder. Last night, he thought, I wasn't so feeble... He flickered a desperate glance at Upjohn, then half shrugged. Well, if I don't ask, maybe she won't tell me.

Meg patted his cheek warmly and left the room, swinging her hips for his appalled benefit. Upjohn laughed at him openly.

"Can't you remember, cock?"

Blanchard shook his head helplessly. But I sure must have been fighting drunk to lay a hand on that worn-out doxy, he said to himself.

"Well, I wouldn't worry about it," Upjohn said reassuringly. "Meg probably has you confused with one of the hairy types in greasy buckskins who slip in and out of town all the time." He eyed Blanchard's seedy appearance with a critical eye. "Is it really necessary to wear such savage regalia?"

The arrival of his rum flip spared Blanchard the need for reply. He endured Meg's questing finger against his neck and then he plunged his nose into the foaming beaker, draining the egg and rum mixture in a long gulp.

"Most savage," Upjohn murmured.

Blanchard put his mug back on the table and glanced at his former commander. Upjohn was a short man, unlike most dragoons, though he was solidly muscled in his heavy chest and arms. He sat very much at his ease, lounging back in an oak armchair with one spurred heel caught on another chair. His face had a top-heavy look, with the brow wide and bulging at the temples, the jaw sharply pointed, the mouth a thin restrained line. His deep-set tight-lidded eyes were nervously active, giving the lie to his habitual pose of indolence. He was shaved to the quick and his thinning hair was lightly powdered. His linen was glistening, his shirt ruffles were discreet though intricate, his silken cravat was resplendent but there was something slightly military in the cut of his plum velvet coat. Probably the way the gold lace followed the regimental pattern, Blanchard thought. He leaned back in his hard chair and smiled at Upjohn.

"You're getting fat, Benny," he said amiably.

Upjohn grinned widely and patted his stomach complacently. "After five years in the field, I regard every ounce of fat as a gallant triumph that attests to my indomitable determination," he murmured. "My wife treasures an old coat of her father's at the house. I try it on now and then. According to my estimate I'll be able to wear it in another three or four years. Then I'll know I'm a civilian for good."

"You're doing well in Pittsburgh?" Blanchard asked with little interest. His eyes followed the barmaid as she brought in a huge wooden trencher loaded with sliced ham and fried potatoes. My God, he muttered, did I really ... He snatched up a fork and knife as soon as the dish touched the table.

"Well enough," Upjohn said. "Not as well as I'll do when we get the Indians cleared out of the Ohio country."

Blanchard grunted something through a large mouthful of ham.

"Settlers are coming in slowly, too slowly for profit. Mostly they're scared of Blue Jacket, but that fat fool Harmar scares them too, I'll wager. I wouldn't trust my neck to him."

"Hmmm?" Blanchard murmured.

"St. Clair's treaty did the real damage," Upjohn said, his languid tone sharpening with evident anger. "When he was named Governor of the Northwest Territory, he drew up a treaty for the Indians to sign. And he stupidly talked about it before he sent it to the Indian nations. The settlers began coming in then and we deserving souls in trade made a tidy profit. But then the Shawnees refused to sign. Blue Jacket not only didn't sign for the Shawnees but he made big medicine and barred all white settlement beyond the Ohio. Of course, Little Turtle and the Miamis backed him up. So the settlers turned right around again, taking all my hard earned profit with them." Upjohn sipped lightly at his rum flip and tapped his mouth elegantly with a laced handkerchief.

"Blue Jacket never bothered Putnam any," Blanchard said casually.

"Not a bit," Upjohn agreed. "Together the Shawnees and the Miamis are too much for most settlers though. Putnam can take care of the Ohio Company all right but what's needed is an Army campaign to break the Indians. The Army could push them out of the way in no time at all. But we have that flatulent ass, Harmar, commanding our valiant forces, so the Army does nothing and that deserving, hardworking young merchant, Mr. Benjamin Upjohn does without his due profit. But not for long, I assure you."

Blanchard choked down a large bite and grinned at the short dapper man. "Going back to war, Captain?"

"Heavens no, I'd get thin again. No," Upjohn said. "I had it in mind to let someone else fight this one. I just want to get rich. My bet still rides with St. Clair. He's Governor of the Northwest Territory and that is a farcical job if one ever existed. The Territory is American in name only as long as the British still hold the forts along the Great Lakes. And the British are arming the Indian nations. The only chance St. Clair has of being governor of anything more than a map is to chase the Indians and British out. He'll force Washington to replace Harmar within the year."

"So you say," Blanchard grinned.

Upjohn glanced around cautiously and then leaned forward, pitching his voice low. "I have it from General St. Clair himself. Now I won't say he was any great shakes as a general, but he was President of the Congress long enough to learn about politics. Knox is his friend and Knox runs the Army now. St. Clair assures me that he'll be named to head an expeditionary force by Washington, probably sometime next Spring."

Blanchard whistled softly. "Maybe I can get a job."

Upjohn nodded quickly. "If you want one. But the Army's a dog's life, Nick, unless you're a politician, and you're not. And St. Clair's a bad-luck General, has been ever since he surrendered Fort Ticonderoga without a fight. He's no man to throw in with. No, Pittsburgh's the place. A man should be able to make a fortune here within the next ten years."

Blanchard pushed back his empty plate and picked up his friend's rum flip. He drank half of it and handed the glass back to Upjohn just in time to forestall an angry bellow. "Right good breakfast, Captain," he grinned. "Think maybe I'll recover now."

Upjohn finished his drink and rose gracefully, dropping a coin on the table. He swung his gold-laced hat from one finger and said, "You think over what I said, Nick. I'll need help soon if things go the way I expect."

"I'll remember, Benny," Blanchard said, "but I've been thinking of going on down to New Orleans and putting in with General Wilkinson. I hear…"

Upjohn clamped down hard fingers on Nick's shoulder. "Don't," he said flatly. "Stay away from Wilkinson, Nick."

"What…?"

"He's bad medicine, Nick, believe me, I know," Upjohn said seriously. "I've seen strong evidence tying him up with the attempt to secede Kentucky county from Virginia and join it to Spain. General Putnam suspects he's sold out to the Spanish. Anybody who tied in with him would be playing with treason. You don't want any of that, Nick."

"No, but..."

"Well, think it over, anyway, Nick. Don't go rushing off." Upjohn settled his ornate hat carefully. Then he looked up and studied Blanchard's face thoughtfully. "Why don't you go home, Nick?" he asked with real curiosity. "The Tidewater country is almost the only place a man can live a really comfortable, civilized life, and here you are turning your back on it for no reason at all that I can see..."

"Reason enough," Blanchard interrupted. "I'm the youngest in a family of four boys, Benny. One plantation just isn't big enough or rich enough to support four establishments. Somebody had to look around for some other means of support..." he paused, then shrugged, a gesture picked up from the French *émigrés* who seemed to find that it expressed almost anything. "Somebody was me," he finished.

For a moment Upjohn was silent, then he became brisk and businesslike again. "Now then, when am I to expect your people to arrive at my boatyard?"

"Couple days," Blanchard said. "I'll send a man in or come myself so you'll have warning enough. Better arrange for a bait of feed for the horses." He walked toward the open door with Upjohn. The tavern was still deserted in the late morning, incredibly quiet and somnolent to Blanchard's ears. The blistering heat had chased everyone inside; only one rickety wagon rumbled through the dust toward the river docks.

Upjohn raised his ebony stick to his hat. "My best regards to Colonel Crosbie, Nick."

"Goodbye, Benny." Blanchard leaned against the open door, staying back in the shadows where the air was slightly cooler. He stretched his arms wide and yawned. Time to think about getting back to the wagons, maybe. No rush though. Might be kind of nice to walk through town for a while.

A man strolled slowly from a tavern doorway down the street and walked past Blanchard, wiping his forehead with a scrap of cloth. Seemed as if people who lived in a swampy place like Pittsburgh would get used to it after a bit, but somehow the people who belonged here appeared to take it the hardest. The man across the street was too fat and he wore his clothes loose on his body; he was puffing like a wind-broken mare by the time he passed Blanchard.

Two more men came slowly out of the other tavern and with the first glance, Blanchard froze. He leaned farther back in the shadow of the doorway, squinting his eyes to focus through the hard sunlight.

The tall man was dressed in white and from where Blanchard stood, his beautifully cut clothes shimmered like satin. His knee and shoe buckles threw sparks. The man's face was in deep shadow from his lacy cocked hat and Blanchard could not be sure who he was, not sure enough to shoot, but sure enough to stand immobile as an Indian, staring fixedly across the street.

A light carriage drawn smoothly by a glossy chestnut pacer slowed to a stop in front of the two men and the tall man mounted to the seat behind his driver. Leather springs creaked faintly as the man sat and raised his cocked hat negligently to his companion. The tall man gestured forward with his hat and then Blanchard saw the face clearly.

Mr. Oliver Budd. By God, it was ! No grimy riding coat and soiled wristbands now. And no unkempt horse, either. Mr. Budd's long sallow face was shaven and powdered, his white wig shone bravely and the rings on his fingers were impressive.

All told, Mr. Budd was more credible as the dandy than he had been as the seedy rider outside Alexandria. But what was he up to? Why the disguise?

Blanchard slipped inside the doorway until Budd's carriage passed. He would follow then, if he couldn't keep up with it. Certainly anything he learned about Mr. Budd was going to be useful to Crosbie. And even if he learned nothing, there was always the little matter of the Colonel's wounds. Budd would pay heavily for them.

Blanchard stepped warily outside as the carriage swept by and then stopped again suddenly. Budd's companion was walking across the street, heading toward him, taking his time and moving carefully through the dense layers of powdery dust.

Which one, Blanchard wondered ? If he followed Budd, then he himself could be followed. And while he waited, Budd's carriage was going up the road at a spanking clip. He could never catch him on foot. But why not Budd's friend? The other man might know as much as Budd if they were in cahoots, and from the look of him, this was a prime scoundrel.

The man was fairly tall and incredibly thin with a ratlike face in which the sharp waxy nose and protruding teeth were featured while both chin and forehead receded. He strode along on thin stilt-like legs, placing his narrow feet cautiously as though he had painful bunions. Both long bony hands were clasped tightly over his drab waistcoat and his mouth worked constantly as if he were chewing with his teeth clenched. The man's eyes were almost shut against the glare of the sun as he went past Blanchard's doorway.

Blanchard stayed back in his concealing shadow until the thin man reached the corner and turned at the blacksmith's shed. Then he stepped out, walking with long easy strides that covered ground swiftly without apparent haste. He slowed at the corner, sauntered around the shed and lounged against the wall.

No one was in sight. The wide dusty street was still and sleepy. Nothing moved near the stone and timber houses. A squalid frame tavern with a badly hung front door was equally deserted. Blanchard felt the pounding ache begin in his head again as he swore softly at himself. He eased slowly onto the puncheon bench outside the blacksmith's entrance and held his head in both hands.

What a damned fool. He'd had Budd right in his hands and watched him ride away. Then the stork-like man had vanished, simply vanished, not leaving even a set of footprints in the dust.

No footprints. Blanchard's head rose quickly, then dropped to his hands again when he heard quiet voices inside the smithy. Of course. The thin man had gone inside. No wonder he hadn't left a trail in the dusty street.

Blanchard twisted sideways on the bench, putting his ear close to the open doorway. But the voices were too faint, too far away for him to hear. And the smith kept tapping his hammer on his anvil, making a metallic ringing tone that covered up whatever was being said.

A horse stamped restlessly inside and something warned Blanchard. He slumped on the bench, head against the shed, mouth open, eyes closed, obviously still a man bemused by last night's liquor. He ignored the clouds of flies that swooped and brushed against his lips. The horse moved again and this time continued its movement into the street. Blanchard heard feet padding over the cushioning dust. He murmured and shifted slightly on the bench.

"Garn," a thick voice growled. "Garn outa here. This ain't no hostel for drunken …"

"Chrisman!" This voice was hard and demanding. Blanchard heard another low, inaudible growl, then the smith went inside his shop again.

"An hour then," the hard voice said. "I'll not wait a minute longer. I'm devilish late as it is."

"Not a minute more, sir. And I'm right sorry to …"

"That's settled." The hard voice ended the exchange.

Blanchard heard no movement. After some minutes, the smith's crackling bellows began to pump wheezily, but Blanchard kept his eyes closed, his posture relaxed on the bench. Finally he shifted again, opened one eye slightly and closed it again. The skinny man was only a step away but he faced toward the tavern with his back to Blanchard. He had stood over him then, watching, listening, for some time. Only a fool's luck had saved Blanchard. He closed his eyes again, firmly determined to wait for most of the hour before he moved. His man would return. For his horse, most likely. Blanchard would be waiting for him.

He risked another glance and saw the thin man enter the slanting door of the dingy tavern across the street. The fox was in his hole. No need to watch him now.

The torpid heat, the lazy buzzing flies and the rhythmic pleasant tones of the smithy relaxed Blanchard after a few minutes. He stretched with genuine sleepiness and actually dozed for a brief moment. He woke with a sudden guilty start, stretched again, scrubbed at his matted hair and pushed himself wearily up from the bench. He returned to the Indian Princess, walking with the extreme deliberation of a man who has learned to distrust his gait.

His apparent lassitude vanished entirely when he entered the tavern. He bounded up the stairs two at a time, brushed aside Meg's hot importunities with an impatient hand, snatched up his rifle and gear, searched for and found his cocked hat under the bed and was downstairs again, heading for the stable, all in a matter of seconds. He would have to wait for his man, but the stable was a safer place to wait than the tavern where Meg watched his every movement with possessive interest.

He left money for his bill with the hostler and saddled his bay gelding carefully. This was no moment for a slipping girth. He walked his gelding to the street and mounted there.

Blanchard rode in a wide circle, coming back toward the dingy tavern where his man was waiting, approaching from the west, using the Forbes Road. He stopped at the tavern openly and hitched his horse at the railing outside with no attempt to hide. The chances were slim that he would be recognized and Blanchard was willing to take no further chances on losing his game again. He would let the thin man get his horse, if that was what he planned, but from then on, he and Blanchard would travel together—to Colonel Crosbie.

CHAPTER THIRTEEN

Young Jock threw himself down in the shadowed area beside his wagon, snuggled close to his mother's warm shoulder. He watched her easy rhythm as Cammie worked deer's fat into corn meal, adding water and salt sparingly. He dipped his finger into the tasty mass just once; that was his allotment; another dip would bring a clout he'd remember for a week.

"You drip like a little water rat," Cammie said lightly.

"It was glorious," Jock sighed. "But the Colonel Crosbie made us leave so that the girls might bathe, too. You should go with them, *maman*."

"There will be time enough after dinner," Cammie said. "We are very early today."

Early enough so that she had found time to wash Jock's soiled clothes and most of Crosbie's, early enough to prepare dinner by full daylight, and early enough to sit by her wagon and watch Duncan Crosbie restlessly prowling the campsite on Braddock's Field like a wounded bear beleaguered by a thousand enemies. He had hardly stopped to eat, driving himself constantly, though he was careful to give the men time to rest between jobs.

Jock scrambled up quickly, reached through the rear port to get his *cornemuse*. He, too, had seen Crosbie's immense bulk outlined against the sky. Cammie grabbed his thin arm in a hard grip and pulled him down beside her.

Not now, *mon petit*," she murmured softly. "Dooncahn is too busy to hear you play." She smoothed Jock's damp and matted hair. "We will wait till nightfall, when he has a moment to rest.

Why don't you go help François?" She pointed to the open campfire where the stowaway boy was bent carefully, tending a small pot of melting lead. Shortly he would get to his feet, hold the pot high over a bucket of water and dribble the molten lead slowly into the bucket, making bird shot for Edmond de la Foure's fowling piece. Jock squirmed irritably away from his mother. He had no time for François now. He stood where he could watch Crosbie, and Cammie turned with him.

Even at night, Crosbie would not rest, she knew. He would eat, if someone reminded him he should, but he would eat absently, without appetite, and leave his meal unfinished if he saw the least reason to start again on his endless rounds of the bivouac. And at last when he would come to bed, he might sleep but it would be a restless, muttering sleep during which he would stir continually, turn over and over with flailings of his huge arms. Cammie touched a tender bruise on her shoulder and half smiled. Sometimes, though, he could rest. Sometimes when he came to her...

"Dooncahn never has time for the *cornemuse* any more," Jock pouted. "And now I can play it well, too. It is not as though it were a pain to hear..."

"I know, I know," Cammie said softly. "When Dooncahn gets his great bagpipes at Marietta, then he will again find time. But until then, you must not coax him. He is too... too busy for us now. There are so many things to distract him."

Two wagons lost in the gorge today, Cammie thought. They would weigh heavily on Crosbie's mind and he would blame himself for the loss, though neither wagon was stout enough for the journey as he had often warned. But the Marquis had been sarcastic, almost insulting, about his wagon and Cammie had seen the fury mount to Crosbie's eyes as he restrained himself from an angry response. Then to overturn the wagon that contained the last of their ground corn, that was close to tragedy. But all the women had been issued rations and most of the sodden corn had been baked into hard bannocks that would last for a few days longer.

And Duncan, the dear silly man, would brood upon the two lost wagons and never stop to count the number he had safely brought across that horrible stream. The deep scowl would etch deeper into his forehead and the dour biting anger would be very near the surface for weeks now, but only for himself, though few could understand that. Cammie's hands clenched in her lap as she watched Crosbie prowling the skyline. She could do so little to ease the tension which Crosbie imposed upon himself.

Jock twisted away from her and rose quickly. The boy was always restless when Duncan had no time for him. Jock wandered with a spurious aimlessness through the campsite, working his way in long arcs that brought him closer and closer to Crosbie's route. The boy hitched the *cornemuse* bellows to his elbow and pumped solemnly, keeping a slow march-time as he mounted the long hill. Cammie could hear very faintly the thin reedy tones of his pipes and something abruptly made her heart pound as she saw Jock approach Crosbie, saw the heavy soldier pause irritably, then crouch solidly on his haunches to talk to her boy.

Even she could not have interrupted Crosbie with impunity, Cammie knew, but Jock was another matter. Crosbie loved the boy, but wasn't there more to it than that? Mightn't he also …

Two horsemen breasted the hilltop on the far side of the camp, saluted the sentry and cantered quickly along the ridge toward Crosbie. A strange pair, Cammie thought. That long leggy bay looked like Nicholas Blanchard's gelding, but whose was that distinctive gray? And why did the other rider remain at a cautious distance ahead of Blanchard who carried his long rifle across the cantle of his saddle.

"Stop right here," Blanchard ordered. "Just rein in and wait. Don't even think of moving before I tell you."

The rider of the stubby gray pulled his overheated horse to a halt and muttered something under his breath. Blanchard couldn't hear what he said but he refused to bother about it; his skinny companion had been mumbling all the way out from Pittsburgh.

Blanchard trotted forward toward Crosbie, dismounted quickly and laid his long rifle across his saddle, aiming it at the gray horse.

"Got a visitor for you, Colonel," he said easily. "Private matter, I'd say." He winked at Jock and gestured with one hand. "Scoot, young-un. *Allez vous-en.*"

Jock glanced at Crosbie, saw the heavy frown and shrugged resignedly. He marched down the hill toward Cammie's wagon, pumping hard at his pipes.

Crosbie winced at the shrill sound and muttered to himself.

"Remember a gentleman named Budd, Colonel? Oliver Budd?" Blanchard asked. "We met him outside Alex, then I saw him at the City Tavern just before my head was bashed in."

"Aye," Crosbie said. "A seedy fellow. I remember." He looked toward Blanchard's captive. "But this isn't..."

"No, sir," Blanchard laughed. "But this is a good friend of Budd's. I saw Budd in Pittsburgh just now, dressed like the Duke of Buckingham and riding in a carriage as good as I've ever seen at home. Nothing seedy about him today, Colonel. I think Mr. Budd was playing a part in Alex. Trying to fool somebody."

Crosbie nodded silently and waited.

"I lost track of Mr. Budd," Blanchard went on. "His carriage moved faster than I did. But I caught up with his friend, here, and invited him to come have supper with us. I thought you might like to have a little talk with him. Maybe he can explain the actions of Mr. Budd. Maybe he can even tell us about a certain mysterious map marked with crosses..." Blanchard reached out and halted Crosbie when the Colonel started toward the man on the gray horse.

"He wasn't anxious to answer questions, Colonel, so I sort of riffled through his belongings. According to a letter from a girl in Pittsburgh, his name is Daniel Fiske, a gentleman from Richmond, Virginia, but he carries a pair of matched pistols marked L.N. He had something close to five hundred dollars cash in his pockets. Just a couple dollars short, as if he collected the money recently and just bought a couple of drinks and paid for some new shoes for his horse. I picked him up outside a blacksmith's place."

Crosbie looked up quietly at Blanchard. "I understand," he said solemnly. "Let's have Mr. Fiske over now."

Blanchard signaled with his rifle and the strange rider moved forward at a cautious walk, halting when Blanchard raised his hand.

"Climb on down, Mr. Fiske," Blanchard grinned. "I want you to meet Colonel Crosbie. A few days with the Colonel and you'll have no more use for Oliver Budd."

"I do not know an Oliver Budd," the man said automatically, as though he'd said the same thing often before without anyone believing him.

"You left a tavern with him this afternoon," Blanchard said flatly. "You were mighty close then, considering you don't know the man."

Fiske rubbed his prominent nose slowly. "That was Mr. Michael Foreman, a member of Governor St. Clair's staff. I told you that before and I can add nothing to it."

Crosbie glanced briefly at Blanchard.

"Could be," Blanchard said lightly. "He had a different appearance in Alexandria. Maybe he used a different name there, too. But I doubt it," he said more thoughtfully. "Chances are this rascal just picked a name out of the air, hoping maybe if he said it long and loud, I'd think I might have made a mistake."

"Did you?" Crosbie asked quietly.

"No, sir."

Crosbie nodded and turned back to Fiske. "My wagon train has been attacked twice, Mr. Fiske. I have reason to believe it may be attacked again before we arrive in the Ohio country. For several reasons I believe Mr. Oliver Budd has a great deal to do with those attacks. Do you understand?"

Fiske flicked a glance at Blanchard, then turned squarely facing Crosbie and put his hand dramatically on his drab waistcoat. "I solemnly swear that I do not know Oliver Budd and I have no knowledge whatever of the attacks against your wagon train." Fiske raised his eyes soulfully to the sky and Crosbie had difficulty restraining his impulse to kick the man.

"I mentioned all that, Mr. Fiske," he growled, "so that you would understand why I will not accept any evasive answers from you. I want to know about Oliver Budd—by whatever name you know him—and I want to know why he gave you five hundred dollars today."

Crosbie's shot in the dark had some effect, he thought. Fiske reddened and his small mouth dropped open. He glared wildly at Blanchard, then controlled himself with visible effort and forced a faint sneer that wobbled uncertainly under his pointed nose.

"No such thing," he said in a shrill voice. "No such thing. That money is mine. Always has been mine. I never ..."

Crosbie waved his huge hand impatiently. He pivoted on his heel. "Mr. Blanchard, find a wagon to keep him in. Tie him up well and let him think it over. He can talk to me whenever he wants to. No one else is to go near him. Report to me when you have him taken care of properly."

Blanchard brought his rifle up to the "present" briefly. "Very good, sir."

Blanchard ignored the loud bleatings from Fiske. He prodded him with his rifle to move him toward the wagons on the campsite below. Crosbie could hear Blanchard drowning his prisoner's complaints as he bellowed for his scouts to come help him. All told, Blanchard was gone less than five minutes and Crosbie stayed on the skyline, holding the reins of Blanchard's bay and Fiske's tall gray until he returned.

Blanchard walked easily up the slope, knowing Crosbie was watching him. He chose his footing carefully and tried not to stagger as he climbed. Now that the strain of guarding Fiske was over, Blanchard was feeling again all the agonies of his drunken night. His forehead was wet and feverish and he would have given a dollar right then for a cold glass of water.

He stumbled over a polished stone, kicked it forward as he approached Crosbie. Blanchard stooped to pick it up, intending to throw it into the creek. But he didn't complete the throw.

"What have you found, Mr. Blanchard?" Crosbie asked heavily.

Blanchard glanced up at the Colonel and saw him suddenly as a tired, worn man with a drawn, almost haggard face in which hard blue eyes seemed the only vital element.

"Piece of a jawbone, Colonel," he said slowly. "Least I think it is ..." He held it out to Crosbie.

Crosbie took the long curved section of bone, looked at it quickly and half shuddered. His face was bleak and deathly as he kicked his moccasins at the heavy loam of the hillside, digging a six-inch hole with his toe. "The filthy bastards," he muttered. He bent stiffly and placed the bone deep in the earth, covered it with handfuls of soil patted down hard.

" 'Tis a better burial than his own people would give him," Crosbie said bitterly. "But we'll not make a practice of this, Mr. Blanchard, else we'll be here for years."

"Braddock's men, is it, Colonel?" Blanchard asked.

"Aye," Crosbie growled. "Braddock's men. They lie all across the field and down along the creek. But it was a long time ago and their bones aren't so noticeable now." Crosbie tamped the small mound with the sole of his moccasin. "Their king never found time to bury them."

After a long silent moment Blanchard took the reins from Crosbie's hand. "About this Fiske fellow, Colonel," he said hesitantly. "I'm beginning to think I made a mistake bringing him out here. He doesn't look scared enough to talk and ..."

"But he can't do whatever Budd paid him to do," Crosbie said quickly. He laid his solid hand on Blanchard's shoulder and smiled. "You've done well, Mr. Blanchard. Now, what of the boats?"

"All ready, sir," Blanchard said. "We can load any time we're ready. Benny Upjohn's got the boats at his yard on the Mon so we won't have to go in through town."

"Fine. Fine," Crosbie said. "We'll start early tomorrow. Five wagons at a time with mounted guards. A double guard here at the bivouac until all the wagons leave."

"Right," Blanchard said. He led the horses down the slope toward the wagons, keeping pace with Crosbie. "Benny was plumb full of the latest gossip, Colonel. Said Johnnine Burnham was sent downriver by General Putnam a couple months back. He had 36 men with him to build cabins for our people."

"Thirty-six!" Crosbie roared. "Was that all? Thirty-six men to house over three hundred people? What's Burnham building, a set of barracks?"

Blanchard shook his head slowly. "Don't know, Colonel, I never thought to ask. But Benny said Burnham had some tough-looking boys and he's allowed to pay them 26 cents a day and whiskey, so I reckon he's planning to get plenty of work out of them."

"Ridiculous," Crosbie snorted. "I'll have a word to say to Putnam when we reach Marietta. By God, I'll ..."

"He's not in Marietta, Colonel," Blanchard said mildly. "Went upcountry last month. Benny doesn't know when he'll be back."

Crosbie stopped abruptly, glaring at his lieutenant, his mouth a meager slit in his taut face, his eyes burning. He said nothing.

"He'll probably try to get back right soon," Blanchard said ineptly, trying to think of something appropriate. "Don't reckon he expected us to make such a fast trip." He tethered both horses to the rear of Cammie's wagon.

Crosbie waited until some of the tension had left him. "I'm beginning to wonder," he said hoarsely, "whether anyone expected us to get here at all."

CHAPTER FOURTEEN

Blanchard braced his feet firmly against a rock in the middle of Turtle Creek and let the swift water pour along his body. It was chilly now that the sun was gone and night was closing in, but Blanchard felt as though new life were entering his tired frame with the hard running water. Earlier he had shaved with hot water at Cammie's fire and now for the first time in a long day, he was clean and relaxed.

As he lay on his back he could see through the foam of the creek the dim outline of a sentry's head above the gorge. Twice since he'd been there, Crosbie's immense bulk had loomed up restlessly on the horizon. The old man was wearing himself to a nubbin, doing the routine chores of a guard sergeant along with his other work. Well, another day or two should see them aboard the bateaux and then Crosbie could sleep for a full day if he chose. And the Colonel needed it, too. He was beginning to look his fifty years lately. But who wouldn't with his entire future tied up in the success of this journey? Blanchard knew vaguely of the five hundred acres which Putnam had promised Crosbie for a safe passage. And he knew very well that Crosbie had no other prospects if this should fail. Well, maybe the Colonel would come along to New Orleans with him, or even sign on with Governor St. Clair if there was really going to be an expedition against the Indian nations as Benny had hinted.

Blanchard rolled twice in the fast water, tried vainly to swim against the current and then angled toward the bank where he had left his clothes. The towel Cammie had given him was rough and scratchy against his skin but he enjoyed the tingling sensation that came when he rubbed. He pulled on a pair of loose breeches and slipped his feet into clean moccasins.

Over the rushing sound of the water he heard another sound, the sudden snap of a dry stick under a foot trying vainly to make stealthy progress along the creek bank. Blanchard froze, peering through the dimness. The stick snapped again as the foot was withdrawn. A second later a figure appeared, the figure of a woman. Her pale hair and her pale dress were almost luminous against the darkness. Blanchard relaxed and drew a deep relieved breath. Only one woman had hair like that.

"Mademoiselle Lucie—" he called softly.

The woman gasped in sudden alarm.

"Who...?" she stammered. She paused but seemed poised for instant flight.

Blanchard moved toward her, identifying himself in quiet tones.

"Monsieur Blanchard," she breathed. "I...I was afraid..."

"You should not be out here alone, Mademoiselle," he reproved gently. "It is not safe." She must know that, she had known it was not safe for Adrienne to go roaming off alone back at Halfaday Creek.

For a moment she said nothing. He thought she was trying to decide how to answer. He could see the gleam of her eyes as she watched him but her face was an indistinct blur. She was a strange girl. So appreciative of the small kindnesses he had shown her now and then, like finding moccasins to replace her worn-out, inadequate shoes, or building a proper cooking fire for her when all the available wood was green or wet. Lucie was very little a part of the ordinary life of the wagon train. Even less was she akin to any lady's maid he had ever seen before.

"I was not alone, Monsieur," she said softly. "I was walking with...with a friend. It is sometimes pleasant to have a small

space of time to oneself. There is so little privacy possible, traveling as we are ..."

That was true, of course. Lack of privacy did not trouble
Blanchard greatly; he had been in the army too long. But for these
people, unaccustomed to the cramped quarters and the necessary restrictions of the wagon train, it might be hard indeed.

"Your friend should not have left you alone, Mademoiselle,"
he told the girl.

Again she hesitated before answering. Blanchard thought
she sounded oddly defensive, and he wondered why.

"It was, for the moment, necessary, Monsieur. A task to perform at the wagon train. He knew I should be quite safe. As you
see, we are within view of the camp fires."

She was right, Blanchard saw. On the bluff above them, half
a dozen fires twinkled their cheerful yellow light.

"Still, you must be careful," he warned. "This is a wild rough
country. Not like the fields and parks of France, I'm sure. Not
like Virginia, either ..." For a moment he felt a homesick surge
of remembrance. Probably because he'd been talking to Benny
Upjohn about it earlier in the day, the warm sweetness of a
Virginia night, the salt tang of the sea in the Tidelands breeze
were sharper in his memory than they had been for a long time.
He wondered if he would ever see Virginia again.

"I know the dangers, Monsieur Blanchard," Lucie was saying
in her soft voice. "A wild country, as you say. But ..." a new note
disturbed the softness suddenly, he thought it sounded almost
exultant. "But a *new* country, Monsieur. A *free* country. With
new ways, new freedoms, the right to build a new life without
the barriers of the old ..." Abruptly she broke off the words, as if
remembering that she was confiding in a near-stranger. "I must
go now." she said, and her voice was soft again, almost flat. "For
me, too, there will be tasks to perform at the campsite."

"I will see you back to your wagon," Blanchard offered.

Again that odd hesitation. "No," Lucie said at last. "I am grateful for your concern, Monsieur, but it would be best if you did not accompany me."

Blanchard shrugged and glanced again at the campfires. The distance was short, she would be safe enough. And he could keep an eye on her until she reached camp.

"Good night, Monsieur," Lucie said. "And…thank you." She sounded genuinely grateful. "You have been most kind to me always, Monsieur Nicholas. I wish…" she paused and he did not learn what it was she wished, for when she spoke again it was a conventional phrase of thanks. "I am most appreciative, Monsieur," Lucie said.

He said good night and watched her move slowly up the path to the rim of the gorge. A strange girl, he thought again. After a moment he wondered idly what man she had slipped away to meet. But that, of course, was none of his business.

Blanchard walked back down the gorge. No wonder the Colonel had wrecked two wagons here, he thought, if this was the best place to ford the creek. He toiled up slowly to the bank, waved his hand at a sentry and stood for a moment outside the ring of wagons, looking up at the clear dark sky.

"The king of all he surveys," a low mocking voice said behind him.

Blanchard whirled and laughed. The woods were full of wanderers tonight. "I can't see a thing in this light," he said. "So it's a mighty poor king I'd be this moment."

"But such arrogant posture I have not seen since we were last at Versailles."

Blanchard edged closer to Adrienne. "Just the effect a bath has, mamselle," he murmured. "Makes me feel light enough to float."

"Come sit beside me," Adrienne said from the darkness. "I have been deserted by Edmond and Monsieur de Flaville. I suspect they have run into Pittsburgh for a taste of the flesh pots."

She giggled lightly at something his words recalled. "If bathing has such a wonderful effect, Monsieur, possibly you can explain why you stopped me from bathing at Halfaday Creek?"

Blanchard felt his way cautiously up the slope and sank to the ground where he thought Adrienne might be. Her wide white skirt was a pale blur in the darkness.

He draped the damp towel about his bare shoulders and tried to see Adrienne's face. It was strange, he thought, how a nice girl likes to talk about an embarrassing moment in the past. She sort of toys with the notion and giggles about it, but if you were to suggest we try it again, you'd get your ear mighty near burned off.

"I made a mistake then," Blanchard said easily.

"But I thought you said ..."

"I should have waited just one more second," Blanchard added. He waited tensely in the dark stillness, wondering whether she'd scratch his face again or merely slap it. Adrienne's breath stopped with a catching sound in her throat and then she laughed again. Blanchard relaxed. It was all right.

"My uncle would then have been compelled to call you out, Monsieur."

"A blissful death," Blanchard said happily. "Listen to me, will you? Anybody can catch on to this macaroni chatter with a little practice. And a pretty girl to egg him on. I told you," he added softly, "my friends call me Nick."

"Another name for the Devil," Adrienne said softly. Her voice seemed much closer now, Nick thought, but he wasn't sure enough to make a move. He let his towel slide to the ground and under the pretense of groping for it, ran his hand around in a quick arcing motion.

"But I am on this side," Adrienne murmured surprisingly, "Nick."

Blanchard turned swiftly, reaching with avid fingers. Adrienne came into his arms lithely and her mouth met his in a warm writhing movement. Her hands were icy, digging hard against his bare skin. But her lips were soft, warm, demanding. Blanchard heard himself groan deep inside his throat. This wasn't real, any part of it. It couldn't be happening. This couldn't be Adrienne, who had laughed at him, teased him, scratched his face with the slashing claws of an angry cat. "A hellion, that girl. A spoilt minx… Marquis's niece or no…"

And still it was Adrienne, stroking his damp hair and holding him close.

The quiet murmurs around the campfires seemed far away and meaningless now, all the long tensions of the journey were wiped away in a blind driving instinct. Blanchard knew with a reasoning part of his brain that he should go back to the wagons now, leave Adrienne to her own world, her own people and the life she knew. This was a girl who wanted no part of a wilderness, no part of the raw new world that was the only world Nicholas Blanchard could give her. He knew that deeply, but the knowing carried no meaning for him. His breath seemed to sear his throat and he could manage to say nothing. But his hands moved independently, seeking, molding, warming a flesh that needed no warming. Adrienne lay back in his arms and he could see the faint shimmering reflection of stars in her eyes as she looked up at him.

"Nick," she whispered sleepily, "my darling Nick."

The stars were blotted out by the silver light of the rising moon and the moon in turn was obscured by scudding clouds. Sleepy sentries were replaced by even sleepier sentries and Colonel Crosbie stamped angrily up and down the long sloping hill from the wagons. Adrienne and Blanchard were aware of none of it.

At length Blanchard lay still and quiet, his head on Adrienne's breast, his hand holding hers in a loose, familiar grasp.

"Your hair is very damp," Adrienne said quietly.

"Yes," Blanchard cleared his throat roughly before he could speak. "I was…"

"And you are cold." Something soft and filmy wrapped itself around his bare shoulders, a shawl, he guessed, light and silky and smelling faintly of roses, roses warmed by the sun of a gentler world than this one; a silken something a girl might wear to stroll the mannered path of a distant place called Versailles ...

"Adrienne ..." he groped for words to ask her if there could be any reconciling of worlds so very far apart. In that moment he would have promised her anything. He would have taken her back to that Tidewater country Benny Upjohn said was the only place a man could live in a comfortable, civilized manner; if she had insisted on going back to Paris he would have promised her that, too, blindly. "Adrienne, could you ..."

"Mr. Blanchard!"

A bull-like voice bellowed from the campsite. "Mr. Blanchard!" That was Colonel Crosbie and no doubt of it.

Blanchard tried to shut out the sound. Of all the fool times for the Colonel to roar commands ...

Adrienne's arms tightened. She pulled his head down and she kissed him eagerly. Then she pushed him away gently and smiled up at him.

"Go to your tactless commander, my darling. I shall wait here."

"Mr. Blanchard! On the double!"

"Uh ... yes," Blanchard stammered, confused and angry as a man might be who has been rudely jolted out of the most wonderful, incredible dream of his life. "Yes, I suppose ..."

"Go quickly, dear Nick, before your infuriating Colonel bellows again." Her voice was teasing, now.

Nick bent for a fleeting kiss and then rose hastily, pulling his damp towel about his shoulders as he raced down the dark slope toward the wagons.

"Where are you, Colonel?" he called.

The fire nearest Cammie's wagon had been built to a roaring blaze and some fifty people were milling about the wagon. Blanchard could not identify Crosbie in the mob.

"In the wagon, Mr. Blanchard," Crosbie's voice shouted angrily. "Come in here at once."

Blanchard pressed through the cluster of people, murmuring his apologies, shrugging his shoulders when they asked him the meaning of Crosbie's sudden alarm. He climbed in the rear port, suddenly aware of his odd appearance, hoping the Frenchmen would assume he had just wakened and had covered himself with the first thing that came to hand.

Inside the wagon, Crosbie knelt on a packing case, facing away from Blanchard. The Colonel looked around and grunted.

"A fine mess," he muttered, almost to himself.

Blanchard moved forward, bending low under the canvas to see. Before Crosbie lay a long, incredibly thin man. That was Mr. Fiske, he thought numbly. The man's hands were roped behind his back and his skinny legs were tied to one side of the wagon. A fat wad of linen made a gag under his high prominent nose. And under his chin was a wide scarlet gash across his throat. The bed of the wagon was almost awash with blood.

"How could a man so skinny have so much blood?" Blanchard asked aimlessly, saying the first thing that came to mind.

"You put him in this wagon, Mr. Blanchard?" Crosbie demanded furiously.

"Yes, sir," Blanchard replied. "I guess I figured Cammie wouldn't mind ..."

Crosbie snorted. "You gagged him?"

"Yes, sir," Blanchard said. "You said to keep him from talking to anybody. I didn't figure he was worth a special guard."

"You were wrong, Mr. Blanchard. Did you leave his five hundred dollars in his pocket?"

Blanchard nodded.

"It's gone," Crosbie growled.

Blanchard had no suggestion to make regarding that. "Do you know who killed him?" he asked.

Crosbie turned slowly and glared at his lieutenant. "No. But I can guess why he was killed. Can't you?"

"I reckon so, Colonel," Blanchard said slowly. "I think I was right about this Mr. Fiske being one of Oliver Budd's men. Maybe he would have told us why our wagon train is worth stopping. Maybe somebody didn't want him to tell us that."

"Only that would explain it," Crosbie agreed. "Fiske alive was a threat to someone. Fiske dead might be the means of stopping us."

"Will he be that, Colonel?"

Crosbie's face was deathly in the dim light within the wagon. "He will not," he growled. "We'll bury him, you and I, later tonight. One more body on Braddock's field won't make much difference. Later, perhaps, after our people are settled...an investigation..." he was wandering, thinking aloud. "Now," he said crisply, "get outside and send everyone to bed. Tell them anything, but get rid of them. I'll come for you when I want your help later on. Stay with this wagon until then."

"Yes, sir," Blanchard said. "But I'd like...for just a moment..." he fumbled for words. He couldn't tell Crosbie that Adrienne was waiting. "Something I have to do..."

"I have told you what you are to do, Mr. Blanchard," Crosbie said angrily. "Nothing else has any importance. One more blunder..." he stopped. It was not necessary to continue.

Blanchard shrugged. "Yes, sir," he said flatly. He watched coldly while Crosbie strode away across the campsite. There was no help for it. He would have to stay with the wagon. What Adrienne would believe when he didn't come back, he hated to think. He stared down at the still form of the man who had called himself Daniel Fiske. Already Adrienne with her warmth and softness was retreating into a sort of dream. He thought, as he had thought before, that it couldn't have happened. He couldn't have held her in his arms like that, couldn't have heard the whispered eager words she said...

He watched for Adrienne to come back to camp, half frantic, not only for what she might be thinking about his not coming back to her, but for her safety as well. Across the campsite he saw Lucie step from Adrienne's wagon and look searchingly out into the darkness. He called to her softly but she did not hear. He wondered whether she was looking for Adrienne or for the mysterious friend she had been walking with earlier in the evening. At last he whistled François from his task of polishing the boots of the Marquis's son, and sent him to find Adrienne. But before the boy returned, Adrienne herself crossed the firelit area to her wagon. Even at a distance Blanchard could see how angry she was. Her shining dark head was carried at a high arrogant tilt and her long skirt swept across the grass at a furious pace. He was too far away to see her face clearly, but he knew the dark eyes would be flashing angry sparks, as they had flashed at him that day in Alexandria when he had mistaken her for a laundress and reached out to pat the fine curve of her hip.

He called to her but she would not hear him or look at him. Deliberately she walked on to her wagon and disappeared inside it.

Blanchard sighed. It would not be easy to explain why he had not returned to her. He wasn't even sure Crosbie was going to let him explain, what with a killing on their hands and the necessity of keeping secrecy about it.

He stirred restlessly. Maybe it was better this way. Some sane part of his mind had told him all along that he had nothing to offer Adrienne. He was a soldier ... right soon now, an *ex*-soldier ... with no prospects beyond joining up with Wilkinson in New Orleans. Crosbie and Benny Upjohn were both mighty scornful of Wilkinson. And for all his wild hopes, he couldn't take Adrienne back to the Tidewater country, to land that might support one establishment elegantly enough, but four not at all ...

Still, the gloom of his thoughts deepened as the night deepened, as all but the sentry fire died out, leaving the camp silent and dim.

CHAPTER FIFTEEN

Duncan Crosbie followed the last group of five wagons through the log gateway of Upjohn's boatyard. Two of Blanchard's young scouts heaved at the gate to close it behind him. Through the light drizzling rain Crosbie could dimly see the long line of squatty bateaux rising and falling lightly in the dark gray water of the Monongahela. Crosbie rode slowly behind the wagons, his heavy chin low on his chest, his cocked hat pulled down against the slanting rain. In the large enclosure of the boatyard, children were yelling and running from the wagons to the boats, men staggered under immense loads, stepping cautiously across the treacherous muddy yard, but all of them were gay enough, Crosbie noticed. They called cheerily from the boats and their light happy voices echoed from the log walls. None of them knew that Crosbie and Blanchard had buried the body of the late Mr. Fiske under a tree on Braddock's Field early that morning and if Crosbie had his way, none would ever know. But the knowledge weighed heavily within his mind, the brutal hidden shamefulness of smuggling a man's body into the earth without any acknowledgment other than a deep grunt of relief when the job was done. Crosbie's thin mouth clamped in a hard tight line. He checked his tired wet horse.

"Right on schedule, Colonel," Blanchard called from his perch on the roof of Upjohn's office building. "A lot of stuff is getting soaked and the women are raising hell about it."

Crosbie tipped back his hat to see Blanchard sitting astride the ridgepole in the misty rain. "Keep them at it, Mr. Blanchard," he said with a briskness he didn't feel. "Where's Captain Upjohn?"

Blanchard pointed at his feet. "Down in the office, keeping dry," he laughed. "He's plumb lost his taste for wet weather."

Crosbie wondered vaguely how Blanchard could maintain his easy lightness after last night, but he didn't think about it for long. He dismounted, tied his heavy gelding to a post and walked stiffly toward the small log-and-frame office. Inside a small fire crackled cozily and Crosbie saw Benny Upjohn sitting languidly back in a comfortably padded armchair, reading carefully through a thick canvas bound ledger. Upjohn tossed the ledger on a table when he noticed Crosbie.

"Greetings, sir," he said cheerfully. "Come in and join me in a tot of something to keep the chill out. I've some prime Demerara I think you might relish."

Upjohn's linen was sparkling in the flickering light and somehow he had avoided getting rainspots on his velvet coat. Crosbie felt disheveled and unkempt by comparison.

"Later, sir," he said gruffly. "Right now I'd like to know when you'll be able to clear my boats from your docks?"

Upjohn raised both palms in a bored gesture. "Whenever you like, Colonel. Blanchard should be finished loading before nightfall if he keeps at it. But there's a storm brewing, I'd say. I told Nick this morning it would be foolish to take inexperienced people downriver in bad weather. But it's your responsibility." Upjohn reached down two small glasses from a cabinet and poured thick dark rum into them. "Your health, Colonel Crosbie."

Crosbie drained the glass impatiently. "Excellent rum," he said politely. "You've found a good pilot for me?"

"Two," Upjohn said, rising to stretch his arms wide. "That gives you an extra man so you can have two watches if you like. But you'll have to furnish steersmen from among your own people, Colonel. And if just one of them should lose control and broach to ..." Upjohn shrugged.

"Yes, yes," Crosbie growled. "What of the wagons and the excess animals?"

"I have receipts for you." Upjohn riffled through a stack of papers, selected two and passed them to Crosbie. "The Ohio Company will take over the wagons and teams you bought in Virginia and we can also buy any wagons your Frenchmen might want to sell. As it happens, we've a warehouse full of Monongahela whiskey. I'd welcome a chance to send it East for a better market."

"Yes," Crosbie nodded. "Well, that's all then, Captain. I'll take the boats out at daybreak, storm or no storm."

"The decision is all yours, Colonel," Upjohn said blandly. "I don't envy you. But let me wish you well, sir. And have another taste of rum before you go."

"No more," Crosbie said bluntly. He pulled open the door and ducked his head to keep the persistent drizzle from his face. Across the Monongahela dark ropy clouds lay in a thick layer against the black Ohio hills. The high flat bateaux rose clumsily at their moorings, rolling constantly as fitful winds lashed the dark water into a roiling froth. The boats didn't look at all safe but Crosbie had seen too many of them weather bad storms to have any misgivings about the trip from the Forks of the Ohio to their final destination. It wasn't the boats that worried him, nor the lack of pilots.

He stood solidly before the small log building, looking sharply around the boatyard. Blanchard had posted sentries at the gate and at each corner of the yard. Only the water side was unprotected and he would have lights burning all night. Only a fire could stop them now and Crosbie blessed the annoying drizzle that effectively dampened the timbers of the bateaux. And rain would also discourage the more active young men from going down to Pittsburgh for a last spree.

Crosbie almost smiled at himself as he watched the boats being loaded. Only a few more days now and he would own five hundred acres in the Ohio Company tract. A week ago he would have sold his chances for a Continental shinplaster. Now he was fifty hours from Marietta, another day or so more from wherever they were going.

"Ready to load the stock, Colonel," Blanchard bellowed overhead. "Everything else is aboard."

"Come down, Mr. Blanchard," Crosbie shouted. "We'll load the animals at daybreak. Put them in one of the boathouses and see they get a good feed."

Blanchard called to his men. He pointed out an empty boathouse for the stock and then he slid down the sloping roof and dropped lightly beside Crosbie.

"Get a nice view from up there," he said easily. He wiped his dripping face with an equally wet sleeve. "The river looks a little rough."

"We'll leave at daybreak, Mr. Blanchard," Crosbie said quickly to forestall any argument. "Are we ready?"

"I'd say so, sir," Blanchard answered thoughtfully. "Maybe you'd like to walk around with me and ..."

Crosbie signaled him to proceed and he followed Blanchard carefully along the slippery path to the river bank, stepping aside whenever a man went stumbling by with a last-minute load on his shoulders.

"Two of the boats are fresh off the ways, Colonel," Blanchard reported. "One of them I've had fitted out with eyebolts and slings for the livestock and the other one I figured could be the command boat."

Crosbie nodded soberly. He could see the low boxy shapes of the boats ahead. Each was nearly fifty feet long and almost fifteen feet wide. Because of bothersome sandbars, they were shallow, drawing less than three feet of water, but each could easily carry fifty tons. The boats looked rather like ice skates, Crosbie thought, considering their long up-curving ends and their flat square deck covers. They weren't fast, and life aboard them would be even more primitive than on the road, but they were safe, provided they were properly controlled.

"I checked all the steering sweeps, Colonel," Blanchard said quietly. "And the sculls are in good shape, too. We may need them if this storm kicks up any more."

"We'll leave at daybreak," Crosbie said flatly. He closed his eyes briefly to ease a growing tension that was beginning to blur his vision. A faint edge of nausea burned in his stomach. Not enough sleep lately, he told himself.

Blanchard glanced absently at the silken sheen of the wet timbers glistening in the steady rain, looking everywhere except at Crosbie. The old man is looking all-fire tired lately, he thought. His face is thinner and the skin is pulled back so tightly it looks almost transparent under the clusters of freckles. Crosbie stood there heavily, paying no attention to Blanchard, apparently concentrating on a private thought. Blanchard turned away and looked out across the boatyard. Be a damned good thing when we get these people on the boats and then the old man can get some rest for a change.

"The women got some of the boats fixed up pretty well, Colonel," Blanchard said softly. "A couple look just like parlors. I found some big metal pots so each boat can have a little stove where the folks can make a hot drink or soup in case we don't want to come in to shore. I figured you might be planning to go straight through."

"Straight to Marietta," Crosbie said tonelessly. "But I'll not go aboard until we're ready to start. Which is the command boat?"

"First one, sir, up ahead. You can tell by the fresh wood. Looks like it was varnished. Madame Carel and Jock are aboard now," he added slyly. Then when he saw a lowering frown on Crosbie's face, he said, "I put the Marquis's party there, too. And both the pilots. Makes a full enough load, I'd say."

"Very good, Mr. Blanchard." Crosbie forced a lean smile for his lieutenant. "Have you received any attention from the local authorities?"

"About Mr. Fiske, sir? Not a word. I reckon you had the right idea about that, Colonel. Whatever Budd hired him to do to us sure ain't going to get done now. I'm counting on a quiet time until we leave."

"Yes," Crosbie said bleakly. "I hope you're right." He regarded Blanchard with some wonderment. That young man had been up half the night waiting for the Frenchmen to get to sleep and then he had dug a grave for the murdered Fiske, carried him half a mile on his back and then a few hours afterwards had led the first contingent of wagons from Braddock's field to the boatyard. He had been continuously busy since then, and not just routine going-through-the-motions, either. Blanchard had given real thought to the problem of loading the boats. But he stood lithely before Crosbie now, eyes fresh and alert, looking well rested and fit for anything. No one would ever suspect he had been doing anything more strenuous than sampling Benny Upjohn's excellent Demerara.

"You aren't worried about Fiske, are you, Colonel?" Blanchard asked with a mild surprise. "Nobody saw us burying him."

Crosbie stared blankly at Blanchard. "Plenty of people saw him when he was alive, though," he said grimly. "And anyone could have been watching, anyone who had a real interest in the man, interest real enough to warrant killing him. Someone knows about him, all right."

"Sure, whoever killed him knows," Blanchard agreed quickly. "But *he* would have made tracks just as fast as possible after he did Fiske in. *He* wouldn't stay around waiting to be discovered..."

"He didn't leave," Crosbie said in a quiet, matter-of-fact voice. "He didn't leave at all. Whoever killed Fiske stayed with us last night."

There was only bewilderment on Blanchard's face as he stared at Crosbie. "But, Colonel," he protested. "Colonel, that couldn't be. We ... somebody in the wagon train ... would have noticed any stranger hanging around like that..."

"It was not a stranger," Crosbie said flatly "Whoever killed Fiske before he could talk, before he could betray not only the plot against us but the reason for it and the people behind it...whoever killed him is, I am sure now, one of our own people."

"No!" Blanchard whispered hoarsely. The healthy glow of his face paled slowly as he thought of the implications of what Crosbie was saying. "It couldn't be that way..."

"It is that way," Crosbie affirmed quietly. "I thought it over very carefully on the way here, and I talked to the men on sentry duty last night. I'm sure." His voice was tense and cold and the words came out with heavy certainty. "Last night I made three rounds of the sentries at the campsite, all of them within an hour of the time I found Fiske's body. Not a soul could have passed those guards without being seen. No one did. De Flaville and the Count and a couple of other young men rode in to Pittsburgh; Lucie and Mademoiselle Adrienne both went wandering off into the woods for a time..." Blanchard flushed slightly at the faint ghost of amusement in Crosbie's tone when he spoke of Adrienne. "But no one else passed our lines," Crosbie went on. "The killer stayed with us."

Blanchard leaned both arms against an empty wagon and put his head down, stared blindly at the wet ground. His eyes followed an aimless rivulet of water streaming from the wagon tongue.

"It never even occurred to me," he said in a patient voice, as though through patience he could negate Crosbie's sureness.

Someone, a lean young man bent under the weight of the wide polished mahogany table he carried across his shoulders, slithered along the muddy path behind Crosbie and the Colonel whirled suspiciously, glared at the rain-wet wood of the Marquis's dining-table and turned back to Blanchard.

"I can't believe it," Blanchard said. "One of these people betray us? Not just us, but three hundred of his own countrymen?" His tone was completely incredulous. "Who, Colonel?" he demanded. "Which one ...?"

Crosbie had no answer.

There was a long silence, as if both men were going through a mental list of all the members of the wagon train. The Marquis, soldier, leader, gentleman. He, with all his flowery speeches about the new world and his hopes for his people. That was not possible. But who, then? De la Foure, his son? De Flaville? One of the other young scouts? Then there were the women. Cammie, Lucie, Adrienne ... but that was unthinkable. Adrienne resented the whole business of journeying to a wilderness to find a new home. Almost everything about Lucie was a mystery. But betray their own people? Again, it was impossible. Yet someone had surely plotted with Oliver Budd. Someone had drawn a map on fine parchment and marked it with crosses to show where the wagon train could be attacked. And someone had bloodily murdered Daniel Fiske ...

After a long time Blanchard said irrelevantly, "Some of the kids were up and down the river all morning, looking for crawdads. They said Cammie was going to make soup of them. Crawdad soup." His voice said it was just one more improbable thing.

Crosbie touched Blanchard's shoulder lightly. "Crayfish bisque," he said soberly. "And very good, too." He tapped Blanchard's shoulder again, more heavily this time. "Wake up."

Blanchard blinked his eyes several times rapidly, then lifted his head and shook it. "Yes, sir," he said in a normal tone. "Then ... we've got a murderer riding along with us? An unknown murderer?"

"Worse," Crosbie said flatly. "We have an unknown traitor with us."

CHAPTER SIXTEEN

The long black line of boats crept slowly down the Ohio, gliding silently, wraith-like over the murky water, passing in and out of the dappled moon patterns that brightened the still, wet darkness. Duncan Crosbie paced restlessly across the stern of his command boat, keeping clear of the massive steering sweep which his pilot held clamped tightly under his right arm. For hours the only sound had been the soft liquid bubbling of water lapping against the boats, an occasional splash of tobacco juice on the river when the steersman spat. Crosbie moved softly in his worn moccasins, his tired mind obstinately busy with plans. Should he tell General Putnam of the secret murder committed by one of the Frenchmen ? Should he insist upon a complete explanation of all the mystery with which Putnam had cloaked his mission ? And what of the constant threat of attack, which might still be hanging over the *émigrés?* As for himself, where should he look first for his five hundred acre parcel of land, his payment for a successful mission. The land along the Muskingum, hard by Marietta, would be worth a lot of money soon if he wanted land for an investment, but for farming, he'd do better up the …

The steady breeze veered suddenly and he could hear the thin lilting strains of music from the boats following. A lively sort of tune, a gavotte probably, Crosbie thought vaguely.

From the high-decked cover of the boat, Blanchard leaned over toward Crosbie.

"Three days almost they've been singing and dancing," he said casually. "I think somebody must have bought a barrel of red-eye back in Pittsburgh You want me to go back and ask if they've got a spare dram for us?"

"No," Crosbie snapped irritably, annoyed at having his attention distracted.

"Wouldn't even mind swimming back in a good cause, Colonel," Blanchard suggested in a bland, laughing tone.

The steersman behind him chuckled abruptly, a clattery sound that ended in a strangling cough. He spat again noisily.

"Go back to sleep, Mr. Blanchard," Crosbie said coldly. "You'll have a busy day in Marietta when we dock."

Blanchard yawned, stretched widely and rolled to the edge of the flat deck. He lowered himself carefully beside Crosbie and reached up for his leather shirt.

"Just be another couple of hours at the most, Colonel," he said. "That slat ridge back there is just a spit from the Muskingum, if I remember rightly."

"It will still be full dark, then," Crosbie said almost to himself. "I doubt if they'll let us land."

"Putnam's off up-country somewhere," Blanchard said mildly. "We'll be able to land all right. The boys never play it rough when Old Put's away."

The steersman choked again and muttered something corroborating Blanchard's opinion.

"Very well," Crosbie said briskly. "You remain at the dock until all the boats come in safely. Try to discourage anyone from going in to town if you can. There's nothing there anyway. Then meet me at the Adjutant's office."

"Right," Blanchard agreed. "Don't know how successful I'll be keeping people on board, but..."

"Not the least successful, Lieutenant," Adrienne's voice said lightly from the darkness. "One's first view of the wild Ohio! I wouldn't miss it. Would you, Edmond—Charles?"

Murmurs of agreement came from the two men standing beside her.

Crosbie growled something incoherent. He resumed his fretful pacing, an almost automatic motion now but one which seemed to relax nerves that had been pulled tight to the snapping point.

Blanchard rested his chin on the cover deck, trying to see Adrienne in that poor light. Perhaps her face would tell him more than the light, casual voice. It was the first time she'd spoken to him since the night at Turtle Creek. He didn't know whether to consider it a good sign or not. She had spoken, true, but something in her voice seemed to mock him with its light condescension. And she had one hand resting gently on the arm of each of the two gentlemen escorting her. She flashed her sparkling smile at first one and then the other.

"Marietta's a mighty poor town, Mamselle," Blanchard said in his vile French accent. "But I guess it'll be some better than the place you're heading for downriver."

"Ah...?" Adrienne asked coolly. "But it is a town named for our own Marie Antoinette. Despite one's opinion of l'Autrichienne, one must pay one's respects."

Edmond de la Foure laughed and said something Blanchard's recently acquired French was inadequate to catch. Charles de Flaville bent forward and whispered something in Adrienne's ear. All three laughed together, then Adrienne turned and walked away, along the narrow aisle toward the bow of the boat. The two young men followed her.

Blanchard watched them go. For one who'd tried so hard to convince himself that a quarrel with Adrienne was all for the best, he felt surprisingly dejected. She was acting as though what had happened between them meant nothing at all. And he'd have sworn... well, he'd have sworn that night at Braddock's Field that she understood how he felt about her. That it was certainly no casual, momentary affair he wanted... He'd have told her all that, of course, if he'd been able to go back. He sighed. It seemed something was always keeping him from saying the right thing to Adrienne, the thing he wanted most to say. Well, he guessed now that he'd been wrong about what it meant to her. It seemed to him she was going out of her way to show him just how wrong.

The voices faded slowly, mingled with the night noises and were lost in the darkness. Inside the decked part of the boat, someone blew lightly on the banked coals in a metal pot, coaxing them to flame again with scraps of dried bark. By the growing light of the fire, Crosbie saw Cammie's round, kind face, her red cheeks glowing in the flickering light, her long dark hair held loosely in a night-time braid that fell over one plump smooth shoulder. After a moment Crosbie stooped clumsily and came inside.

Cammie smiled at him warmly. Her full red mouth pouted deliciously and Crosbie felt the deep dour lines of his face soften in response. Cammie could always do that to him. Merely the sight of her dark eyes that glittered with a mocking challenge and Crosbie was a fumbling cadet again, gulping and stammering, but never able to remove himself from torment. Cammie touched his hand lightly, stroking his sunburned skin with a sureness that made Crosbie shiver like an overtired horse. And Crosbie thought of himself as a clumsy horse, too large for normal folk, much too large altogether for this tiny rounded woman who looked at him with sleepy eyes.

"What … what are you doing up?" Crosbie asked in a hoarse whisper. "It's pitch dark still."

Cammie reached up slowly, rubbed her warm palm against the sandy stubble that covered Crosbie's huge chin. "If you are to see your General, then you must shave, *non*? So I have the water for heating. And I have prepared your fine handsome uniform and even repaired your poor plume. It now stands up brave and martial as it properly should." Her hand rested against Crosbie's heavy shoulder muscles as she tipped her head back to look at him. "As my Dooncahn does," she murmured gently.

Crosbie locked his arms around her, holding her as he would hold a baby robin, tender as only a big man, frightened of his strength, can ever be tender. His hard lined face seemed bleak and purposeful, stern with intent, but his blue eyes were moist and he found it hard to speak.

"I have been thinking," he said thickly, "of five hundred acres which I am to have. I have been thinking of..."

"And I, Dooncahn," Cammie said softly, her warm lips against Crosbie's, moving quickly, gently.

Forward, young Jock called something in his high boyish treble, evidently speaking to Blanchard. Crosbie pulled back in a guilty movement and then grinned shamefully at Cammie.

"One might think Jock was your father," he said, "and I a young scoundrel with..."

Cammie kissed him quickly and moved away to test the heating water. Her face was averted and she said nothing for a long silent moment while Crosbie stood fidgeting, knowing he had said something wrong and not knowing how to correct it.

"I...I think of the boy as my own," he said with a strange stiffness. "A man could take pride in..."

And Cammie whirled swiftly, a blue of flying skirts and wild hair, whirled to meet his waiting arms and find there what she needed most to find.

The strong solid clump of martial boots along the narrow catwalk parted them again but there was no misunderstanding this time. I've done it now, Crosbie thought. All these years, all the too many times I've run away and never thought of coming back, the too-many women, the too-many places, all that's behind now and I'll settle down and watch Jock grow up and raise a crop on my farm and grow a big belly and maybe even take a hand in government. I'll do all that and I'll forget I've ever been a soldier or ever wanted to. And I'll be a happy man.

Jock swaggered under the deck cover, stepping high in Crosbie's boots which came far up his thighs and made him wobble uncertainly. He swept off Crosbie's cockaded uniform hat and bowed low to his mother. Cammie knelt to clasp him and over Jock's shoulder, Crosbie saw her eyes large and warm on his, full of acceptance, full of a knowledge he might once have feared but now welcomed wholeheartedly. Crosbie spanked his heavy hand against Jock's bottom and laughed in a full-throated bellowing roar, a rare joyous laugh that surprised Cammie as it did Jock.

"Ye'll hold me looking glass for me, Jocko," he boomed, "for today is a holiday and I must look neat."

Crosbie shaved with infinite care, kneeling on the rough timber of the deck while Jock held his polished steel mirror high in the fitful light of the small fire. But when he was finished, he refused the fresh uniform and again pulled his voluminous leather shirt over his heavy shoulders.

"I've done with the uniform, lass," He said gayly, chucking Cammie's cheek. "From this day I'm a sober-minded farmer with weighty responsibilities." The conceit so pleased him that he laughed again, so infectiously that Cammie and Jock joined him. "But merely for the look of things," he said, "I'll have the fine hat with the brave martial plume," and he winked at Cammie in high good humor.

The fine humor stayed with Crosbie during the bothersome delays of docking. He had worries and responsibilities and a sense of bewilderment that would have split the skull of a sensible man, but at the moment Crosbie was above such matters; he was busily planting twenty acres to corn, preparing his meadow land, selecting timber that would serve for a cabin large enough for three and possibly even more. He debated with himself about the comparative merits of brood stock, determined to take no more risks with blooded stock. He stood straight and firm in the bow of the boat, staring sightlessly at the densely wooded Ohio shore, seeing only a farm grow slowly, surely, from a wilderness plot, seeing a life without savor grow rich and meaningful.

He shook off his pleasant preoccupation when Blanchard leaped lithely ashore to moor the boat. He climbed sedately up to the dock, as became a sober-minded farmer, turned to raise his hat to Cammie in a crisp military salute, then headed for the hill where the log fort of Campus Martius loomed darkly against the morning sky.

CHAPTER SEVENTEEN

Duncan Crosbie sat at his ease in the Adjutant's office at Campus Martius, having been ushered in by a distracted sergeant of the guard who didn't know what to do with a high-ranking visitor who came calling before reveille, before any self-respecting Army officer could possibly be expected to be out of bed.

Crosbie helped himself to a fat loosely wrapped segar from a bundle on the Adjutant's desk. He lit it from a stinking tallow candle and sank back in his comfortable armchair that someone had painstakingly covered with the nappy hide of a woods buffalo. A most comfortable chair and a fine segar. Crosbie breathed in the oily smoke and sent it spurting in high looping rings toward the ceiling. It was quite all right to take a segar, if Old Wide Mouth was still Adjutant. Old Wide Mouth would want him to have a smoke, he told himself. And if someone else had the job now, why then Crosbie just wouldn't mention the segar at all. He grinned foolishly at the smoky ceiling, thinking of a future that seemed more sure and desirable than any he had ever outlined for himself.

The hobnailed boots of the guard sergeant clumped along the hallway, stopped at the entrance and Crosbie heard him speak to someone outside. Crosbie reached backward easily and pulled the door open. Outside in the hallway, Nicholas Blanchard stood uneasily.

Blanchard's eyes roamed around the empty room and his hesitation visibly diminished.

"Something's come up, Colonel," he said quickly. "I thought you'd want to hear about it before you saw the Adjutant."

"Eh?" Crosbie blew out a gush of segar smoke. "Well, what is it, Mr. Blanchard?"

Blanchard entered the room quickly. When his back shielded his hands from the guard sergeant, he pointed his thumb backwards, indicating to Crosbie that the problem called for privacy.

"Maybe you'd like to take a turn along the walls, Colonel," Blanchard said. "Always a pretty sight come daylight."

"All right," Crosbie said resignedly. Blanchard was being all-fired dramatic about something, but Crosbie knew him too well to doubt his judgment. He rose heavily, puffing mightily to keep his badly rolled segar going. He followed Blanchard up the narrow stairs and ladders to the log wall that commanded the pier of land where the Muskingum rolled sluggishly into the Ohio.

Blanchard led the way to a point where the nearest sentry was five yards away. Then he halted and faced Crosbie soberly. His face was running sweat from his swift chase after Crosbie. He coughed to clear the dust from his throat and took off his cocked hat, wiping his streaming forehead.

Crosbie clamped his teeth hard around his segar and glanced sharply at Blanchard. The young man's posture was tense and the lines of strain around his mouth were sharply clear. Crosbie watched as Blanchard thrust a hand inside his leather hunting shirt and brought out a folded parchment sheet.

"After we tied up the boats I had a talk with the Marquis," Blanchard said thickly. He coughed again as he offered the folded parchment to Crosbie. "He let me borrow this. I told him you were a mite curious about it."

"About what?" Crosbie asked through a wreath of smoke.

"It's his deed for the land he thinks he owns."

"*Thinks* he owns?"

"Yes, sir," Blanchard said heavily. "You figured these people bought land from the Ohio Company, didn't you? So did I. But no one actually said so, did they? I heard the Marquis talking so much about his big estate that I asked him to show me his deed." Blanchard flapped the parchment, making a thin brittle sound in the morning breeze.

Crosbie frowned in puzzlement. He shifted cautiously on the parapet so that he could more easily see Blanchard's face. "I don't..." he began.

"These deeds were issued by the Scioto Company, Colonel," Blanchard growled. "Somebody has swindled our people."

Blanchard gestured angrily with the parchment deed. "This says that *Monsieur le Marquis* François Etienne de la Foure D'Aucourt owns lands in the Scioto Company tract, all paid for. And it looks legal as a dollar bill. There's only one thing wrong with it, Colonel. The Scioto Company doesn't own any land."

"What!" Crosbie bit so hard on his segar that it came apart in his mouth. Angrily he spat the remnants oved the parapet.

"That's right, sir," Blanchard said tonelessly. "I know all about this because I helped General Putnam when the Ohio Company was formed."

Crosbie's face was cold and stiff. His lips barely moved as he spoke. "What has General Putnam or the Ohio Company to do with this... this..."

"Let me explain, sir," Blanchard said slowly. He rubbed his eyes with grimy fingers. "The Ohio Company of Associates was formed by General Putnam and the Reverend Doctor Manasseh Cutler and a lot of other people, mostly soldiers. After a lot of dickering they persuaded Congress to let them buy one-and-a-half million acres in the Northwest Territory for a dollar an acre, mostly for resale to veterans."

"Yes, yes," Crosbie said irritably. "I know all that. But what has..."

"Congress took a lot of persuading, sir," Blanchard said bleakly. "If it wasn't that Doctor Cutler made a deal, the Ohio Company would most likely never have been formed."

"A deal?" Crosbie growled. "What kind of a deal?"

"Doctor Cutler fixed it up with the Secretary of the Board of the Treasury. A man named Duer. Colonel Bill Duer. A Scot like you, sir, but not a Colonel like you and not a man, either. Well, Duer had a plan to start a land company of his own. That was the Scioto Company of Associates. Duer promised to deliver the votes in Congress for both companies provided Cutler and Old Put and the others went in with him on his company, sort of to make it look respectable. And that's what happened. Duer also arranged a Treasury loan for the Ohio Company. It was $143,000, just enough for the Ohio Company to make its first payment to the government for its land purchase. And Duer gave Cutler and Putnam and the others thirteen shares in the Scioto Company to whack up among themselves. They paid nothing for them."

Blanchard shook his head in a confused gesture. "I've forgotten some of this. Wasn't really my business, but I remember the important facts. Duer delivered the votes approving both companies at the same time. The Ohio Company got its purchase of one-and-a-half million acres and the Scioto Company got three-and-a-half million acres just due west of the Ohio Company tract. But the point is that the Ohio Company bought its land while the Scioto Company bought only the pre-emption rights, an option to buy the land later on. They don't own an inch of it."

Crosbie grunted. His fingers toyed with the jeweled dirk in his belt. "Exactly what does the Marquis's deed say?"

"Outright sale, sir. The Marquis himself read it to me. He's got this deed that says he owns land, owns it outright. Actually, all he could possibly own is an option to buy. He doesn't own anything worth paying money for. He's been swindled."

"Are you sure of your facts, Mr. Blanchard?" Crosbie demanded.

"Yes, sir. Maybe the Scioto Company bought its land since I last heard. But one thing I'm positive of: When the Scioto Company sold these deeds in Paris, they didn't own any land."

"But didn't the Marquis or anyone do any investigating?" the Colonel groaned. "Surely they didn't just…"

"As I get it, Colonel, this *Compagnie du Scioto* in Paris was a very solid-looking business. Mr. Joel Barlow was representing the company and be brought a lot of influential Frenchmen into it. Ohio was all the rage in France then, a very fashionable subject, and right after the mob stormed the Bastille last year, why the people who were afraid of the revolution bought these deeds and emigrated. I guess Barlow did a fine job of peddling. And that's not all. The Marquis told me who wrote that pamphlet, the one about the sugar and the cotton and the candles growing in the streets. It's been toned down some by the people who worked with Barlow, but it was written originally by the Reverend Doctor Manasseh Cutler."

"I know Doctor Cutler as a man of honor," Crosbie said coldly, glaring at Blanchard.

"I know nothing of his honor," Blanchard said in a mild tone. "I just know he's a sly old fox and if he wrote that lying pamphlet we saw, then I have no belief in his honor."

"Are you telling me," Crosbie asked angrily, "that Doctor Cutler and General Putnam are parties to this swindle?"

Blanchard shook his head. "I can't believe that, sir. Not about the General, anyway. I know when Colonel Duer approached them, they didn't like his scheme. But he was the man they had to have, so they agreed, but never willingly." Blanchard stared down at the deed in his hand. "Didn't General Putnam explain any of this to you, sir?"

Crosbie shook his head slowly. "No details," he said with some bitterness. "Only his statement that it was a matter affecting his personal honor."

"He must have known," Blanchard said in a musing tone. "Surely his agent in Alexandria saw these deeds. Old Put would know they were worthless."

"Possibly," Crosbie growled. "I'll not believe it until I hear him admit it to me."

"And," Blanchard asked softly, still not looking at Crosbie, "why did General Putnam send us to bring these people out here, knowing as he must have known, that their deeds were worthless?"

Crosbie turned slowly until he was facing out over the log parapet, feeling a deep distaste and revulsion at Blanchard's news. He had known and respected Putnam for a long time; it would be very hard to change his opinion of him now, but more than that, the very air around him seemed somehow polluted now. Crosbie's eagerness to free himself and his future from the French Army and the French attitudes was rotted in his instinctive disgust at the basic corruption of all organized activity in France. Until now, America had seemed singularly free of those ancient evils.

Blanchard cleared his throat softly and Crosbie closed his eyes wearily. "Most of our people have no more money," the Colonel said heavily. "I know that. There isn't any point in returning to Alexandria, even if we could. Captain Upjohn told me that General Putnam is building houses for our people downriver, so at least they'll have some place to stay." Crosbie paused. "But possibly you have another idea in mind, Mr. Blanchard?"

"Je ne sais pas," Blanchard said with a faint grin. "Not an idea, sir."

"Then we'll go on. But first I'll have a talk with General Putnam's adjutant here." Crosbie's face was grim and stern as he looked at Blanchard. "You'll say nothing of this to anyone. No one at all, Mr. Blanchard."

"I wouldn't want to, sir," Blanchard said in his soft Southern voice. "I'd hate to be the one to tell them."

"Yes," Crosbie swallowed heavily. "It is a frightful affair," he almost whispered. "You did well in discovering the facts,

Mr. Blanchard. All this explains one thing that has been bothering me."

"Yes, sir, I know," Blanchard said quietly. "Now we know why our people are in danger, why these attempts have been made to stop you. Nobody will ever be punished for this swindle unless our people make a formal claim for restitution. If they never get to Ohio, why the swindlers are fairly safe." Blanchard shivered as if a cold wind blew on his back.

Crosbie nodded grimly. "Let's get back," he said stiffly. "I want to see the adjutant."

Blanchard walked slowly a pace behind Crosbie, seeing the wide shoulders of the Colonel stiffen as Crosbie stamped along the parapet. The old man's head was up high and from that angle his jaw would look like the working end of a sledge, his eyes would be hard and bright, looking through you with an intensity that was almost frightening. Blanchard felt vaguely sorry for the Adjutant.

Crosbie pounded heavily along the wall toward the stairs, not noticing when the wary sentry ducked out of sight as he saw the Colonel's grim figure stalking toward him. Crosbie's eyes were fixed in a hot blind stare, seeing nothing but the red shadow of fury in his mind. His people were ruined, ruined beyond any power of his to repair. A madman had thrown them into a wilderness completely unprepared, almost without weapons, entirely without resources to make a life for themselves now that their land claims were valueless. For a long moment Crosbie could think of nothing else, but as he paused outside the Adjutant's office, he was suddenly conscious of the fact that he, too, was ruined, as completely as the poorest of the French, for he could never accept Putnam's payment for bringing the *émigrés* safely to Ohio, for those five hundred acres would be the profit from a successful swindle and by accepting them, Crosbie would make himself a party to that swindle. The Colonel's teeth clenched until his jaw ached. He turned the knob and threw the door open with a force that sent it crashing against the wall.

At the desk sat a round faced Major in worn blue regimentals, a man of forty with a head that was completely hairless. Even his eyebrows were gone and his face seemed to be something crafted of spongy pink leather. He frowned irritably as the door opened without warning and he rose angrily when it slammed against the wall.

"Damn you," he shouted in an odd gobbling voice, "Get the flaming hell out of here until I send for you!" The Major glared furiously at Crosbie, taking no warning from the Colonel's grim expression as he approached the desk. "Sergeant of the guard!" he roared.

"You address me as 'sir,'" Crosbie snapped. He pulled out an armchair and sat, resting his heavy hands on the desktop. "This is Lieutenant Blanchard," he said.

Blanchard wisely chose to stand. He held his face set in formal lines, not even smiling as the Adjutant growled incoherently. A man hauled from his bed at this ungodly hour had a right to some vile temper, but he picked a bad man when he lit into the Colonel, Blanchard thought.

The guard sergeant stamped into the room, brought his musket to the "present" and waited for orders. Some whisper of wisdom or caution restrained the Adjutant from telling him to eject his visitors.

"Who are these men, sergeant?" he snapped.

"Why," the sergeant hesitated briefly, "why, this here is Colonel Crosbie, Major, and this here ..."

"That's all," the Adjutant broke in. "Carry on."

The sergeant stamped out martially and closed the door behind him.

"Apologies, Colonel," the Major said stiffly. "I had no ..."

Crosbie shook his head in a curious gesture, rather like a dog shaking off water. "Never mind," he growled. "Where are my people supposed to go from here?"

"Your people?" The Major plucked at his fleshy underlip and slowly an understanding smile came to his face. "Ah, yes, the

Frenchies." He turned to a wall, pointing to a small map pinned on the rough timber. "Just about here, Colonel," he said. "Place that Major Burnham calls Fair Haven. Just downriver a piece."

"Fair Haven," Crosbie said with a snort. He shoved up heavily from his chair and went to the map. It wasn't the usual military chart of the Ohio country that he had so often used. This one seemed somehow old-fashioned in its draftsmanship, the ink was faded a pale brown and many of the place names were misspelled. Printed in the lower right hand corner was the familiar signature of George Washington. Crosbie almost smiled at the sight. Of course a land company that desperately needed Congressional assistance would make a point of using the map prepared by the President, even though Washington had then been a young surveyor with little skill and poor instruments. Dark lines marked the area purchased by the Ohio Company, the tract running from the seventh to the seventeenth range of townships. Immediately west was the Scioto Company's land, clearly marked in black ink. Fair Haven was an indentation made by the Adjutant's thumbnail. The site lay within the Scioto Company tract, opposite the mouth of the Kanawha River, only a few miles from the Ohio Company's *land*.

"That's in the Scioto tract, " Crosbie said sharply.

"Well ... uh, yes," the Major said clumsily.

"What's the meaning of that? Why should the Ohio Company transport people to the Scioto lands?" Crosbie's eyes held the Adjutant closely.

"Just ... uh, co-operation," the Major stumbled. "Matter of friendship, I believe."

"Whose friendship?" Crosbie demanded harshly.

The Major drew himself up as erect as his pudgy figure permitted. "It is not my custom to question General Putnam's orders, Colonel," he said with a note of true dignity that made Crosbie stare in surprise. "Nor, I respectfully suggest, is it your province to question those orders."

Crosbie turned slowly, gazing thoughtfully at Blanchard who stood on the other side of the room. Blanchard shrugged lightly. "Mighty fancy language, Colonel," he said easily. "I think he means you should mind your own business."

"You will remain silent," the Major said frigidly, "or I'll have you removed under guard, Lieutenant."

Blanchard grinned suddenly, a wide beaming flash of teeth that made him look years younger. "The Colonel forgot to mention, Major, that I've just been separated. I'm a civilian and I'll thank you to mind your tongue when you address me, sir."

Crosbie laughed shortly, a quick barking note that held little humor. "If you please, Mr. Blanchard," he said, "I should like your opinion on this matter."

"My pleasure, sir," Blanchard said with a low bow. "I've been standing here wondering what happened to Old Wide Mouth."

"Yes," Crosbie agreed. He turned to the Major. "How long have you held this post, sir?"

"Ten days," the Major answered stiffly. "I relieved Colonel Belcher temporarily when he left with General Putnam."

"Left for where?" Crosbie snapped.

"I ... I really don't know, sir," the Major said. His round face contorted oddly and for a wild moment Crosbie thought he might cry. "They didn't tell me."

Crosbie stared at the smudgy map blindly, not seeing the brave dark lines that marked the soaring ambitions of the great land companies, not reading the painfully misspelled lettering that President Washington had penned, seeing only the long stretch of perilous river yet to be traveled and the faint depression that indicated the raw new town of Fair Haven.

"What do you know about the Scioto Company, Major?" Crosbie asked bluntly.

"Not much, sir," he replied. "I don't even know much about the Ohio Company. I've only been detailed to this post for a month now."

"Do you have any information about the value of Scioto Company deeds?" Crosbie insisted. "Are they worthless?"

"Worthless?" the Major's round jaw dropped comically. "Worthless? Impossible. Utterly..."

Crosbie gestured angrily, cutting off the Major's sputtering voice.

"Did General Putnam leave any instructions for me?"

"No, except that you should proceed to Fair Haven as soon as possible. I got the idea that he planned to be back before you arrived. Of course, I might be mistaken, but..."

"Very well," Crosbie growled. He looked across the room to Blanchard and half smiled. "Well, Mr. Blanchard?"

Blanchard shrugged. "I'll nose around some, Colonel," he said thoughtfully. "Might pick up some gossip."

Crosbie nodded soberly and Blanchard left the room. The Adjutant seated himself pompously behind his desk and fiddled erratically with a quill pen that had a badly frayed nib.

"I'm very busy today, Colonel," he said with a trace of his former truculence. "I trust you'll..."

Crosbie looked down at him grimly, his mouth a hard line. "Tell Putnam," he said in a flat toneless voice. "Tell him I want to see him."

CHAPTER EIGHTEEN

Nicholas Blanchard sat well back under the shadows of the boat deck, holding his slim brown rifle across his knees. On the flimsy landing, Colonel Crosbie directed the loading of the last heavy sacks of grain which he had requisitioned from the Campus Martius storeroom. Crosbie had earlier sent his trunks and boxes of personal possessions down to the boat and seen them safely aboard. Neither Blanchard nor Crosbie had yet been able to find a way to tell the Marquis and his people about their worthless deeds. Blanchard had spent a profitless day with his friends of the Marietta garrison without learning anything useful and Crosbie had been a flaring, raging fury in his demands for additional supplies of food, seed and tools for the *émigrés*. He could himself do nothing about their land, but he could do much to insure that they would be able to live through the coming winter.

On the upper deck, a light silken ribbon rippled gently in the faint breeze. That would be Adrienne, Blanchard thought numbly. He had much to say to her, but somehow he didn't want to see her yet, not with the dragging weight of his knowledge weighing heavily on his mind. He could think of nothing else, not even Adrienne.

From the corner of his eye Blanchard could see the wide dark Ohio which rolled northward to a peak at Marietta and turned sharply southward from there, flowing between smooth rounded hills that appeared solidly black from the dense timber that covered them. Blanchard recalled with a rueful memory the near-mutiny that had developed when the Frenchmen had seen their heavily laden bateaux lead out from Pittsburgh in a northerly direction. They had no lack of faith in Colonel Crosbie, but the map clearly showed Marietta to be south of Pittsburgh, so a northern route could not possibly be correct. Blanchard almost chuckled at the thought. There would be other northern reaches along the Ohio before they came to Fair Haven, but now the French, always disinterested map-readers, understood that a river might occasionally turn back upon itself in its southerly progression.

Blanchard turned his attention to the dock where Crosbie incessantly toyed with his long murderous dirk as he shouted orders. He pulled the blade slowly up from its enameled scabbard, plunged it back again, sometimes took it out to test its cutting edge on his heavy thumb, never for long did his fingers leave its ornamented hilt, as though, Blanchard imagined, he hoped that any moment might bring him a target for its keen blade. And Crosbie's stern drawn face was the face of a man ready, even eager, for murder. Blanchard vaguely recalled a piece of poetic drama a school master had once read to him, a story full of dark and evil plottings, of the Scot who murdered his king, and Blanchard shuddered slightly as he remembered. For Duncan Crosbie today was a man who made Blanchard believe in the existence of Macbeth.

Crosbie drove his French assistants constantly and actually had them working almost as well as a trained waterfront crew, but they were not gay and laughing as they responded to his harsh commands. Blanchard noted none of the quick willingness that had been so much a part of the Frenchmen in past weeks, tired though they often were. In them now seemed to be a certain wariness of Crosbie's grimly restrained fury, an edgy reaction that was close to fear.

Crosbie came aboard with the last grain sack. He leaped from the dock to the gunwale of the command boat and beckoned for Blanchard.

"Spread your armed guard among the boats, Mr. Blanchard," he said. "All weapons loaded at all times."

"It's been done, Colonel," Blanchard said easily. "Where do you want me?"

Crosbie looked at Blanchard as though seeing him for the first time. He half smiled and touched him lightly on the shoulder. "Good," he said with evident relief. "You stay with me. I'm having a pirogue brought aboard. I'll want you to patrol the line of boats tonight."

"We're going on right away, Colonel?" Blanchard asked in surprise. "Without..."

Crosbie nodded slowly, his eyes bleak and cold. "We can do nothing more here, Mr. Blanchard. The great need now is to see our people settled before the weather turns. They have no idea what winter will mean to them in this country." Crosbie rubbed thoughtfully at the coppery bristles on, his chin. "Putnam," he said slowly, almost spitting the name, "Putnam can make his explanation to me at Fair Haven, if he has any explanation to make."

"Yes, sir," Blanchard said softly. "But what... what about..."

"Yes," Crosbie interrupted in a heavy tone, "I was forgetting, wasn't I? You're no longer on the active list, are you, Mr. Blanchard? So you can't be expected to accept my commands or to..."

Blanchard waved an irritated gesture. "I signed up for the duration, Colonel," he said gruffly, shaken for the moment from his rigidly maintained air of indolence and infinite leisure. "I had it in mind to ask what we were going to do about the Marquis."

Crosbie's fingers absently dragged the dirk from its scabbard. "Thank you, Mr. Blanchard," he said seriously and Blanchard knew he was not referring to the question he had asked. Crosbie flicked his blade at the solid wood on the upper deck. "I don't know," he said in an odd voice. "I just don't know." He stared with blank eyes at the polished steel of his dirk, jabbed it fiercely at the wood and then slowly worked it loose again. "I...I can't seem to think how to tell him," he almost whispered. "I've thought all day and...I have no words to tell him."

Blanchard eased the butt of his rifle to the desk and cupped his hands over the muzzle. He stared out dully at the slack, sluggish water of the broad river. "I...I reckon it wouldn't hurt if we waited till we got in," he said in a soothing voice. The Colonel looks like he's been jabbing that fancy sticker into himself all day, Blanchard thought and for one quick moment he saw something of the complex horror that was plaguing Crosbie, for a man cannot easily accept a respected friend in the role of swindler any more than he can stand by and see people he had come to like, even to love, be swindled of everything they owned by a pack of greedy land company rascals. No matter how it turned out, Crosbie stood to lose something and Duncan Crosbie was not a man to go easy on himself; he'd think that somewhere along the line he'd made an error, trusted the wrong man, given his binding oath to an evil cause. Blanchard looked at the Colonel with inarticulate sympathy clear in his expression, a vague sadness blocking his throat and keeping him from speech.

Crosbie drew a deep decisive breath and rammed his dirk into its scabbard. "Check the passengers, Mr. Blanchard," he said harshly. "We'll cast off when everyone's aboard."

Blanchard rested his rifle against the railing and jumped lightly up to the gunwhale. "Aye, aye, sir," he said in a feeble attempt at humor.

Crosbie walked toward the rear of his boat to inspect the hollowed log canoe which had been tied to a projecting timber at the stern. It was a small cranky craft which required clever handling to keep from capsizing, but it would be useful in patrolling the line of bateaux as they drifted downstream. There were long dank islands dotting the stretch he had yet to pass, and a few larger islands with sparse timber and thick rank marsh grass growing high enough to hide an ambushing regiment. At several spots where the river curved around, the current would bring his boats close inshore, too close for safety from rifle fire or even arrows for that matter. He or Blanchard would have to inspect every danger spot and if they were not satisfied, then the Frenchmen would have to man the sculls to keep far out in the river. There would be groans and complaints but the French would do as he ordered while they were complaining.

"Hail and farewell, was it not, Colonel?"

Crosbie pivoted abruptly, almost spasmodically, as though he were controlled by a guilty impulse to run. The Marquis D'Aucourt sauntered toward him, dressed once again as a man of fashion. His slippers were a grained red leather with red heels that had small brilliants set in the welt. His coat was a bright cerise ornamented with black braid and his silk small-clothes were a somber black relieved only by winking brilliants on his waistcoat buttons, his long dangling watch fob, his slim knee buckles. His black hat sported a cerise feather which curled below the brim elegantly and he had given up his snuff colored traveling wig for a neat and tightly curled white wig that had showered a faint softing of powder across his cerise shoulders. The Marquis planted his cane firmly, moved his feet into position and swept off his hat in an enormously complicated salute that had the cerise feathers sweeping the dust from a wide expanse of the grimy boat deck.

"It is always an unhappiness to leave old comrades in arms, I have found," the Marquis said politely. "I trust that our speedy departure does not indicate any lack of... of..." The Marquis flourished an eloquent hand as he fumbled for a word.

"Most pleasant," Crosbie broke in brusquely. "However the people I know best were away from the fort, so it was not a social matter."

"A pity," the Marquis said vaguely. He looked out at the high silhouette of Campus Martius. "A strange place," he said quietly. "I wonder what our gracious Marie Antoinette would say if she could see the wilderness settlement to which she has lent her name?"

"A genuine *Petit Trianon*," Crosbie said dryly. "She would admire and shriek with pleasure," he added firmly, "and leave ten minutes later."

The Marquis laughed appreciatively. *"Je suis de votre avis,"* he murmured. He replaced his plumed hat and leaned languidly on his long ebony stick. "I walked through the streets for a moment," he said casually. "From the comments I could understand I gathered that I was not appropriately attired."

"Nothing wrong, sir, but probably such fine clothes are a rare sight in Marietta," Crosbie said soberly, fighting to keep a straight face. "It's the capital of the Northwest Territory, but Marietta still isn't much more than a tomahawk settlement." And a swindler's nest, he thought bitterly.

"So," the Marquis said mildly. He rubbed the gnarled gold tip of his cane against his powdered cheek in a thoughtful gesture. "So much I have to learn," he said almost wistfully. "I trust, Colonel Crosbie, that your duties will not take you from us too soon?"

"I have no further duties," Crosbie said flatly. "I haven't yet decided what to do in the immediate future." And that, he thought sourly, is the truest statement I've ever made.

"Splendid," the Marquis cried with genuine enthusiasm. "I look forward to the opportunity to entertain you in my own house on my new estate."

"I…" Crosbie coughed heavily. "I think that General Putnam's men are building a sort of…town for all of you. All fairly small cabins, I'm afraid, and close together."

"Of course, of course," the Marquis said with a genial expression. "One understands that the first requirement is adequate defense. You have well instructed us, Colonel. But in the near future surely, one may build a suitable house where one's own family may…"

"Yes," Crosbie said, choking again. "Yes, most certainly," he muttered. "If you'll excuse me now, sir," he said in a sudden torrent of words, "I must see to...the boats should cast off and..." Crosbie lurched past the Marquis quickly and almost ran to the bow of the boat.

The pilot straddled the steering sweep casually and spat a resounding splash of tobacco into the quiet water. "Mighty sour man, the Colonel," he said calmly, shifting his chew slightly while he kept his pale eyes fixed blandly at nothing.

The Marquis drew himself haughtily erect before he remembered that he was now a member of a wilderness society where such men as boatsmen might speak freely to a Marquis. He forced a thin smile and nodded amiably. "He has many responsibilities, my friend," he said lightly.

"Cast off!" Crosbie's bullheavy voice roared in the still afternoon and a scurry of action sent men toward the thick mooring lines.

"Still ain't no call for a man to be all that sour," the pilot said in a low tone. He shoved the sweep full over so that the current would carry the boat out into the stream. "Ain't friendly."

"No," the Marquis said as he walked away. Crosbie was not at all a friendly man of late, not that he had ever been effusive, but he had never before been so preoccupied, so...elusive. The Marquis went to stand beside Crosbie in the broad curving bow of the boat, hopeful of a halt in Crosbie's constant activity that would give him an excuse to talk more about the nature of the soil, the climate, the aboriginal savages of the Marquis's new estates in the Ohio country.

CHAPTER NINETEEN

Crosbie leaned far out beyond the gunwale of the boat, peering tensely into the darkness, trying to get his eyes low toward the water so that he might see a moving silhouette against the dark river. On both sides steep wooded escarpments seemed to overhang the long silent line of boats. There was no distracting music tonight: the Frenchmen were weary from the labor Crosbie had put them to during the day and they needed to rest for their endless tours of guard duty which the Colonel demanded. Guard duty on board a boat drifting easily along a wide slow river. What foolishness this mad Scot is capable of, and how vehemently he insists, with what cold murderous fire his eyes glare when one offers the mildest sort of objection! On his trips of inspection, Blanchard had not once found a boat unguarded, had never once come within yards of any boat without being challenged promptly and hearing the double snick of a rifle hammer lifting to full cock whenever he delayed an identification. The French complained, muttered incessantly over their cups of coffee and mugs of brandy, but they stayed awake rather than bring Crosbie's wrath on their luckless heads.

Far in the distance Crosbie caught a brief phosphorescent flash of dripping water. A carelessly lifted paddle, he thought. Blanchard knows better than to stir up sparkles like that; it must be de Flaville who lifted his paddle, even though Crosbie had devoted an hour to teaching the young Frenchman how to drive the clumsy pirogue forward with a circular motion of the paddle, never lifting it nor pulling so hard that the water rippled or gurgled under the blade. An Indian trick, but one worth knowing if you wanted to move silently on the river at night. The paddle dripped its flickering spray again and Crosbie cursed softly.

He whistled faintly once against the water and heard an answering whistle from Blanchard before he raised up to the gunwale.

The pirogue came alongside quietly and Blanchard jumped to the bow of the bateau, swinging himself lithely inboard with one hand, carrying his rifle cradled easily in the crook of his left arm.

"Clear for about six miles, Colonel," he said softly with his mouth against Crosbie's ear. "Then we hit a bend and a long string of little islands. The channel goes to the right and it's not very wide right there. And we didn't find anything on any of the islands."

"And the Ohio side?" Crosbie asked.

"Charlie prowled around for an hour. Didn't stir up anything."

"De Flaville!" Crosbie snorted. "Why didn't you…"

"Hell, he can see," Blanchard said wearily. "And you know damned well no Indian would let a man with hair like Charlie's get by him, no matter what kind of a scheme was planned."

"All right," Crosbie said stiffly. "I'll want you there when we go by. Have de Flaville come aboard and both of you get something to drink before you go out again." Crosbie's heavy hand rested on Blanchard's shoulder. "Looks cold on the water," he said.

"Misty," Blanchard said, warming to the sympathetic tone in Crosbie's voice. "There's a wind kicking up around the bend. Makes waves that might give the steersmen some trouble. Maybe I better warn them."

"Rest first," Crosbie said. "There's time enough."

Blanchard reached over the side and tapped the pirogue with his knuckles. A moment later, de Flaville scrambled onto the boat and tied the pirogue to the gunwale.

"A long miserable night," he said pleasantly. "Have we time for a drink, Colonel, before we canoe again?"

"Madame Carel has some coffee on the stove," Crosbie said stiffly. "And take more care with your paddling or you'll not live to canoe for long."

"To hear is to obey," de Flaville said lightly as he ducked under the deck into the covered portion where Cammie tended the fire, and Lucie sat talking to her. Lucie looked up when de Flaville came in and the soft murmur of her voice ceased. The firelight glinted on her blonde hair and it was kinder to the pallor of her face than the harsher light of day. Absently Crosbie had noted the increasing degree of that pallor and the signs of strain etching themselves into the girl's face in deep lines and shadows. She had always been quiet and unobtrusive but for the past few days she had hardly seemed with them at all.

He put the irrelevant thoughts about the girl out of his mind and turned again to Blanchard. "Keep an eye on de Flaville, Mr. Blanchard," Crosbie said tightly. "I could see the flash of his paddle half a mile away."

"Right," Blanchard muttered. "I'll put him in front next time." He stretched himself to his full length on the damp boards of the boat and half smothered a wide yawn. "That's a mighty small canoe for a man my size," he complained mildly. "Seems like it shrinks in the water."

Crosbie lowered himself to the deck stiffly, feeling a stitch of pain in his chest. The wreaths of mist rose from the still river like steam and the boards of the boat deck were running with moisture. Every vagrant breeze seemed doubly cold as it drove through the night. Crosbie leaned against the gunwale, moving cautiously. He and Blanchard let a companionable silence stretch out without either of them feeling a need for casual speech.

"Rain before morning," Blanchard said at length. "Clouds building up pretty high in the west."

Crosbie expelled his breath slowly in a sound suspiciously like a sigh.

Shouldn't have said that, Blanchard thought suddenly. No point in worrying about our folks getting wet. That's mild compared to what might happen to them and the Colonel's fixing to worry about the rain now, on top of everything else.

He saw Crosbie's face taut and gray with fatigue and realized that his minor complaints sounded ridiculous compared to the Colonel's problems. He searched his mind for a subject that might distract the Colonel.

"Used to be an old man back in Albemarle County," he said with a soft chuckle. "Fellow had a bullet in his leg, he said. Claimed he could tell when rain was coming. Bullet used to make his leg ache if the weather turned wet. Long time afterward I found out he didn't have no more bullet in him than I did. Just had a twisted leg from where a mule kicked him one time when he was drunk. But that old fellow always knew when it was going to rain. I never could figure it out." Blanchard's voice was low and quiet and somehow mournful as voices often are late at night when memories flood in with the mist. "Mightly pretty country, Albemarle County," he murmured. "Night like this puts me in mind of it. But I miss the salt smell. Got mist a lot back home but you could always smell the salt mixed up with it. And the seaweed and the dead fish," he added with a faint chuckle. "But you get used to the salty way everything smells. Sometimes, when I'm thinking about it, all I can remember is the way everything is salty when the wind blows off the sea."

"Aye," Crosbie said heavily, thinking with no pleasure of the long dreary procession of provincial French houses that had been his boyhood homes. Nothing worth the bother of remembering in any of them. "Do you plan to return, Mr. Blanchard?"

"Not me," Blanchard said quickly thinking it was only a little time ago that Benny Upjohn had asked him the same question; only a little time since he had held Adrienne in his arms and thought wild thoughts about taking her home to the Tidewater country, in spite of his three brothers, in spite of a single plantation split up four ways... "No," he said soberly. "No, I won't be going home. But someday..." he paused, thinking about that day and how little it might mean without Adrienne. Damn the girl, anyway! What right did she have, confusing his life like this? "Someday I plan on having me a place bigger and fancier than my daddy ever had. Someday I'll..."

"I had forgotten," Crosbie said politely. "You mentioned your plans before. New Orleans, Wilkinson and a quick fortune, wasn't it?"

"The scoundrel Wilkinson," Blanchard laughed wryly.

"I may have said that," Crosbie admitted heavily. "I have reason now to doubt my judgment of men."

"Didn't mean that, Colonel," Blanchard said, sitting up beside Crosbie. "Wilkinson's a right scoundrelly fellow and no mistake. He was mixed up in that business of trying to get Kentucky County to secede from Virginia and then when the Spanish raised a stink about it, why he made them buy him off. Now he's got trading rights with the Dagoes and he'll make a fortune if he doesn't get killed first. No doubt about Wilkinson," Blanchard said honestly. "But I do reckon Old Put deserves a chance to explain himself."

"He'll get it," Crosbie said grimly. "I can assure you of that. He'll get his chance."

And he'll be lucky if Crosbie doesn't slip that fancy dirk down his throat and rip him inside out, Blanchard thought. I sure wouldn't like to be Old Put with a man like Crosbie after me.

"What about you, Colonel?" Blanchard asked after a long silent moment. "Where will you go from here?"

Crosbie sat unmoving, saying nothing and Blanchard wondered whether he had heard the question. Finally Crosbie cleared his throat roughly.

"Can't leave these people in a position like this," he said in a bleak tone.

"No," Blanchard agreed quickly. "Reckon you can't." He rose to his feet and picked up his rifle, inspecting carefully the deer hide wrapping that protected the pan. "If you're going to stay around for a while," he said in an off-hand voice, "why I reckon I might as well stick around, too."

Neither of them needed to speculate on the problem. The names of Cammie and Adrienne were unspoken but the two women were more forceful arguments for remaining with the *émigrés* than Crosbie's sense of responsibility or Blanchard's lack of definite direction.

"Thought you might plan to," Crosbie said dryly.

"Well…uh…" Blanchard hesitated, cursing his fumbling tongue. "Guess I'd better get Charlie away from that fire and head downriver. You'll be at the bend pretty soon."

Blanchard moved quickly, relieved at the chance to escape from Crosbie for the moment. He tapped de Flaville's arm, untied the pirogue and climbed down into it, holding the light log canoe against the heavy bateau until de Flaville took his seat on the forward thwart.

Crosbie watched the frail dugout vanish upstream. Blanchard would inspect the guards on each boat and warn them of the approaching bend with its chain of marshy islands, before he headed down again to patrol the narrow water through which the line of boats would have to maneuver. Young Blanchard was probably the most dependable junior officer Crosbie had ever known, particularly when the situation required a degree of initiative and inventiveness. Then something wild and undisciplined in Blanchard bubbled to the surface and he found his solution in a cheerful casual easiness that sometimes disturbed Crosbie. But there was much to be said for the American attitude, Crosbie thought, even though it often put sound military procedure at a serious disadvantage.

Probably it was the mental approach one needed to face the wilderness for a life-time without growing frightened or bitter or cruel. If ever a man was adequately equipped for such a life, it was Nicholas Blanchard. Crosbie turned slowly and looked toward the tow-cloth curtain that shielded a portion of the boat from his view. Behind there somewhere, Mademoiselle Adrienne was lying on a makeshift bed, trying to sleep, maybe thinking about Blanchard. For a time there, Crosbie remembered, she seemed to regard young Blanchard with real favor, though ever since Turtle Creek she'd been avoiding him in a manner so ostentatious it could not be overlooked. Some sort of quarrel, no doubt. That probably accounted for Blanchard's harried attitude the past few days. Near Adrienne would be Edmond de la Foure and the Marquis. Gentlemen who had run from impending revolution to build new lives in a wild untouched country, new lives on the wide estates purchased from the smooth-talking Mr. Joel Barlow in Paris. Crosbie's fingers clenched tightly on the gunwale of the boat. The first thing in the morning, he promised himself, or right after breakfast, anyway, he would take the Marquis aside and try to explain exactly what he knew about the Scioto Company deeds. And, he thought bitterly, exactly what he suspected about his old friend General Putnam and the greedy crew who made up the Ohio Company of Associates.

It was sometime later that he recalled his other problem, the fact that one of these people he was protecting so tenderly from harsh reality was a traitor, a traitor and a murderer.

During the next hour Crosbie twice inspected the five guards who protected his boat. He checked the priming powder of his rifle, gulped a cup of steaming coffee from Cammie's supply and went out to patrol the deck nervously in the dark. None of the guards spoke to him, he noted absently. Usually the voluble French couldn't be restrained from their constant chatter, but tonight for some reason, they had little to say. Crosbie didn't bother speculating about their quietness. He kept his eyes forward, trying to discern the first sign of the approaching bend.

The pilot edged slowly toward the right bank, anticipating the turn, knowing from long experience where the best channel lay between the islands. While they were still some yards from the first low-lying marshy island, the water developed a choppy character that made the heavy boat bob like an errant cork. Crosbie heard the steersman swear luridly as he fought the huge sweep, struggling to keep it deep in the water so he could control the boat. But despite the wicked swooping motion, the boat maintained its course smoothly along the bank.

Crosbie's glance constantly scanned the shores ahead, wary of ambush in this narrow defile. On the right bank the high dense foliage of the trees almost swept across the boat. Crosbie brought back the hammer of his rifle, smoothing out the motion so there was no sound. He waited tensely as the boat silently slid past the river bank.

Crosbie's bateau neared the second island, approaching the acute bend of the river. The danger point was behind him, he thought. Surely if attack were coming, it would come from that narrow stretch back there. Crosbie walked quickly back along the right side of the boat, watching as the second bateau moved toward the overhanging trees and the narrow channel.

Then a rifle cracked spitefully from the Ohio side. Crosbie jumped slightly as it fired, thinking for a moment he had pressed his own trigger.

Just the one shot, no more. A decoy, Crosbie thought abruptly. Maybe they can't see us against the water.

"Hold your fire!" he bellowed lustily. "Hold your fire!" At least he wouldn't give them a target to shoot at.

"Colonel!" That was Blanchard's voice shouting. "Colonel! Take the left channel! The left channel!"

On the riverbank twigs snapped loudly as someone ran desperately, crashing through the underbrush toward the river.

Crosbie heard a splash, a wild thrashing in the water and then silence.

"Left!" he roared to the boats behind. "Take the left channel!" He shoved the steering sweep of his boat so that its bow pointed between the islands, toward the shallower channel on the far side of the river. "Hold it there," he snapped.

A flailing paddle drove the small pirogue quickly under the stern of Crosbie's boat. When the line was thrown aboard, Crosbie snatched it quickly, looped it around a timber and reached down to help Blanchard aboard. He pulled heavily and brought de Flaville swinging up to the deck in a long swooping motion. De Flaville's rifle clattered to the deck from the force of Crosbie's assistance. The sound was very loud in the quiet night. It brought Cammie and Lucie running from the warm area beneath the shelter. They stood watching though neither spoke.

"Where's Blanchard?" Crosbie demanded quickly of de Flaville. He looked over the gunwale at the pirogue. No one. No one at all. "Where's Blanchard?" he snarled.

"Colonel," de Flaville said placatingly. "Colonel, I do not know. There was shooting and I …"

Crosbie's hand was tight around the steering sweep and he almost had it cramped hard when he stopped abruptly. Twenty people were aboard his boat and hundreds more in the boats behind him, all of them trusting to his leadership. He fought against accepting what he knew had to be accepted. Even for Blanchard he could not risk an attempt at maneuvering in an unknown channel at night. Slowly, he relinquished the sweep to the pilot and stood stiffly, staring blindly out at the dark roiled water.

"Colonel," de Flaville said hesitantly. "Colonel, I am sure that …"

Crosbie didn't turn his head. He didn't look at de Flaville but his flat hard hand swept wide through the air, smacking against de Flaville's face like a pistol shot. The young Frenchman reeled back to the upper deck support and barely kept himself from falling by a wild clutch at the timber.

Lucie made a small sound and started forward. Cammie caught her arm and held her.

De Flaville wiped a hand at his mouth, stared at the thin ribbon of blood on his knuckles. *"Cochon,"* he spat viciously, *"Espèce de cochon!"* His smooth young face was contorted furiously and the heavy mark of Crosbie's hand made an angry welt against his cheek. De Flaville snatched a long hunting knife from his belt and dove toward Crosbie, holding the knife low as he flung himself at the Colonel's back.

The pilot reached forward easily, raised one foot and let de Flaville run wildly against the sole of his boot. Then the pilot shoved him back with a strenuous push.

"You don't want to do that, yonker," he said agreeably. "The Colonel's a mean man. He'd as soon kill you as not. You just rest easy there for a minute and cool off." He spat a gob bet of tobacco juice over the gunwale, but he kept his eyes fixed carefully on the Frenchman.

Crosbie turned very deliberately, looked solemnly at de Flaville, saw the young Frenchman leaning back against the upper deck support with the long heavy blade in his hand. In the darkness, de Flaville could see little, but he was sure then that Crosbie was smiling, an evil deadly smile, as he slowly lifted his jeweled dirk from its scabbard. It would be a fair fight, de Flaville knew, and it would be a fight he had sought. But in that moment, while he was whole, breathing deeply and vitally alive, while he still held a longer, heavier weapon, he saw death before him. The huge Scot moved toward him, the slim blade of the dirk held slightly forward. De Flaville glanced desperately at the pilot, saw him staring blandly over the top of the deck at the boiling water ahead. And when he looked at Crosbie, the Colonel was closer still, with the dark steel blade moving forward and back rhythmically like the tongue of a thirsty snake. De Flaville raised his own knife gradually, fighting against a panic that welled within his throat.

But something halted the Colonel's inexorable progress. Lucie shook off Cammie's restraining hand and darted forward. She caught Crosbie's arm with both hands.

"Colonel," she gasped. Crosbie paused, looking down at her but only half seeing her in his blind rage.

"Monsieur Blanchard, he has not returned?"

Crosbie swallowed to relax the hard knot of tension in his throat. "No," he said with harsh fury. "No."

The girl clung to his arm. He could feel the tremor of her small hands and he could see the taut whiteness of her face as she looked from him to de Flaville and back again.

"You will go back for him?" she pleaded. "You will search?"

He stared down at her in silence. Why was she so concerned for Blanchard? He let wild suspicions race free in his mind for just a moment. Could it be Blanchard who was... how had Cammie put it? "The man Lucie loves." The man she had braved a wilderness journey in her condition to be with? But the thoughts were brief. They were clearly impossible, of course. Only at such a moment of confusion and rage could he have suspected their possibility.

But he had no answer for Lucie. She read that into his bleak silence.

"You cannot leave him like this!" she cried. "He may be hurt. He must have help."

Still no answer. She beat on Crosbie's arm with small clenched fists. "It is a coward's decision. You cannot do it. He is your friend, Colonel. Do you think he would leave you like this?"

She whirled to face de Flaville, still half crouched at the rail of the boat, frozen in the sudden wild tension that gripped them all. "Or you, Charles. He has been your friend, too. Yours, Edmond's, the Marquis's. A friend and protector to all of us. How can we all betray him? Has there not already been enough... too much...betrayal?" From the darkness there was a half-stifled gasp. Lucie's voice broke and was abruptly silent.

Her unexpected outburst had at least the effect of sobering Crosbie's murderous rage. "Mademoiselle," he said as gently as he could, aware that the narrow space on front of the shelter was crowded now. He could see the Marquis, Edmond de la Foure, even Adrienne, wrapped in a long dark cloak, her hair a cloud of black over her shoulders and around her startled face. "Mademoiselle, we cannot go back. We cannot turn here and even if we could there is great danger in doing so. Would you have us endanger the lives of three hundred people on the chance of saving one? Mr. Blanchard would not have it so, himself."

He did not think she really heard him. Her eyes were wide and staring in her white face. It was as if some long controlled tension had snapped abruptly within the girl, as if something had touched off a store of hidden fears and resentments and she no longer knew what she was doing, or why.

Adrienne moved forward through the crowd and put her arms around Lucie's shoulders. They trembled under her touch. Adrienne started to remove the cloak from her own shoulders, then evidently remembered the inadequate state of her night-robe and turned to call softly to her cousin.

"Edmond, bring me your cloak, please. I..."

At the sound of her voice, Lucie started, looked wildly from Adrienne to the Marquis's son, then to Crosbie and on to the crouching figure of de Flaville. The dark gleam of the water behind him seemed to catch and hold her gaze. Without a word, she tore herself from Adrienne's light embrace, flew across the deck and grasped the low rail of the boat. There she hesitated only a second, as if she knew now exactly what she had to do. Both hands seized the rail, there was a flurry of wide pale skirts against the dark water and Lucie was gone.

Immediately the frozen group on deck exploded into action. Crosbie cursed furiously and ran for the rail. Adrienne screamed and followed with de la Foure at her heels. But it was de Flaville whose actions were quickest and most decisive. Closer to the rail than any of the others, he seized the rough wood, vaulted over it and struck the water in a clean dive. He came up a few yards from the boat, let his heavy knife drop in the water, shook his head to clear his vision, and struck out for the spot where Lucie had disappeared.

It was too dark for those on board to follow his progress clearly. A moment passed in silence. Another. Then Adrienne cried out and as she did, de Flaville reappeared. In three deep thrusts, he swam to the side of the slowly drifting boat. There were willing hands to relieve him of the burden he was supporting. Lucie was unconscious, her long pale hair streamed over Crosbie's arm as he carried her toward the shelter, where already Cammie was building up the fire and bringing out blankets. She murmured soothing, useless words that Lucie could not hear. Adrienne rushed to help her with blankets and towels. Under their ministering hands, Lucie stirred, moaned and then opened her eyes. She looked up at the anxious faces surrounding her. Crosbie, Adrienne, Cammie, Edmond, de Flaville, still dripping from his plunge into the river. She looked but her eyes were blank and unseeing. Her fingers plucked at the blankets Cammie had wrapped around her and her eyes moved from one face to another.

"... safe?" she whispered.

"You are safe," Commie soothed.

Lucie tried to shake her head. She was still thinking of Blanchard, Crosbie realized with a shock. No one spoke. After a moment Lucie whispered again.

"So much betrayal," she murmured. "So much wrong..." she paused again, almost as if she waited for someone else to speak. "There must be an end." The sound of her breathing was slow and heavy. No one else said a word. Her eyes closed and for a moment there was only silence. But suddenly they opened again. When she spoke this time, her voice was clear and strong. "I know," she said firmly as if she were saying something she had waited a long time to say. "Since the crossing at Turtle Creek I have known that I must tell you ..." she bit her lip and a spasm of pain twisted her mouth as she stared up at Crosbie's startled, worried face. The pain deepened, she gasped and turned to Cammie like a child instinctively recognizing the source of help and reassurance.

"She is delirious," Cammie said swiftly. "Please ..." her eyes found Crosbie's pleadingly. "Please leave me alone with her. I am afraid there may be injuries. I must get her out of these wet clothes."

Crosbie nodded wordlessly. With a wide gesture he ordered everyone out of the shelter. Adrienne begged to stay and he permitted it on Cammie's agreement. He herded the others forward in the boat and returned to his post beside the steersman. Only then did he realize that he had held his *skene-dhu* tightly gripped in his hand all that time. He sheathed it carefully.

"Ahoy there," a voice called softly. "On the boat. Ahoy."

Crosbie whirled on the ball of his foot, crouching automatically as though he feared a new enemy might be attacking him from the rear.

Over the low gunwale a thin finger of steel slid quietly, then raised up once to tap against the wood. A rifle barrel, Crosbie thought vacantly, stupidly. A rifle barrel come up out of the river.

"Ahoy. Give me a hand, somebody."

Blanchard! Crosbie leaped for the gunwale, snatching eagerly for the rifle barrel protruding above the rail. He heaved desperately, putting the weight of his solid shoulders behind the effort. Nicholas Blanchard came up lightly from the water like a deeply hooked trout, dripping water and gasping for air.

"Wet in there," he said foolishly. He leaned against Crosbie as he struggled to catch his breath. "Never thought ... these *boats* ... could drift so ... fast," *he* gasped "Ever ... ever try swimming ... with a rifle ... in one hand ... Colonel?" He grinned at Crosbie's tense face. "Don't try it," he said.

"What happened?" Crosbie snapped. "Did you fire?"

Blanchard nodded. He shook his head briskly and rubbed his hands against his hair to scrape off the water. He looked forward, saw de Flaville's white drawn face staring at him. "Hi, Charlie," he said lightly. "Wondered if you'd get back." His eyes widened as he looked at de Flaville. "You swim back, too?"

"Did you send him back?" Crosbie growled.

"Well, no," Blanchard said, "but he'd have been a fool to stick around after I fired."

"Why did you shoot?"

"Never did like Injuns," Blanchard grinned. "Saw me a big greasy buck lying down behind a log right at the edge of the water, so I snapped a shot at him for luck." Blanchard's face lost its pleasant expression. "Fellow had a lot of friends with him. I didn't stop to count them, but the woods were full of them."

Crosbie flicked a bleak glance at de Flaville. "And this young man patrolled that stretch an hour earlier?" he asked grimly. "And then later he ran away without waiting to help you?" Crosbie's voice was low and controlled, but de Flaville felt the same creeping coldness sweep over him that he had experienced when Crosbie had held his dirk blade toward his throat.

"Hell, Colonel, those rascals had a good hour to get into position after Charlie checked the bank. And he wasn't the only one who didn't wait. I didn't do any daisy-picking myself. Soon as I shot, I went right into the water. I shouted to you and then I ducked under. Tried to swim under water and that rifle damned near drowned me. But I made it to one of the boats and hung on for a while. I been moving up a boat at a time for some little while now. And a nasty night for a swim if I ever saw one."

Crosbie nodded dourly without looking at Blanchard. His eyes remained tightly on de Flaville, waiting.

"Colonel," de Flaville said eagerly, "I swear…"

"Sure, sure," Blanchard broke in. "Never mind, Charlie. Colonel, how about a tot of grog for the swimmers?"

"Yes," said Crosbie ambiguously.

Blanchard quickly pushed de Flaville ahead of him toward the covered deck. The Colonel was some peeved with Charlie right now and this was no time for anyone to start trading words with Crosbie. A man could wind up dead that way.

Crosbie stopped them, remembering what had happened. He told Blanchard about Lucie and watched his lieutenant's eyes widen in amazement.

"She's ... she's all right?" Blanchard asked.

Crosbie nodded. "She will be, I think," he said curtly, and went himself to fetch the rum, hot coffee and dry clothes.

Half an hour later, Crosbie rested both elbows on the stern rail of the boat. Behind him came the long silent line of bateaux creeping across the river. The bend was behind them now and smoother water carried them easily downstream. Crosbie closed his eyes briefly.

"That Blanchard fellow," the pilot said easily, "he's some goer, ain't he? Regular half horse, half alligator."

"Yes," said Crosbie hoarsely. And all soldier, he said to himself. He couldn't say as much for that young Frenchman, he thought, despite his earlier impression of his willingness and ambition. But it was true he'd gone overboard after that girl mighty fast and with no regard for his own safety. That was something in his favor. And it was good to see how Blanchard protected him from Crosbie's anger. A fine soldier, he repeated softly, and was surprised at the depth of relief he felt at Blanchard's safe return from the river.

He rested, too tired even to think clearly. Except to be grateful that, for, the moment at any rate, all was well. But gradually, after a little time, he became aware of sounds coming from the deck shelter where the fire still burned and Cammie still watched over Lucie. The sounds came at intervals, rising and falling, choked and agonized. They were human sounds, and yet somehow not human.

Crosbie got to his feet and moved quietly toward the shelter, fear growing in his mind that he had spoken too soon about all being well with his people. Cammie looked up at him from the blanket-swathed figure that was Lucie, and Cammie's face told him that his fear was well founded. She rose swiftly and came to meet him.

"Lucie..." he asked carefully.

Cammie nodded. "She is ... oh, Dooncahn, I am afraid!"

He had never known Cammie to be truly afraid before.

"The baby?" he asked.

"She ... injured herself, somehow, in her fall. She is in pain, great pain. There is hemorrhaging ..." Cammie's eyes stared up at Crosbie, wide and darkly shadowed with despair. "There is so little I can do, Dooncahn," she said, "so very little." She paused and he saw her fingers tighten on a fold of her shirt as Lucie moaned again. "Only wait," Cammie said. "And pray."

He waited with her, and if he did not actually pray, his thoughts were close enough to it. Except for their confused, incoherent quality. Pity for Lucie was somehow mixed up with pity for all these foolish unlikely settlers of a wild new country. Settlers of land they did not even own. Crosbie thought about their laughter, their foolhardy disregard for discomfort and even danger. He remembered great bravery, too; Cammie's and Jock's, Adrienne's when she came to his rescue with a tiny, almost useless weapon against armed and desperate men. Even poor Lucie, for there was bravery in what she had done, too, though it was hard to understand her reasoning. But he knew now that he had to get them through safely to that new world they wanted so badly. Even Lucie, if that was possible...

But it was not. All through the long dark hours of the night her slow, heavy breathing went on. The agonized moaning stopped and Cammie said the girl was unconscious. She said it with a catch in her voice, but with something that sounded almost grateful, too. Lucie was no longer suffering. Just before dawn the slow breathing got slower still, more labored. When the first gray light of morning began to trace the banks of the wide river, the breathing stopped.

Crosbie stirred, easing his cramped muscles. He had sat without moving for hours. Only now did he feel the discomfort. He watched incredulously as Cammie drew a fold of blanket across the still face. It could not have happened, he told himself. Not so quickly, so completely without warning, so needlessly cruel. He swallowed and tried to say something of that to Cammie.

Cammie reached to touch his hand lightly, as if she were the one to do the comforting. Her face was pale and drawn in the gray light. She spoke very softly.

"She did not want to live, Dooncahn. Not enough to fight for life. I do not know why that was so, but I know that it was. It was caused by something that happened to her in the past few days. That was when she changed. Until then she had confidence enough to hide whatever concerns she carried with her, she thought the future was bright and fine enough to wipe away the past, to give her a new life ..." There was something beneath the softness of Cammie's voice, something with the hard touch of steel and something Crosbie knew she wanted him to understand. And he remembered Lucie saying, as she studied the faces around her: "'so much betrayal. So much wrong...'" And later, as though she had come to some sort of decision: "'I know, since the crossing at Turtle Creek I have known I must tell you ...'"

Something stirred slowly in Crosbie's tired mind. Knowledge, betrayal, the wild outburst that had led to Lucie's death. He could guess what it was the girl felt she must tell him. She meant to tell him who their traitor was. Their traitor and the murderer of Daniel Fiske. And she must by then have known it to be the man she loved.

He had thought once, when he first heard of Lucie's condition and the secrecy surrounding it, that a man who could be responsible for such a thing would be a man you could not trust.

He did not know then how right he was. Lucie had trusted that man and Lucie had paid with her heart, her honor, her hope of a new world. At the end she had even paid with her life.

"Who is the man, Cammie?" he demanded. "What is his name?"

Cammie did not answer directly. Her thoughts were still with Lucie herself.

"She was no servant, Dooncahn," she said softly. "She came here as Adrienne's maid because it was the only way she could be included in the party. And Adrienne helped her, or tried to help her. Perhaps it would have been better if she had not, if..."

"I know all that!" Crosbie interrupted furiously. "Cammie, if you know the man you must tell me. There may still be danger..."

Cammie's eyes focused on him vaguely. "Danger?" she repeated the word. "Dooncahn, I do not understand. I ..."

Crosbie drew a sudden sharp breath.

"Was it Oliver Budd?" he demanded. "Did she plan to meet him in Pittsburgh? Was he to join her later at Fair Haven ... ?" It was possible. Budd was certainly in Alexandria before the wagon train left there. Blanchard had seen him in Pittsburgh only days ago. Budd had obviously known all the plans and the movements of the *émigrés*. It was not beyond possibility that he had also been in on the very beginning of this great swindle ... that he had been in Paris with those lying, cheating promoters of the Scioto Company ...

Rage darkened his face and tightened his huge hands into clenched fists. Watching him, the vagueness of Cammie's gaze turned slowly into fear.

"Dooncahn ..." again she reached to touch his hand comfortingly. Her voice was a whisper. "Dooncahn, I do not know what Lucie's plans were. I do not know a man called Oliver Budd."

Crosbie got to his feet. For a moment he stood staring down at her, and at the blanket-wrapped body of the girl who had wanted so much of this new world and this new life.

"Mademoiselle Adrienne," he asked, "does she know who the man is?"

"Perhaps," Cammie faltered. "If she does not know, she may at least suspect. Lucie would have confided in her, I think, more readily than in me."

Crosbie was silent for a moment.

"All right, Cammie," he said gently. It was no time to devil her with his suspicions, his anger and his despair.

It was a little time before realization came to him that if Oliver Budd was the man Lucie had loved, then she herself must have been their traitor. It must have been her hand that drew the careful map, and marked it... The thought sickened him and deepened his despair.

CHAPTER TWENTY

Blanchard tied the light pirogue to the stern of Crosbie's command boat and climbed quickly up to the deck. He paused near the pilot for a moment, bending deeply backward to ease the cramped muscles that still ached from his narrow seat in the dugout. The pilot eyed him lazily while he cut a fresh chew from a roll of dark-fired tobacco. When Blanchard looked at him, the pilot shifted his gaze to the upper deck and nodded twice.

Blanchard put one foot on the gunwale and leaped lithely up to the deck cover. There Crosbie reclined in his leather and timber chair, staring out fiercely at the sun-dappled Ohio land and nursing a small beaker of brandy in both hands, sitting in a tense posture as though he had frozen there during the long tiring ride.

Blanchard flopped wearily on the hard deck beside Crosbie's chair and waited to be noticed. For a long moment Crosbie sat motionless, then his eyes blinked twice as Blanchard shifted his moccasins with a rasping sound on the deck timber. Crosbie glanced down at the small glass in his hand as if he were trying to recall how it had come to him. Without a word he held it out to Blanchard.

"Thank you, sir," Blanchard murmured. He reached up for the glass, drank the brandy in one gulp and gasped as the fiery liquor scraped his throat. "Whew," he whistled. "That's as rough as Monongahela any day."

"Everything all right, Mr. Blanchard?" Crosbie asked, automatically, as he had asked the question every time Blanchard returned from a tour of inspection.

"Most everyone's asleep, Colonel," Blanchard said slowly. "Plumb wore out. I told them it was all right just to keep one guard on duty in each boat, provided all the others slept on deck."

"Very good," Crosbie said, again automatically. He had come of late to have a strange respect for Blanchard's views and he often agreed to his lieutenant's decisions before he had actually taken time to consider them. But in any event he was far too drugged with sleeplessness to consider anything seriously. No one wanted to think or to talk of what had taken place early that morning. Lucie's sudden death had left its mark of shock and horror on all of them. There seemed to exist only a desire to forget the hasty burial on a green hill overlooking the river. Young *Père* La Font had done his best to give the sad occasion the dignity and solemnity it demanded, but there was all the necessity for haste, which resulted in a ceremony that was to Crosbie's weary and confused mind almost furtive. They had chosen a towering walnut tree as a marker for the grave. Small blue flowers carpeted the place and seemed somehow fitting for Lucie. Crosbie stood by the grave as *Père* La Font spoke the brief service, but his own head was not bent as the others were because he could not help wondering whether, with the girl they buried here, they also buried their traitor.

Blanchard slipped down until he lay flat on the upper deck. He pushed his hat forward to shade his eyes from the sun and pulled his long rifle up to the crook of his arm. He hoped the Colonel would not bring up the subject of Charles de Flaville again. Just to avoid a discussion of Charlie's merits as a scout, he had taken the young Frenchman to another of the boats. Charlie certainly was upset enough about the whole thing, tight-lipped and miserable. Maybe so long as he was out of sight Crosbie would forget about him. But it would be best to distract the Colonel's mind, just in case he was still brooding about Charlie's "desertion" last night.

"Been wondering about that ambush business last night, Colonel," Blanchard offered quietly.

"So have I," Crosbie muttered.

"I can't see why those Indians weren't out on the islands as well as along the bank," Blanchard said quickly before Crosbie could speak further. "That way they could have done us some damage, even if they were spotted early."

"Fiske," Crosbie said cryptically.

"Sir?"

"Fiske," Crosbie repeated, turning to Blanchard. "You can thank yourself for upsetting the attack, Mr. Blanchard," he said grimly. "I've been thinking about it all morning. I'm convinced that by removing Fiske, you removed the guiding force behind last night's attack."

Blanchard shoved his hat back on his head and sat up. "I didn't remove Fiske, Colonel," he said mildly.

Crosbie made an irritable gesture. "Didn't mean you killed him," he said. "You intercepted him after he had received his instructions to attack us and before he could pass on those instructions to the actual attackers. Last night's attack," he said firmly, "had all the signs of a hasty affair and like all hasty jobs, it was botched."

Blanchard's face was just as serious and bleak now as Crosbie's. "Have you learned anything more about our … well, about the matter we discussed in Pittsburgh?"

"The traitor, you mean?" Crosbie said bluntly. "I don't know, Mr. Blanchard. I am not really sure."

Blanchard looked at him in surprise. And perhaps because he could no longer tolerate his solitary suspicions, Crosbie told him all that he knew, all that he suspected and feared.

Blanchard listened in silence, shocked at first, then angry. When Crosbie finished, Blanchard shook his head.

"You may be right about Budd, Colonel," he said. "He's an oily sort, all right, and I wouldn't put anything past him, any sort of thievery, even murder if he stood to profit by it. No, sir, I wouldn't argue about Budd. But Lucie…" His voice was clearly dubious, his face showed both wonder and regret. "I can't see Lucie plotting with a seedy character like Budd. I..."

"You said he was far from seedy when you saw him in Pittsburgh a few days ago," Crosbie said relentlessly. "Elegant was the word you used, I believe. And you said also that he seemed far more at home in this elegant role than he did in the earlier, seedy one."

"Yes, sir," Blanchard admitted unhappily. "Yes, sir, I did and he was."

"Well, then, isn't it likely that Lucie might have known him only in that role? Might have met him in Paris, an elegant gentleman and sponsored in Paris society by some of our own government officials, men of good name and character?"

Blanchard nodded slowly and had no words to deny the possibility. "I'd like some ... some proof, sir," he said. "It could be the way you say it is, but ..."

"I know I don't have the proof yet, Mr. Blanchard," Crosbie interrupted impatiently. "But I will have it. I will have it when I find Mr. Oliver Budd." He looked down at his lean strong hands and tightened them slowly as if they held something in a relentless, iron grip. "I'll get it, if I have to choke it out of him."

Blanchard nodded again.

Crosbie thumped the arm of his chair. "And then there are the worthless deeds, Mr. Blanchard," he growled. "That's the final link in this filthy chain of evidence. We know now that those worthless deeds are the reason why our people had to be kept from the Ohio Country."

"Yes," Blanchard said hoarsely, remembering all that had been done to keep them from getting here. "Yes, if they never got here, then nobody would ever go to wondering whether the Scioto Company deeds were any good. As soon as word gets around now, there won't be any Scioto Company."

"Exactly," Crosbie said heavily. "A daring gamble. A tremendous fortune for the lives of a few hundred friendless, deluded French *émigrés*."

Blanchard swept back his hat and wiped his damp forehead. Even in the strong heat of the sun, he felt suddenly chilled. A thin trickle of iciness touched along his spine.

"But it's all over when we get in this afternoon, isn't it, Colonel? There isn't anything that can be done after our people get to Fair Haven."

Crosbie's mouth pinched in to a tight thin line as he glanced up, looking forward over the boat to the distant shore. "Possibly," he said coldly. "Last night's attempt, mishandled as it was, seems to indicate that our people were never intended to reach the river at all. Otherwise, more intelligent plans would have been drawn to stop us. Last night was a desperation effort. And who can anticipate what desperate men will do?"

Blanchard came to his feet easily and stood with his legs wide against the gentle motion of the boat. A soft breeze whipped at his long hair. Crosbie gazed at him curiously, saw the flaring nostrils, the tensely set mouth and he almost smiled at the sight. Blanchard at any time was a worthy aide, but Blanchard keenly on edge was the best man he knew.

"Our people are safe," Crosbie said in a low confidential tone, "or will be safe, only when the world knows of the deception that has been practiced against them. Only then, Mr. Blanchard, and not until then."

Blanchard's chin rose angrily and both fists clenched tightly. "You think…"

"I think we'll remain on guard," Crosbie said. "We will have some opposition from our own people now that we are about to land, but between us I'm sure we can exercise control. We'll stay ready at all times."

"Yes, sir."

"Now get below and try to rest, Mr. Blanchard," the Colonel said softly. "We'll be landing late this afternoon. While it is still daylight if we're lucky. I'll need you then."

Blanchard glared fiercely at Crosbie, saw what he needed to see in the Colonel's worn, drawn face, in the hot hard eyes that looked calmly at him. Then he nodded silently, picked up his rifle and swung down to the main deck, landing on moccasined feet without a sound.

The afternoon passed quickly for Crosbie. For most of the time he slept, dozing lightly in his chair, waking whenever the pilot went about or when one of the Frenchmen climbed to the upper deck to speak to him. By now his dour silences had become routine to the *émigrés* and none tried more than once to induce the Colonel to chat. He roused himself to some interest when young Jock clambered up with Crosbie's heavy bagpipes clutched in his arms, eager for his first lesson on the pibroch. Crosbie's fingers stroked the woolen tartan of the Clan Crosbie with affection; it had been almost a year since he had seen the family cloth. Jock picked up the trick of inflating the bag, that steady pressure of air blown constantly while the elbow squeezed and the fingers rippled along the chanter pipe. The full nine-note scale of the pibroch baffled the boy for a while, but he managed from the first to force a recognizable air from the strange instrument. And the volume he could produce was staggering. Even Crosbie was compelled to call a halt.

"Ye'll frighten every Indian for miles about, boy," he smiled. "Now give over for a time and go help your mother."

Crosbie watched Jock as he lowered the pibroch carefully to the main deck and jumped down after it. A bright gay fad and one a man could find pleasure in, biddable but not so obedient as to be annoying, and a boy with real spirit. His fiery playing at Halfaday Creek had proven that, for Jock had never before played so well or surely as he had when he had ambushed the ambushers in the darkness.

Crosbie was wakened firmly when every Frenchman on the boat came climbing up to the upper deck.

"The pilot says we will be within sight of our Fair Haven very soon," Cammie called at him, pulling him up from his comfortable chair and tugging him until he followed her to the forward edge of the deck.

And Cammie's excitement was mirrored in all the *émigrés*. Even the sedate Marquis who could usually be depended upon to retain his imperturbable attitude was positively capering and his niece joined him in a superbly ridiculous burlesque of the minuette while Jock blared a slow-paced but raucous version of "Charley Is My Darlin'." They had a lot to forget. Maybe their manner of forgetting it was right, after all.

This moment which Crosbie had so eagerly anticipated as the end of his responsibility was the most trying experience of the long journey. None but he and Blanchard knew the French were celebrating an arrival that would be the beginning of their greatest time of trouble.

Crosbie managed a smile, he patted Jock's tousled head and forced a few light comments on the splendid occasion, but his eyes betrayed him. Their pained and angry expression worried Cammie and she remained close by his side, curling her small warm hand into his hard palm and trying with her presence and obvious affection to remove Crosbie's anguished tension.

The wide reach of the Ohio was a vivid blue in the late afternoon sun, except for streaks of muddy brown where swift thin creeks emptied into the river. The banks on both sides were low and sloping with occasional escarpments where the current had undercut the ground and toppled tall trees into the water. Thick rushes made a dense mat along the edge of the water and behind, the trees stood high and dark, blotting the sun and making almost a solid shadowed wall. Thick grapevines, as large as cannon barrels, twined through the trees, tangling with berry vines until the ground was covered with an unbelievable fertile mass that seemed forbidding and impassable to any man. The Frenchmen caught the quality of the new country, too, and after a time they no longer exclaimed over the wild, savage beauty. Another element crept into their awareness and without knowing why, without identifying any specific object, they felt the undertone of danger and their gay phrases quavered slightly with the note of fear.

Long ago the great glaciers had swept over this country, pushing huge granite boulders so far that they were polished to a glossy shimmer, tearing at the earth, uprooting, squeezing, prying with an incredible force, upending the inner structure of the earth itself, baring the privacy of layers that man had not seen for a million years. And as the ice cap receded, man had come again. A strange race first, a race of farmers, craftsmen, sedentary, timorous folk about whom little will ever be known. The wild jagged country had long since grown wooded with a profusion of growth that was frightening to a European accustomed to neatly pruned parks. There was nothing timorous about the race of men who claimed the sweetly fertile land now. The Shawnees, the Wyandots, the Miamis, the Hurons, all the nomadic, hunting fighters who had endured where the earlier people had failed, whose dedicated angry people had drawn the line of the water of the Ohio as the westernmost line of settlement of the white people. They had a complete and sure knowledge of the great Iroquis confederation—and of its end at the white man's untrustworthy hand. They wanted no further encroachment. And the nature of the land itself was with the Indians. A dark country, where the sun was rarely seen except in water-bordering meadows and then only at high noon, a country of amazing fertility that had never been asked to grow more than a few hills of beans and corn and almost seemed grateful for its easy life, judging by the difficulties it placed in the way of the white settler.

In this savage country the white men and the red men lived in much the same fashion. If either lived better it would be the Indian. Against that advantage the white men had only their ability to organize and to foresee the needs of the future. But it was a land whose fertility had become a lodestone, an irresistible attraction that could bring eager settlers from as far away as France, men induced to come by lying, stupid reports, knowing nothing of the ways of the land, of the needs of the land, knowing only the driving right of their own need to own and occupy an untouched virgin part of the world and bothering not at all about the rights of the race who lived here, hunting a little, farming even less, but retaining the land and holding it in their culture as they held their gods. The land would be taken, the gods would lose their power, the people would dwindle until only a handful grubbed a meager living from tiny farms along a river far to the west, forgotten as they once were in their meaning and their pride, forgetting themselves that they had ever been anything more. But what the future held was hidden now and without meaning. The Shawnees watched the long line of bateaux, loaded deeply with the hated people, the hated and feared things, as the boats drifted toward Fair Haven. They too had their leader in the tall arrogant Blue Jacket, a strong man who stood as high as any white man, well over six feet, and spoke with the hard tight words of authority. The three white feathers of Blue Jacket had bowed to the white man only once, when he had stooped to draw the line that barred settlement of the land beyond the blue Ohio.

Now the Shawnees watched and the gay music, the frivolous happiness of the *émigrés* was shadowed ominously by the watching. The music sounded as loudly, the impromptu dances were as lively and the deep relief of arrival after long months of journeying had its effect, but still ... there was something ...

Crosbie shook his head briskly, smiled down at Cammie and squeezed her hand gently.

The pilot eased away on his sweep and the boat began its slow graceful turn. Below them lay Fair Haven.

CHAPTER TWENTY ONE

The music dwindled as boat after boat came within view of the landing at Fair Haven. In the solid wall of dense greenery, a slim gash had been slashed, and there on the bank that raised only fifty feet from the water of the Ohio was the town built for the Frenchmen. Four rows of log cabins paralleled the river. The rows were less than one hundred yards long and were broken at hundred-foot intervals for cross walks. Two-storied blockhouses stood at each corner of the town. At the far end was a ramshackled stockade, obviously the first structure built, and near it were four large double cabins which had been designed for the wealthier *émigrés* or possibly for the larger families. A low timber rampart ran along the crestline of the river bank. On the other three sides the shadows of the forest closed in tightly around the cabins.

Crosbie heard a low sigh from Cammie, a quiet, disappointed sound that touched him. And, momentarily, a quick raging anger colored his thoughts. What did these people expect after all he had told them ? They had willingly come some thousands of miles to an untouched wilderness, sure that somehow, by some magical process, the wilderness would be manicured to resemble the Bois de Boulogne by the time they arrived. But the gasps of disappointment were general among the people in his boat, and the genuine note of surprise made Crosbie feel somehow apologetic for their reaction.

The Marquis touched Crosbie's elbow diffidently. "We have arrived, *mon colonel*?" he asked quietly, hoping to hear that

Fair Haven was another, prettier place farther down the river. "This…this is our new home?"

Crosbie turned to the thin dapper aristocrat. The Marquis's eyes were gentle, almost pleading, and Crosbie choked back his impulse to growl at him.

"Fair Haven, sir," he said softly.

The Marquis sighed and then shrugged, making a comical face as he glanced around at his compatriots.

"*C'est bien remarquable,*" he murmured, almost inaudibly. Then he shrugged again. "*Chacun à son gout, eh, mon colonel?* So it is that we come to the end of our journey to the Promised Land."

For the Frenchmen, it was the Promised Land, Crosbie reminded himself sourly. It held the same meaning of peace and safety. It was land promised, indeed, but the land would not be delivered—not the land the Marquis was speaking about.

D'Aucourt rumpled Jock's hair as Crosbie had done. "A brave tune, my boy," he said cheerfully. "Something to honor our arrival." The Marquis fumbled for a coin, slipped it into Jock's shirt pocket and patted him again. "Something gay and we shall dance again for joy."

Jock puffed mightily at the pibroch, inflating the bag and tuning the drones while Crosbie looked at the Marquis with new respect. The Marquis was a fop and sometimes a fool but he would never let his people become depressed, particularly when their lives might well depend upon their eager willingness to build a world for themselves.

On the raw clay embankment, more than a dozen men had gathered as Jock's bagpipes blared bravely through the still afternoon. The men waved their hats, capered and shouted as Crosbie's boat swung wide in the swift current and glided smoothly toward the rude log dock in front of the town. One of the men turned and ran quickly along the row of cabins toward the stockade, throwing up streamers of pale dust as he ran.

As always, it was Blanchard who did what had to be done. He was standing in the bow of the boat as the pilot brought it close to the dock and he leaped out quickly, spanning the two feet to the bank. He pulled at the thick mooring line as the boat glided after him. Just as the current was about to pull the boat downstream, Blanchard tossed the line over a bitt and snubbed it short. The pilot threw over the after line and Blanchard together with several others hauled the stern of the boat close to the dock and secured it there.

The second boat was moored to the other side of the dock minutes later and following boats were warped after them, lying in long double lines along the bank, tied boat to boat. But Crosbie had leaped to the dock before the second boat landed. He took Blanchard's elbow and walked swiftly up the clay embankment with him toward the cluster of cheering men on the log rampart.

"Housing will be a problem," he said crisply. "You find out what facilities are ready and then get together with the Marquis and allocate the cabins. And get the stock unloaded first thing and inside a barricade somewhere. You'll have to be quick. The sun won't stay more than another two hours."

"Yes, sir," Blanchard said readily.

One of the shouting men grounded his double-bitted axe and swept off his disreputable hat in a deep clumsy bow. "Kay vooley voo, mownseer," he grinned, showing wide gaps between his yellowed teeth.

Blanchard aped the bow. "Bien, mon vieux," he said in his vile accent. "Je suis…"

"Stop this nonsense," Crosbie barked. "Where's Major Burnham?"

The axeman replaced his hat and stared suspiciously at Crosbie. "I thought you was all Frenchies," he said with obvious disappointment. "That's what…"

"Where's Major Burnham?" Crosbie roared with exasperation.

"Right here, sir." A tall heavy man approached at a fast walk, buckling on his sword belt as he came. He was dressed in an approximation of infantry uniform, at least the trousers were regulation, but the boots and gaiters had been replaced by leggings and moccasins and he wore a dark calamanco shirt with no insignia of rank on it. He doffed his cocked hat to Crosbie and bowed slightly. "You'll be Colonel Crosbie, sir?" he asked in a harsh New England voice.

Crosbie returned the salute briskly. "Can you get my people under cover tonight, Major?"

"Just about, Colonel. We got two roofs to finish yet, but maybe we could crowd some of them a little bit."

"Good. Send someone with Lieutenant Blanchard so he can assign the quarters."

Major Burnham pointed to the grinning axeman and Blanchard took him aside for a fast tour of the town. Crosbie in the meantime had looked through the small window of one cabin and he pivoted toward Burnham with an angry face.

"Dirt floors," he said hotly. He strode swiftly around the cabin and kicked his moccasined foot at the clay fireplace. "No stones here. What sort of work is this, Major?"

Burnham's thin face reddened and his wide mouth clamped shut before the first retort could escape him. He swallowed gravely once and said in a quiet tone, "The job prescribed by General Putnam, Colonel." From his trouser pocket he withdrew a much-folded sheet of paper and opened it out. "My instructions, Colonel," he said dryly, "'four blockhouses and a number of low huts agreeably to the plan which you have with you. Clear the lands...'" Burnham looked up apologetically. "Haven't cleared much of the land yet, Colonel. Most of the trees are girdled but we haven't had time to cut many yet. Didn't expect you to be here for another month and I wanted the cabins ready." He bent his head again to the sheet of instructions. "'You will remember,'" he quoted, "'that I don't expect you to lay floors ... nor put in any sleepers or joyce for the lower floor ... and as I don't expect you will obtain any stone for the back of our chimneys, they must be made of day first, molded into tile and dried.' That's what General Putnam ordered me to build, Colonel," he said finally, folding up the paper. "And if you have any complaints, I suggest you take them up with the General."

Crosbie nodded grimly. "Have no fear," he growled, "I shall." He glared irritably at Burnham before his natural good sense returned. Then he held out his hand. "My apologies, Major. We have had a trying journey. None of us is in a good mood."

"Quite all right, sir," Burnham said, taking Crosbie's hand eagerly. "Will you take a tour of inspection with me?"

"Yes, but first, what of your men?" Crosbie asked. "How long will you remain here?"

Burnham shook his head. "No definite time, Colonel. As I understand, General Putnam may want the men to stay through the winter to help the new settlers. But I'll have to get specific instructions before I can be sure."

"Thank God for that," Crosbie said fervently. "They'll need all the help they can get."

"Shucks, Colonel, won't be much of a trick to stay alive in a place like this. Usually we just send out one man with a gun and he brings back enough meat to keep us for all week. Never saw game any place thick as it is here. Deer, elk, wild hog, pheasant, pigeon, all a man would want. And the woods are full of berries and fruit. We planted a few seeds when we got here and we can have a mess of garden greens any time we take a notion. And just about a mile up Chickamauga Valley, there's a salt lick. Couldn't want for a better place. You just come along with me and I'll show you."

Burnham led the way down one of the cross streets, heading for the forest opposite the river. Behind him Crosbie heard the eager gaiety of the French as they tumbled from the bateaux and ran up the slope to inspect their new homes.

At the edge of the cleared area, the air smelled pungently of leaf mold and pine with a sweeter note that was probably sassafras. Crosbie breathed in deeply. Then he stopped and looked back, trying to see the raw new settlement with the eye of a potential attacker.

The girdled trees came close to the cabins. That could be set right easily enough. Even the Frenchmen weren't bad axemen, not after their long training on the route from Alexandria to Pittsburgh. The two blockhouses that fronted toward the forest were stout enough and they were properly designed, with an overhanging second story that was pierced for loopholes. The doors of the cabins opened toward the river; only a tiny window in each one looked toward the trees. And that was sound, too. Then Crosbie looked to the right and his uncertain temper exploded again.

"What," he snarled, pointing his finger, "what in hell, Major, is that?"

"Huh?" Burnham turned to sight along Crosbie's finger. "Why, that's one of them Indian burial mounds. See them around a lot…"

Crosbie glared at the Major, glanced down at his trousers, eyed his cocked hat closely. "You're an Infantry officer, Major?" he demanded.

"Eight years," Burnham said stiffly.

"Then you have heard some mention in your long career," Crosbie growled, "about the meaning of high ground? How high above the surface is that mound?"

Burnham squinted, his face red and tense. "About sixty feet, maybe," he muttered.

"Nearer seventy," Crosbie said flatly. "So why in the name of everything holy, didn't you build a blockhouse up there? You'd have commanded this area for several miles."

"Weren't supposed to build a fort," Burnham said testily. "Supposed to build a town. Built it." He looked up at Crosbie's furious face and said hastily, "Besides, Indians are touchy about burial mounds, I hear tell. No point in riling them up."

Crosbie drew in a deep breath and waited for his anger to subside. "These Indians," he said in a more normal tone, "are Shawnees. They do not build burial mounds. They didn't build this one. A race of Indians who came long before the Shawnees built them and the Shawnees don't know what they are, nor care a damn about them one way or another."

"We…ell," Burnham said, rubbing his hand across his jaw, "I sure didn't know that, Colonel. But anyway…"

"I want a blockhouse on that mound," Crosbie said bluntly.

"When General Putnam says so," Burnham said lightly. "I been told to take orders from you, Colonel, but not about that."

Crosbie's huge hands clenched into hard fists and he stood silent, slightly trembling as he eyed Burnham. A dark, murderous rage beat at his brain, almost frightening him with its intensity. Crosbie was no man to admire a loss of control, particularly not in himself. He held himself tightly for a moment and then walked blindly past Burnham, heading back toward the dock.

Blanchard was deep in conversation with the Marquis. They stood just behind the log rampart overlooking the river. Blanchard looked up as Crosbie neared them.

"Sixty-three cabins we can use right away, Colonel," he said blithely. "Plenty of room. The Marquis thinks one to a family would be the best idea. I reckon we could try it that way and see how it worked out."

"Very good," Crosbie said crisply. He stepped aside quickly as Cammie bustled up the path from the dock, paying no attention to her footing in her haste to be settled in her new home. "Doucement," he said gruffly. "Doucement."

"Ah, Dooncahn," she laughed. "Such a sweet little house. Mr. Blanchard says I may take this one with the splendid view of the water and the lovely golden bank of the far side. I hasten to prepare a window against the rain, but which will still admit light. It is a trick I have from a lady of Alexandria." She displayed proudly a slim roll of heavy brown paper.

"Aye," Crosbie said, trying to fall into the gay spirit, grateful to see that she had recovered from the trials of the night and the shock of Lucie's death. "Well-oiled paper. Nothing better for a good window." He felt that he sounded rather pompous but Cammie took no notice.

"You will come to dine," she said, brushing by him. "But not too early. There is so much to do."

"We men have become unwelcome," the Marquis chuckled. "I too have been dispossessed from my home. Mademoiselle Adrienne has advised me not to appear until called for." He shook his head. "A trying time, sir. However, to business. I have told our people to select whichever cabins most suited their fancy. Does that meet with your approval?"

"If you approve," Crosbie said shortly. "Frankly, I'd anticipate some squabbles, sir, if two ladies set their minds on the same cabin. And what have you done with the four large ones?"

The Marquis flushed slightly. "Well, one of them is occupied by Major Burnham, and Mr. Blanchard and I thought one would do for you and him, and if you would care to share a cabin. And..." he hesitated. "I have taken another. The last we thought it best to leave for an occasional guest, thinking as you did, that too many differences of opinion might arise if..."

"As you wish," Crosbie said. "I find it best to make a firm decision at the outset if I wish to avoid discussion, but this is your decision, sir. In fact all decisions are yours from now on. I'll be on hand if you want my opinion, but the control of this settlement is entirely your affair. However, I'll undertake to arrange for its proper defense..."

"Defense?" the Marquis challenged. "But surely..."

"You are living in the land the Shawnees said will never be open for settlement. They may leave you alone for a time but even that isn't too likely." Crosbie's voice was cold; he was prepared to beat down any objection the Marquis might raise and that determination was clearly evident in his tone. "You must have at least two men on guard at all times. All weapons must be kept loaded. No animals loose after sundown; you'll have to build pens in the stockade. Only parties of five armed men or more will be permitted to go into the woods out of sight of the blockhouses. And all the able-bodied men must be prepared to stand a regular tour of guard-duty at night, though it should mean only one night's watch out of seven, no more. Unless, of course, we are attacked."

The Marquis nodded gravely. "I had not thought..." he began. He chewed his lip for a brief moment and then shrugged amiably. "We shall be guided by your advice, Colonel, as we have been in the past. And," the Marquis smiled warmly as he bent his neck back to look up at the tall Scot, "I am pleased to hear you say 'we' when you speak of our problems. You are not, then eager to take your leave? We may hope..."

"I'll stay for a time," Crosbie said. "At least until General Putnam arrives." He glanced at the Marquis's powdered wig, absently noting a spot where the whiteness had been smirched with dirt. It was on the tip of his tongue to speak of the worthless deeds, to tell the Marquis of the Scioto Company, of Putnam and...

"Me, too," Blanchard said quickly, sensing the Colonel's confusion. "I kind of like the country."

Crosbie nodded gratefully to Blanchard. He felt strangely affected by the Marquis's obvious pleasure in his decision to remain, and for a moment he wondered how much pleasure d'Aucourt and his people would find in him when they learned the truth. He turned to Blanchard and said gruffly, "You're seeing to the unloading, Mr. Blanchard?"

Blanchard laughed at his dour commander. "Hell, Colonel, couldn't nobody make them work faster if he used a whip."

And as Blanchard had said, the Frenchmen were zealous in their work, almost running up the smooth embankment with staggering loads on their heads, slipping and falling, bumping into each other in a confused pattern of eagerness, but always gay, always laughing, as though this business of fitting out a tiny cabin was the greatest possible fun. A more sedate group freed the horses, oxen and cattle and led them toward the stockade. The boats would require several days to unload completely, but by nightfall, most of the vital items should have been brought up to the cabins. Nothing Blanchard or Crosbie could do would possibly speed the process.

"I'll want you to come with me, Mr. Blanchard," Crosbie said crisply. "With your permission, sir." He bowed to the Marquis and turned away, taking Blanchard's arm.

"You'll have to establish a defense plan," Crosbie said as he walked with Blanchard toward the heavily shadowed trees surrounding the settlement. "Map out the ground here for several hundred yards in each direction. Pick the most likely avenues of attack and we'll put Burnham's men to clearing fields of fire so we can defend ourselves. And don't put any of Burnham's men on your guard roster. They'll be working hard every day from now on and they'll have to rest. We'll consider them as our reserve force."

Blanchard nodded without answering. The massive bulk of the trees seemed to fascinate him and he walked up to the nearest one, putting his hand flat against the bark. He looked up to the leafy top and then turned to Crosbie. "Over two hundred feet high and a good thirty feet thick," he said with a note of awe in his voice. "It will take a man most of the day to bring one of these down. They all seem to be black walnut and that's a mighty hard wood, Colonel. And then what? You can't burn them until they dry out and ..."

"Back this way," the Colonel said, pointing over Blanchard's shoulder, "there's a ravine, fairly deep, with a shallow creek. Cut the timber up to the edge of the ravine and take all the oxen teams to drag the timber to the ravine and then you can throw the trees down there. That will block the ravine as an approach route and get rid of the trees."

"Very good, sir," Blanchard muttered. He continued to survey the enormous trees with a speculative eye. The Colonel, he thought, had no objection to outlining big jobs for him. Those trees were going to be a problem for years. Take months to clear enough ground for a kitchen garden.

Blanchard pivoted to look back at the settlement, viewing it with the same attitude as Crosbie's. Not a difficult place to defend, but the advantages of the ground had been wasted. He opened his mouth to say something about that high mound, and then closed it again. Crosbie wouldn't need to be told about it. Blanchard contented himself with pointing to a low marshy spot that crossed the settlement. "That's a soggy patch right there, Colonel," he said. "I think it better be filled in or we'll have swamp fever on our hands."

"Good," Crosbie agreed. "Tell Major Burnham to assign a detail for it. Now come along. I want to see what the country looks like around here. We have an hour of daylight yet."

Crosbie and Blanchard spent their last daylight hour in traversing the outlying country around the new town. The ground was oddly clear in many places, for the sun seldom penetrated beyond the tops of the trees. But wherever the sun did reach, thickets of thorned underbrush impeded every step. The trees had grown so high in their constant battle to find the sun that most of them had never put down adequate roots. A storm always brought down dozens crashing to the ground where they lay rotting, tangling the underbrush so densely that only rabbits and squirrels could move through much of the country.

Blanchard stopped abruptly on the brink of the ravine behind the settlement. He dropped his hat beside his knee as he began to paw industriously among a thick growth of low bushes.

"Late blackberries, Colonel," he grinned. "Mighty small, but sweet enough for anybody." Blanchard stripped out enough to fill his hand with each thrust, picking out the leaves and dropping the berries into his upturned hat.

Crosbie sat heavily on a fallen tree trunk and pushed his hat back from his streaming face. "This is the ravine I want filled with timber," he said quietly, shifting his posture to take his neck out of the direct sunlight.

"Right," Blanchard mumbled through a mouthful of blackberries. He offered his loaded hat to Crosbie and held it in invitation until Crosbie took a few. "Have to take a big mouthful to get the flavor," he insisted hospitably, showing his meaning by cramming in a double handful. Then he paused to dig out a small thorn from one stained finger.

"Very good indeed," Crosbie said politely. After a moment he rose and led the way down the ravine and up the opposite slope. Only a trickle of water ran in the stream but that trickle was enough to maintain a thriving crop of sumac and ferns, hazel and wild rose bushes. The air was warm, damp and oppressive and Crosbie was breathing heavily when he reached the far side. He promptly set off on a circular route that would carry them along the perimeter of the new settlement. Blanchard followed easily behind the Colonel, carrying his fruit-laden hat in one hand, eating the tiny berries in huge mouthfuls as he walked. The problem to him seemed simple and he paid little attention to the details of terrain that obviously fascinated Crosbie. As far as Blanchard was concerned, the solution lay in clearing a wide swath of ground around the cabins, thus making a surprise attack impossible. The settlers would always be defenders, so a specific knowledge of the outlying ground would be of little more than academic use. But Crosbie wanted to see it and Blanchard had no objection to a quiet stroll through the virgin country, particularly not as he noticed how the exercise served to soothe Crosbie and relax his overwrought nerves. The Colonel actually smiled at one of Blanchard's comments before their trip was completed.

They came within view of the settlement again just before the last rays of the sun were sinking into the Kentucky hills. The forest behind them was dark and gloomy, already a place of danger.

Blanchard shivered slightly as he stepped out from the cool shadows into the open area around the cabins. He looked at the town quickly and turned to Crosbie in bewilderment.

"Where is everybody?"

The new town seemed deserted. Where busy Frenchmen had milled in the streets, up and down the bank where the boats lay moored, now no one could be seen. A few dim lights burned in the cabins, but nothing moved. As Blanchard spoke, a door opened wide at the far end of the main street, a wide streamer of light swept across the darkening street and a man stood silhouetted for a moment. From the open door, came the soft strains of a gavotte and Blanchard laughed suddenly at the rollicking sound.

"That's the Marquis's house," he grinned. "I'll bet they're having a ..."

"*Mon Colonel*," the Marquis called in a high demanding voice.

Crosbie checked in midstride to let the Marquis come up to him. The dapper Frenchman picked his way carefully across the rough ground, using his slim cane skillfully. His long snug coat was a dove grey velvet picked out with silver lace in intricate patterns. His red heeled slippers gave him an additional three inches in height, and brilliants set in his buckles twinkled in the dim light. The wide embroidered clocks in his silk stockings reached almost to his knee buckles. As he bowed ceremoniously to Crosbie, the spill of silver lace at his throat swept forward dramatically.

"I have been searching everywhere for you," he said plaintively. "We plan a surprise for you, then you are not to be found. A distressing situation. But all is well now." The Marquis smilingly included Blanchard in his insistent invitation. "This way, gentle-men," he urged. "We must not delay."

Crosbie fitted his pace to the Marquis's, taking long slow strides to keep up with the hurrying Frenchman, paying little attention to d'Aucourt's constant clatter of conversation, dourly fixing his gaze on the ground before his feet. Whatever d'Aucourt was planning, Crosbie assured himself, it would not take much of his time. It was now nearly full dark and the few lamps and candles in the new settlement would hardly be wasted on social gatherings.

Blanchard, anticipating the reason behind the Marquis's invitation, went past the Colonel quickly, pushed back the door of the lighted cabin and waited for Crosbie to enter first.

The Marquis posted himself stiffly erect opposite Blanchard. He bowed gracefully as Crosbie approached and Blanchard, unwilling to be outdone in formalities to his chief, repeated the bow as best he could.

As Crosbie's moccasined foot came down on the floor, three violins and a viol wavered uncertainly into "The Campbells Are Coming." The notes came hesitantly and without rhythm at first but gradually the musicians settled into the tune and Crosbie could faintly discern the basic melody. They played sweetly and quietly as though the Scottish air had originally been written as a lullaby. But however badly it was played, it was meant as a compliment and Crosbie doffed his cocked hat automatically as he entered.

CHAPTER TWENTY TWO

The Marquis's double-sized cabin was tightly packed with most of the adult Frenchmen and their ladies, all obviously garbed in their very best. Major Burnham, now shaved and dressed in an irreproachable dress uniform, stood grinning widely before the small orchestra. The scene was a shapeless blur to Crosbie, his eyes dazzled by the bright lights. He saw a shimmering movement of brilliant color, but little else. He stopped in surprise, just inside the doorway.

The music picked up in tempo and volume. At Major Burnham's signal, the gentlemen bowed deeply, the ladies swept the floor in curtsies. Crosbie turned, bewildered, to the Marquis.

"The first evening in our new home, *mon colonel*," the Marquis said warmly. "We mark the occasion properly with a ball, such as our resources permit. And fittingly, we honor the gallant soldier who has safely brought us to this new world."

The Marquis finished his speech in a roaring tone and the assembled company cheered wildly. Crosbie glanced around stupefied, his eyes blinking quickly to come into focus, seeing little more than the violently colored blur, hearing the twisted strains of the Scottish battle song, feeling suddenly gross and filthy in his worn buckskins, his old moccasins, not even a clean shirt while everyone else, save only Blanchard, looked fit for a court levée. It was a deeply embarrassing moment for Crosbie. He stood rooted, his thin florid skin slowly flushing a dark, angry red.

Then young Jock saved him from further torture. In later days Crosbie never remembered that evening without a surge of warm feeling for Jock. The badly rendered version of "The Campbells Are Coming" must have tested Jock's musical taste to the breaking point for he paraded stalwartly out before the Colonel, balancing Crosbie's great pibroch on his narrow shoulders. He stood with both short legs spread wide, and the mad shriek of the bagpipes blared through the cabin, drowning the ineffectual strings, skirling bravely the old song, making Crosbie's pulse tingle in response. The bad moment of tension passed. Crosbie laughed abruptly and bowed to the Marquis.

"A great honor," he said, pitching his voice to carry above the keening of the pibroch. "Now if you will permit me to retire for a few minutes." He made a brief gesture at his travel-stained buckskins.

"Mais non," the Marquis insisted. "The grande marche is to commence at once. You will lead, of course." He placed his hand on Crosbie's sleeve and smiled gaily. "A happy moment, is it not, sir? I know how a soldier feels when he has successfully completed a trying mission. My felicitations, Colonel Crosbie."

Crosbie clenched his teeth savagely, biting back the bitter comments that crowded his throat. Felicitations, indeed. A happy moment, no less. Duncan Crosbie choked in his secret fury, a deep anger swept through him, for this compliment, the most elaborate within the power of the émigrés to present, was given to a man who deserved nothing good of them. He had not himself betrayed them, not knowingly. But he had been the stupid dupe, the tool, through which the Frenchmen had been brought penniless to a miserable wilderness village. Crosbie brought himself stiffly erect and glared out at the happy crowd, trying desperately to control his emotions.

He focused his attentions on the cabin furnishings as Jock went on blaring with his bagpipes. Crosbie knew the Marquis's heavy load of baggage had included household goods, but he never suspected that a sensible man could think of transporting such things to the bleak Ohio country. Opposite him was a glittering mahogany cabinet that touched the roof, a wide and elegant piece with glass decanters and a dainty Limoges porcelain clock shining behind the glass doors, gilt mounts at the corners and feet, ornate gold buttons on the door. Some of the ladies were seated on fragile gilt and velvet chairs whose tiny balled feet had sunk deeply into the packed earth flooring of the cabin. On the wall hung a huge mirror, a shapeless rococo design of gilt that was not at all to Crosbie's taste, but looked incredibly fine all the same. At various sites along the gilt frame were crystal vases which someone, Mademoiselle Adrienne, probably, had filled with wild flowers. Behind the orchestra hung a dim faded tapestry depicting an involved battle scene, a softly muted pattern of fury and death that suited Crosbie perfectly. He stared intently at it while the music continued. He had just made out the tense snarling faces of two opposing swordsmen when the Marquis clapped his hands briskly as a signal to the orchestra.

The pibroch sighed to silence and the outplayed violins rested. The Marquis bowed again to Crosbie. "We await your pleasure, sir."

Crosbie moved his feet into position stolidly, bent forward in his best bow, an involved and elaborate piece of maneuvering that always gave Blanchard a fit of giggles. The young lieutenant ducked behind the Marquis, fighting to keep a straight face. The Frenchified bow coming from a rigid old soldier like Crosbie wasn't anything but downright funny, even if it was a perfect bow.

Crosbie winked solemnly at Jock and tossed his cocked hat into the boy's hands. The violins swept into a lively tune and only the necessity for catching Crosbie's hat kept Jock from joining the orchestra again. As Jock snatched the hat, a thoughtful Frenchman skillfully grabbed the pibroch, putting it safely up on a high rafter where Jock could not reach it.

Crosbie passed slowly along the line of gayly dressed ladies. The niceties of protocol demanded that he should choose a lady of rank as his partner to lead the march. That would properly be the Marquis's niece, since d'Aucourt was the host tonight. Crosbie's meticulous mind registered the requirement of manners automatically. But when he saw Cammie's round glowing face wedged in the far corner, the question of protocol was forgotten. He stalked through the press of people, thinking only that he would dance with Cammie, if dance he must. He bowed before her, again with that Parisian bow that convulsed Blanchard.

Cammie looked very fine as she curtsied before him, Crosbie thought. That shade of red went perfectly with her bold coloring, her dark hair and brilliant dark eyes. Crosbie didn't see that Cammie's velvet gown was rubbed at the seams, strained at the bodice, obviously made for someone else. He didn't see that it was a style not worn for the past three years, nor would he have cared had he known. When she took Crosbie's arm, her hand trembled slightly on his sleeve, her glance was warm, unbelievably welcoming, and Crosbie smiled broadly. A sudden light-heartedness swept over him as the music rippled and Cammie's shoulder touched him as she came into position.

The Marquis d'Aucourt shrugged at Crosbie's choice. An attachment of some meaning, doubtless, but hardly the thing for the ballroom. However ...

He presented himself to his radiant young niece, bowed and watched her silver and scarlet gown sweep gracefully as she responded. He offered his arm and took his place behind the Colonel and Cammie. The first twenty couples who could assemble lined up behind them and the remainder wisely stayed on the sidelines so that the dancers might have room to maneuver. Blanchard, thwarted by the Marquis's move, stationed himself near a long low table covered with a fresh white cloth. If that was the refreshment buffet, he thought, then Adrienne would find her way to him sooner or later.

Crosbie paraded stiffly with Cammie but as the dancing figures formed and dissolved, taking Cammie away, bringing her to him again, his spirits grew more lively, his steps more sure and relaxed. For the first time in months, Crosbie permitted himself to forget his responsibilities, even his deep sense of guilt. The wild gay tone of the music touched him and Cammie noticed the contrast between this easy smiling man and the drawn-faced bitter soldier she had comforted for many weeks. Her hands clutched his feverishly when the figures permitted, a warm touch of reassurance and affection that intoxicated Crosbie.

Blanchard leaned against the rough cabin wall, folded his arms across his chest and watched Adrienne move lightly through the involved patterns on the dance floor. Someone had cleverly dampened the ground and only rarely did a puff of dust rise from the dancing feet. Adrienne looked like a wild rose bobbing in a high wind, Blanchard told himself, especially when the movement of the dance brought a flush to her cheeks. He hadn't been able to talk freely with Adrienne since that night at Braddock's Field. He followed her progress jealously, now, cursing himself for not having straightened out their misunderstanding long ago. It would not have been an easy thing to do, in the face of her icy disdain, but he could have made her listen if he had been willing to swallow his pride and forget his timorous fears about the future... After all, her own future was no more secure than his, now. Why, when the news of the land swindle was finally told to them, all the French *émigrés* would have to face poverty and possible ruin... maybe even the elegant Marquis and his family. It was not a pleasant thought. And yet it did make Adrienne seem more... accessible.

The music faded to a close and Blanchard pushed away from the wall, determined to wait no longer. He threaded his way hastily through the crowd to Adrienne's side.

"I've got to talk to you," he said abruptly, "it's nonsense, this business of ignoring each other!"

Adrienne's dark eyes lifted to study his face blankly, as if it were a face she couldn't remember having seen before. Under that cool remote stare, Blanchard found himself fumbling for words. "About that night at Braddock's Field…" he blundered on. "I want to explain…"

The cool eyes went colder still. "You owe me no explanation, sir," Adrienne said with icy politeness. It was more cutting than hot anger, by far. The music struck up again, gay and lilting. For a moment Adrienne hesitated, then she said, "You will excuse me? I am engaged for this dance. Monsieur de Flaville…"

"Charlie?" Blanchard asked in relieved tones. "Oh, Charlie won't mind if you just…well, forget about his dance. He'll understand…"

"That I doubt, Lieutenant," Adrienne cut him off sharply as de Flaville started toward her across the crowded floor. "I think you overestimate the understanding of Monsieur de Flaville. And…" again that little hesitation… "And I wish to dance with Charles just now!" She turned away. Incredulous, Blanchard watched her go. Something was wrong, her behavior told him that, a lot more wrong than he had thought. He meant to find out what it was. Angrily he took a long stride forward and caught Adrienne's wrist in a firm grasp. Adrienne gasped, a high startled tone of outrage that stopped Blanchard abruptly.

Nearby, Edmond de la Foure left his partner suddenly stranded and pushed through the crowd to Adrienne. He placed himself squarely before Blanchard, glaring hotly at him, one hand belligerently gripped on his sword hilt.

"Do you insult my cousin, sir?" he demanded angrily.

"Why…why, no," Blanchard stammered, his face reddening furiously. "I…I…just…" He glanced at Adrienne helplessly, silently praying she would call off the Count before he had to fight a foolish duel. The whole bewildering thing was getting well out of hand.

Adrienne's eyebrows were lifted slightly, her eyes were dangerously bright as she returned his gaze. For a second, he thought he saw an odd, almost questioning look on her face, but then she tugged her wrist from his grip and turned away, taking Charles de Flaville's arm and smiling up at him. It was a gay and charming smile, the smile she had used to lighten, or to conceal, hardships on the long journey to the Ohio country.

The devil, Blanchard said to himself, the little devil. She's doing this just to make me look a fool. It must be that, it's clear as anything in her eyes.

The Count de la Foure had no patience with Blanchard's hesitation. His fiery anger boiled quickly. He flipped back the dangling lace of his cuff and swept his slender hand forward at Blanchard's flushed face.

Blanchard blocked the blow easily enough with one arm. He would then have welcomed a fight with almost anyone, but he couldn't fight Adrienne's cousin. And probably she knew that, too.

"That's enough," Crosbie's stern voice said coldly. He placed himself between the Count and Blanchard, facing de la Foure. "It was a misunderstanding, sir," he said flatly. "I'm sure Mr. Blanchard would be delighted to apologize to your cousin through you." He pivoted to Blanchard and demanded, "Sir?"

"Exactly right, sir, a misunderstanding," Blanchard said hastily, knowing the Colonel couldn't possibly have seen what happened. "Deepest regrets."

The elderly figure of the Marquis d'Aucourt interposed also between the two young men. He bowed to Crosbie when the Colonel turned. "Is that satisfactory, sir?" Crosbie asked him.

The Marquis met Crosbie's glare for a silent moment, then shrugged lightly. "A lamentable misunderstanding," he murmured in agreement. "I, too, must apologize. Edmond, you will convey Mr. Blanchard's compliments to your cousin. And I remind you that you have deserted your partner most rudely." He waited until his son had bowed coldly and walked away.

Crosbie's stiff posture relaxed abruptly and his eyes sought Cammie's again. She took his arm in a tight clasp, twining her fingers through the heavy fringe that ran down the seam of his buckskin sleeve.

"A glass of wine with me, gentlemen," the Marquis said pleasantly. "To wipe out all misunderstandings. I insist."

Crosbie eyed Blanchard carefully, obviously ready to interfere actively if Blanchard showed signs of wanting to continue the quarrel. Blanchard looked once toward Adrienne. She stood in her brilliantly white and scarlet gown, framed against the pale tapestry talking intently to de Flaville as they waited for the music to resume. Blanchard shrugged, his anger cooling for the moment, and let Crosbie lead him toward the table at the far end of the room.

The Marquis pulled open the glass doors of his cabinet, took down a decanter of wine and several glasses. He poured the wine with careful precision, giving the first glass to Cammie. Crosbie took his and waited as the Marquis helped Blanchard and himself.

"A great moment, Colonel," d'Aucourt said with evident sincerity. "A moment most happily anticipated for years, and now…" he gestured widely. "We held a meeting to consider a name for our new home. Not that we object to Fair Haven, but somehow we thought we might find a name more suitable to our people. And we have, sir." He lifted his glass high. "I give you, gentlemen and Madame, the City of the Gauls. Our new home, Gallipolis!"

"Gallipolis," Crosbie echoed.

"Gallipolis," said Blanchard uncertainly. He gulped his wine and choked heavily on the syrupy drink.

"A pity," the Marquis murmured as Crosbie thumped Blanchard's back. "I fear this wine has traveled badly. Only an indifferent Oporto at best."

"Ex…excellent wine," Blanchard sputtered. He brought his spasms under control and sipped again. "Splendid wine," he said staunchly.

"I am so pleased you approve, sir. I shall take the liberty of sending a bottle to your quarters if I may."

"Delighted, sir," Blanchard said, wondering if the Marquis thought he had been asking for the bottle. He looked in confusion at Crosbie.

"And what, Colonel," the Marquis said lightly, "do you think of our town's new name? I do not ask Madame Carel, for I know she shares my opinion."

Crosbie sipped at his port. He smiled at Cammie and felt her hand tighten on his arm. "With such advocates, sir," he said, aping the Marquis's light tone, "I am sure the name of Gallipolis will never be successfully challenged." He lifted his glass and bowed to Cammie. "To the ladies who will make Gallipolis a fair haven for all who are fortunate enough to come here."

"Splendid, sir," the Marquis laughed. "I must remember that. Indeed I must. Gallipolis a fair haven for all. Excellent."

Blanchard eyed the Colonel over his glass. He noticed the ardent byplay with Cammie and almost grinned. The old man was a gay dog when he eased off a bit. And he could talk macaroni with the best of them.

"You might care for some refreshment, Colonel," the Marquis said hospitably. He turned, sweeping back the linen cover from a long mahogany table. On the matching plates were thin cakes of coarse corn meal, each shaped in a flower pattern, mounds of sliced meats, and piled on the last platter, something Blanchard could not identify. The Marquis deftly plied a knife and fork, serving each of three small plates with meats and corn cakes and adding several of the other items. He balanced a fine silver fork on each plate, handed the first two to Cammie and the Colonel.

"A rare treat, sir," he smiled. "One of our gentlemen made a most fortunate discovery this afternoon." He gave Blanchard his plate. "In a pond just outside were many frogs, large succulent frogs. You can well imagine how welcome they were. Do try them, sir. Not the frogs of Artois, but frogs of some merit, nonetheless."

"I do agree indeed, sir," Crosbie said readily, stripping the flesh from one leg with a practiced motion. "Magnificent."

Blanchard watched Crosbie carefully. The Colonel chewed and swallowed happily, exchanging compliments with the Marquis while he ate four frog legs. Frog legs, Blanchard thought, what in God's name comes next? In his life Blanchard had seen a million frogs at a conservative estimate, but never before had he seen anyone eat them, or even mention eating them except as a joking reference to the French. Blanchard had put no credence in such reports. He hadn't believed that Frenchmen ate frogs, any more than he was prepared to believe that they ate snails. But the facts were against him.

He picked up a frog leg gingerly. Looks a little like a chicken leg, except for its scrawny size, he told himself. Just forget it's a frog, then it won't be bad. He sensed that Crosbie and the Marquis were watching him, so he bit manfully at the frog leg, stripping the fragile bone bare as he had seen Crosbie do it. He forced himself to smile agreeably as he ate, but he tried to chew quickly and get the thing swallowed before he could taste it. Then his eyebrows lifted in surprise and the false smile became wide and genuine. That stuff was good ! By God, there wasn't a finer sweeter meat he knew. Nothing was nearly so good as frog legs. They reminded you of chicken in a way, but the flesh was more delicate, almost creamy. Blanchard quickly finished two more, gobbling with real interest.

Crosbie chuckled softly. "Surprising, eh, Mr. Blanchard?" He leaned toward Blanchard's ear. "I'm afraid we'll have to give up our plans to drain that pond outside."

"Yes, sir," Blanchard said forcefully. "I'll personally shoot the man who wants to drain it. These things … why, my God, Colonel, these things …"

"Yes," Crosbie laughed. "They're all of that." He bowed to the Marquis in apology. "You must forgive us, sir. Mr. Blanchard and

I had thoughtlessly planned to drain your frog pond in order to avoid swamp fever. We are now agreed that such a thought would be criminal."

"You so enjoy the frog legs? Then this will be your first taste, Mr. Blanchard?" The Marquis swiftly brought up the serving dish and spooned half a dozen more on Blanchard's plate. "They will always be a delightful dish, but never again will they taste quite so pleasing to you. One should always be immoderate with one's first experience, for the first appetite of discovery will never come again."

Blanchard bowed clumsily and applied himself to his replenished plate eagerly. The Marquis retrieved empty plates from Cammie and the Colonel and filled their glasses with wine again.

"The merest taste, Colonel," he said, shrugging. "A shame that one can no longer offer an ample hospitality to guests. But one must be adaptable, no? There will be many demands on our flexibility, I assume, before we become thoroughly adapted to our new environment."

Crosbie nodded dourly, all enjoyment gone for the moment. There would be many adjustments necessary for the French. In his unusual sensitivity, Crosbie seemed to find in the Marquis's every word some reference to the swindle which he and Blanchard still held a close secret. Crosbie faced the fact that he lacked the courage to acquaint the Marquis and his people with the true situation. This was Putnam's doing, all of it, and Duncan Crosbie meant to let General Putnam himself make whatever explanation could be made. As for Crosbie, if Putnam's explanation was inadequate, he had no doubt where his sympathy, his entire future, would lie. He looked down fondly at Cammie and touched her hand gently with a wide calloused fingertip.

"If you can tear yourself away from your charming partner, Colonel Crosbie," the Marquis said in a quiet tone, "some of our gentlemen would enjoy very much an opportunity to ask some questions regarding our estates here. We hope to make a tour of inspection shortly."

Crosbie's muscles stiffened. Cammie felt the abrupt tension and her eyes widened in alarm.

"No," Crosbie said hoarsely. He turned to look at the Marquis. Let the man believe he still owns estates, he told himself. Let him believe that as long as he can, until General Putnam arrives to tell him that scoundrels have sold him worthless paper.

"No," he repeated, "I regret I cannot leave, sir. Madame Carel has only now consented to become my wife and I..."

Blanchard's empty plate slipped from nerveless fingers. He lunged desperately for it, barely deflected it so that it spun harmlessly to the earthen floor. He picked it up and placed it on the table with extreme care, watching his hands as though he had never seen them move before.

The Marquis's long years of social diplomacy led him to recovery before Blanchard could speak. He bowed to Crosbie, offered his congratulations, then moved to Cammie, taking her soft round hand in his and bowing to touch his lips to the roughened skin. "I am overwhelmed with joy, Madame," he murmured.

Cammie's round face flushed deeply. She flicked a glance of wild desperation at Crosbie, saw the stern set lines around his mouth. And she smiled, suddenly beautiful, sparkling in a way she had never been before. An auspicious beginning, too, for the Marquis had never before kissed her hand in honor. Surely with such a beginning, all would be as well as she had often dreamed it might.

Crosbie saw the stricken glance, saw Cammie's flush and in that moment knew he had done a brutal, shameful thing. To conceal his own discomfiture, he had announced their engagement, never once mentioning the matter before to Cammie, never doing her the simple justice that was hers by every right. He laid his hand softly on hers, fully covering it in a hard, hurting clasp. Cammie's expression as she looked up was forgiveness enough for any man. Duncan Crosbie glanced into the soft warm brown eyes and knew himself to be at home for the first time of his life.

Blanchard waited patiently for them to notice him. When Cammie looked up, he bowed, unconsciously copying Crosbie's elaborate court bow with careless precision.

"Back in Albemarle County, ma'am," he said in his soft Southern voice, "we don't kiss ladies' hands. Not often anyway. But we have a tradition about kissing the bride." He moved closer. "Sometimes we ask the groom's permission and," he stooped swiftly and kissed Cammie's cheek, "sometimes we don't."

Tears sprang quickly to Cammie's eyes. She turned to shield her face against Crosbie's chest.

Blanchard stiffened solemnly, saluted. "Warmest congratulations, sir. I hope you will always have such good fortune."

"Thank you, Nick," Crosbie said simply. "Thank you."

The Marquis had promptly spread the news and the dance floor was deserted in a matter of minutes as eager ladies centered around Cammie and Crosbie. Blanchard was eased first into the corner, then he worked his way slowly to the door and stepped outside to be free of the crush. He felt somehow pleased and lighthearted at the Colonel's decision, as though marriage were the finest idea any man could think of on a night when the moon is just full enough and the music is sweet and gay.

Blanchard walked slowly around the cabin, stopping to look in through the open window at the happily chattering crowd around Crosbie. He waited for a long silent moment, silhouetted against the pale light. He couldn't see Adrienne anywhere. Probably she was hidden in the press somewhere and anyway, this wouldn't be the time to approach her. Not after that scene, earlier. Not when she ... But maybe this was just the time, he thought suddenly. They say weddings have a powerful effect on females. Maybe Adrienne might be relenting a little. Maybe ...

Blanchard turned again toward the open door. On the second story of the blockhouse above his head he could hear the steady, sure pacing of the sentry on duty and something of the rhythm entered his pulse. He stepped quickly toward the door and then he stopped.

The other window of the Marquis's cabin threw its soft beam of light across the open ground and there, lovingly outlined in the rays, stood Adrienne, her scarlet and white gown unmistakable even in the dim light. With her was a man whose dark, gold-laced coat was immensely becoming to his tall slender figure and sleek blond hair. Charles de Flaville looked more at home in gold-laced velvet than he ever had in a buckskin hunting shirt. He was of Adrienne's own world, seeing them together brought that home to Blanchard with a sudden painful sureness. And Adrienne's world was not just a matter of security, as he had so blindly thought earlier. It was also a matter of background and manners, of shared interests and shared memories...

Blanchard could not hear the words de Flaville was saying to Adrienne, but the tone, and the expression of his lean handsome face were both unmistakably pleading. And Adrienne was listening to him with complete willingness. Her dark eyes were intent on his face.

Blanchard pivoted on one heel and walked off into the darkness, holding both fists clamped hard. He had been a fool, he guessed, not to see that de Flaville's relationship with Adrienne was more than the cousinly affection that existed between the girl and de la Foure. But he'd never thought of Adrienne and Charles... not seriously, at any rate. Perhaps because he had not wanted to think seriously of Adrienne and anyone but himself. His shoulders were stiff as he strode heavily across the cleared ground toward the darkness that lay along the quiet river.

CHAPTER TWENTY THREE

Stretched out flat on his back in the rough cabin he shared with Blanchard, Duncan Crosbie tried to compose himself and quiet his nerves for a trying experience. In the three days that had passed since the Marquis's party, the ladies of Gallipolis had done little save prepare for his wedding. By virtue of incessant demands, they had prevailed upon the Marquis to floor his cabin for the ceremony and all had generously given up any hope of flooring their own until much later. Crosbie rolled a segar from one corner of his mouth to the other and blew a soft greasy smoke ring toward the roof. A sparkle of sunlight glinted through a chink in the roof, throwing its tiny beam directly on his eyes. Crosbie shifted his head to escape the light.

Mr. Blanchard had done a good job in fixing the cabin for their use, Crosbie thought. The beds were simply squared logs pegged together in a rectangular shape and filled with pine tips with a blanket thrown on top. They were couches more comfortable than many Crosbie had slept on. In a corner Blanchard had hung a wooden water pail, suspending it with a rawhide thong so that it was a simple matter to tilt it enough to fill the wooden basin below. A most ingenious device that saved much stooping. The table was a rude piece of work but it served to hold shaving gear. Best of all Blanchard had pegged their polished steel mirrors to the log wall, setting them one above the other, the upper one suiting Crosbie's height perfectly. His years of rough living during the war had given Blanchard a surprising adaptability; in just a few days he had constructed a room in which he and Crosbie could live quite comfortably. But Blanchard didn't intend to live there, comfortably or not.

Against the far wall were four leather trunks. The two rough rawhide ones were empty now. They were Crosbie's and the most of his clothes were hanging inside a bark closet Blanchard had made. But the pair of matched trunks of dark polished leather with heavy brass fittings were Blanchard's and save for clean clothes he had removed for the wedding, they remained packed.

Outside on the landing dock, hung from a high stripped pole, floated a red flag. That was Blanchard's signal. The first boat going downstream would have a passenger. Crosbie glared dourly at the heavy trunks. Whatever had happened between Blanchard and the Marquis's niece at the party had completely altered Blanchard's plans. He had been apologetic when he told Crosbie, but his apology had stemmed from the fear that he might be leaving Crosbie with an unmanageable problem. Crosbie had quickly disabused him of any such idea, but he now admitted to himself that he would miss Blanchard drastically. The young lieutenant had a genius for organization, a talent unusual even among men trained in organizing. And, Crosbie thought, he was more than a subordinate. In a sense, he never had been that, for Crosbie's commission had been inactive when they met and now Blanchard, too, was separated from active service. In Gallipolis, there was no disciplinary bar to friendship and Crosbie realized, now that he had to face the fact of Blanchard's departure, that he had been counting on that friendship, planning his future in some part on Blanchard as he did on Cammie and Jock.

Crosbie rolled to his feet restlessly, went to the open door and pitched his segar stub out into the dust. The small town seemed strangely deserted. At the far end a few children were playing around the blockhouse. From the surrounding forest, Crosbie could hear the slow rhythmic sound of chopping axes where the men were clearing the heavy timber. The small girls and their mothers would be gathered in the cabins with Cammie, he thought, twittering and squealing about dresses and such-like. Crosbie looked up at the sun with a practiced eye. About four o'clock. That gave him a couple of hours before the Marquis and Blanchard would come for him. At the thought, a wild embarrassment seized him. He turned back to the gloom of the cabin, welcoming the dimness that masked his flushed face. At fifty, a man should have his marrying over with, or at least he should be used to it, he shouldn't quiver and twitch at the idea, go nervous and shy like a skittish colt.

Crosbie crossed the cabin quickly, drew another segar from the box the Marquis had sent him, lit it from his tinderbox and poured a glass of d'Aucourt's sticky port. He sat stiffly on the end of his bed, chewing his segar, occasionally taking a sip of the heavy wine, staring blankly out the open door, thinking of nothing until high-pitched female laughter broke the silence. Then Crosbie rose again to pace the packed earth floor, moving from door to window in a restless prowl that relaxed his tense muscles even if it did nothing for his nerves. The laughter sounded again, seeming farther away this time, and Crosbie found himself wondering what it was the Marquis's niece had done to change Blanchard's plans so quickly. He had seen the by-play at the party, but that alone didn't seem enough to warrant Blanchard's decision to leave for New Orleans as soon as he could obtain passage. Crosbie shook his head savagely. Adrienne was a wild, headstrong filly for all her gentle training, and even if Blanchard had got her, she'd probably have led him a fast and furious pace. Just as well, Crosbie thought vaguely. Adrienne was nothing like Cammie, had none of Cammie's warmth and kindliness, none of her ease, didn't even, to Crosbie's taste, have her beauty, though no man could say the Marquis's niece wasn't a snug little armful at that. But Crosbie liked a little softness in a woman, something that gave under pressure and warmed when it did. Strength was all right, but Crosbie had strength enough for two; he wanted a woman who enjoyed being a woman.

Gradually, the tension left Crosbie and he sat again, smiling aimlessly across the room as he sipped his wine and drew deeply at the short Spanish segar.

"Looking mighty fat and lazy, Colonel," Blanchard said cheerfully. He lounged in the doorway, grinning down at the Colonel. "Ready for the big doings?"

"Ready as I'll ever be," Crosbie grunted.

Blanchard whistled. "Got that hemmed-in feeling, Colonel? Want to make a quick run for New Orleans before you're hooked?"

Crosbie glared silently up at the young man and waited until Blanchard's grin broke and sobered.

"Small joke, Colonel," he said amiably, coming inside. "Thought I might give you a hand with something." He fingered his old buckskins that had weathered to the color of wood smoke. "Have to do myself better than this for the parade."

Crosbie smiled thinly. He put down his glass and came slowly to his feet. "Not uniform, Nick," he said heavily.

"Not…?"

"I've little taste for the uniform now," Crosbie muttered. It was clear to Blanchard that he was thinking of Putnam, and Putnam's unexplained betrayal of the Frenchmen. Crosbie untied his thong belt and slipped off his *skene-dhu* carefully, putting it on the shaving table. Then he bent forward to strip his shift over his head.

Blanchard regarded the Colonel soberly. A big man by any standards, he thought. Big enough to stand almost any punishment but not big enough or strong enough to endure the sort of betrayal he suspected he had from General Putnam.

"I'm a civilian, myself," Blanchard said lightly. "Sort of figured I'd wear clothes to match. Borrowed me a pair of silk stockings from the Marquis. I'll be a real macaroni. You wait and see."

"Aye," Crosbie said. He took down a rolled doeskin carrier and put it down on his bed, flipping one end to unroll it. He untied the fasteners and spread the hide back, revealing several coats and half a dozen pairs of trousers. He stirred among them with an aimless hand, remembering vaguely where he had bought each, under what circumstances, how seldom he had worn any of them, for his uniform had long been the only clothes he needed.

Blanchard came to look over his shoulder and as the Colonel lifted a drab brown coat, he stayed Crosbie's hand.

"What is that, Colonel? The gay thing there?"

Crosbie silently lifted a black velvet jacket into the light. Gilt buttons and gold braid shone bravely against the blackness and under the jacket was folded a deep spill of heavy Alençon lace for a neckcloth. Blanchard whistled admiringly.

"Very elegant, sir," he said. "You'll be the brightest cock of all in that."

Crosbies let the velvet fall and picked up the brown coat. " 'Tis a jacket to be worn with a kilt," he said dryly.

Blanchard grinned suddenly. He stooped and rummaged through the wad of clothing until he found what he sought. Then he straightened, fluttering the elaborately pleated kilt, the brilliant red, green, white and yellow of Crosbie's tartan.

He bowed extravagantly and held it out to Crosbie. "Your wedding suit, Colonel," he said lazily.

Crosbie snorted and went on shaking the wrinkles out of the brown jacket.

"Why not, Colonel?" Blanchard insisted. "Those Frenchies all look like birds of paradise. Who wouldn't stand a chance to shine. And," he cleverly played his best card, "just think how Cammie would feel if you showed up for the wedding in an old brown coat like a farmer when the Marquis was right there in something so bright the eyes couldn't stand to look."

Crosbie eyed Blanchard suspiciously. He'd not worn the tartan since he came to America. Probably wouldn't fit him anymore. He actually kept it only as a sort of memento; except for the skene-dhu and the pibroch, he had nothing else to remind him of the clan of Crosbie, of its lost lands at Craigsmuir, its broken, wandering clan. But why not wear it? After all, Cammie would soon be a Crosbie, too, as would Jock. It would be fitting, he thought. He nodded slowly and put down the drab brown coat, ignoring Blanchard's wide gleeful smile.

The kilt was snug, but Crosbie had been a big man when it was made and he had never run to fat. The buckles had to be let out to the last hole, but the kilt went around him well enough. The big goatskin sporran was a little rubbed from long storage but it fluffed out with a bit of shaking. Crosbie sat to pull on the gay tartan stockings, tied them with a scarlet ribbon before he shoved his feet into the heavy silver-buckled brogues. Over his shirt he draped the lace spill, tying it deftly so that the heavy folds billowed out from his throat. The black velvet jacket was perilously tight across the shoulders and Crosbie was almost afraid to breathe. Rather than bend down, he lifted one leg high to slip the scabbarded skene-dhu into his stocking. The jeweled hilt came high enough to touch the top of his kilt, just where it could easily be reached if a man needed it quickly. Crosbie straightened and settled the lacy frills at his throat. In a pocket of his jacket he found two tightly rolled hands which spread out into lace cuffs. He tied them in place, pushed them up under his sleeve and flipped the lace back up over the black velvet sleeves.

Blanchard applauded vigorously from his post in the doorway. When Crosbie turned irritably, he bowed ceremoniously. "Pure admiration, Colonel, I assure you. Nothing but admiration and a speck of envy. Won't a soul look at me today.'

"Damn foolishness," Crosbie muttered. But inwardly he was pleased with the figure he made. He knew well how the velvet and the tartan set off his big burly body, the body which never seemed quite at ease in anything but kilts.

"Shall I summon the pipers, me laird of Craigsmuir?" Blanchard asked, uncontrollable merriment obvious in his glance.

"Ye may search for me bonnet," Crosbie growled, the deep Scottish brogue becoming more pronounced every moment. He flicked a sidewise glance, trying to catch his reflection in his tiny shaving mirror. He could see only a brief hint of velvet and lace but that was enough. If married he'd be, then there'd not be a man present to rival him. And it was a fine, stirring sensation to be wearing the tartan once again.

The strident notes of a bugle shattered the stillness, echoed and re-echoed from the hills. Blanchard straightened abruptly from his search, dangling Crosbie's tartan-trimmed bonnet from one finger.

"A boat!"

The bugle blared again, twice, signaling for a landing. Blanchard tossed the bonnet to Crosbie and dashed for the door. "Back in a minute, Colonel," he called over his shoulder.

Crosbie shrugged. Boats were rare along the Ohio, but not rare enough to distract him now. Blanchard evidently was in full earnest about his intentions to leave as soon as he could, and Crosbie frowned to himself, angry and frustrated at his inability to retain the young man whom he had come to trust and like.

Crosbie turned the gay bonnet in his hand. He fitted it carefully over his thick grizzled hair, turned it slightly to bring the silver and cairngorm brooch into position on the left side. Then, with a cautious glance toward the open door, he stepped quickly in front of his steel mirror.

Unconsciously, he smiled, widely and without restraint. A braw figure, by God, and one worthy of a bridegroom. As he raised his chin, the lace at his throat fluttered elegantly. Crosbie moved back to bring the brilliant tartan into view. Splendid indeed, he thought. And won't Cammie be pleased, though?

Blanchard's running feet padded across the open ground outside. He skidded to a stop at the door and knocked before he entered. Crosbie glanced up in surprise.

"General Putnam, sir," Blanchard announced in a formal tone. "Coming up the bank this minute."

The rare sense of lighthearted pleasure that Crosbie had been enjoying vanished immediately. He looked at Blanchard and his face was lined again and gloomy. This was a moment he had been anticipating for nearly a month. In his mind were several formal and elaborate statements wherein Duncan Crosbie would express his deep contempt for thieves and swindlers, his suspicions of Putnam and his shady associates. At that moment, Crosbie could remember none of them. In the brief time it took Putnam to reach his cabin, Crosbie was conscious of only one thought—Putnam, having already ruined the French settlers, was now capping his offense by ruining Crosbie's wedding. The hard habitual lines of tension deepened in his face. He brought his bulky body slowly to a stiffly erect posture and he waited like that, facing the door squarely, his gray eyes hot and tight with controlled fury.

"Do I stay, sir?" Blanchard asked quickly, looking out the door.

"Aye," Crosbie growled heavily. By rights, the Marquis should also attend any conference with Putnam. Crosbie was willing to give his General a separate interview, but not, however, an interview without witnesses.

Blanchard brought his heels together silently, doffed his hat in salute as footsteps sounded outside the cabin. "General Putnam, sir," he said sharply.

Blanchard maintained his stiff posture until Putnam had passed him and approached Crosbie. Then he relaxed and turned to watch. Putnam had come alone, leaving his staff outside with Major Burnham. Probably his staff people would have business with Burnham, but the business couldn't be that urgent.

Not a muscle moved in Crosbie's dour face when Putnam entered. He bowed a fraction of an inch, said, "Sir," in a chilling tone and straightened again.

General Rufus Putnam was considerably shorter than Crosbie, though he might weigh as much. He was a round man and he looked soft at the first glance. But the round belly that swelled his white uniform waistcoat was hard as a stone; only the drooping jowls indicated a self-indulgence that was belied by the hard mouth, the cold eyes that met Crosbie's glare evenly without wavering.

"Not a warm welcome, Duncan," Putnam said easily. He flicked a glance at Crosbie's startling costume, raised one eyebrow but wisely said nothing.

Crosbie opened his mouth slowly as if the effort were almost too much for him. "You expected warmth, General?" he asked bleakly.

Putnam removed his cocked hat precisely, slipping it under his elbow. With one hand he dusted his blue uniform sleeve, turning to look at Blanchard as he did so. "We'll speak alone, Duncan," he said lightly, still maintaining an even tempered attitude that amazed Blanchard, experienced as he was with Putnam's fiery temper.

"Mr. Blanchard remains at my request," Crosbie said stiffly.

Putnam's mouth opened slightly. He raised his head to look directly at Crosbie, a necessity that always put him in a bad mood. "Alone, Colonel," he snapped.

Before Crosbie could answer, Blanchard stepped forward. He had seen Crosbie's anger mount in response to Putnam's peremptory tone and he still had hopes of avoiding a serious argument.

"We're civilians now, General," he said in a lazy drawl. "This elegant Scot is Mr. Duncan Crosbie, Laird of Craigsmuir, and my name is..."

"I find your levity offensive, Mr. Blanchard," Putnam rasped. "Go..."

"He stays," Crosbie said flatly. "I prefer a witness to hear whatever you have to say to me."

Putnam turned swiftly to stare at Crosbie, his round face flushed with resentment. "Very well," he said, obviously controlling himself with a major effort of will. "I should think that old comrades might…" He permitted himself a brief shrug. "However…"

"Outside," said Crosbie heatedly, "are some three hundred swindled people. That crime outweighs any rights an old comrade might have with me."

Putnam's flush deepened, but this time with embarrassment. He looked at the earthen floor, rubbed his boot sole at a ridge of dust. After a long silent moment he sighed heavily. "Let's sit down," he said in a weary tone. "I have much to say to you."

Putnam seated himself on the foot of Crosbie's bed, put his gold-laced hat beside him and waited for Crosbie.

The Colonel planted himself squarely before Putnam, his heavy legs spread wide. From Putnam's viewpoint, he seemed nine feet high and three wide, an ominous glowering figure in his brilliant kilt.

"Please sit down, Duncan," Putnam said pleasantly. "You hover over me like the avenging fates."

"Would to God I could be just that," Crosbie said with genuine feeling.

Putnam's face was drawn and sad, very weary now that his original affability had disappeared. "Do you, then, have no regard for me?" he asked in an odd tone.

Through Crosbie's mind ran swift memories of Stony Point, of the second Saratoga, of the long and trying days when he had seen Rufus Putnam in battle. Then he was a fine soldier, Crosbie thought grimly, a man worth respecting. Crosbie's promotions had come largely through Putnam's flattering recommendations. But the man seated before him was not the Rufus Putnam he had in his mind. This was a man to whom Crosbie felt he owed nothing, save the mere right to speak in his own defense.

Putnam cleared his throat briskly and looked up. "The Scioto Company has gone into bankruptcy," he said in a harsh tone. "I forced them to it. Colonel Duer is in jail this moment for failure to meet his obligations. I have just returned from seeing to that. Doctor Cutler has remained behind to try to salvage something when we liquidate the company." Putnam drew a deep breath and his eyes dropped to the floor again. He shifted his gilt small-sword slightly.

"And what," Crosbie said tightly, "of the people…"

"Do I intrude, gentlemen?" the Marquis's voice called from outside the door.

Blanchard had his hand on the open door, his eyes upon Crosbie for instructions. When Crosbie said nothing, he pulled the door wider for the Marquis.

No splendor the Marquis had previously achieved could compare with his present grandeur. He wore the full white court wig, preposterously high and his suit was a white satin sprinkled with tiny golden stars. A larger star decorated his fragile white pumps and another was pasted to his chin. Putnam rose to his feet in a clumsy scramble, his eyes wide and staring, his mouth open at this astonishing sight.

"Permit me, General," Crosbie said with stiff punctilio, "to present you to the gentleman who leads the settlers of Gallipolis, His Excellency, the Marquis d'Aucourt."

"No, no," the Marquis cried, "it is rather I who should be presented to the General Putnam. We have all learned how much our future lies in the hands of the gallant soldiers in this forbidding land." He bowed precisely and Putnam swallowed heavily, looking in frantic bewilderment toward Crosbie.

Putnam hastily contrived a bow in reply. He replaced his cocked hat under his elbow, holding it tightly as though there was reassurance in the act. He held his left hand gripped around the hilt of his sword, toying with it as he goggled at the fanciful Marquis.

"All of us are eager," the Marquis said slowly, gathering his precise English carefully, "to see our new estates. The Colonel has advised us that we must await your arrival."

Crosbie glanced sharply at Putnam, making sure that the General caught the significance of the Marquis's statement, understood that the French still did not know of the swindle. Then Crosbie spoke heavily. "A pity," he said, "that..."

"How ungallant of you, sir!" the Marquis exploded. "A pity, indeed ! Ah Seigneur Dieu, that one should hear a bridegroom speak so at the moment of his wedding." He smiled warmly at Putnam, as if he shared a gleeful secret with the General. "But we should expect that from such elusive game, eh, *mon general*? A bird caught late in life makes a poor captive."

General Putnam forced a stiff meaningless smile. "There is to be a wedding, then? I had not..."

"Not even to you?" the Marquis said, breaking in. "He does not tell you of his wedding, to which I have even now come to summon him?" He touched Crosbie with his elbow; from another man, Crosbie would have thought he was nudged, but the elderly Marquis was too dainty for such a broad gesture. "And did he not explain why he has adorned himself as the lilies of the field?"

The Marquis's coy whimsy pleased Putnam no more than Blanchard's heavy-handed humor, but he maintained his blank grimace, his facial muscles beginning to ache from the strain.

And Crosbie liked it no better. He had forgotten about the kilt and now that he was reminded, his only reaction was anger. Somehow he felt less capable of handling Putnam when he was wearing clothing that would seem outlandish to the General's Yankee eye. Crosbie interrupted the Marquis's endless comments with a voice that was loud and cold.

"Madame Carmelite Carel," he growled, "has done me the honor to become my bride. We shall have to postpone our discussion of business for a short time."

"A short time!" the Marquis laughed. "The Colonel knows little of his duties as a bridegroom, eh?"

Putnam chuckled with him. And his heavy round face seemed for the moment free of the worried frown it usually wore. "When does the ceremony take place, sir,?" he asked the Marquis.

"At any moment. At any moment. I have come to summon the laggards." He turned to Crosbie plaintively. "The men have returned early from their labors to attend. The musicians have practiced all the day long and I suspect Madame Carel has endured all the congratulations she is capable of enduring. The moment awaits only the bridegroom. I should warn you, however, that Père La Font plans a dismally long service. Nothing I can say will dissuade him."

While the Marquis was talking, Blanchard had swiftly pulled off his clothes, taking up the gray silk suit he planned to wear to the wedding. He rolled his borrowed stockings carefully up over his legs, cinched them snugly and climbed into the skintight silk breeches.

"Only need a minute, Colonel," he grinned as he wrestled with his cravat. "Go on ahead if you like. I won't be late." He searched quickly through his discarded leather clothes, held up a thin circlet of gold and waved it at Crosbie. "All prepared, sir."

"I trust, Duncan," Putnam said in a voice so low that Crosbie could barely hear, "I trust I shall be welcome at your wedding? I should like to meet your lady if I may."

"But we insist," the Marquis declared forcefully. "It is an honor we shall long remember. And I can promise, sir, that you will not only be permitted to meet the bride, but may even with good fortune, expect to kiss her."

Crosbie glared at d'Aucourt. The Marquis's elation made it impossible for him to force the issue. He nodded Stiffly to Putnam. "An honor, indeed, General," he said heavily.

Only a practiced scoundrel, Crosbie thought, would be able to attend a social gathering with people who would shortly learn that he had been responsible for cheating them of their life's savings, their entire fortunes. Yet somehow, when he saw Putnam walk to the door with the slim Marquis, he could not restrain a feeling of ease, a slackening of strain, as though something had been solved. And the feeling persisted despite the fact that Putnam had practically admitted complicity in the swindle.

He followed them, his heavy shoulders swinging within his tight velvet jacket, his face set and hard. Blanchard's hand touched his arm and he turned.

"Cammie doesn't know," Blanchard whispered.

"Eh?"

"Not knowing," Blanchard said, "she might think you were no happy bridegroom."

Crosbie nodded, grateful for Blanchard's warning. He walked outside the door, fighting to erase his frown, to wipe out from his mind all thought of Putnam and his rascally companies, to think only of Cammie, of the soft, sweet Cammie who was waiting for him, her eyes warm and tender with the love she never tried to shield from him.

CHAPTER TWENTY FOUR

Around the Marquis's cabin, Burnham's rough frontiersmen who had built the town of Gallipolis stood ranked in depth, leaving clear a narrow path to the doorway. Their dark tanned faces spread in wide grins when they caught their first glimpse of Colonel Crosbie in his kilts and they split the quiet air with boisterous yells and catcalls. Crosbie nodded his thanks as he passed through.

Inside, the raw new puncheon flooring of the cabin had been covered with a pair of Ispahan carpets in jewel tones with a thin lane of red velvet marking the aisle that led toward Père La Font who waited patiently before a makeshift altar under the muted tapestry. Crosbie could hear an eager buzz of conversation when he entered, but the moment he stepped across the threshold, silence claimed the room. After one incredulous moment, the ladies and gentlemen broke into spontaneous applause. Crosbie stopped in momentary confusion, then smiled and stepped forward again, followed by Putnam and Blanchard. The Marquis paused a moment to whisper to one of Burnham's men before he entered.

To honor Crosbie, the French had turned out as if for a levée and as they would at court, most wore the Bourbon white and gold, the dark-skinned ones cleverly limiting themselves to scarves or sashes in those difficult tones, but the blonder women were spectacular in sweeping white gowns slashed with golden accents. Blanchard's simple gray suit, fine as it was by normal standards, was completely outshadowed by the gaudy clothes of the French, as was General Putnam's undress uniform. But Duncan Crosbie was more resplendent than any. The dramatic black velvet set off the brilliant tartan perfectly and Crosbie's immense bulk brought sighs of rapture from the ladies. The Colonel strode down the red carpet, his face set and determined, bowing slightly right and left. He took his place beside Père La Font, just in front of the padded stool.

Blanchard followed uneasily, pale and contained. His fingers nervously sought for the ring which the Marquis had thoughtfully provided. He touched it reassuringly and his shoulders relaxed. Beside him General Putnam pressed back into the crowd, clearing the red aisle. Putnam kept one hand knotted tightly around his sword hilt and he stood stiffly erect, absorbing the incredible roomful of incredible people with brief flickering glances, keeping his face sternly composed, betraying nothing of what he might have felt. Rufus Putnam was a Brigadier General, was now the Superintendent of the Ohio Company, had for many years associated with the French who came to serve under Washington in the war. He was a man of stature and attainment, and his fifty-three years had seldom been put out of countenance. He had learned to control his instinctive resentment when people confused him with his cousin, General Israel Putnam, that blustering back-slapping braggart who had been magnificent at Bunker Hill and had become progressively more stupid and noisy as the war proceeded. Diplomacy came hard to Rufus Putnam and Crosbie's wedding was a severe test of his equanimity. He could hardly bring himself to look into anyone's eyes and whenever a lady smiled at him, he bowed in a jerky manner and looked quickly away, his bewilderment well hidden, but nonetheless upsetting to him. The furnishings of this rude cabin were beyond belief, especially the soft rugs underfoot and that amazing tapestry. And the clothes these people wore ! They had come to start a new life in a new country; they were almost the first white people to settle here, but they dressed as if their future days would be spent in pleasant walks along manicured boulevards. The towering white court wigs were like banks of snow and the heavy musky scent of the ladies' warring perfumes was making the air too thick to breathe. He could feel a light sweat break out on his forehead and he would have given a great deal to be able to ease his tight collar.

Blanchard slyly observed his General's discomfort. It was rare to see Putnam ill at ease in any company. Somehow Putnam's evident embarrassment permitted Blanchard to relax and he looked about the crowded room curiously.

The French had separated into two groups divided by the vivid red velvet carpet and they had withdrawn slightly from the altar so that Crosbie and Blanchard stood apart with Père La Font. The priest waited patiently, his thin hands clasped at his waist, his head bowed and his eyes almost closed. His lips moved gently as if he were whispering to himself. And Colonel Crosbie beside him had the look of death on his face, an expression that made Blanchard want to say something, anything, to remove that haunted tension. That was Putnam's doing, he thought savagely. The Colonel was having a fine time today till Old Put showed up.

Blanchard glanced idly down the room. They were all waiting for Cammie, he assumed. The Marquis, fidgeting restlessly in the doorway, eyed the path outside as if he were trying to hurry her to the altar. And not far away from her uncle was Adrienne. She too was in white and gold, a white silk gown that was almost creamy against her skin. Her face was lifted in animated conversation to a tall blonde man whose back was turned to Blanchard. Blanchard looked away. Even now, he felt no differently toward de Flaville. Charlie had been a good friend during their long journey and Blanchard had no hatred for him, but rather a deep tired numbness and a determined intent to get away from Gallipolis, from Adrienne, from anything that reminded him of the foolish plans he had once made for their future together.

From the doorway the Marquis signaled peremptorily to someone outside. Blanchard caught the gesture and he turned toward Crosbie, letting his hand touch the Colonel's shoulder in warning. Crosbie nodded once, absently. He turned his head to stare straight at General Putnam for a brief moment, then he turned forward again, his heavy jaw thrust out angrily. Behind them Père La Font coughed softly, then again in a basso tone as though he wanted to test the resonance of his voice.

A wild shout went up from Burnham's men outside the cabin and all eyes focused on the door as Cammie came in, her hand resting on her small son's shoulder. The massed Frenchmen pressed back to permit them adequate room on the velvet carpet. Cammie paused in the entrance, her eyes wide and sparkling with excitement. The frenzied days of consultation and borrowing had produced a wedding dress that rivalled any of the splendid court costumes of the high-born ladies. Cammie wore a softly draping gown of rose color, as befitted one who was a widow and not a bride for the first time. About her neck hung a delicate filigreed rivière of gold and rubies that warmed her skin, giving her a high flush. She wore no wig but her abundant hair had been piled intricately high and dredged with powder, so that it shone softly above her rosy face. A tiny heart-shaped patch lay on her cheek, just below a dimple that kept appearing and disappearing. Her plump hand, adorned with a handsome ruby ring, lay lightly on Jock's shoulder, as if in support, but actually guiding the boy along the carpet. He strode determinedly forward, his mouth firm and resolute, but he could not resist stealing little sidewise glances as he went. His face was dangerously flushed with the strain of remembering just what he was to do, and once he almost stumbled. As he did, Crosbie came forward, bowed gracefully and waited as Jock returned his bow and took his mother's trembling hand, kissed it regally and then laid it trustingly on Crosbie's arm.

Colonel Crosbie touched the boy's head lightly, then led Cammie proudly up to Père La Font. Blanchard moved out to take his position beside Jock. He put his hand on Jock's shoulder and let him feel the pressure, just for reassurance. The small boy glanced up nervously, then smiled his quick smile. They faced forward soberly as Père La Font spoke the first solemn words. Blanchard fumbled once more for the ring, slipped it up the first knuckle of his little finger and held it there safely, waiting for the moment.

When the first shots sounded, they were received with irritation by everyone in the large cabin. Major Burnham really should restrain his ruffians until the ceremony was ended. Four or five rifles fired in quick succession and Putnam turned toward the open door when he heard the ragged volley. But no one stirred. Père La Font droned on, his light voice held low and tense.

A loud roar almost shook the rafters of the cabin. And Putnam frowned heavily. That was the light field piece mounted in the bow of his boat. It wasn't to be fired without his express permission. Blanchard half turned, then hesitated.

"Shawnees!" an angry voice bellowed. "Shawnees, God damn it! Get your rifles!"

Blanchard's instinctive reaction got him out the door one step ahead of General Putnam. Crosbie pounded along behind them, swearing incoherently as he ran for his cabin. Blanchard entered first, tossed Crosbie's rifle to him, gathered his own and their powder and shot in a swift movement and rejoined him outside.

The bewildered Frenchmen streamed out of the crowded cabin, their gay clothes incongruous against the bare ground of the new town, the towering dark trees, the rude log cabins. "Aux armes!" the Marquis cried. "Vite, mes amis! Vite!"

Long months of practice during their journey had developed a rudimentary form of discipline among the French. The young men who had served as scouts were assembled in a matter of minutes before the Marquis's cabin, their brilliant white and gold court suits crisscrossed by hanging powder horns and shot pouches. Charles de Flaville and Edmond de la Foure dashed toward the Marquis for instructions.

General Putnam mounted the first blockhouse stiffly and Major Burnham leaned far over the ladder, pointing down toward the deep ravine behind the town.

"War party there, General," he yelled. "Must be a hundred of them."

Putnam mounted sedately, his round face betraying no emotion. He pursed his full lips thoughtfully as he considered the problem.

"Mr. Blanchard," Crosbie said quickly. "Put most of the French scouts in the far blockhouse facing the forest. Keep two or three men back of the first row of cabins."

Blanchard nodded readily. Crosbie's plan was the only sensible one. Attack, if it came, would be mounted from the forest side and the blockhouse at the far end would have few men at the moment, since most of them had been excused for the wedding. But there was another factor to be considered.

"What about the General, sir?" Blanchard asked softly.

Crosbie glared hotly at his lieutenant. "I command here, Mr. Blanchard," he growled.

Blanchard grinned. Old Put would huff and puff like a tea kettle, but Crosbie would turn him off mighty quick. He waved his arm for Charlie and ran toward him.

Burnham's men scrambled for their positions in the blockhouses, most of them concentrating in the two facing the trees, leaving only a handful in the riverside positions. They squirmed up the ladder past the descending General. Colonel Crosbie planted himself firmly at the foot, waiting grimly for Putnam.

"Colonel, I'll want a detail to go downstream and come up behind them," Putnam said before he was on the ground. He dropped safely beside Crosbie, sidestepped a running rifleman. After a quick glance at the sun, he said, "We'll have almost two hours of daylight to ..."

"No," Crosbie said in an oddly flat tone. He folded his arms over his rifle muzzle.

Putnam's concentration broke. His thoughtful frown vanished in bewilderment. "What...?"

"I command here," Crosbie said. "And no one gives orders but me." He waited for a silent moment, saw Putnam's surprise would not permit an immediate answer. "We didn't finish our discussion, General," he said grimly. "And there's no time now. But stay out of my way."

Putnam gobbled incoherently. A violent flush swept over his face as he stammered for words.

"This, General," Crosbie said in a hard quiet voice, "is the eighth attempt to attack these people. I don't know who is responsible, but I'll not permit you to command the defense of this town until I do know."

Putnam's jaw dropped wide. Then he closed his mouth deliberately and swallowed heavily. "This isn't the time, Duncan," he said stiffly, "as you say. I credit your concern for the settlers, but..." Then he made a quick angry gesture. "Hell, man, we can't stand here talking. I have a field piece on my boat. Get it into position while we still have time. We'll settle our differences later."

"I command," Crosbie insisted.

Putnam's jaw muscles knotted heavily before he answered. "You command," he said. "Now move!"

The brief respite won by an alert sentry ended with a wild ululating shriek from the woods. By that time both blockhouses were crammed with riflemen. Blanchard had half his detachment in the cabins facing the trees where they could fire through the narrow windows. And Crosbie's foresight in clearing the forest had given them a fifty-yard field of fire across which it would be suicide to pass.

The Indians in the ravine opened fire, screaming wildly, working themselves up to attack. But for the moment, it was a fire fight, rifles against arrows and muskets, with no casualties because the targets were still too elusive. Crosbie ran toward the river, gathering a group of Frenchmen as he went. Among them the Marquis and young de Flaville led the way. The two boatmen still on General Putnam's command bateau helped them dismount the light cannon and muscle it up to the flimsy dock. They wasted nearly five minutes getting the wide wheels on the axles, and the ungainly brass monster threatened a dozen times to topple into the mud. The boatmen attached thick ropes to the cannon and four men leaned against the dead weight of the field piece while Crosbie and the Marquis shoved at the high wheels. When the gun moved away, groaning across the logs, Crosbie relaxed and let the ropes take the strain. The men ran the gun up on the bank in a quick rush.

"Leave it there," Crosbie bellowed. "I want all the powder and shot in the boat. All of you come back here."

Less than four solid cannon balls were available together with a dozen canister charges, but it took a long time to get them up on the bank. Crosbie was in a frenzy of excitement, eager to get back where he could see what was happening. He could hear only the sporadic fire from the woods, the answering rifles from the blockhouses, but nothing to indicate any change in the situation.

The Marquis struggled with his last small keg of powder, working his way slowly from the lazaret while the younger men ran up the bank with their loads. Crosbie didn't want to goad the aging Marquis, but he couldn't bear to wait any longer. He followed the others to the bank, leaving d'Aucourt to come behind.

The Colonel stooped to pick up his rifle, not bothering to lower his powder keg from his shoulder. He pointed to the right, intending to give directions to his men, when the Marquis screamed.

The shrill piercing sound knifed into Crosbie's brain. He let the keg slide from his shoulder as he turned. D'Aucourt stood frozen on the dock, his arms still straining at the powder keg. Behind him, Putnam's boat seemed to swarm with Indians.

A lithe warrior, his face black and red in vivid stripes, leaped from the boat after d'Aucourt, tomahawk poised. A taller Shawnee with two shimmering peacock feathers in his scalp lock, stood on the boat deck, aiming deliberately with an ancient musket.

Crosbie fired at the Indian aiming the musket. The peacock feathers jerked backward, the musket exploded harmlessly, and the tall Indian fell back into the boat. But the painted warrior had reached the Marquis. He swung his hatchet down and d'Aucourt ducked quickly, taking the tomahawk blade on his shoulder. The powder keg slid forward and the hatchet glanced from the tough oak.

Behind Crosbie, the men of his detail fired swiftly, but none dared aim at the Indian attacking the Marquis. Crosbie ran down the sloping bank, knowing as he ran that he would be too late to help.

The Shawnee knocked d'Aucourt to the dock with the force of his rush. He shortened his grip on his hatchet and gripped the Marquis's hair tightly to pull his head up for a killing blow. But the Marquis's hair was a wig and the Indian's hard clutch merely pulled it loose, sending the warrior back on his heels abruptly with a look of incredible astonishment on his face that almost made Crosbie bellow with laughter.

Before the Shawnee recovered from his shock, Crosbie swept his skene-dhu from his stocking. He straightened as he ran, let the blade rest easily between his fingers and then hurled the dirk. The jeweled hilt sparkled in the sunlight as it turned, then the jewels darkened as the blade took the Shawnee in the throat.

Crosbie leaped over the Marquis, yanked his dirk loose and leaped up on the boat. But the diversionary raid was over. Only one canoe had slipped downriver to take the settlers by surprise and it was already some yards away, being driven by desperate paddles toward a sheltering bend in the Ohio. Crosbie reloaded his rifle with hasty motions, but the canoe had disappeared before he could fire again. The four Shawnees lying dead in the boat, he ignored.

"I ... I have much to thank you for," the Marquis said shakily. His fingers trembled against Crosbie's shoulder. "I was taken by surprise ..."

Crosbie tried not to look at the strangely bald Marquis. The dazzling court wig lay forgotten in the mud and the Marquis's shaven poll seemed oddly shrunken to Crosbie's eye. He bit his lip, striving to maintain a straight face. He patted the Marquis's back and nodded, not daring to speak. He shouldered the powder keg that had saved d'Aucourt's life and walked quickly up the embankment.

In the clearing outside the Marquis's large cabin, he concentrated his supplies and the small cannon. Then he bellowed for Blanchard.

"Get me all the men you can spare," he shouted. "Picks and shovels and plenty of riflemen. I want to emplace this gun."

Blanchard stared unbelievingly at the cannon. "Yes, sir," he said automatically. "Where?"

"What?" Crosbie snapped. "On the mound, of course. Don't you know anything about cannon, Mr ...." Then he stopped short and almost grinned. "Of course you don't. Dragoons aren't supposed to know guns. Get the men, Mr. Blanchard."

Exposed in the space between two cabins facing the trees was General Putnam, standing on a high stump, trying to see what was to be seen of the Indians. He quartered the field carefully then stepped down and behind the cabin as a volley of muskets banged from the ravine. An arrow whizzed just past his shoulder, drawing no attention. He walked slowly along behind the cabins and mounted the blockhouse ladder. Seeing Putnam as imperturbable as he had been at Stony Point somehow shook

Crosbie's suspicions of his old commander. But there was no time to consider that now.

When Blanchard brought up some twenty men, Crosbie quickly issued his orders.

"Riflemen first," he snapped. "Stay behind the crest and keep up a steady fire against the ravine. Then a detail of men with shovels. I want them to build a ramp to take the gun up to the top. Throw the earth forward to make a rampart, but leave an opening facing the enemy. Signal me when you have a level space for the gun. The rest of you wait here. I'll want four thick logs about three feet long to buttress the rampart. Get them ready and wait. When the site is prepared, the gun and supplies must go with a rush. Everyone understand?"

With Blanchard to lead the way, the high burial mound was invested in a matter of minutes. When the riflemen were in place, Blanchard worked his way back, crossing the exposed ground with long springing strides, bending low to make a shifty target. The men with picks and shovels soon had earth flying high above the mound, while Burnham's steady riflemen maintained an accurate fire against any Indian they could glimpse among the trees.

"Alert the blockhouses, Mr. Blanchard," Crosbie growled. "The mound is becoming a target. I'll want a heavy fire when the gun goes forward. Everyone is to fire. I don't want an Indian to stick his head out of that ravine."

Blanchard dashed off on his errand and Crosbie leaned momentarily against the Marquis's cabin, suddenly weary, feeling a quivering tension in his leg muscles. But a flickering smile crossed his face as he thought of d'Aucourt's wig. By God, a wig-maker would make a fortune if he could insure his clients against scalping. And any Shawnee would prefer a fancy court wig to an ordinary scalp. The Marquis's frightening experience should increase Monsieur Grennelle's business enormously as soon as word got around.

And as he smiled at the notion, Crosbie thought suddenly of the Marquis's cabin as he had last seen it, of Cammie, of their interrupted wedding ceremony. He turned toward the door, wondering if Cammie...

"Dooncahn," she smiled. "You are well?"

"Yes, my dear," he said clumsily. "Perfectly safe."

She came into his arms for a moment, holding him close. "Do not let me distract you from your duties," she said softly. "I shall wait here and I...I have Jock to protect me."

"Yes," Crosbie murmured. "I wish..."

Cammie's soft hand blocked his lips. She kissed him gently on the cheek and managed a wavering smile for him. "We have so much time," she whispered. "We can wait."

Crosbie bent his head. Behind Cammie the candles shone a soft glow on the elaborate furniture, on the ornate gowns of the ladies who still waited inside.

Jock ran out quickly from the press of wide skirts. "Shall we again attack the savages?" he demanded shrilly. "A surprise attack again, Dooncahn?"

Crosbie smiled absently. His heavy hand touched Cammie's forehead gently. "I hope so, my boy," he said. "Guard your mother well. I..."

"All ready, Colonel," Blanchard said from the doorway.

"Coming." Crosbie brushed his lips against Cammie's cheek, ruffled Jock's carefully powdered hair and went out again.

An eager, grinning mass of men were gathered around the small brass cannon, clutching at the heavy drag ropes. The use of field armament was extremely rare in the wilderness and all of them were eager to see the fun.

"No more than six on the drags," Crosbie said amiably, catching some of the suppressed excitement. "Any of you lads know anything about guns?"

Edmond de la Foure grinned quickly, a darting gambler's smile. He began to work his way through the crowd. But a thin man with a prominent, bobbing Adam's-apple reached Crosbie first. He tugged at his forelock with an embarrassed gesture. "Powder boy, I was, Colonel," he said in a tense voice. "Aboard of the Esmeralda that was. I kin load and swab and like that."

"And I, *mon colonel*," de la Foure said quickly, "Have received a cadet's training in the sighting of small pieces."

"Fine," Crosbie said heartily. "A fine team. Canister to start," he said, clapping the Count on the back. He turned to the thin man. "What's your name?"

"Fisher, Colonel," the tall man said, gulping rapidly. "Jeb Fisher, Major Burnham's command."

"Very good, Jeb," Crosbie smiled. "Load with canister. Medium charge. Don't use ball as long as you have any canister left. Now, you first six men can run up the piece after Jeb has loaded. The rest of you get your rifles and take positions behind the mound. And keep down. We don't want those Indians attacking before we're ready for them."

Edmond de la Foure watched Fisher carefully as the thin man measured out his powder charge and inserted the thin metal can of musket balls. Then the Count dribbled powder gently into the touch hole, priming the cannon.

During the delay, Blanchard moved closer to Crosbie and whispered, "What do you reckon is keeping the Shawnees back? It'll be dark pretty soon."

Crosbie shook his head slowly. "Senseless," he agreed. "But Indians sometimes need a little time to work themselves up. They had a chance when they were first discovered. But every minute they wait reduces their chances. They're finished when we get the gun emplaced, though we may have to give them a few rounds to prove it to them."

Together the Colonel and the Lieutenant turned west, estimating the dwindling sunlight. After dark, the Shawnees would quit as they always did. Possibly they might besiege the town but until sunrise the next day, there would be little danger from them. They had wasted their advantage by lying in that ravine and trading long-range shots after they'd been discovered. If they had made a concerted charge then, they might have overrun the settlement, but now Crosbie was sure they could be easily stopped. It was a strange problem, for of all the military errors they could make, warring Indians seldom wasted a chance at surprise.

"Reckon they'll come at all, Colonel?" Blanchard asked, his mind concerned with the same problem that worried Crosbie.

"Needn't be so fretful," Crosbie said. "You can go chase them if they don't, but we'll give them a little time first." He smiled at Blanchard. "Stay back here. I'll go up and lay the gun. Then de la Foure can take charge."

Willing hands had rushed the unwieldy cannon up on top of the mound before the Indians could possibly have been aware of what Crosbie was planning. From every loophole in the block-houses, a withering spatter of rifle fire intimidated any Shawnee who was not under cover. Crosbie had his field piece behind its embrasure before the first shot was fired at him.

"Point blank range, sir," he said to the Count. "No adjustments to make. Aim directly at the mouth of the ravine. Keep your slow match burning briskly all the time. You may have a long wait."

Fisher's Adam's-apple danced erratically as the former powder boy listened to Crosbie. "Canister all the time?"

"That would be best," Crosbie agreed gravely. He ducked down carefully below the low parapet and motioned de la Foure to get down. "Maybe those Shawnee don't know about field pieces, so hold your fire until you get a good target. When they charge, let them reach the cabins before you fire. And then fire as often as you can as long as you have a target."

Fisher grinned widely. "By Gawd, Colonel, I guess it'll scare 'em spitless. Ain't been a big gun west of Pitt since I been out here." De la Foure's grin matched Fisher's.

Crosbie nodded and slid down the mound, his loose kilt bundling around his hips. Burnham's men grinned but only one said anything and he choked his words off short in his throat when he saw Crosbie's hot glare. That fancy skirt affair was sure funny, but when a man as big as Crosbie looked that mad, why then maybe it wasn't quite so funny after all. Crosbie shook his kilt into place, saw to the security of his skene-dhu and then dashed quickly across to the cabins.

General Putnam waited stolidly with Blanchard, his round red face almost placid. He nodded at Crosbie amiably as though they were working together in close harmony.

"Do you plan a diversionary movement, Colonel?" he asked.

"Not yet, sir," Crosbie said frigidly. "We'll let the Shawnee attack if he plans to."

Putnam shrugged faintly. Apparently the Indians were stupidly massed in that long ravine. If they were, a few men could do great damage by moving around behind them. But then again, they might have scouts out all around the settlement and a raid wouldn't even get clear of the cabins. It was a commander's decision and he had relinquished command to Crosbie.

The attack came as Indian attacks always came. The sporadic firing died slowly. Then from the ravine came the first daring young warriors, eager for a reputation. The organized effort followed. A sweeping flood of dark bodies flitted among the trees at the edge of the ravine. Then, as the Shawnees massed, their dreadful war-cry sounded high and frightening, making even Crosbie feel an ominous tightness in the pit of his stomach. The hideous screeching rose to a frenzied pitch with the Shawnees goading themselves to the attack. From the Marquis's cabin, Crosbie could hear women whimpering at the evil sounds. As the tense expectancy mounted almost unbearably, the younger men stationed in the blockhouses shot toward the dark forest, shot without aiming merely to relieve their nerves. The Shawnees attacked in disciplined waves, with nearly half of them firing from the shelter of the trees while others dashed across the open ground, bent low and sprinting desperately to reach the cabins.

Crosbie aimed with slow deliberation, picking a glittering mica breast ornament as his target, squeezing his trigger gently. The bravely painted warrior leaped in agony when Crosbie fired and then slid along the ground, plowing a deep furrow. Crosbie waited to see no more, but ran behind the Marquis's cabin where he could see the mound where his gun was emplaced. He reloaded automatically as he ran, his mind busy with plans.

Along the top of the mound, riflemen exposed themselves dangerously, rising or kneeling in order to pick a target. But Edmond de la Foure kneeled patiently beside the cannon, his long thin face tense with strain as he held the slow match poised above the touchhole. A good man, was Crosbie's surprised thought, a daring man with a gambler's sense of timing. Just the right sort for a gunner. He turned to watch the field, saw the first Indian reach the line of cabins and go down under a flailing rifle butt. The open ground was alive with swiftly running Indians. Crosbie shouted at the Count and as he shouted, his words were blown away in the blast from the cannon.

For a moment, all sound seemed to stop short, the defenders seemingly as shocked as the attackers. Then from the close-lying trees went up a loud screaming wail of terror. For the canister had swept across that open area like a giant scythe. Hundreds of musket balls had chopped a wide deadly path through living flesh. The attack was over. Less than a dozen Shawnees returned to the trees and not one of them was unwounded. De la Foure and Fisher reloaded swiftly, fired again without an adequate target, but the same frightened yells came from the woods. To Crosbie's eye, it seemed as though the Indian commander had concentrated his men at the point of the ravine nearest the mound. But Blanchard had his men under some rudimentary cover by that time and they returned the increased fire with good will, shooting in staggered volleys after the fashion of seasoned Indian fighters so that each man had a chance to reload while the others fired.

With no warning, an Indian whooped and went racing toward the mound in long buck jumps. He was a thin man, tall for a Shawnee and completely naked except for the vivid smears of paint on his body.

The Marquis tugged urgently at Crosbie's sleeve. The Colonel ignored him while he watched the running warrior. The Indian reached the foot of the high mound and came sprinting up the slope, brandishing a long, feather-decorated tomahawk, screaming his high war cry defiantly. From the trees came an exultant echo of the whoop and Crosbie tensed, wondering if this might be the beginning of a new concerted attack.

Edmond de la Foure squatted imperturbably behind the cannon, holding his slow-match close to the touchhole of the reloaded gun. He eyed the racing Shawnee without excitement, not moving his match. One Indian was no target for a cannon.

Four rifles cracked in unison. The Shawnee screeched in shrill agony and flopped forward on the slope, digging his tomahawk deep in the turf with a savage swing of his arm. His fingers clutched at the earth, then relaxed. His lifeless body rolled back down to the foot of the mound. Jeb Fisher half rose to see him. He spat a fat gobber of tobacco juice over the parapet before the Count pulled him down to safety.

Crosbie let out a pent-up breath with an audible sigh. He turned to the Marquis. "Your son's a good gunner, sir."

The Marquis's eyes glittered proudly but he contented himself with a brief bow.

"Only six men have been wounded so far, Colonel," d'Aucourt said softly in a voice meant only for Crosbie's ears. "And one poor fellow was caught out among the trees when the savages attacked. General Putnam asked me to advise you of the situation."

"What's being done with them?" Crosbie asked harshly, angered at having given no thought to the wounded and no provision for their care.

"The ladies," the Marquis answered. "They have appropriated most of the bedding and all the large cabins. Doctor Saugrain directs the proceedings. There is already enough hot water for all of us to bathe when this is over."

Crosbie frowned. It was no work for a well-born lady, but he hated to take men from the loopholes. Best let it go until the number of wounded became serious. "Please keep me informed, sir," he requested politely.

"Certainly, Colonel." The Marquis looked up at the mound, watched the stolid riflemen at their work. "Do you think the savages will dare to charge your gun, sir?"

Crosbie shrugged. "No way to tell," he said slowly, knowing the Marquis was fearful for his son. "But it's their only hope. I'd waste no..."

Like the yapping of hounds the yells from the woods rose to an excited pitch, a rising and falling shriek that spoke of decision. The Shawnees debouched from the ravine, a hard knot of running men who spread wide as they came. Crosbie saw the Indians massed among the trees, swift and elusive, streaked with vermilion and black and white.

The rifles of the settlement focused on the head of the ravine where the Shawnees were concentrated. The Indians had already reached the foot of the mound, lapping around on all sides to evade the deadly rifle fire that was cutting them down rapidly.

Edmond de la Foure sat quietly, waiting for the most useful target. As the number of Shawnees before him mounted to twenty or more, he touched the match to the primer vent of his gun. A blast of acrid white powder obscured the field briefly. When it blew away, there were a dozen Indians sprawled before the cannon. The Count rapidly hauled back the gun and Fisher reached for his swab.

As though the cannon had been their signal, the Indians broke from the sheltering trees, racing straight for the cabins, ignoring the mound. The half dozen leading warriors carried fat pine torches, whirling them viciously around their heads as they ran, sprinkling the bare ground with flaring sparks.

As he aimed his rifle, Crosbie had a moment to appreciate the sense of timing, the judgment of the Indian commander. With the gun out of action for a short time, Crosbie had lost his best weapon. This was the only moment for a charge across open ground and the Indians were charging. Crosbie, together with every rifleman in the settlement, aimed at one of the torch-bearing Indians. He pressed the trigger easily. The running Shawnee seemed to trip and fall. But in falling he threw his touch high toward the cabins. It fell short by some feet and lay burning on the grass, setting fire to a small mass of twigs and bark.

Crosbie ran down behind the line of cabins, reloading quickly. Blanchard stood squarely between two cabins, aiming his rifle. As Crosbie ran toward him, he fired carefully, then he spouted powder down the barrel and spat a bullet into the muzzle, ramming it down with a long even stroke of the ramrod. He primed his pan with a small powder flask he kept in his shirt pocket.

"Water, Mr. Blanchard," Crosbie snapped. "Organize a bucket brigade. Some one of those torches might reach the cabins."

Blanchard nodded, his cheek oddly swollen with a dozen rifle balls he carried there. He dropped them in his shot pouch, took a moment to fire his rifle once more and then dropped back toward the river, shouting for assistants as he went.

Crosbie ran the entire line of the cabins to see what harm had been done. The fire was not yet critical but if the stockade were burned, the new town would be seriously damaged by the loss of its work animals. The Indian attack might reach the cabins, but it didn't seem likely. Vaguely, he heard the sullen growl of the small cannon and realized that the open ground would have been swept clean once more. The Marquis's son had been a good choice for gunner.

With a long quavering defiant whoop, the Shawnees retreated again ; the same howling wail followed the blast from the cannon. But this time they had left their mark behind.

Three cabins burned briskly, their raw timber still damp with resin. Behind him, Crosbie saw Blanchard staggering up the bank with buckets, followed by small boys and a growing line of men, all with some sort of container to carry water. Crosbie signaled the Marquis to divert some of them to the farthest cabin. He assigned de Flaville to the middle one and left the other for Blanchard. The fires had a good start, but having caught them so quickly, the settlers could easily get them under control.

General Putnam strolled easily up to Crosbie, nodded pleasantly, his customarily sedate air somewhat spoiled by the wide burnt-powder marks on his cheek. Putnam had been serving a rifle energetically for some time, but now he moved with the easy stride of a man with no cares.

"Well done, Duncan," he said agreeably. "Firefighting detail in hand?"

Crosbie indicated Blanchard's line of bucket carriers. "Should be, sir," he said heavily. "Unless we don't have time …"

"We don't," Putnam barked. "Here they come again !" The General sprinted off to find a vacant loophole, leaving Crosbie to stare at the third wave of painted Shawnees dashing from the line of trees, screaming exultantly as though they hadn't been twice repulsed with severe losses.

Crosbie posted himself near the blockhouse where he could see the entire field. De la Foure had waited too long, he thought. The Indians were coming closer, so close that the men fighting fire were endangered. The Marquis had managed to put his out and Blanchard's was nearly under control, but de Flaville's cabin was directly in line with the Indians and the young Frenchman recalled his men. Why didn't the Count fire? Crosbie heard himself cursing wildly, fearful that the Marquis's son had been shot. There was no replacement available, if he ...

The cannon roared, cutting through Crosbie's thoughts. But three shots had thrown it off aim. The cannon shot cut a great bare patch through the trees, bringing howls from the Indians still under cover, but doing little damage to the new attackers. But the riflemen were steady. Their deadly aimed fire began to cut into the ranks of Shawnees.

Blanchard threw the last bucket of water on his cabin roof and saw the last flicker of fire die away. He jumped to the ground and ran for cover. But he stopped, seeing one cabin still afire. He snatched up a bucket and sprinted along the front of the cabin in full view of the approaching Indians. With a wide sweep of his arm, he threw water up over the burning torch on the roof, then withdrew for a full bucket. De Flaville seeing his determination, grabbed a bucket, handed it to Blanchard and ran back for another.

Blanchard pivoted, hurling the water. He bent well forward and made himself as small a target as possible. But then, instead of running for cover, he bent lower still, and lower. He fell so slowly it seemed almost an act of deliberation. That couldn't be, Crosbie thought, that was senseless. Then he saw the feathered tip of a Shawnee arrow shaft protruding from the gray silk back of Blanchard's best coat as Blanchard crumpled slowly to the ground.

For a moment the scene had no reality. Crosbie's only feeling was that queer bewilderment. And then, from the nearest of the double cabins being used to shelter the wounded, burst a figure that gave the unreal scene even greater unreality. Gold and white gown caught high in strained, clutching fingers so it would not impede her flying feet, towering court headdress awry on her dark hair, Mademoiselle Adrienne came racing down the wide battle-swept street between the double row of cabins. She paid no attention to shouts ; bullets and arrows obviously did not exist for her. Crosbie was shouting too, now, but miraculously the fool girl was not hit. She reached the spot where Blanchard lay, dropped to her knees in a bone-jarring plunge that was the final ruination of her satin gown, and began tugging Blanchard toward the doubtful shelter of the nearest cabin.

Crosbie dropped his empty rifle without thinking. He ran with the earth-shaking strides of a heavy man, his face a hard mask. Another arrow quivered in the ground beside Blanchard who was trying to crawl on his hands and knees while Adrienne tugged at his shoulder and, incredibly, scolded at him in furious little bursts of panting French. Crosbie leaned down in full stride, picked up Blanchard as if he had no more weight than a small satchel and carried him quickly around the cabin, shouting at Adrienne to follow. As the best target available, they drew concentrated fire from the advancing Shawnees. A thrown tomahawk ripped through a paper window in the cabin as they ran.

The Colonel raced on in his lumbering pace, carrying Blanchard in both arms, heading for the double cabins at the far end of town. Cammie had the door open and she stood there, waiting. Crosbie lowered Blanchard easily to a bed.

"Wait ..." Blanchard gasped. "Colonel, wait just a second." He groped for Adrienne's hand and only then did she cease the rapid-fire little scolding phrases. "A nice charge, Mademoiselle," Blanchard panted the words. Christ, he sounds happy, Crosbie thought unbelievingly. Happy, at a time like this ! "But..." Blanchard choked a little ... "but you forgot your little gun this time..."

Adrienne made a sound like a sob.

"Enough," Crosbie growled. He pushed the girl aside, turned Blanchard on his stomach, yanked out his skene-dhu and cut the coat and shirt, barring Blanchard's back. The arrow had struck glancingly, scraping a long furrow along the rib before it entered Blanchard's body. It didn't seem to be far under the skin.

Crosbie fumbled for a bullet from his shot pouch, held it to Blanchard's mouth. "Bite," he commanded. "I'm going to take it out.'

Blanchard bit the bullet tightly, braced both hands against the timber of his bed and waited, keeping his head turned away from the Colonel. He heard, as from a great distance, Adrienne's thin cry as Crosbie cut with his blade. The Colonel seemed to take hours with his work and Adrienne crammed both hands against her mouth, trying not to cry out again. But fear verging on panic swelled her throat. Cammie, catching Crosbie's impatient gesture, drew the weeping girl into her arms and led her outside until Crosbie had finished.

Crosbie made four shallow cuts to let the blood flow freely in case the arrow might carry infection, then he dug deeply once, gripped the shaft with one hand and pulled steadily as his razor-sharp knife felt for the arrow-head. The arrow came loose gradually. As it cleared his skin, Blanchard twitched, then shuddered heavily and for long minutes. Crosbie deftly bound up the gash with a length of Blanchard's shirt and put his bloody hand beside Blanchard's face.

"Don't swallow it," he said.

Blanchard spat out the flattened bullet into Crosbie's palm. Teeth marks had bitten so deeply that the shot was nearly in two pieces. "Fire ..." he gasped, fighting the waves of pain and weakness. "Fire out?"

"All out," Crosbie said, having no idea whether it was or not, but wanting Blanchard to rest. "Lie back while we clean up."

Crosbie ran toward the door, suddenly mindful of his irresponsibility in leaving the field when the Indians were attacking. Thoughtlessly he still carried the bloody dirk clutched in his hand and Adrienne moaned when she saw it. Then she buried her head on Cammie's shoulder.

Crosbie frowned. "What ails her? She was brave enough a few minutes ago ..." If, he thought, you could call her foolhardy actions brave.

Cammie managed a small smile. "Are you blind, Dooncahn?" she murmured. "It is the young Lieutenant, of course. And I think she no longer doubts her feeling for him. I think she has learned much of... of human values in this wild new world she was so reluctantly a part of."

"Ah," Crosbie said. He bent quickly to Cammie's lips, kissing her hungrily.

But his brief moment was broken by Jock's insistent tugging at his elbow. "When do we attack, Dooncahn? When do we attack?"

"Soon," Crosbie snapped, recalled to his duty by an effort of will. He forced a smile for Jock, then ran again in his heavy strides down the line of cabins.

Jock's insistent young treble followed him toward the block-house but Crosbie had no time for the boy. The Shawnees were among the cabins, only a few of them, but enough to endanger the town.

Men who had been firing from the loopholes in the leading row of cabins had wisely retreated to the second row and their steady fire was rapidly cutting down the number of Indians. But the critical fighting went on behind the cabins.

In the growing dusk, a fitfully brilliant light was thrown over the town by the burning cabin that Blanchard had been wounded trying to save. Friends were not easily distinguishable from foes and the tight knots of struggling men were unrecognizable, nightmarish shapes to Crosbie. He made out the distinctive frieze of a Shawnee scalp lock silhouetted against the light and he dove at the Indian who had his arm upraised with a tomahawk poised. His skene-dhu, already wet with Blanchard's blood, went deep into the warrior's armpit, grating nastily on bone. Crosbie wrenched it loose, plunged it deep once more and then stepped back, letting the Shawnee brave slide forward off the blade.

Riflemen poured from the two blockhouses that faced on the river. Now that the fighting was hand-to-hand, every spare man was vitally needed. Crosbie saw the portly figure of General Putnam following the extra men. Trust Old Put to take prompt action, Crosbie thought.

As the newcomers joined the melee, the light field piece crashed viciously once more, drowning all other noise. The high quavering war whoops rose and fell with a note of desperation. This was the critical moment, Crosbie told himself. In a matter of minutes, the fight would be over. And if Edmond de la Foure had swept the bare ground clear, then there would not be another attack.

From the open space between the town and the line of densely packed trees came the high wild keening of bagpipes, a shrill insistent drone that froze everyone momentarily. Crosbie turned quickly, running with all his speed toward the open stretch, hearing himself cursing monotonously, savagely, as he ran. That fool boy, Jock. He'd get himself killed, sure.

The boy paraded bravely along the ground, pacing off his short strides with the timeless arrogance of a veteran pipe-major. The great pibroch towered high above his head and he needed all his strength to keep the bag inflated to a proper tension. Crosbie noted unconsciously that the boy was playing well. His notes were clear and sharp, rising high above the excited yelps of the Shawnees. Jock made a slow stately turn, faced the cabins and blared the strident battle cry of the Campbells. Crosbie ran desperately, his breath choking him as he strained for air.

But the Shawnees reached him first. While Crosbie was still yards away, a tall sprinting buck smashed his tomahawk contemptuously at Jock. Luckily the Indian was more attracted by the pibroch than the boy. He snatched the bagpipes greedily and ran on toward the woods, flourishing the tartaned pipes as he ran. But others followed and another war hatchet swooped down at the defenseless boy on the ground. Behind him Crosbie could hear the hoarse angry curses of the men who followed on a charge that swept the Shawnees before them.

Crosbie left his feet in a low dive, took the leading Indian around the waist before he could strike Jock with his tomahawk. They rolled over and over in the dirt, the Shawnee struggling to shorten the stroke of his hatchet, Crosbie plunging and plunging with his dirk, not aiming the blade, but merely jabbing it in whenever he found flesh beneath the point. When the Indian relaxed and rolled over, Crosbie pushed up on his hands and knees, felt a racing Indian trip over him and fall. He ignored the Shawnee completely and ran on toward the fallen boy.

But another had reached him first. Over his recumbent tousled head, Cammie wrapped her arms warmly, sheltering her son from the yelping Shawnees that surrounded them.

Crosbie roared heavily, a deep rumbling growl like a wounded bear. His skene-dhu was a flashing streak of red fire as he struck first at one, then at another. A weighted blow struck his head, dimming his vision momentarily, sending him wobbling to his knees before he recovered his balance. Then he sank to his knees again and touched the powdered elegance of Cammie's scented hair lying still against the deep dust of the ground.

The maddened men of the settlement swept past Crosbie, pursuing the retreating Shawnees with a determined charge that would not stop short of the ravine.

The danger was past. The Shawnees had retreated and they would not return. But Cammie lay still, unmoving, her warm arms still protecting her weeping son, even in death.

CHAPTER TWENTY FIVE

The hours immediately following Cammie's death were forever hazy in Crosbie's memory. He could recall brief episodes, particularly the moment he ran after the retreating Shawnees and stumbled over the lifeless body of a Frenchman lying flat on his back, arms spread wide as though he were displaying the ornate design of his court clothes. The Parisian had worn his own hair, heavily powdered. A ring of white hair still remained above his ears but the top of his head was smoothly red where the scalp had been stripped away. His facial muscles sagged with the release of tension so that his cheeks folded down to his chin and his eyelids were pulled down, exposing great staring eyes that followed Crosbie accusingly as he scrambled to his feet again and ran on toward the ravine, mouthing heavy curses at the top of his lungs, a constant spate of swearing that left him with a throat that felt raw for days.

The bulk of the retreating Shawnees had leaped the ravine and were in full flight. But a simultaneous charge from the mound and the blockhouses had cut off a small detachment of about a dozen at the head of the ravine. Most of the pursuing riflemen kept after the main body, but a small number kept the dozen surrounded. Crosbie joined them, racing in among them with a wild yell and continuing through them toward the beleaguered Indians. The riflemen rose cheering and followed.

Younger men, faster on their feet, passed the Colonel before he plunged into the last thicket. Only that saved the burly Scot who, crazed with grief, seemed determined to crush the Indians with the sheer massive weight of his body. His example was enough to inspire the riflemen to equal recklessness. They trampled down the wild thorn that concealed the last pocket of resistance, firing as they ran, then discarding rifles for swords, hatchets or bayonets. Crosbie, still armed only with his bloody skene-dhu, hurled himself at full speed against a Shawnee who knelt with his musket at his shoulder, waiting for a sure target.

The musket ball carried away much of the bedraggled late that still hugged Crosbie's throat. Then the Colonel hit the greasy painted body, felt lithe muscles bunch and strain under his hands. And Crosbie laughed, a high insane laugh that went unnoticed in the fury of the fight. He stabbed the Shawnee again and again, digging the blade deep and watching the warrior's eyes as first fear, then a sort of resignation came into them and, at the last, defeat and death. Crosbie rose then, shaken but sane again. He shuddered involuntarily.

The fight was over. Burnham's veteran woodsmen had made short work of the small body of Indians. Crosbie saw one of them stoop, sweep his knife in a quick circle and yank loose the high roached scalp of a Shawnee. Beside him, a watching Frenchman leaned suddenly against a tree and vomited heavily. Crosbie's legs trembled under his weight at the abrupt ending of strain. He walked slowly, unsteadily toward the head of the ravine, the shortest distance to level ground.

"Gawddamed renegade, I reckon," one of the riflemen said contemptuously, lifting a dead man's head by the hair. "Christ, I hate a white Injun wuss'n them red hellions any day." He spat a heavy stream of tobacco juice and felt at his hip for his skinning knife. "This un ain't dead yet, don't appear."

Crosbie put his hand on the man's arm, leaning his full weight against the knife while he bent forward to look at the exposed face of the renegade. From the waist up, he was naked. He wore long leggings, a breech clout and plain heavy moccasins.

A cylindrical parfleche bag hung at his belt. His hair, unlike most white Indians, was untrimmed, falling in tight short braids on either side of his face. But naked or dressed, painted or washed, it was a face Crosbie would never forget. And looking at it, Crosbie felt no least surprise that he should see it here, at this moment.

"Take him up to town," Crosbie ordered in a hoarse tired voice.

"He's mine," the rifleman objected. "I reckon I ..."

Crosbie merely tightened his grip on the man's arm, tensing his muscles until the knife fell to the ground from numbed fingers.

"Up to the town," he repeated mildly. "We need him." He let his grip relax and looked hard into the rifleman's eyes. "His name is Oliver Budd. He'll have a lot to tell us if he lives. He's the man behind this attack."

"Ain't goin' to live long," the rifleman muttered. "Derned near got his head cut plumb off." He shoved his boot idly against Budd's body. "Mike, give me a hand here with this. Cuhnel wants himself a souvenir."

Crosbie waited stolidly while four men agreeably swung the limp body of Oliver Budd between them and walked slowly up the uneven ground of the ravine toward town. Crosbie followed then, taking stiff heavy strides on his weary legs, his head down, his eyes half closed with fatigue. He carried the dainty deadly skene-dhu still gripped unconsciously in his fist.

Cammie's body had been removed by the time Crosbie returned from the ravine. The bare open stretch between the trees and the first cabins of Gallipolis seemed miles long to Crosbie, a space that was too much for his waning strength, a journey he had no real wish to complete. There was nothing at the end for him now.

"Put him outside my cabin," he told the men carrying Oliver Budd's limp body. "And leave his hair on."

The men chuckled appreciatively and then slowly, the good humor vanished when they saw the Colonel's stricken, deathly expression.

Slowly, from the line of cabins, a small group of men came forward to meet Crosbie. The men with Budd's body turned away toward his cabin.

The portly solid frame of General Putnam reached Crosbie first. He stopped and let him approach.

"I have only just learned . ." the General began.

Crosbie made a weary gesture. Putnam's eyes widened as the reddened dirk flashed in the air near him. Crosbie grunted and bent down slowly to ram the blade home in its scabbard He wiped his stained fingers on the tattered remnants of his velvet jacket and went past Putnam without saying a word. The others, led by the Marquis, still elegant and erect even though he had not yet recovered his wig, stayed discreetly at a distance, not wanting to intrude upon the Colonel's sorrow.

Crosbie went slowly toward his cabin. The four men carrying Budd had dropped him beside the door and gone away, bothered not at all by the possibility that the renegade would surely die without medical attention. Crosbie leaned with one hand against the log wall of the cabin and looked down at Budd. The renegade lay on his side, breathing in shallow gasps. Crosbie wearily drew his skene-dhu again and bent down to cut loose the parfleche bag that hung from Budd's belt. Then he put away his blade and went inside the cabin, holding the pale rawhide pouch in his huge fist.

Adrienne turned when the door opened, raised her tear-stained face and looked at him.

"How is he?" Crosbie asked in a croaking voice.

"Bien," Adrienne said almost inaudibly, as though there were nothing more she could say.

The wounded were still few. No more than ten men were lying on pallets on the floor. There would be more, though, Crosbie thought numbly. More would be lying out among the trees waiting for someone to come for them. And the two inept French doctors and all the people who knew anything of medicine would be outside, helping their own. It would be some time before anyone had time or effort for Oliver Budd's wounds.

"All," Adrienne said slowly, her tongue stumbling with her uncertain English, "all here are well, *mon colonel.*"

She rose from Blanchard's bedside when Crosbie nodded vaguely. There was so much for him to do and he tried to think of what should come first. Patch up Budd, he supposed, and see what he could find out from the renegade. Unconsciously, he turned the parfleche bag he had taken from Budd in his fingers, opened it idly as he stared down at Blanchard's flushed face. A thin sheaf of English money came out, the bright flimsy bills wrapped around something stiffer. Crosbie unwrapped the folded money. Inside was a sheet of paper that displayed a well-drawn map of the new town of Gallipolis, a map drawn expertly to scale, with particular attention being paid to the ravine that approached the settlement. Crosbie turned the sheet and read the short lines of writing on the reverse side. Then, with solemn deliberation, he folded the paper again and rammed it, together with the English money, into the capacious pocket of his sporran. His face was drawn and ghastly. They had not buried their traitor when they buried a fair-haired girl named Lucie. Their traitor was still active, had come closer to success this time than ever before. Only now he knew who that traitor was.

He started in surprise as Adrienne stretched up on the tips of her toes and kissed him gently on his grimy cheek.

"We were all... all so fond of your Cammie. We... we cannot tell you..." her voice broke and she dropped again beside Blanchard's bed, burying her face in her hands and sobbing.

Crosbie looked down at her, then bent for a close look at Blanchard. The boy was sleeping heavily and his color, though high, seemed good enough. He did not have the pallor of approaching death. Well, he and the girl could take care of each other. Neither of them need know about the next grim step. Perhaps Adrienne did know, or suspect. He could not be sure of that. Maybe she suspected only a part of it. Or perhaps her suspicions had been as far afield as his own.

Crosbie turned and went outside. The pale light from his cabin flooded the ground beyond the door. Far down the street was a cluster of men standing near another light; a group that included the Marquis, his son and General Putnam. But near at hand was Oliver Budd and he came first in Crosbie's view. He left the door standing open so that he could see his way.

Budd lay still and straight near the cabin, just beyond the splash of light. Crosbie took one step toward him, then froze in his tracks when he noticed a quick movement. It seemed for a moment that Budd had lifted his arm. But slowly, silently, a second figure rose from the ground, a tall lean man whose hand clutched something that glinted in the dusk. And not only glinted, Crosbie knew, but was also dulled with blood.

Budd was dead now.

Charles de Flaville stood erect and with his left hand brushed back the long hair that had fallen forward around his face. "A dangerous souvenir, Colonel," he said smoothly. "The men told me you had taken him. I came here to find him alive, waiting to attack again when you came out into the darkness..."

"Put down the knife," Crosbie interrupted flatly.

De Flaville gestured with his stained blade. "But I have..."

"You were too late," Crosbie said tonelessly. "I found the map first." He crouched tensely, waiting for the young man's response, guessing what it had to be. But for a long moment there was no response. De Flaville stood rooted, frozen. Crosbie could see his face only dimly. How wrong could you be about a man, Crosbie asked himself tiredly. How could you see only good when so much was there of evil? For Cammie's sake he should have known. For Lucie's sake. Lucie, who loved this man and to whom the shock of his betrayal was the end of all hope. She had tried to warn them the night she died. She had given de Flaville his chance to speak, and when he did not, only death had kept Lucie silent...

His thoughts were achingly bitter. When the young Frenchman charged him suddenly, Crosbie had no warning.

But his dirk was only inches from his fingers. He flicked it from its stocking scabbard and remained as he was, crouched low, reaching forward with blade and open hand. De Flaville reached him swiftly in a hard lunge, blade striking up in a tight controlled arc that should have reached Crosbie's belly.

Almost contemptuously, the Colonel swept his left arm wide, knocking de Flaville's blade aside and spinning the younger man about. Then the burly Scot clamped his left arm around de Flaville's neck, bending him back over his knee while he placed the point of his skene-dhu at the cadet's throat.

"Drop it," he growled heavily. He tensed his left arm, bending de Flaville back farther in an iron grip.

Wildly the Frenchman stabbed in tight desperate arcs with his knife. The frantically seeking blade could not reach the Colonel, but there was a small margin for safety. Crosbie exerted his full power, hauling at de Flaville's neck with his crooked elbow, unwilling to use his dirk against a man who should be made to face his own people for punishment.

De Flaville relaxed abruptly, slumping on Crosbie's arm. Far down the street, the collected group of men began to run toward Crosbie's cabin, their footsteps soft in the deep dust. A voice that sounded like the Marquis's shouted, "Qui va la?" Crosbie shifted his position slightly, still retaining his grip on de Flaville's neck. And as he moved, the Frenchman made one last desperate bid for freedom, surging mightily to turn so that his blade would reach Crosbie. The Colonel stepped back, braced his knee and yanked quickly. A dull thin crack sounded ominously loud in the stillness. De Flaville gasped. Another sharper crack and de Flaville slumped.

Crosbie let the young Frenchman's lifeless body slip to the ground. His head was strangely out of position, as though even in death, he strained his neck to keep a sharp eye on Oliver Budd, who could have talked and in talking, betrayed him. Slowly, Crosbie sheathed his dirk and straightened as the Marquis reached him.

Crosbie turned his sporran, extracted the sheaf of English money and the folded map. These he thrust into the Marquis's limp hand.

"Where is Jock?" he growled.

"But what..." Putnam insisted. "Duncan, what in God's name..."

"The Marquis has a map," Crosbie said impatiently. "That will tell you what you need to know. Where is my boy?"

The Marquis stared down at the two bodies, de Flaville and Oliver Budd, unable to comprehend what Crosbie had said. Edmond de la Foure knelt beside his friend, moved his head gently into its proper position.

"The boy is in that cabin, *mon colonel*," a light voice said. An arm covered in grubby white satin extended, pointing at a closed cabin door.

Crosbie nodded his thanks. He pushed between General Putnam and the Marquis, ignored their sharply insistent questions as he strode directly toward the cabin.

Two slim scented ladies hovered around the high carved bedstead inside the cabin, one holding Jock's limp hand in hers, the other slowly stroking his rumpled hair. The boy's eyes were tightly closed. In the corner of each, a large tear gathered to roll down the furrows of his cheeks. As Crosbie entered, the ladies smiled at him without rising.

"I would be grateful for a moment alone with my boy," Crosbie said gruffly.

Jock's eyes opened wide when he heard Crosbie's voice. His lips began a smile, but never completed it. He turned his face to the wall.

The ladies withdrew silently, their manner slightly disapproving. They glanced at the heavy Scot with such obvious sympathy that he felt a momentary rage to kick them both. He restrained himself, bowed them out the door and shut it firmly behind them.

"Maman...?" Jock asked in a broken voice. "They wouldn't tell me."

Crosbie put his hard hand on the boy's arm with a gentle touch, the clumsy, sure gentleness of a very strong man. "We are just the two of us now, Jock," he said softly. "Only the two Crosbies, Duncan and Jock."

Jock turned quickly on the bed, pillowing his teary face against Crosbie's massive chest. "Am I," he mumbled, "am I your boy now?"

"Aye," Crosbie insisted. "Didn't I marry your lovely mother?" He himself couldn't remember. The ceremony had proceeded, but had it reached that point? Had Blanchard passed the ring, had Père La Font pronounced the words? It didn't matter. As surely as he drew breath, he knew that Cammie had been his wife, knew that Jock was his son. "You're my boy now," he said firmly, feeling the racking sobs that shook Jock's small back.

The boy twitched, pushed away to look up at Crosbie. "They took the pipes," he said. "They took them away from me. I couldn't help it. A big savage..."

"It doesn't matter," Crosbie soothed. "I'll find another set for us, my boy. It doesn't matter."

"But why didn't they run?" the boy insisted. "When I played the pipes, they didn't run!"

"But they did," Crosbie said flatly. "They ran right over you, they were so anxious to get away. And then later, a few resisted until the last, but they weren't Indians, Jock. Not the men in the ravine. The Indians ran away. Only a few renegade white men stayed behind to fight after you piped the battle cry."

That wasn't true, either, he thought. But then, in a way, it was true, as his other lie had been true. The disciplined Shawnees would never have broken at the sound of the pibroch, not before they had been cut to pieces by the cannon. But, nonetheless, it was Budd's evil influence over the Indian leader that had kept them fighting so hard against such odds. Crosbie shuddered to think what might have happened had Putnam not mounted the brass cannon on his boat.

Jock's worried face smoothed slightly. Professionally then, he had not been a complete failure. His sharp piping had once again turned the tide of battle and there was some satisfaction in remembering that. But maman was gone. The warm hearted tender woman he had learned to call Cammie, as Crosbie did. She was dead and he had to stay alive without her, remain in a world that already seemed too large and complex ever to conquer.

Crosbie's hand pressed Jock close. "We'll not forget," he said gently. He put the boy down in bed again, pulled the blanket up loosely to his neck. "Now, sleep, my boy. I must see to the men. But I'll be back soon. You sleep now."

Crosbie sat watching Jock as the boy dutifully closed his eyes. The boy was dead tired from the terrible day. In a moment, he'd be asleep, if he would only lie still. Crosbie stayed in the dim cabin, patiently immobile, until Jock's breathing evened out into a regular cadence.

Once Jock opened his eyes, fright standing large in his expression, but when he saw Crosbie, he smiled mistily before he dosed them again and slept.

"Sleep, my boy," Crosbie whispered, bending to kiss the damp cheek.

Softly, he rose from the bed, stood for a moment to be sure his boy slept soundly. Then he picked his way softly to the door, opened it and went out into the dusk to find General Putnam and the Marquis.

CHAPTER TWENTY SIX

The cabin was lighted by a single candle that shed its dim glow over a small table where General Putnam sat opposite the Marquis, both men leaning forward tautly with their elbows on the table, faces intent and slightly angry. Beside them Edmond de la Foure stood patiently, holding himself erect by his grip on the back of the chair. Colonel Crosbie pulled the door shut behind him and dropped the locking bar.

Putnam pushed back from the table, leaning into his armchair and smiled thinly up at Crosbie. "Well, Duncan, I'm glad you managed..."

Crosbie had stopped at the Marquis's cabin before going in search of Putnam. He had seen Cammie, her round quiet face still rosy in the soft candlelight. And in Crosbie's eyes as he looked at Putnam was the blank black awareness of death. Putnam's voice dwindled away and he locked his jaw tightly as he tried to meet the steady glare from the Colonel's tired red-rimmed eyes.

The Marquis sat without moving, staring blindly at his folded hands. Between them he held the expertly drawn map Crosbie had found in Budd's parfleche bag. Underneath lay the slim pad of English money and nearby a fat roll of American currency. The Marquis shifted his hands slightly and the stiff paper in his fingers rustled with a soft sound like mice far away.

"We have all of us endured much today," the Marquis said in a frail, whispering tone. "You most of all, I believe, mon cher colonel. I should like to..."

Crosbie gestured impatiently. He could endure no sympathies. He couldn't bring himself to speak of his loss. Cammie was dead. The knowledge—and the hurt—lay within him in a hard hot lump.

When Crosbie spoke, it was not to Putnam nor d'Aucourt. He turned to Edmond de la Foure who stood near the table.

"You did well today, sir," he said bleakly. "Superb gunnery, by any judgment." He pulled a stool from the wall and eased himself slowly down. He put his heavy forearms on the table and folded his hands, unconsciously aping the Marquis's posture. With a strange dull curiosity he noticed that a long muscle in his thigh had begun to twitch rhythmically.

De la Foure bowed slightly and smiled at the Colonel. His thin face was taut with worry, cheekbones protruding sharply from a face that had been almost pudgy in Alexandria. The heavy dusting of powder had been shaken from his black hair, leaving it streaked with gray as though the young cadet had in the course of one short day become an old tired man, far too weary to speak.

The Marquis dropped the map on the table. "This was sent by Charles de Flaville," he said, his voice tight and brittle. "C'est incroyable, but Edmond recognized his handwriting immediately, though it was hardly necessary to have such corroboration." D'Aucourt shifted the wad of American currency, uncovering a folded paper. "In his pocket was this letter from the man Budd, which makes Charles's villainy quite obvious to all. In addition was this money, nearly five hundred dollars in American currency. And Charles had no money at all, save a small sum I advanced and a little more he had won at Poque from Edmond. This money, then, must have come from ..."

"A man named Fiske," Crosbie said heavily. He spread his feet wide apart on the floor to maintain his steadiness. Suddenly an intense weariness seized him and he had no energy for talk, none for worry or thought.

The Marquis blinked his eyes slowly at the Colonel. "You said…"

"Fiske," Crosbie repeated in a thick tone. "A man Blanchard met in Pittsburgh, a man who worked with Oliver Budd. Mr. Blanchard brought him out to Braddock's Field. We tied him in a wagon. Then he had five hundred dollars in his pocket, minus a few dollars. In the morning he was dead, murdered. The money was gone."

"And you think…"

"De Flaville killed him," Crosbie said flatly.

"What in God's name are you talking about?" General Putnam said angrily. "What…"

Crosbie's hard gray eyes swiveled toward Putnam. "We were speaking of a traitor, General," he growled. "Of a man who sold out his people, planned to murder them all, just to keep your swindle from coming to light." A growing fury deepened Crosbie's voice.

"My swindle!" Putnam bellowed. He half rose from his seat, hands reaching forward to grab Crosbie.

Edmond de la Foure struck swiftly. His long thin hand slashed at Putnam's wrist, numbing his entire right arm. "We will hear the good Colonel," he said softly, standing ominously above Putnam.

"There is no need for that, Edmond," the Marquis said sharply.

De la Foure laughed once, a high crackling sound that suggested his calm control had been won at considerable cost. "Look at the Colonel," he said to his father. "Had I not stopped General Putnam, he would have been killed." He leaned close to the enraged General and said lightly, "En bref, the Colonel Crosbie does not realize we have already spoken of this matter."

Crosbie's folded hands had spread open, waiting eagerly for Putnam to move closer, a high exultance tensing his muscles, flushing his face as fatigue washed away in a wave of fury. At de le Foure's words, he forced himself slowly to relax, realizing that the situation had somehow drastically changed.

Putnam sank back in his chair, nursing his numbed arm, his red face flaming with anger. "Very well," he said furiously. "You tell him. And advise him to keep his tongue under restraint until you've finished." He turned partially in his chair so that he could no longer see Crosbie squarely.

The Marquis's voice was low and shaky, but clearly audible to Crosbie. "The General has told us of the Scioto Company," he began. "It is now bankrupt, out of existence and we ... all of us are also bankrupt and ..."

"No," Crosbie said in a dull tone.

The Marquis smiled faintly. "Do not interrupt, my dear Colonel. I know you would counsel some daring course, but the facts are against you, against us all. We have no right to this land and the little money which our people still have would hardly purchase the land which comprises the village of Gallipolis. No more, certainly. We could buy no farming acreage, no land for stock or ..."

"No," Crosbie repeated. He glanced at Putnam tensely. "What became of the money paid for the lands, General?"

Putnam shook his head. "Never forwarded from France. Or so Colonel Duer claims."

"And the members of the swindling Scioto Company, sir," Crosbie said softly, "what responsibility have they toward the French settlers here?" When Putnam didn't answer immediately, Crosbie went further. "You're a member of the Scioto Company, aren't you, sir?"

Abruptly Putnam turned, facing Crosbie and leaning forward until their hands nearly touched on the table. "Duncan, listen to me," he said in a tone of deep sincerity. "I do not approve of the practices of the Scioto Company and I have never had any hand in controlling that company. But what they did is hardly the rare and dastardly swindle you think it to be. Every land company in the world—including the Ohio Company of Associates—has sold deeds to land upon which it legally held only an option and has later redeemed the option and validated the deeds. What makes the Scioto Company especially guilty in this matter is that there has been no serious attempt to purchase the land for which they sold deeds."

"What responsibility, sir?" Crosbie insisted implacably, obviously listening to nothing Putnam was saying.

"The company is bankrupt," Putnam said stiffly. "The members have no individual responsibility. Colonel Duer may possibly go to jail if he is prosecuted for fraud, provided sufficient evidence can be found. Otherwise he will most surely stay in prison for indebtedness."

"And nothing more?" Crosbie insisted.

"In God's name, Duncan, what do you want?" Putnam exploded. "I came here to try to work out a solution to this terrible problem. None of my colleagues take it lightly, I can assure you. The Marquis and I have been talking for an hour without …"

"First," Crosbie said sternly, "before we consider the matter of a solution, let's conclude the issue I raised. Who is responsible for the swindle? Who hired Charles De Flaville? Who employed Oliver Budd to waylay our people again and again?"

"A man named Oliver Budd was a member of the Scioto Company," Putnam snapped irritably. "A crony of Duer's, I believe. An oily fellow. I met him once and didn't like him. Why do you ask me these questions?"

Crosbie turned thoughtfully at Putnam's angry face. "Because, General," he said, his voice a soft purring note that Putnam had never heard before, "because Oliver Budd is lying dead outside my cabin. He led the Shawnees against this town today. And because, General, you are close to death yourself at this moment."

Crosbie's clear threat brought Putnam erect in his chair, his hand reaching for the smallsword at his belt. Then after a long silent moment, he shook his head. "No, Duncan," he said in a quiet, unworried voice, "It was not my order that brought Budd here, nor was it an order from any member I know." He leaned forward urgently. "We have built an honorable business in the Ohio Company. In order to form it, we were compelled to deal with scoundrels such as Duer and Budd, but believe me Duncan, we did not then know them as scoundrels, though we may have disliked them and their methods. We thought, God help us, that they were efficient men of business. And now, I and the other members of the Ohio Company want to do everything we can to straighten out the mess left by the Scioto swindle."

"And why," Crosbie asked in an accusing tone, "why did you insist that I maintain secrecy about my mission ? Why could no one know where these people were bound when they left Alexandria?"

Putnam shrugged. "I had to give Duer his chance to clean up the mess himself," he said quickly. "And I wanted to avoid a scandal if I possibly could. That may not have been noble of me, but I think it is understandable. But I repeat, Duncan, that none of my associates had any part in this terrible crime."

Crosbie nodded slowly. He knew Putnam too well to have any doubt of the General's honesty. He pressed one hand against his eyelids. "My apologies, General," he said heavily.

"You owe me no apology, Duncan," Putnam said firmly. "I asked you to serve me in protecting these people. You've done far better than I had a right to expect. If apologies are due, then I must ask your forgiveness for sending you on such a trying assignment."

The Marquis sighed audibly, his face relieved of tension for the moment. "I am pleased to see we are together again, gentlemen. I think we can take it as established that this Mr. Budd whom the Colonel mentions was the hireling of swindlers who wanted to keep us from the Ohio country. And that Charles de Flaville was his servant?"

"Fools, the lot of them," Putnam said sharply.

"No," Crosbie said. "If we had not arrived here safely, there might well have been no exposure of the swindle. The Scioto Company could have continued to sell worthless deeds for some time to come."

"Nonsense," Putnam growled. "Oh, I won't deny that these scoundrels may have thought just that, but I've been watching them. Not closely enough, I'll grant you, but well enough to learn from our agent in Alexandria that the deeds your people held were worthless. I assumed of course when I arranged for you to escort them, that they held their options and understood that they would have to make additional payments before they owned their land. Colonel Duer gave me to understand that was the case when he asked me to help in bringing these people to Ohio and preparing some sort of shelter for them. Later my agent told me of the deeds and I went straight to New York. I demanded that Duer pay for the deeds or refund the money. He was able to do neither and I forced the Scioto Company into bankruptcy."

Crosbie slumped at the table, fighting to control the rising hysteric laughter that welled within him.

"Then," the Marquis observed dryly, "our trials were needless? There was no reason for Mr. Budd and his henchmen to attack us ? Nothing to be gained by them, nothing to be lost by us, save only our lives?"

"Nothing," Putnam said flatly. "Though they obviously did not know that."

The three weary men sat silently around the table, none of them looking at another. The tiny candle flame wavered in a faint breeze, throwing grotesque shadows on the rough timber wall.

"Who is this man you mentioned?" Putnam asked, after the long silence had built into a tangible thing. "The traitor among you?"

Crosbie gestured wearily at the Marquis. He didn't want to think about de Flaville again, not when the memory of Cammie was so fresh in his mind.

"A young cadet," the Marquis said in a thin cold tone. "An intimate friend of my son's. He was eager to come with us when he learned of our plans and because of my son's friendship for him, I advanced the necessary funds. Charles was of good family, impoverished by recent happenings in France. He was eager to improve the family fortunes..." the Marquis hesitated, and Crosbie wondered if he, too, could be thinking of the way in which de Flaville had chosen to mend his lost position. "He was a young man we all liked and trusted," the Marquis went on steadily. "He served well as a scout during our journey here." D'Aucourt eyed the dour Scottish Colonel thoughtfully. "When we found it was Charles whom you had killed outside your cabin, I was hard pressed to restrain Edmond from seeking you out. Only the map and Edmond's instant recognition of the handwriting..."

"What does all that mean?" Putnam interrupted.

"De Flaville sent a map to Budd," Crosbie said. "With a note on the back saying that my wedding would distract everyone so that an attack would easily carry the town. I found it on Budd and de Flaville attacked me when I charged him with it." Crosbie glanced briefly at the worn old face of the Marquis and decided not to mention that de Flaville had also wantonly murdered the badly wounded Budd for fear the dying man might expose his part in the plot.

"But I do not understand how you could have been so sure..." the Marquis said hesitantly. "And what did you say earlier about a man named Fiske?"

Crosbie took a deep breath. It all seemed so long ago now and his mind focused with difficulty on the problem. "Fiske had just left Oliver Budd in Pittsburgh when Mr. Blanchard intercepted him and brought him to Braddock's Field. He rode a distinctive gray horse which was tethered to the outside of the wagon where we kept Fiske overnight. De Flaville learned we had him. Possibly he recognized Fiske's horse and realized the danger he would be in if Fiske could be made to talk to us. Maybe Budd told him something, for you'll remember de Flaville was in Pittsburgh that night for a while ..."

Edmond de la Foure made a convulsive movement that distracted Crosbie. "Yes," he said eagerly, "it is possible. He deserted me for nearly an hour and when I mentioned it he said he had a rendezvous with a girl ..."

"A girl," Crosbie said flatly. "De Flaville was a great one for girls, wasn't he?"

De la Foure flushed. "You knew about Lucie, then," he said, "that it was Charles ..."

Crosbie shrugged. "No," he said honestly. "I thought the man was Oliver Budd. I thought that it was Lucie who sent him the maps and the information he needed to attack us. I did not realize until tonight that the chain had three links, not two ... one of them an unwilling and deluded girl." He eyed de la Foure briefly. "You see, if the man Lucie loved were a member of our party, it could have been you, sir, quite easily. The girl kept the secret faithfully and well, though I am afraid some did suspect you were the man. Lieutenant Blanchard said the girl talked to him of social barriers, and of finding a new world in which those barriers would not exist. That fitted you, sir, better than it did de Flaville. Fitted you well enough, I think, to convince Mademoiselle Adrienne, your cousin, that you were the man."

De la Foure was too startled to speak. The small, half-smothered sound came from his father, the Marquis. So he'd been right about that, Crosbie thought. D'Aucourt had suspected his son. Both the Marquis and Adrienne had probably been most of all concerned with protecting the young Count.

"Charles asked me to keep his secret," de la Foure said at last. "He told me it was a matter of money, or reestablishing his future before he married Lucie. It was I who asked Adrienne to bring

Lucie along as her maid, so she could be with Charles, but it was Charles who thought of it. And I ..."

Crosbie waved the young man to silence irritably. He wanted no more discussion of de Flaville. He had liked the boy, too, admired his ambition and his drive. Never thinking, any more than the others had, that if ambition and drive are blocked in one direction they will find another, and take it, for good or evil. The Marquis had felt the same way about the boy. And Lucie must have weighed heavily on the Marquis's conscience, thinking his son responsible for her condition ... and, indirectly, for her death. At least now he could feel a certain relief about his son.

"And then he stole this man, Fiske's, money?" the Marquis insisted, somehow unable to stop talking about de Flaville, as though the thought of the young man held a bitter fascination for him.

Crosbie shifted in his chair. "We can't be sure," he said softly. "Any more than we can be sure that he killed Fiske. No one saw him ..." But even as he spoke he remembered that someone must have seen him, after all. Lucie. She had said, dying, "I know. Since the crossing at Turtle Creek, I have known ..."

"I am sure," the Marquis said in a faint voice. "I did not know of this man Fiske or his death. You were most discreet about that, Colonel. But late at night when we were at Braddock's Field, I saw Charles cleaning a bloody knife. He stabbed it many times into the ground and then carefully covered over the spot. I turned the earth over later, in the morning, saw the blood and assumed merely that he had skinned a wild animal."

Crosbie nodded. The Marquis's voice sounded frail and very tired. Suddenly Crosbie saw that the Frenchman was a man of many years, no longer able to withstand the pressure that had come to him constantly since they had left Alexandria. He liked de Flaville, Crosbie thought again, observing the Marquis, he liked and trusted the boy and now he's trying to take some of the guilt upon himself.

"It's all over for him," Crosbie said gently, the gentleness for the Marquis entirely, not for the memory of de Flaville. He turned to Putnam with slow ominous purpose, his eyes focusing on the General tightly. "But it's not all over for you, General. Not yet."

Putnam flushed but he controlled his explosive temper admirably. "I'll do what I can," he said simply. "Major Burnham and his men will remain here through the winter, both for protection and as hunters. They'll help your people get a crop in the ground next Spring..."

"And then the Frenchmen will be evicted from government land they have no right to, won't they?" Crosbie insisted. "As soon as the Scioto Company lands are returned to the government, as they will be?"

Putnam pursed his meaty lips and his glance dropped to the tabletop. "This town is not within Scioto boundaries," he said grudgingly. "It's Ohio Company property."

He looked up at Crosbie's amazed expression and made a hesitant, embarrassed gesture. "We used an old survey," he said thickly. "The boundary of the Ohio Company should be opposite to the mouth of the Kanawha we thought, and we told Burnham to put the town there. But the land wasn't very good and he moved the site upriver. Actually, it's within the Ohio Company boundary."

Crosbie chuckled, a grim sound that disturbed Putnam.

"Your people can remain until we work out something," Putnam said angrily, annoyed at the revelation of error he had been forced to make. "But I can't do more than that. The Ohio Company is not wealthy yet. Payments for our land take most of our available capital. We can't afford to subsidize..."

His voice drifted to a halt at a brusque gesture from Crosbie.

"There are three hundred people here..." he began furiously.

"And a couple of hundred more on the way," Putnam said miserably. "I don't know what we'll do with them."

"My God," Crosbie breathed. "You'll damned well have to find something! I won't..."

"Gentlemen, gentlemen," the Marquis expostulated. "We will solve nothing through heat. Let us consider our problem rationally. I assume there is little possibility of recovering any of the money we have paid to the Scioto Company?"

Putnam shook his head. "Highly unlikely," he admitted. "Impossible, I should say."

"Then we must remain here," the Marquis said calmly. "And somehow endure what comes to us." His voice was resigned, beaten, the voice of an old man who has no more resiliency, who clings steadfastly to a proven endurance as his only hope.

"No," Crosbie said flatly. He sat forward impatiently. "We have one hope left to us." When both men looked at him with quick interest, he said, "Congress can make a grant of land to our people in restitution. And General Washington will hear our petition sympathetically. He knows how much this country owes to the French." Crosbie's tone gained in enthusiasm as his idea developed. "You have a lot of influential people in the Ohio Company, General. When the public learns that most of them were also members of the Scioto Company, it will be hard for them to prove they weren't involved in the swindle. In any event, their reputations would suffer seriously. But if they all joined in our petition to Congress, they can help us and themselves at the same time. Nobody would be likely to believe that swindlers would go to that much trouble to help their victims." The thinly veiled threat in the Colonel's statement brought a deep frown to Putnam's forehead.

Crosbie's eyes were hard and insistent. He would make a very dangerous enemy, Putnam thought. The Marquis's gaze was intense with renewed hope, slightly masked with a civilized control but clear enough for anyone to see. A fine man, Putnam told himself, a man who had led his indomitably gay people through much peril, had withstood a savage series of attacks with them and now asked only an opportunity to regain some portion of the vast lands that had been swindled from him. The portly General looked from one to the other, his round red face lined with thought, darkened by powder burns and dirt, his eyes somber. Slowly, General Putnam nodded.

CHAPTER TWENTY SEVEN

Duncan Crosbie sat stiffly erect on the forward edge of the padded seat, keeping his eyes on the floor, deliberately avoiding the anxious glances that sought to catch his attention. He felt that some vital energy had been drained from him during the months of difficult discussions in the clammy breathless heat of summer in Philadelphia. A vagrant beam of light flickered and sparkled from the carved silver buckles on his shoes. His feet seemed strangely small in the polished black shoes and they felt infernally hot and cramped, too. Young Jock shifted restlessly on the brocade divan beside him and Crosbie reached out an immense hand to soothe the boy. He was growing every day, Crosbie thought suddenly. Already inches taller than he had been when Crosbie first saw him, Jock was nearly Cammie's height now. He had her warm smile that brightened Crosbie's dour existence and her dark burnished hair, with the same quick dancing eyes with tiny flecks of silver deep inside. Crosbie smiled at the boy, saw him straighten proudly, saw his small hard brown hand drop to his belt and grip the ornamented hilt of the Crosbie dirk with a possessive pride. His name was Jacques Carel and one day he might care to use that name again, but for the weary Colonel, he was Jock Crosbie and no one had a better right to the skene-dhu of the exiled family.

Nicholas Blanchard rose with an easy grace, winked at his wife and crossed the polished floor toward Crosbie. Both arms swung with a smooth rhythm; only in extreme cold did the wound bind and grip, making Blanchard move slowly and stiffly as an old man would move.

"Marquis's about to bust a gut with waiting," he said softly, leaning across Jock to reach Crosbie's ear.

Crosbie smiled and nodded, an absent gesture that had become habitual during the long months of negotiation. "It's over," he said heavily. The words sounded dull and discouraged to his ear. It was over and with it Crosbie felt himself finished, his years weighing on his shoulders and crushing his interest in any of his remaining life, except for Jock alone. There was no world for a retired soldier, he reminded himself. Not one in a million ever finds another meaning, another form of usefulness after he has left the Army. For every George Washington there would be a thousand Duncan Crosbies, men still competing from a sense of habit and the need to live, but men long since tired of their lives because there was no longer a challenge for them to meet.

Blanchard returned to his seat between Adrienne and the old Marquis. He touched his wife's hand lightly, stroking his finger across the wide gold band on her finger. Then he leaned to whisper a word to the Marquis.

He'll have a good life, Crosbie told himself. Blanchard would miss the excitement and the labor he had known, but he had the new excitement of Adrienne, the new labor of building a stable life for her. And when he was Crosbie's age, he wouldn't have to look back before he could find the meaning of his days. He could look ahead, if the faint swelling beneath Adrienne's waistband meant what he thought. Blanchard would not be a lonely man. And no matter how much fun his life with Adrienne might be, she would see to it that the concrete and essential elements were never forgotten. For the Scioto Company swindle had been a great shock to all the *émigrés*. None would ever again consider life to be truly gay and enjoyable, not so long as the frightening memory of the early days at Gallipolis remained fresh in their minds.

None of them knew the terms of the grant Congress had made, with the single exception of Crosbie. He knew, too, how high their hopes had once flown, and how deep they had fallen into despair. The actual grant would please no one, save a Congress guiltily aware of need for redress but determined to make no outlay of cash or land that had a present value to any-one else. A ridiculous affair from start to finish. And the finish was a mere twenty-four thousand acres lying at the juncture of the Ohio and Scioto Rivers, a tract that would not possibly be safe to use for another twenty years, if then. But it could be sold. And from the sale, the French could purchase their lands around Gallipolis, though there would be no such immense estates as they had once purchased. Small tidy farms, easily defended, but no more than that.

Crosbie looked quickly around the small pleasant room. Spindly gilt chairs had hurriedly been brought in so that all the French delegation from Gallipolis could be seated at one time. The room was crowded, but the high windows were opened wide and a faint breeze stirred the heavy curtains. Outside a carriage rumbled over cobblestones, drowning the constant tide of low-toned conversation. Everyone present had hopes and suspected in his heart that they were not going to be granted, but none would discourage his neighbor, so the talk was light and bantering, that frivolous, civilized chatter that had once so irritated Crosbie and which he now regarded as a display of incredible courage. They were a good people, he thought. He didn't actually like them bet-ter, but his respect for them was deep and positive now.

In the hallway beyond the open door, a light scamper of foot-steps sounded momentarily, then slowed to a stately pace. A white-wigged footman entered briskly, brought his heels together with a military crash that made the chandelier ring softly. That heel-clicking would be von Steuben's training, Crosbie thought mildly. Strange how it hung on as a habit despite the years. The footman inflated his chest, timed himself by the crisp steps outside the door,

"The President of the United States," he bellowed.

The tall man who paused in the entrance looked as tired as Crosbie, his face as lined, his eyes quiet and reserved. His clothes were almost as much a uniform as the buff-and-blue hunting clothes he had worn during the years of the war. Black, almost always now, with the old-fashioned white wig, the delicate silk stockings, the fabulous diamond buckles at knee and ankle. But for all his slim elegance, a big man, a man who had once had to work hard to control the arrogance that comes from enormous strength. The strength was still there, tempered now, controlled always without effort, visible mostly in the small blue eyes that delved deeply at men to see what lay hidden within.

Crosbie rose quickly, bringing young Jock up with him. The Marquis hurried forward to bow.

"This is a great honor, Mr. President," Crosbie said when he had straightened again. He had once addressed Washington as "General" in a forgetful moment and the President's immediate reaction had made Crosbie careful never to offend again.

"It is entirely a pleasure, Colonel," Washington answered. "One I could not forego." He gestured to General Putnam who stood immobile a few feet to one side. "General Putnam has the bill which I have this moment signed. And he has prepared a small map which will show exactly where the lands of the French Grant are situated. A strange occupation for the Surveyor General of the United States but one which he approached with keen pleasure."

The French clustered around a table where Putnam had spread out his map. Washington looked over their shoulders, hearing their exclamations of pleasure with a warm smile. Crosbie moved closer to him.

"In the excitement, sir," he said heavily, "we might forget to express our gratitude for the assistance and guidance you have given us. We are indeed..."

"Tut, tut, Colonel," Washington said pleasantly. "I am gratified that you should come to me and allow me to take part. If gratitude is due, I suggest it go to Doctor Franklin." The President bent toward Crosbie and spoke lower. "I do believe the old fox has enjoyed guiding your bill through Congress far more than he would allow. It has been almost his only interest for months."

"I shall call upon him this afternoon," Crosbie said. He glanced down at the map Putnam was displaying. The French Grant made a brave appearance but the delight of the Frenchmen would be rather less when they realized it was only twenty-four thousand acres. Better than nothing, though, and even that would have been impossible without Washington's sponsorship of their cause.

"General Putnam has informed me of your part in helping these people," Washington said softly. "It is no more than I should have expected of you, sir, but I should like to express my feeling of respect. It was noble work, Colonel."

"My duty, sir," Crosbie murmured in embarrassment. He looked quickly around for a new subject of conversation, saw Jock standing close, his eyes wide with admiration as he stared dumbly at Washington.

"I should like to present my foster son, sir," he said quickly. "Jock, make your bow to the President."

Washington returned the boy's clumsy salute, then put his large white hand on Jock's shoulder. "A braw laddie, eh, Colonel?" he laughed.

"Braw enough, sir," Crosbie said, trying to mask the pride he took in his boy.

"I.. I heard from Putnam of your tragic loss, sir," Washington said simply. "I trust you will find consolation in..." His voice softened and the tired blue eyes that had met and conquered tragedy beyond most men's endurance, held Crosbie's in a warm sympathetic gaze.

Crosbie looked pointedly at Jock and the President nodded, eager as Crosbie to let the subject drop there.

"And where will your future take you, Colonel?"

The two tall men stood at the edge of the excited group, hearing the exclamations of pleasure, gratitude and excitement, but paying little heed, as fathers might regard children at play. The long journey was over now. The worst perils of the wild Ohio had been overcome and the French were safe as men are ever safe in a troubled world. Crosbie's last work for them had been accomplished. It was something to know that it had been successful but with success had come the finish. And Crosbie had no thought or plan for the future.

He looked up at his old commander, knowing the sympathetic inquiry came from a deep sincerity, that Washington's good wishes would accompany him wherever he went. But the memory of Cammie was still a sharp emotion, not one to be eased or forgotten. He fought down the depression that threatened him again.

"I have no plans, sir," he answered. "A good school for the boy, then ..."

Washington nodded briskly, pinching his wide thin mouth into a thoughtful line. He stepped forward, touched Putnam's shoulder and spoke in a low tone for a brief moment. Putnam straightened and left the room at a quick pace.

The President remained within the excited group. He answered many questions about the grant of land, patiently explaining details that should have been evident without explanation, maintaining always an agreeable and even interested concern in the gay, volatile people who pressed closely around him. At last he glanced up wearily, caught Crosbie's eye and laughed softly.

"The town of Gallipolis," he said, chuckling, "should have been sited within the Scioto tract. Somehow an error was made and the town was built on Ohio Company lands. The mistake is meaningless now, I am happy to say, but it might have been serious." The President ran his eye over the map Putnam had prepared for the Frenchmen, and a small smile lifted the corners of his wide mouth. "As a young man I once prepared a survey of the Ohio country," he said. "It may even be that General Putnam and his colleagues used that very survey when they plotted the Ohio Company tract. I find I have not the courage to ask." He shook his head in mock sadness. "The young make many mistakes. However, ladies and gentlemen," he added with a slight bow, "I, too, must share some of the blame for your unhappy experience. I can only hope that the action of Congress in making the French Grant will leave you with the conviction that we wish you well and do most sincerely welcome you as citizens of our new country."

The President drew in a deep breath, obviously relieved at having come to the end of his formal statement. Crosbie almost smiled. Washington was never a man to enjoy making speeches and the Colonel was convinced that he had spent anxious moments preparing this one, delving deep into his memory for the lighthearted reference to his own errors as a surveyor—real or imaginary.

The French responded as Crosbie was sure they would. But the Marquis d'Aucourt cut the responses short, skillfully maneuvering his people away from the door so that the President might withdraw. As the assembled Frenchmen bowed low, Washington beckoned to Crosbie. Then he made his farewells and escaped before he could be cornered again.

Crosbie hesitated momentarily, unsure of Washington's meaning. Then he crossed to the table where Blanchard was rolling up the map and the deed to the French Grant. "Take Jock under your wing for a time, will you?" he asked. "I'll rejoin you at the tavern."

Blanchard nodded absently. With a flourish, he presented the rolled papers to the Marquis and, grinning, took Adrienne's hands in his, unable to restrain his high good humor. And it was a memorable moment for Blanchard, Crosbie thought dourly as he crossed the room. He had funds enough to establish himself properly wherever he wished. In Ohio, Blanchard would be a comparatively wealthy man and now that his wife's people were no longer penniless, he could build a good life for himself. Crosbie went out the door slowly, one hand fiddling with a small collection of gold coins in his pocket. He would have to find a source of income soon or he and Jock would not be able to remain in Philadelphia much longer. The five hundred acres of Ohio Company land which was his payment for bringing the French safely to Gallipolis had brought only three hundred dollars when he sold his deed and that sum had been spent in financing his long dreary work with Congress. Putnam and the Marquis had added full shares but they still had resources they could draw upon while Crosbie was at the end of his available funds.

As he stepped onto the blue carpet that ran along the hall, Crosbie saw a footman signal to him from a door toward the rear of the building.

"The President is waiting, sir," the footman whispered urgently. "Right in here, sir."

The room was a small library, fitted with the oddly shaped but extremely comfortable chairs that Mr. Jefferson had designed. At the big dormer window stood Washington, gazing out at the busy street, cocked hat on his head, long slim walking stick in hand. He was poking the silver ferrule impatiently at the carpet.

"My apologies, sir," Crosbie began.

Washington turned swiftly. "Nonsense, Colonel," he said gruffly. "The impatience is Mrs. Washington's, not mine. I fear I am delaying her." He rolled the stick in his palm, looking down at it intently, as if he had never seen it before.

"What, Colonel," he said deliberately, "is your opinion of the value of the Northwest Territory?"

"Why..." Crosbie hesitated. Washington knew more than he could possibly know of the situation. It must then be a personal attitude he was asking about.

"It will be immensely valuable, sir, as soon as a man can take his family out there in safety."

Washington nodded casually, still not looking up.

Crosbie regarded the silent figure, wondering what more he should say. "As long," he observed thoughtfully, "as the British control the Great Lakes with their forts, they'll keep the Indians fighting us, maybe even fight us themselves again ..."

"Yes," the President said softly in a voice that was almost a sigh. "The Revolution is far from over but we must do nothing to provoke the British until we are much stronger. It is a terrible responsibility ..."

The President seemed momentarily lost in a reverie of his own and Crosbie was not eager to interrupt. But when the silence had dragged on for minutes, he said softly, "We all had hopes that General St. Clair ..."

Washington made an impatient gesture. "St. Clair was defeated, as was Harmar before him. The Indians can assemble a larger force in the Ohio country than we can send against them and, God help us, a better force. But the Indian coalition is the key to continued British control of the Great Lakes. It must be broken. But in breaking it, we dare do nothing that will bring the English troops against us."

Vaguely Crosbie wondered why the President chose this moment to outline the difficulties of his official policy. And mostly, Crosbie wondered why Washington chose to tell him.

With a decisive gesture, Washington grounded his walking stick and his hard tense eyes caught and held Crosbie's. At moments, one could forget he was General Washington. In a drawing room he seemed merely a well-dressed affable Tidewater planter, better educated than most and rather more gallant with the ladies, but nothing particularly outstanding except for his height and erect carriage. But when he put those hard eyes on you, Crosbie thought, then he was a soldier, and the best soldier you're ever likely to see.

"It is not publicly known yet," the President said in a tight voice, "and you will say nothing of it, but I have appointed General Anthony Wayne as commander of a new expedition against the assembled tribes in Ohio."

A growing warmth spread through Crosbie. He hardly dared breathe for fear it would distract Washington. Did that mean...

"He will lead a force adaptable to the terrain and I trust we have learned something from our previous defeats. He'll build a road north of Cincinnati for supply. He'll have mounted dragoons to help him exploit any momentary advantage. He'll build and maintain a line of fortified positions. And he'll have Artillery."

"Yes, sir," Crosbie breathed softly.

Washington looked at him keenly. "Does that interest you, Colonel?"

Crosbie nodded, unable to speak.

"I'd give a great deal to be able to go myself," Washington said with a grim smile. "I haven't seen that wonderful country for a long time. However ..." He raised his stick and cracked it down on the shiny floor. "General Wayne has fought Indians in the South and his success against the Cherokees was splendid. But I am sure he will welcome an Artillery commander with your peculiar range of experience. Go see General Knox, Colonel," he said briskly. "He will be expecting you. In fact you will probably find Putnam with him. And," he thrust his right hand forward abruptly, "good luck, Colonel."

"Thank you, sir," Crosbie said in a thick voice.

He bowed as Washington pulled the door open and left him alone. He gripped both heavy hands together in a convulsive clenching and large knots of muscle stood out prominently along his jaw. For a long silent moment he stood like that, eyes half closed, until the wild surging elation within him had been brought under control.

Crosbie's step was almost jaunty as he strode to the door and down the hallway. His weariness and depression were entirely forgotten. His mind was suddenly busy with a multitude of new concerns. A good school for Jock, not too far away from head-quarters, so he could visit occasionally. Uniforms, a good field kit, horses. And a new training program for his gunners to teach them a more mobile attitude toward big guns in the wilderness. There was no time at all now. Every moment's delay would be an irksome hell for Colonel Duncan Crosbie. His dreary antici-pation of retirement, of grindingly monotonous days without meaning, all that was behind him now.

He heard his heels rap briskly on the stone steps as he left the building. At the corner, young Jock, his hand held tightly by Blanchard, was looking back, his face almost obscured by Adrienne's wide skirt. The boy shouted something, pulled loose with a quick yank and ran toward Crosbie, the jeweled dirk winking brightly in the sunlight with each long stride.

Crosbie stopped, waiting for his boy. He would have to go to General Knox at once, but a moment with Jock would harm no one. Blanchard and his wife turned to look, saw Crosbie, waved and went on slowly toward the tavern. Crosbie grinned happily at them. He would be pleased to have Mr. Blanchard with him on the campaign and he would hold a position open for him, but something in the closeness of the two newly married lovers told him that Blanchard had done his last day's soldiering.

The warm damp air filled Crosbie's lungs as he inhaled deeply and it seemed to him as fine as a sea breeze. Soon it would be the cool dryness of the mountains and then the chill of the deep for-est. But whatever, there would be employment for him, work that would stretch his abilities to the breaking point time and again.

Duncan Crosbie knelt stiffly on the cobblestones, feeling foolishly that the posture was singularly appropriate to express his sense of gratitude. His wide solid face was smiling hugely as he spread his arms wide to catch his boy.

THE END

Made in the USA
Columbia, SC
21 November 2020